HAMMER MARKS

A PROCESSION OF CONSEQUENCES

A NOVEL

ROBERT MULNIX BROWN

Map courtesy of the Library of Congress, Geography and Map Division.

Brown, Robert Mulnix.
Hammer marks: a procession of consequences / Robert Mulnix Brown.

ISBN-10: 1453891242
ISBN-13: 9781453891247

American West—History. Colorado—History. American Railroads—History. Palmer,
William Jackson, 1836-1909. Denver and Rio Grande Railroad. Mexican Land Grants.

Cover design: Anton Khodakovsky
Interior design: Anton Khodakovsky
Production editing: Lydia Bird

Printed in the United States of America

FOR HELEN ADDY BROWN

BORN APRIL 25, 1916
DIED AUGUST 2, 2009

...like the marks that diminish the value
of an otherwise fine piece of cabinetry.

—*Anonymous*

...a person whose only tool is a hammer
picks every nail for a target.

—*Anonymous*

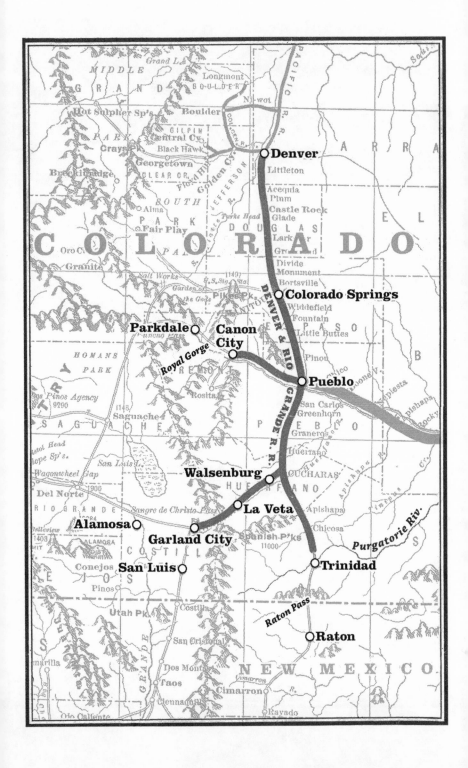

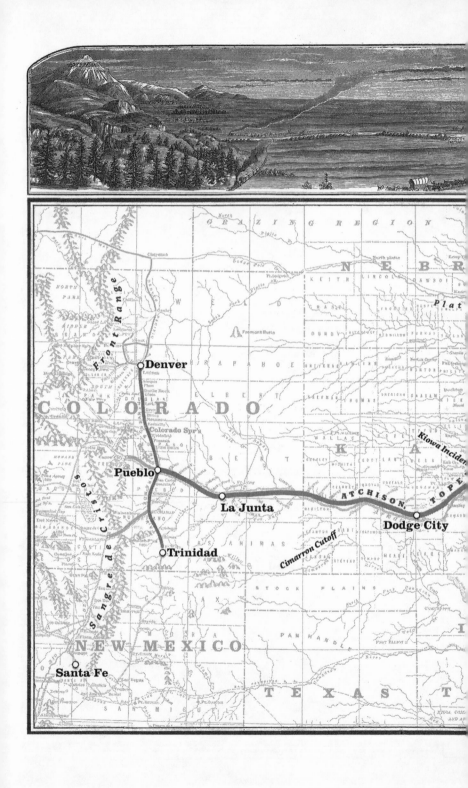

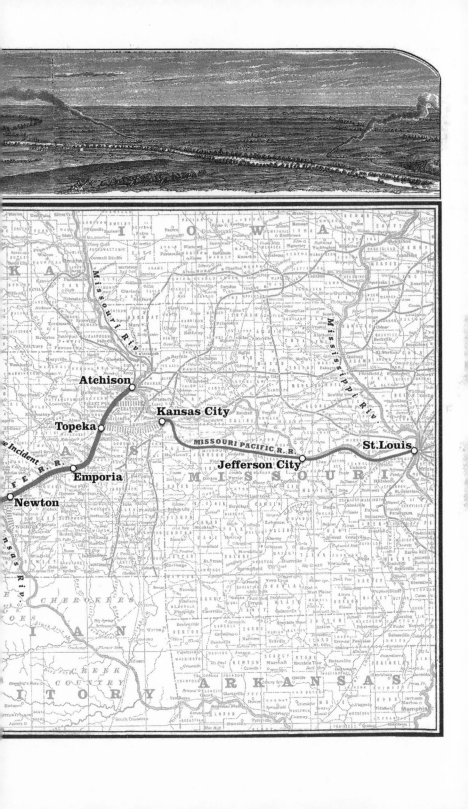

PROLOGUE

A HISTORAMA

THE NINETEENTH CENTURY presented a remarkable picture of America. There were wars: states against states, Americans against Americans, one country against another, Native Americans against "new" Americans and against each other. There were deep distrusts: whites and blacks, Anglos and Latinos, workers and bosses. There was degradation of the air and water—and not yet noticed. There were open wounds that might never heal, like hammer marks on an otherwise fine piece of cabinetry.

But there was discovery, gold and silver in the West, and the West itself was discovered. There were railroads and steamboats for transit. There was steam for power, coal for energy—with petroleum emerging. There were inventions, steam engines, sewing machines, printing presses, and words-on-a-wire, all for the mechanization of society. There was industrialization and the industrial workplace—and conflict therein.

And the Pacific Railroad, Mining, and Homestead Acts were enacted, creating incentives to open up the West, tying it together with steel ribbons and populating it with peoples with a common desire—to own land.

CHAPTER ONE

AN AMERICAN
INSTITUTION

THE SALOON.

S OME CALLED IT "the social institution most threatening to the family"; others viewed it as a way of life; and yet others felt that it should not be so dignified as to be called either. Women were indignant over the existence of such establishments—or perhaps they simply enjoyed being outraged. Miners and the like, from industry's depths, were intensely loyal to a place where they could "come as you are" and drink and argue weather or politics or whatever with their buddies. Gamblers were there trying to make a living. Others would get an honest drink, a little something to eat, and perhaps some entertainment—upstairs rooms were active since most bar girls, singers, and waitresses doubled in prostitution.

The concentration of saloons seemed to have increased ten-fold going from the East Coast to the Wild West and their gentility inversely so. It was possible in the mid-eighteen hundreds to find eastern establishments that would serve—in addition to whisky and beer—ales, gin, brandy, wines, fortified and flavored, and some drinks served over ice. In the West—except for the rare more elegant establishment—it was raw whisky and worse beer.

In New York or Philadelphia one might have found an English-pub-like or even a drawing-room atmosphere. Another type, with similarities East or West, was the coal miners' saloon, maybe one for every sixty inhabitants. Many patrons would be miners or steel workers—many just off shift and still coal smeared and dusty from head to foot. Most would have beer—since it would last longer than whisky—have a free lunch, and listen to the piano, the fiddler, and maybe someone singing. There were newspapers, friends, and lots of man talk. The next type, the "town on wheels," met the railway workers' needs. Here the saloon, the "fancy ladies," the convenience stores, all moved along with the railroad, leapfrogging the railhead every few weeks. Everything was temporary—and looked so. Yet another variation was the cowboy saloon usually located at cattle shipping trailheads. These popular places had everything—liquor, girls, poker and faro, and trail hands with plenty of money and unslaked thirsts. A common denominator of the saloon—either western or eastern—was serious gambling, card games, faro, and dice.

Lighting was provided, day and night, from coal-oil lanterns and candles on walls and tables and decorative candelabra here and there. Typically, the long bar-back was mirrored, sometimes set into elaborate hand-carved frames.

◇◇◇◇◇◇◇◇◇◇◇◇◇

On a particular evening in 1877, in the city of St. Louis—generally known as the "crossroads of westward expansion in the United States"—there was a curious but not uncommon occurrence. As two travel-dressed young men emerged from a crowded saloon and turned up the weathered board sidewalk towards their hotel a short block away, a shaft of light from the open door flashed across the dusk-darkened street. For an instant the beam exposed a group of five men, waiting in the darkness for just this sort of opportunity. They swarmed upon the two, pressing the lesser-sized one against the wall

Shouts rang out.

"He's got a money belt. Cut it off!"

"Grab his purse!"

Then frantically, "Look out behind you! Let's get outta here."

The other quarry, a six-foot-six-inch giant of a man, had slipped between two of the assailants, at the same time extracting an object from his hip pocket. In an ongoing movement, he delivered a forehand left and a backhand right, driving them to their knees. Two more blows and they were on the ground, bleeding from eyes and ears. The thwarted thieves fled—those that were able. Two might not get up again.

Under cover of the dark, moonless night, brothers James and Matthew Molyneaux, the intended victims, looked up and down the street and into the darkness. Seeing no one, they half ran the short distance to their hotel and the small second story room they had taken that afternoon. The hotel, itself, was a two story wood-framed structure about as weathered as the sidewalk. It looked reasonably clean but darkened. The hotel lobby was lit with a single coal-oil lantern on the clerk's counter seemingly casting more shadows than light. The clerk was missing—probably taking a nap somewhere.

They groped their way up the stairs to their room. As the closing door creaked behind them, the young men took off their boots and collapsed on the big brass bed.

Matthew, the younger brother, put into words what both men were thinking, "Jimmie, I think that at least two of those bastards are dead." Somewhat wild-eyed, his words were coming scattershot with the speed of a telegraph operator. "Do you think you hit them too hard? Could you have said something instead? Maybe they were just petty thieves—not murderers. And should we report this to the sheriff?"

"I understand what you're saying," came James' matter-of-fact reply, softening and slowing his words to exert a calming effect upon his overwrought brother, "But we were jumped and outnumbered at least two to one. We didn't start the fracas nor did we hit anyone first, And I totally reject the idea that this was a simple robbery. I was there and I saw murder in their eyes."

He went on, "Mattie, remember this. *If a man's trying to kill you, you can never hit him too hard—or too soon.*"

Matthew hesitated, and then helped his brother rationalize. "I can see that if we stop to make a report we'll miss our train—in any event, they brought it upon themselves. Maybe those felled weren't badly hurt—and besides, this is the *Wild West*. On top of that, you certainly acted in self-defense."

"But how could we prove it? The only witnesses are the attempted assailants themselves, and they might be related to the local sheriff, and then we would be in *real* trouble."

Matthew replied in a more rational tone, "Hell, you're right, of course. I had momentarily forgotten how that son-of a bitch smiled as he backed me against the wall and started to apply a chokehold. I shouldn't even be questioning what you did. But, it's okay. I'm myself, again. I should ask, though, do you agree we should not report this to the sheriff? My own feeling is that as a minimum we would miss our train. And those thugs brought whatever happened upon themselves. On top of that, you certainly acted in self defense."

My little brother doesn't seem at all fazed by this incident, James thought. Matt shook off his nerves in a hurry and he's supposed to be the thin-skinned one. Father would be proud. His younger son is a lot tougher than anyone thought. Being a little bit sensitive doesn't make a man any less a man.

And don't you worry none, Father; I've got Mattie's back. We Molyneaux boys are going to be just fine."

Matt took Jim's silence as agreement and then brought up one of the questions that was still bothering him. "I have to say, big brother, you're a pretty handy travel companion. What'n hell did you hit those guys with?"

"Oh, that's my billy club. I've not used it before, but I've practiced—as you might have guessed." He stood and slipped it in and out of his hip pocket in a sleight-of-hand demonstration.

"Where did you get it?"

"From Carl, the boot-maker at the livery stable back home." Pulling the weapon again from his pocket, he said, "See…he fashioned this little leather bag with wrist strap and hand grip, and filled it with lead shot. It can be carried in a pocket or up my sleeve."

"You didn't mention you had that," Matt said plaintively.

"I didn't really think that anything would happen—no use worrying you for nothing."

"Did Carl say anything about carrying hand guns, as well?"

"Oh yeah. He told me that a small hidden pocket pistol was all right but not really necessary, and not to wear a holstered revolver if I wanted to live to a ripe old age. He said someone my size with a rifle in his saddle scabbard and a black-jack on his hip could handle 'most anything the West has to offer,' but if you have a revolver in hand or even in a visible holster, you'd best be prepared to use it. The old man seemed to know a lot about it—he was out in Cherry Creek in 'fifty-nine and in the Nevada Territory before that. That's why I got those two little single-shot pistols for us."

◇◇◇◇◇◇◇◇◇◇◇◇

Having left the smoke and soot of their hometown Pittsburgh two weeks earlier, the Molyneaux brothers had arrived in St. Louis just yesterday. Already, hometown memories were being crowded out.

The Pittsburgh they left was a city straining at its seams, the result of great numbers of European immigrants, largely Scotch and Irish, pouring into the East Coast and spilling over westward. Even the original name—Fort Duquesne—had been compromised. The French mini-culture was being squeezed out.

Matthew, younger and smaller, an incipient businessman and economist even back in his teens, viewed the West as an unfolding blossom to be plucked (by him). He envisioned that everything beyond the Mississippi River would be wide open and undeveloped with unimaginable wealth underfoot. Matthew urged his brother to sell their inherited property and business and go west. For James, the older and very much more conservative sibling, Pennsylvania, just as it was, offered everything he could ever want; he looked for only the same from the west. But Matthew's pressure was relentless, "We must leave now, or it'll be too late... We'll only get the leavings if we delay..." And on...and on...and on...

Matthew's persistence and intensity reminded James of the gigantic clock on the bank building back in downtown Pittsburgh, always ticking away...ticking away...ticking away. The outcome, of course, was as predictable as a rooster greeting the dawn.

And, finally, "All right, Mattie, you win! You've worn me down. We'll sell the store for a stake in the West.

◇◇◇◇◇◇◇◇◇◇◇◇

It was a fitful night for both of the travelers. Matt, for the first time, was worried about the violent nature of the West; he didn't have Jim's self-confidence about things physical, and he damned well had better stay in his brother's protective shadow, he promised himself

The bed was small and lumpy—the room just large enough for it and a wash basin stand. A coal-oil lamp was provided but the fuel was missing. As the breaking dawn light provided a little natural illumination—the single dirty window seemed nearly as opaque as

the wall beside it—the surroundings started to show their real character. Where the wallpaper had not peeled, there were marks where
pictures had once hung (God only knows what the subjects of those
works of art might have been); ominous water stains on the ceiling
made one happy that no rain was expected. The sheets were clean
enough, but dust heaps in the corners of the room gave proof of inat-
tention; in short, the place was so grim that one could only wish for
darkness to return.

They dressed in the half-light as best they could—practical travel
clothing that didn't show the two weeks of travel to any great extent.
Both wore dark-brown narrow-leg corduroy trousers and broadcloth
shirts, James' plain and un-pleated, Matthew's a little lighter with a
small pattern and color accent. James wore a neck scarf, Matt a four-
in-hand necktie. They both wore very dark brown coats; Matt's was
cut "business style," James' was "Southern-plantation."

Each of the brothers had a carry-on topcoat, James an ankle length
canvas trench coat and Matthew a dressier duster. Each wore a similar wide-brimmed slouch hat. James carried his 30-calibre Springfield in a shoulder holster.

Both were normally clean shaven with trimmed mustaches, a condition difficult to maintain on a long trip. But by and large they presented a respectable appearance.

They each had a tightly packed valise for all other belongings, but
much had been left behind in Pittsburgh.

◇◇◇◇◇◇◇◇◇◇◇◇

The younger man couldn't keep quiet very long. "Do you think those
guys we left on the ground will make trouble for us?"

"I hope not. But they didn't even seem to be breathing...honestly,
I had no idea how much damage I could do."

Matthew smiled a tight wry smile. "Well, that's it for armaments.
We both seem to have pop guns that we won't use, but at the right
time you'll come in with heavy stuff from up your sleeve."

"At least on horseback I'll be well armed," said James. "In a saddle holster I'll have my Colt revolver—which I *do* know how to use—and in saddle scabbards, my small caliber target rifle and my Springfield. If I get a job bouncing or tending bar, I'll get a scatter gun."

"Is that what you'll make of your life—a saloon keeper?"

"Why not? There are twice as many bars as any other business in Colorado, each with its own whorehouse. And you'll have to agree that's one place where every customer knows exactly why he's there and how to get on with it!"

Despite himself, Matthew had to laugh. And then he said, "Back to the subject, is that all this trip means to you?"

"Well I'm joshing—a little. But as you know very well, Mattie, I resisted this grand pilgrimage of yours until you wore me down. Pittsburgh was good enough for me, as was the family store; and game hunting in Appalachia, to boot."

◇◇◇◇◇◇◇◇◇◇◇◇

James didn't mention, nor did he probably even know, his underlying problem, at this time, was with any kind of a new adventure. He simply didn't have the heart to leave home for good. The loss of both parents had hit him particularly hard, but he couldn't let little Mattie know—he couldn't let the security curtain fail.

Matthew interrupted, "I know all that; we made the right decision and it's behind us. Let's look ahead. The proceeds from the sale of the store and apartment give us a pretty good stake to go on. We could invest in real estate, in farm property, in a manufacturing enterprise, in almost anything where the money starts working for us."

"I'm not going to start saying I like any of that. I think I'll take my half, buy a couple of horses, open a little gun shop, maybe even a saloon of my own—but above all, build a little hunting cabin about one or two days' ride from town." That'll be Trinidad, he thought. I guess I can go hunting just about any place around there. I don't know anything about cattle or sheep, or money either, for that matter, and I don't have a profession, so I have to take a modest approach to my future. I don't have a bunch of phony expectations.

They both pondered on this a little. Then Matthew said quietly, "Don't you ever wish, Jimmie, that your life could make a difference somehow or somewhere or to somebody?"

"Hell, no, I've already said that I have a very modest future."

Matthew sat thinking about James' remark. "You're dead wrong," he said, "You already practically raised me and took care of Mother. You held the whole thing together after Father went to war. I'd say that's making a difference."

"No, that was my duty, pure and simple. It had to be done and I was the only one there. No, 'making a difference' would be something else—in my book."

"Then think of the future you could have out *here*. Colorado, in particular, is booming. There's cheap land. Towns are just getting established and laid out for businesses, public buildings, and homes. Colorado became a state just last year and Trinidad was incorporated this spring. Denver or Pueblo would probably be all right, but I think Trinidad may grow faster. Why, a Trinidad town lot bought now will double or triple its value before we know it. There's gold and silver, coal and iron, and even oil like up in Titusville, back in Pennsylvania. These all require back-up and we can supply that."

"That's what I mean. I can't think of a better backup than a saloon. Across all of America, it's an institution—a social institution." He shrugged. "I'll take what's mine and run. And speaking of running, we better get going out of this town before the sheriff shows up."

As usual, Matthew was not to be diverted. "Jim, don't you realize that if we split things up that way, we'll lose the leverage for doing something really worthwhile with our stake?"

"Like what?"

"I don't know. But I'll recognize it when I see it."

Matthew was quiet for a moment, all the while wondering—not for the first time—how in the world would he get his brother to think bigger, and further ahead. Jimmie, he thought, is a superb physical specimen, strong as a bull, quick as a mountain cat, and the very one to have alongside when things get tough, but why can't we agree on something as fundamental as investing for our future? I'll have to take the right steps without his knowledge, if necessary.

After a deep breath Matt said slowly, almost whispering, "I won't settle for making a difference. I want to *be the difference.*"

CHAPTER TWO

MISSOURI RIVER VALLEY

L EAVING THE HOTEL, with their valises in hand and top coats over their arms, the brothers walked along a back road along the Mississippi down to the depot, a facility shared by both the Pennsylvania Railroad and the Missouri Pacific. It was just another clear, majestic day in the river valley. Off to the left, backlit by the rising sun across the Mississippi, they could see the magnificent all-steel Eads Bridge that they had crossed the day before—a high point of the train ride from Pittsburgh. The Pennsylvania Railroad conductor had a spiel all ready for the edification of his passengers. Like a carnival barker he had presented the bridge as the finest in the world—an engineering milestone with three spans stretching out nearly a third of a mile, all over water. A listener might have thought the conductor had built it, himself.

"And," he said, seeming to address his remarks to James and Matthew, personally, "James Eads, the bridge's namesake, had little formal education and no engineering training at all. Yet when he was twenty-two, younger even than you two, he invented an underwater salvage vessel and made his fortune along the Mississippi River in only a dozen years."

This caught Matthew's undivided attention. My God, he thought, in just twelve years? He must have made at least a *million* dollars.

"Then, during the war," the conductor went on, "Eads built a flotilla of armored shallow-draft warships for the Union army, setting himself up for a contract to build a bridge across the Mississippi."

And to this James listened more attentively—for he had an instinct for the spatial relationships embodied in mountains, rivers, and bridges—then shook his head as though closing his mind. It's too late, of course. I would never be able to learn enough to do that kind of thing. Or could I?

◇◇◇◇◇◇◇◇◇◇◇◇

The situation was about the same as it had been yesterday at the St. Louis station yard. Railroad station houses all seemed to be the same— this one at St. Louis about like Pittsburgh's, taking Matthew back two weeks to when he and James saw their first depot and boarded their very first train. The Pittsburgh station agent back there had been kind enough, much too busy to do other than point to some boarding passengers. "Just follow them and make sure to get on the one marked 'Palace Car.' Put your packs up on the rack above the seats and your rifle, too."

Now, as "experienced travelers," they made their way down a similar boarding platform towards a different train. Matthew led, with James dawdling behind some twenty feet or so, having taken a minute or two admiring the engine that was to pull them some three hundred miles across another state.

Matt's progress was blocked by a trio of work-clothed roughnecks who grabbed collar and arm, twisting him to the station platform. The conductor came along just in time to be shoved back and to the ground along with Matthew. "Don't get the idea you're gonna ride this train, mister," one of the strikers said to Matt. "The bastards that own it treat us workers like shit. We're on strike. And this little monkey with the brass buttons ain't gonna help, neither."

By that time James had caught up, and with his arrival the rules of engagement changed faster than a runaway coal car. "What we mean is," the miner elaborated, "we'd rather you'd support our Brotherhood by not taking this train."

"Well, friend," replied James, looking down at the top of the striker's head, his voice low and firm, "we would like to show our support, but we have no other way to get to where we have to be. So good luck with your strike, if that's what you call it." He helped the conductor to his feet and brushed him off. "We're going to board now."

The protestors faded away.

James was bemused. Why were he and Matt singled out while a trainload of passengers seemed to have boarded without difficulty? I guess the Brotherhood just doesn't have its act together, yet, he thought.

Utilizing a little stool placed at the Palace car stairs, Matthew and James climbed to the vestibule and then into the car, immediately realizing that this equipment was wartime vintage, at best. In short, it was dirty and decrepit—not a good introduction to railroad travel. "If I treated my horse like this, he'd throw me off into the nearest ditch," said James.

The Pennsylvania, and to some extent the Missouri Pacific as well, was considered railroad "standard"—standard gauge, standard service, standard price, but a little sub-standard in amenities and passenger comfort. It was said that some of the Eastern lines were featuring smooth-riding four-axel "parlor" cars and Pullman sleeping cars. There was some talk about on- train dining facilities, but not on these east-west operations. "Better get used to these noisy cars, uncomfortable seats, dirty windows, and dim lights," the passenger agents seemed to be suggesting. Of course, this was first class—the emigrant cars just behind had even harder benches, scanty toilets, and no lights at all.

The brothers made their way to a pair of empty seats about mid-car, trying hard not to touch the soiled red velour covering seats and backs. While the spittoons, few in number and capacity, truly defied description.

Hardly had they taken their seats—the train still not moving—than the conductor came hurrying up. "Follow me, you two, quickly—no questions."

He led them through the vestibule and baggage car and into the crew compartment just ahead. "The sheriff came aboard looking for a couple of men answering your descriptions. I couldn't be sure but I couldn't take a chance," the conductor said, "You're safe here. The sheriff wouldn't dare invade private crew quarters."

"But why did you help us...why?" asked James.

With a half-smile, the conductor said, "I didn't want to lose two paying passengers—the Missouri Pacific can't afford it. But mostly I'm saying, thanks for helping me out back there. I'll come and get you when the sheriff is gone." He turned and walked towards the rear of the train.

"So that other person was a picket trying to stand up for what he thinks are his rights," observed James, as they settled into their seats again and the train got underway. "Christ, that's why they get trampled."

"I don't think they're always that mild," said Matt, "but, face it, Jim, you're a mite intimidating."

"You know, Matt," James said, "a couple weeks ago in the Pittsburgh waiting room, just before we came outside to board the Pennsylvania Palace Car, I read in the *Pittsburgh Gazette* that 'Iron City' was becoming the 'focus of friction' between the steel companies' owners and the steel workers." James had worked a year in the coal fields near Pittsburgh but never in a steel mill, so he had no idea what was in those great buildings with steam and smoke seemingly coming out of every opening.

"I don't really understand what's going on in these shops where they have workers' organizations," he said. "I can't remember any such things in the coal fields.

"And what's this 'focus of friction' thing?" he continued. "I didn't learn anything like that over at the Fifth Avenue School—did you?" Matthew looked up from his task of trying to fix a broken boot lace. "As a matter of fact, I did. You may remember Mrs. Hancock, Jimmie. She's a history teacher and her husband is a foreman at the Carnegie mill. He came up from the ranks, starting as a puddler, and is now worried about what to do if there is a strike. Whose side would he be on? And he's a good man."

James frowned. "That's a tough one, isn't it, Mattie? Even without knowing anything about it, I can see that if he goes down the line with the company position, he'll have a really hard time getting along with the workers—his former fellow workers—in the future when the strike is over. But, if he takes the workers' position, he'll lose his job..."

"Anyway, Mrs. Hancock gave us some background on this unionization thing," Matthew went on. "She said that lines are being drawn in the shops, in government, in society, and even within families, but, she said, if you read only the *Gazette* you'll have to look beyond what's written—try to dope out what they really mean and which side they're really on. In this case they're trying to say that unionism has grown too strong in the steel mills and that the arguments between the bosses and workers are getting ugly."

In these kind of discussions Matthew seemed to draw from memory every word (and meaning) that he'd ever read or heard. He continued, "It was clear that such a combined or collective effort, as they called it, was a lot more effective than the voice of one person. This situation has worsened ever since. The workers have begun to think they have the right to demand better and safer working conditions as well as more pay."

"That doesn't sound so bad," said James. "A man shouldn't be forced to work, especially if it's not safe—and now even colored folk don't have to do everything they're told to do."

"Yes, but neither should that man, either black or white, be allowed to shut some other person's plant down. It doesn't belong to him. And on top of that, someone needs the product out of that plant. Why should *that* person be made to suffer?"

"What about safety?" James asked.

"As far as safety goes, nothing we do or any place we go is absolutely safe. You've got to consider, too, the violence that usually accompanies these confrontations. That's certainly unsafe."

"I suppose so—what you've said makes sense, but what doesn't quite go down for me is something I read about that violence last year in the anthracite coal fields over east. Apparently they hanged, *hanged* twenty miners for strike violence. They were called 'Molly Maguires,' as I remember. Isn't that a pretty heavy price to pay for having an argument?" His voice had risen a little. Then slowly and more softly, he said, "And especially, as someone said, the charges were based upon the testimony of a single detective who sneaked into some Union meetings."

"The workers had a trial, didn't they?"

"Yeah, but the paper said that the special prosecutor happened to be the president of the railroad that owned the largest mine, and was the person who had organized the industry-wide agreement to cut everyone's wages at the same time in the coal mines, steel mills, and on the railroads. And the detective was hired by him."

Matthew paused, digesting James' point. "Jim, there's another way to look at this. The detective agency must have been pretty clever to build such a solid case against the Mollies. If I were a mine owner faced with such a bunch of anarchists, I might want to hire that detective outfit."

A well-dressed middle-aged man in the window seat across the aisle broke in. "Please excuse me for interrupting, gentlemen, but I couldn't help overhearing, and this is a subject close to my heart. I'm Alan Patterson, president of the detective agency you have been so concerned with." Turning to Matthew, he went on, "I agree with your analysis, young man, and you can be sure that our detective has been rewarded. And consider another incident closer to home. Just last year there was a strike of railroad workers on these very lines we're taking. Fortunately, federal troops broke it up, although a lot of people were killed in the process. But they should have known that you simply can't get in the way of armed soldiers. Suppose that strike had happened last week, right when we all wanted to travel?" These men have to learn the rules of society, of law and order!"

His discourse was interrupted when a man with Colt revolver in hand, and wearing a frayed and faded Confederate officer's greatcoat, stood up from his seat three rows behind. He obviously had heard the detective agency president identify himself. "So you're the son-of-a-bitch that sent spies all over the South," he shouted, firing point-blank at Patterson. At that instant the train lurched and the shot went wild. Patterson's seat mate and bodyguard promptly brought the assailant down with two head shots. There were some screams and curses and many passengers sank down in their seats and some to the floor. But there seemed to be little panic; travelers had learned to handle these kinds of occurrences while going out West. Practice made perfect in this wild, wild decade, and even the few women and children traveling down the line paid the unfolding scene little mind. They too had seen it all before.

"Drag him up to the vestibule and roll him out." Alan Patterson said, an instruction expeditiously carried out by the bodyguard who then returned to his seat across from James.

James stood, made a half turn right, towering over the guard. With his right hand, the left firmly pressing down on top of the gunman's head, James delivered a modest bludgeon blow behind the right ear. "That's to get your attention," James said. "Now hand me your revolver—butt first. *Now*, I said." A heavier tap to the skull emphasized *that* imperative. "That's it. Now any other weapon of any kind. Let me tell you, if I find anything else when I search you, I'll kill you on the spot.

"Go straight to hell, mister," the guard muttered as he dropped a knife and derringer to the floor.

"I've got a strong hunch you'll get there first, and here's one for the road," James said, striking the now shell-shocked authority figure with the power of a nine-pound hammer. "Now, here's what you will do. You'll walk up to the vestibule, sit on the floor where I can see you from here, and wait for the conductor—he'll know what to do with you. While you're waiting, you can jump out, if you choose. We're only going about fifteen miles per hour and you might live through it. Here's one more to remember me by." This blow was squarely on the bridge of the nose, breaking most facial bones.

James turned to the detective boss. "You can see Mr. Patterson that I don't like bullets flying past my head. Do you have anything you'd like to say?" Alan Patterson was mute.

The conductor made his way up the aisle, picking up bits and pieces of information from the passengers. Pausing at James' seat he said, "It looks, Mr. Molyneaux, that you've solved another problem for me. Please give me the man's guns. I'll take over now."

Matthew turned his attention back to the bootlace. James leaned back in his seat. Workers' problems and concerns wouldn't interest Matt much, James thought, unless the produced goods stopped coming; *that* could distress the customer and destroy the company. James kept thinking about Mrs. Hancock's husband's dilemma. Just how should a foreman's role be defined?

◇◇◇◇◇◇◇◇◇◇◇◇

The train route west lay along the Missouri River Valley, the tracks, themselves, south of the river at all times. The Missouri Pacific had an overnight stop at Jefferson City for coal and water and the passage of an eastbound train. This afforded rest for passengers and crew.

Jefferson City was a nice little town, large enough to meet the needs of the farmers and ranchers and far enough away from the booming frontier to fit their conservative nature. It looked as though there were more churches than saloons. In a way, the town had been an anomaly, a Union capital of a slave state. It was an old city, founded over fifty years before, mostly second-generation buildings downtown, two and three stories, wood siding or brick, and crushed rock or brick streets. For most of the town's existence it was the state capitol and the site of a state prison. Well, that's one way to build up the population count, James thought.

Back on the train, several passengers, all business types judging from their attire, were fretting over the extra travel day. One smaller man with belly enough for a man twice his size said to Matthew, "They can't make a schedule change this way. Let's demand that the conductor—he's the one who counts—arrange an express to Kansas City."

Matthew was reminded of that old exhortation "Let's you and him fight," and said quietly to his fellow-traveler, "I agree with you, friend, but I really don't think it would work. Now, I plan to use the extra time to refine my business plan for presentation in Kansas City. Maybe you should do the same."

What in the world is Matt talking about? James said to himself.

◇◇◇◇◇◇◇◇◇◇◇◇

It was a long journey, nearly twelve hundred miles, halfway across the country, from Pittsburgh to Colorado, and little more than half of that distance had been traveled to date—not that the land distances were so great, but in addition to the obligatory coal and water stops, it was necessary on these single-track railways to take time to allow passage of the eastbound trains. And it was cumulatively tiring—constant bump and rattle, swerve and sway. The overnight stops were welcome to passengers and crew alike. Even the mighty gods of steel and speed needed to take a break once in awhile.

As James and Matthew settled down in their seats again the next morning, they didn't look any older, but there had been a sudden maturation in each—they now knew that they could cope with the West. As a duo, at least, they were not to be intimidated by new and strange surroundings and older and more experienced individuals. Together, they were as smart and strong as anyone else and even the hot mid-October day was tolerable.

◇◇◇◇◇◇◇◇◇◇◇◇

Just outside Kansas City, the Missouri Pacific train made a short stop at the small town of Independence, which the Santa Fe and the California-Oregon wagon trains shared as an eastern terminus. James noticed that a gigantic Mississippi/Missouri steamboat had just finished loading bales of animal hides, probably buffalo, and the last of a great pile of wool shearings. Apparently this part of the cargo had been offloaded from a pair of Conestoga wagons—two more loaded wagons were waiting their turn. A few more had already been emptied and dragged to a reconditioning area. Oxen and mules from the eastbound trip were corralled nearby.

Around the pot-belly stove in the store back home, James had heard all about the Santa Fe Trail—and not much of what he had heard seemed to fit what he was now seeing. Instead of this handful of wagons, he had been led to expect to see at least two or three wagon *trains*, one hundred wagons each, being unloaded, serviced, and loaded, all at the same time..

It was difficult to believe that of the over two hundred thousand settlers and gold seekers who went overland during the period before the railroad came in, most of them *walked*. From some of the hangers-on around the pot-belly, James had learned why this activity was coming to an end. "It had to," one said, going on to point out that the transcontinental railroad had nearly eliminated the Oregon Trail wagon traffic to Colorado and beyond. James wondered how these traveling-sales types all around him on the Missouri Pacific would have peddled their goods in those earlier wagon-train days.

The Kansas Pacific rail route to Denver was meeting the supply and shipment needs of the northern Kansas and Colorado farmland settlements. In the course of this development, the Kansas Pacific for several years had engaged in lucrative cattle shipments east from a cattle trailhead at Abilene until blocked by farmers and fences. Now, as the Atchison, Topeka, and Santa Fe pushed west on a more southerly route than the Kansas Pacific had chosen, it served one Texas trailhead after another, the ultimate being Dodge City. Furthermore, with its temporary western terminus at the Colorado border, it had intercepted a portion of the Santa Fe Trail trade and would soon get the rest. This was a development plan for commerce; migration was secondary.

James had enjoyed this kind of talk, and it seemed to go on all the time. The business part didn't interest him much, it was the railroads. The maps in his mind showed the rails holding all of the pieces together. James loved maps. Given a compass bearing and a good topographic map, he could pinpoint his position anywhere in the Appalachians. Or anywhere else, he supposed. He should have been a surveyor, he thought, but things didn't work out that way. Well, no regrets. And like we we've been taught, "Don't look back."

◇◇◇◇◇◇◇◇◇◇◇◇

Returning from a round of "see you soon" handshakes in the smoking car, Matthew was ecstatic. "Isn't this a glorious sight, Jim? Before our eyes is the passing of an era. Out with the old and in with the new, obsolescence and progress, the wagon train and the 'iron horse,' firewood and coal, trails and roads, savages and white men. And, at last, we're part of it! Aren't you glad we're riding in a first-class railroad car rather than a Conestoga wagon?"

James said nothing, consumed with a depressing thought. It's kind of sad—that wagon train we saw unloading at Independence may be the last of its kind.

Matthew went on, "Anyway, Jimmie, we'll be in the Kansas City station in just a few minutes. I think we should grab a hotel room for tonight and go up to Atchison tomorrow. The Santa Fe is supposed to leave from there very early the next morning, so we'll have some time to kill."

Disembarking from the Missouri Pacific, a small youngster finally worked up the courage to ask James, "Mister, if you and that fella are brothers, how come you're so much bigger?" James gave some serious thought to this question. Taking off his hat and scratching his head he leaned over and looked the boy straight in the eyes, "Our father dearly wanted to make us the same size, but he ran out of material." The youngster walked away content while James smiled for the first time in a long, long time.

◇◇◇◇◇◇◇◇◇◇◇◇

Matthew and James wasted no time getting out of Kansas City. At first light they hired a horse and rig, took the city bridge over the Kansas River, and drove north on the well-traveled Missouri River road towards the Atchison marshalling yards some fifty miles upriver. Just outside Kansas City they passed the rail sidings, livestock pens, and feed lots of both the Kansas Pacific and the Santa Fe Railroads, fallout of the western migration. A slaughter house had been built in nearby Wyandotte; beef carcasses were iced for shipment to packing plants further east. Passing these stockyards was memorable.

"My God, Jimmie, one thousand cows sure do stink."

"Yeah, I'd rather have a few Pittsburgh smokestacks."

As they drove north it was evident the fields on both sides of the Missouri had been settled and cultivated. James asked, "What's doing out here, Mattie?"

"How'n the world would I know, Jimmie? You're the outdoors guy. But I know they grow corn and what they call long-stem grass for cattle."

"Well," James said, "whatever it is they're doing, they don't look very prosperous. Let's be glad that our father wasn't a farmer."

The road they were on didn't pass very close to Fort Leavenworth, but even at a distance it was apparent that the facilities were falling into disrepair. Leavenworth, like most of the frontier forts, had been built and staffed to protect travelers on the trails from the Indians. "I guess when there's nobody to shoot, the army kind of loses interest," James said.

Arriving in Atchison, they stopped for tub baths and shaves at a shop convenient to the station. James had to laugh to himself—the way Matthew had insisted that he, James, not only have his mustache cut back to size, but his bushy black eyebrows as well. "You've got to look more civilized, Jimmie," Matt said. James didn't bother to explain to Matthew how intimidating he had found those heavy brows could be when brought to a tight scowling "V." Several encounters had been thus diffused. But not the other night, he admitted to himself.

The brothers looked around the nearly empty waiting room at the Atchison depot. The painted walls were clean and unadorned except for a few postings announcing schedule changes and accommodations. On a reading table off to one side lay some newspapers, including the morning edition of the *Kansas City Star* and yesterday's *St. Louis Post-Dispatch*. James carefully leafed through the papers, happy to find no notice of the incident two nights before. Strange, he thought, but then he realized he was now in Kansas. The St. Louis sheriff would have no jurisdiction here even if the incident *had* made the papers...well, that's a relief. On the other hand, I killed those men—you don't bleed like that and expect to live—and they might have an avenging family. Will I have to go on looking back over my shoulder like that guy Patterson on the train?

"You're not very talkative today, Jim," said Matt. "I'm going to find out from the station master the status of the La Junta to Trinidad rail construction." He was also curious about stops that would have to be made across the prairie to accommodate the eastbound trains and the necessary overnight stops. "I'll be back before they call us to board."

Doors and windows were open, permitting a full appreciation of the comfortably warm late-fall morning. The sky was clear and essentially cloudless except for a few puffs on the eastern horizon suggesting a storm in the making. A light southeast wind brought in an interesting mix of odors—mowed hay, horse manure, locomotive exhaust. This last was the most familiar to a Pittsburgh person. There were sounds of horses and carriages on the street side of the station and the thuds of railcars being shunted around on the sidings behind.

The few passengers who were waiting had either come up by road from Kansas City as he and Matthew had done, or possibly had ferried across from St. Joe. Additional westbound travelers would board at Topeka. In any event, it would be several hours until the train would be ready. James didn't mind—it was his first opportunity to relax since he and Matthew decided that a hasty departure from St. Louis was prudent.

As the arriving passengers came into the station, they almost invariably did a double take upon seeing James. Even seated, he was an imposing figure. His six-foot-six well-muscled frame was topped with an unruly shock of anthracite-black hair matching his trademark handlebar mustache, in striking contrast with sapphire-blue eyes and long lashes. And the heavy black eyebrows were truly remarkable. His naturally ruddy face, with somewhat flattened nose and high cheekbones, had been sun-darkened to near brick red through countless hours hiking, hunting, and fishing on his beloved Appalachian Plateau. A couple of barely visible scars above his eyebrows and on his left cheek attested to more than a few boxing matches over at the fairgrounds. James, Senior, a large man himself, had said, "James, it looks like you're going to be pretty good size. That will make you a target for every ambitious tough that comes along. You must be able to defend yourself. Now, put your hands up, like this, and stand over there…"

◇◇◇◇◇◇◇◇◇◇◇◇◇

A shrill voice interrupted. "Hey mister." It was the boy from the Missouri Pacific train. "My brother said it don't work that way—it's not true what you said."

"Well, he just might be right," said James. "But to be perfectly sure, you better ask him if he was there."

The boy started off, then quickly turned. "My name's Peter, mister. What's yours?"

"They call me 'Big Jim' and you can, too."

"You're pretty big, but I seen a guy over in St. Louis that was bigger."

And it looks like this boy will be with us all the way to Pueblo, James said to himself. I'll have to be a lot quicker on the uptake, but it's a lot of fun talking to the youngster. I wonder if I'll ever have kids. I'd kind of like to, I think…but they'd have to be boys. I wonder how that could be worked out. I'll ask my little friend—his brother probably knows.

◇◇◇◇◇◇◇◇◇◇◇◇◇

Matthew, returning from the station office, broke into James' reverie. "I just learned that we'll be boarding in about an hour and we'll have overnights at Emporia, Newton, and Dodge. They say the Santa Fe tracks have reached Pueblo, but from there we'll have to take the Denver and Rio Grande narrow gauge down to Trinidad. He indicated that the Santa Fe branch down to Trinidad from La Junta is under construction, but a few months from completion. As I've said, this route to Pueblo and beyond is the most valuable part of our journey. The Pennsylvania and Missouri Pacific legs were not really important—just tedious. Now we'll put our big cards on the table! You can be sure that everyone on *this* train will be going to Colorado, and the people we want to impress are in first class."

"Do we impress them with how we're dressed, for God's sake?"

"Yes—and what we say, how we say it, and how we act. It's all part of the show, Jimmie."

"Christ, Matt, I'm shaved and I'm wearing my Sunday clothes. I'm damned if I'll do any more play-acting."

"It's not really play-acting, Jimmie. It's about convincing some bank president that he needs a personal assistant, or perhaps it's about marrying his daughter." Matthew smiled at his own suggestion and continued. "And remember, *it's all show.* Don't spoil it for both of us!"

◇◇◇◇◇◇◇◇◇◇◇◇

It was a mixed group that gathered in the waiting room as the departure time approached. A quarter of the people, dressed about as James and Matthew, seemed destined for the first-class accommodations. The balance would travel in second or emigrant class. Some of these, judging by their dress, looked to be workingmen, drovers, stockmen, shopkeepers, salesmen, or farmers. Most of the drummers, in order to make contacts, were dressed for first class and were so bound. Most settlers, though, desiring to take along their farm equipment and some livestock, might still travel overland.

And then, at the end of one of the benches, sat the prettiest young woman that Matthew had ever seen—not that he had seen all that many, but this one was unbelievable. The sun shining through the western window enhanced the hint of wheat gold in her hair—almost a halo, Matt thought. She was young and petite and dressed in Philadelphia uptown style. Sensing Matt's interest, she obliged with a profile. At that moment a tallish man in a business suit stepped into the sight-line between Matthew and the young lady. "We'd better get ready to board, Sophia," he said softly.

"All a-b-o-a-r-d" rang through the station, and people started walking along the train, which was pulled head in. Passing the engine, James paused by the massive brute, steaming and hissing and vibrating as though its iron wheels were hooves pawing the track in anticipation. Matthew waited with no apparent interest in the machinery.

"How do you like her?" said a voice emanating from the steam cloud. "She's a brand-new Baldwin four-four-oh. She's got lots of power to get over the mountains. Notice she has four coupled driving wheels, each over two feet high. And she carries enough coal to get halfway across the prairie."

"I'd dearly like to have one," said an admiring James.

"Well, get yourself some tracks and we might be able to oblige."

Matthew looked thoughtful. How does a city boy get into this railroad business, he wondered.

CHAPTER THREE

ATCHISON, TOPEKA
AND SANTA FE

A S THEY SETTLED into THEIR SEATS in the first-class Pullman Palace car, the Molyneaux brothers looked around, somewhat awestruck by the deluxe Santa Fe railroad interior, in stark contrast with the Pennsylvania and Missouri Pacific Railroads' accommodations through Ohio, Indiana, Illinois, and Missouri. Walls and ceiling were dark varnished wood, trim and fittings polished brass. Carpeted floors and padded and upholstered bench seats were in complementary colors. Double-hung sash side windows—with fringed pull-down curtains and fixed-sash clerestory panes above—extended the length of the car on both sides, still leaving room for the ubiquitous overhead racks for passengers' personal belongings. Oil lamps were provided throughout, one for every other pair of seats; toilets and stoves at both ends of the car. All glass sparkled, all brass gleamed. There were eleven rows of seats, a pair on each side of the center aisle; seat backs were reversible to accommodate groups of four. The train consisted of a mail and baggage car, two emigrant cars, a smoking and observation car, and two deluxe four-axel Palace cars, all coupled to a new state-of-the-art coal-burning steam engine with coal and water tender.

The conductor, identified on his badge as simply Mr. Thomas, was responsible for all operations of the train except for the engine. He was a large man, though certainly not of James' stature. He was in a dark-blue uniform, with brass buttons, white shirt, celluloid collar, four-in-hand tie, and uniform cap, whether indoors or not.

At the moment he was engaged in making sure that the very important first-class passengers were properly settled. Nearly all of these persons were clothed as they might have been in Philadelphia or even Boston. Men in shirts, ties, vests, and coats with the ever present gold watch, chain, and fob—watches popped in and out of pockets with a regularity exceeded only by the watches themselves. Women wore city-style floor-length high-necked long-sleeved dresses with delineating corsets and pinched waists. Shoes were high and buttoned. The only concession to travel informality was the placing of valises, hats and some outer coats in the racks above the seats along with sheathed revolvers and rifles, which some men were still carrying to the frontier. Without either spoken or written admonition, smoking of cigars and pipes was relegated to the smoking and observation car at the end of the train. And there were no spittoons! Conversation was subdued—almost muted, as if silence itself was now a language of its own. This all reflected an East Coast drawing-room culture far older than the railroads.

But what *wasn't* quiet was the train, itself. Each of the fifty or more driving and load-bearing wheels struck a rail joint every second— worse than a shod horse on a brick-paved street. Some two hundred carriage windows rattled like a house in a prairie cyclone—even the four-axel Palace car couldn't compensate for a poor roadbed, which also induced unpleasant swaying and swerving. And the huffing and puffing steam engine contributed its share.

"Now, Jimmie, do you see what I meant about our keeping up appearances? We want to look like serious-minded young commercial types—not desperate immigrants, not scared boys. We'll have to act and talk with confidence even when we're shaking inside."

James privately conceded that his brother had made a point, but, as demonstrated the other night, if a man exhibited a soft genteel exterior, he had better have a hardened core in reserve.

Matthew broke through the now almost dirge-like silence. "They told me at the depot that the first stop would be at Topeka, four hours away, for more passengers and to let us have an early dinner in the brand new Harvey House restaurant. Can you believe it? They said that this was to be only the first of a string of Harvey Houses at every major stop across the country. And that soon there would be dining facilities on the trains themselves."

◇◇◇◇◇◇◇◇◇◇◇◇◇

The train moved slowly through the countryside, paced by a small boy bareback on a large horse trotting comfortably along. People and animals are not familiar with these big lumbering monsters, thought James, and could easily be spooked. Out on the prairie, however, the train will probably travel about as fast as a galloping horse. From what he knew, the Missouri River Valley appeared to be pretty well settled, probably because of the Homestead Act enacted just five years before. This is supposed to be bluestem tall-grass country, he shrugged, but I don't see any of that native ground cover around here. I guess it's because the land is mostly cultivated.

The train made an unscheduled stop at a small depot marked, simply, Leavenworth, to allow the boarding of two U.S. cavalry officers with crisp new uniforms and cavalry boots, each wearing shiny new single bars.

"What in the world are those soldiers way out here for?" James asked Matthew. "It seems strange to see them this far from the battlegrounds."

"That's the stop for Fort Leavenworth located a few miles over to the east," replied Matthew. "The conductor told me that a bunch of these forts were built and staffed along the wagon trails and railroads. With the war over, there were plenty of soldiers around to provide escorts. Also, he pointed out that telegraph lines were installed along all of the railroad tracks for instant communication. That's how the Indians were put down."

"I wonder if we'll see any war parties, Mattie."

"I asked that very question at the depot. The dispatcher told me it's highly unlikely; the Sand Creek massacre was more than ten years ago, and except for a dozen or so raids, things are mostly quiet these days. He pointed out that in the year since Colorado gained statehood, Federal military protection has increased several fold. I didn't argue, but he sort of forgot to talk about Custer's problem up north just last year and the situation out west with the Nez Perce—not to mention the uprising at Trinidad. The dispatcher also said we might bump into some isolated and harmless Kiowa, now reduced to begging for food or whiskey around the depots."

"My God, Mattie, is that the condition we've put these people in? They're human beings, too, and entitled to some kind of humane treatment. They shouldn't have to beg in their own land. It's not right, Mattie."

"I guess when they're circling your wagons; you might change your mind. And anyway, they're in the way—we can't let a bunch of natives control our western expansion."

James protested, "But they were here first, before the Spanish and French. And we're a poor fourth. Even *I* know that."

"James, look at this article in the newspaper I picked up in the Atchison waiting room. The *Kansas City Star* says Indians clearly are inferior—they don't have music notes, a number system, or even a written language! And, anyway, it said, we've already given them thousands of acres of land. The Cheyenne, Arapahoe, Lakota, Kiowa, and Comanche have all been removed to their own land in southeast Kansas, about a hundred miles south of here, and to the Oklahoma Territory. And the Army's done the same thing up in the northern plains. The paper goes on to say that as far as the Spanish are concerned, we've honored *millions* of acres of Spanish and Mexican land grants which should have been spoils of a war with Mexico that we won. And the French? We bought *them* out. So, it's all been more than fair, they say."

"Yeah, but you told me the other day that newspaper editorials are opinion and not necessarily true," replied James.

◇◇◇◇◇◇◇◇◇◇◇◇◇

The conductor passed up the aisle collecting tickets and advising passengers of the impending stop at Topeka. "Two hour stop for coal and water and a chance to have dinner at the new Harvey House railroad restaurant.

"Ah...Mr. Molyneaux and Mr. Molyneaux. You two gentlemen are going to Pueblo, are you not? And did I pronounce the name correctly?"

"'Yes' to the first question, and 'almost' to the second—the spelling of our name has been Americanized from Moulineaux, 'Mū-lē-nō,' and we pronounce the 'x.' It comes out as 'Mul-nix.'"

The Palace car was about one-third full, nearly all well-groomed businessmen. When questioned about the empty seats, the conductor said there would be more passengers boarding at Topeka and at Emporia.

In the seat directly across the aisle sat the man whom Matt had seen in the waiting room, accompanied by the same strikingly beautiful young woman. Matthew couldn't get out of his mind the profile she had thrown at him the first time he saw her. Was it just a passing glance or something more?

The man was well dressed with matching gray narrow-leg trousers, suit coat, velveteen vest, and white pleated shirt with detachable wing-tip collar and four-in-hand tie. He was trim, with youthful bearing and a confident manner. Except for his graying rust-colored hair he showed few signs of the maturing years. He was soft spoken but obviously an in-charge person, clean-shaven except for a modest mustache.

He leaned across the aisle to talk to Matthew. "I ate in Topeka on my way east. It has excellent food, nice atmosphere, tablecloths and pretty waitresses. Oh, I should introduce myself. I'm Leonard Llewellyn and this is my daughter, Sophia." He nodded towards the young woman in the window seat. About my age, Matthew judged. She had even features, blue eyes, and fair skin that had seen little direct sunlight. Her blonde hair had been brushed into tight buns on the sides of her head—the latest East Coast style. Altogether, she presented a beautiful picture, acknowledging the introduction with a slight nod and a tight-lipped half-smile, giving nothing away. Perhaps answering my unspoken question, Matt thought.

Matt responded to the introduction. "And I'm Matthew Molyneaux, and this is my big brother, James."

"Molyneaux. That's a Welch name, isn't it?" asked Llewellyn.

"I don't know," said Matthew. "Most of our family's papers have been lost. All I know is that our father's people lived in Pittsburgh when it was named Fort Duquesne. Many Frenchmen anglicized their names after they lost *that* war. Maybe our greater-great-grandfather was one of them."

Llewellyn turned to James. "You really *are* a big brother, James Molyneaux. I'll wager you'll go eighteen stone!"

"Just about," James said with a broad smile, "they weigh me on the cattle scale!"

A hint of a smile on Sophia's face showed that while not being included in the men's conversation, she most certainly was listening.

James then asked. "Do you travel cross country very much, Mr. Llewellyn?"

"It sometimes seems that I live on one train or another all of the time; I'm an officer with the Denver and Rio Grande Railroad, D&RG for short. We're acquiring the rights to some new coal coking and steel manufacturing technology for our Pueblo iron works. The project has taken me to Pittsburgh and to Philadelphia a couple of times this year, with shorter trips to St. Louis and Omaha. This time I picked Sophia up at her school over in Philadelphia.

"I see from your ticket stub that you're going to Pueblo, also," said Matthew.

"Yes, and then down to our home in Trinidad."

"Is it common for a railroad company to get involved in other activities, like coal and steel?" asked Matthew.

"Oh yes, and usually by means of a family of companies with top executive and ownership ties. You must realize that *railroads* need coal for fuel, steel for rails, and people living and working on both sides of the tracks as far as they can see. *Coal* companies need railroads for transport but also as consumers for a large part of their product. *Steel* companies need coke, from coal, for their processing, and rail transport for their ore and products. It is truly a golden quadrangle—railroads, coal, steel...and *land*, which is owned by the government who parcels it out as an incentive for development and settlement."

"Including Indian resettlement?" asked James.

"I wouldn't know, but I can tell you that there are plenty of Indian resettlements in Oklahoma and southern Kansas. Also, south of the Arkansas River, much of the land is owned by the grantees of Mexican land grants—millions of acres—which were supposed to have been honored in the treaty thirty years ago that ended the Mexican War. I've never understood why our country chose to honor these land grants. After all, we won the war."

James drifted off into thoughts he knew he couldn't say aloud in this company. He wondered, and not for the first time, how Americans could so ruthlessly shunt aside entire cultures; Indian, Mexican, and the colored.

Matthew, on the other hand, nodded in agreement with Llewellyn.

"Mr. Llewellyn," asked Matthew, "on one of your trips to the East Coast, did you happen to get over to see the Grand Exposition at Philadelphia? We hear it's remarkable."

"Yes, as a matter of fact. Sophia and I managed to spend a couple days there. I was particularly impressed with Machinery Hall, which has all kinds of working models of newly designed steam engines, dynamos, electric-arc lighting devices, and much, much more."

Sophia chimed in, "and it has a breathtaking exhibition of clothing styles, all from Paris. Dresses have gotten away from the loose-draped look, and returned to multiple petticoats and bustles. I don't think we'll see this very soon in Trinidad." Then, recognizing that she had interrupted the mood and sense of the men's discussion, she blushed a fiery red.

Llewellyn picked that up, as evidenced by a raised eyebrow, but went on, "We saw all kinds of sewing machines that we didn't even recognize at first, and a band-knife machine that could precisely cut many layers of cloth at one time. But the centerpiece of the entire exposition was a steam engine—not unlike the one in the locomotive pulling this train—set up to power literally thousands of mechanical inventions spread out across the fairgrounds. They said there were eight miles of drive shafts. As the steam was powered up, more than fourteen acres of machines sprang to life, pumps, sewing machines, spinning machines, saws, printing presses, you name it.

And off to one side, almost an afterthought, they were demonstrating an instrument they called a tele-phone. The inventor, a Mr. Bell, and his assistant, about two hundred feet apart and each with an instrument, talked to each other!"

"Like a telegraph?" asked James.

"Oh no! There were wires between the devices like a telegraph, but the inventors were speaking with real words—not dots and dashes. However, I heard one spectator say to his companion, 'Hell, look how close they are—I could have shouted easier.'"

"I think there's a 'naysayer' in every crowd," said Sophia.

Matthew asked, "Other than providing entertainment, what were the organizers trying to prove with the...uh...tele-phone and the other machines?"

"They were demonstrating to the world the new inventiveness and imagination, the emerging industrial might of the United States. From being half a century behind Europe a short while back, we're now leading the Industrial Revolution. I'm telling you, it was inspirational!"

James ventured. "Will all this make our lives better?"

"Most certainly," replied Mr. Llewellyn. "Everyone, from every class, every walk of life, every economic level, from laborer to corporation president, will ride along on the back of the 'new technology.'"

Inexplicably, James' mood brightened. Maybe he and Matt were a small part of something grander, after all. On this upbeat note the train screeched and slid to a stop, and a happier group prepared to disembark.

◇◇◇◇◇◇◇◇◇◇◇◇◇

Leonard Llewellyn, while walking over to the Topeka Harvey House, thought about what he had said back on the train, "...*on the back of the new technology.*" It had just slipped out, but it was true and particularly applicable to himself and his very private aspirations with respect to Pueblo Iron and Steel. That's the back I'll ride, he thought. General Palmer is a mountains-and-train man and visionary—and a damned good one. He knows that trains need coal, so he has some good coal men to handle that end. But no one in the organization understands a thing about iron and steel—except me. And I'll keep it that way.

It's just a matter of time until the financial people that control our lives throw the gambling railroaders into a tailspin. When that happens, some of the auxiliary operations like steel may be spun off—and I'll be ready.

◇◇◇◇◇◇◇◇◇◇◇◇

To James, Topeka seemed to be a city unlike any he had seen before. It wasn't a frontier town, a hell-on-wheels railroad town, nor a boisterous cow town as he had heard these prototypes described. It hadn't existed during the Santa Fe Trail heyday; didn't have a saloon in every other building, and looked like any other town its size in Pennsylvania or, he supposed, New York. But it was the headquarters of the railroad they were on—which set it apart, somehow.

Topeka had been founded just before the war by a group of abolitionists who were trying to assure that Kansas would come in as a free state. The streets were crowded with people, horses, and buggies of one kind or another. Topeka had a different flavor than other towns James had experienced. Except for the absence of mountains, it might be a good place to live, he said to himself. It sure was an out-of-place, strange place.

It was, indeed, a nice restaurant, James thought, as they returned from dinner to the train. There had been an announcement that another Harvey House was now open in Emporia, the next fuel and water and overnight stop. As James took a window seat, Matthew turned to the rear of the train. "I'm going back for a smoke. Care to join me?"

"No thanks, Mattie. I'll enjoy the scenery for a while, regardless of who claims to have been here first."

James sat back as the train picked up speed, weaving over the less-than-perfect roadbed and clattering as the wheels passed over the rail connectors—something to simply get used to over the next week or so. The train headed south and westerly past the farmsteads spreading out on both sides of the railroad, all the standard one-hundred-eighty acre homesteads. A few, here and there, were doubled up, he noticed.

Suddenly, in the seat vacated by Matthew, two small bodies plopped down. "Hello, Big Jim, here I am again and this is my brother Michael."

"Why hello, Peter, and hello to you, too, Michael."

Peter jumped right in—he apparently had been saving up for this. "Michael says you're an Indian fighter, Big Jim."

The older boy was quiet, as if suspicious of anything that James might say.

"What makes you think that, Michael?"

"Well, you're big enough and you look tough enough, and besides..."

"Yes?"

"And besides, I saw you put a rifle up in the coat rack when you come in."

James then took all of the banter out of his voice and manner. Facing the boys he said, "I must talk to you two very seriously and very honestly. Do you understand?"

They nodded.

"I hope not to disappoint you, but I have to tell you that I would never fight an Indian unless he was a really bad one, say like if he scalped women and little kids. And I've never seen one that would do that. Up in the woods back in Pennsylvania I had a lot of Indian friends, mostly Shawnee. They taught me all I know about hunting and fishing, how to stalk a deer downwind of a watering spot, how to shoot a duck in flight, how to trick a wily trout. They showed me how to make a camp at night in a forest filled with wild animals and how not to get lost in the hills. They never taught me how to fight—my father did that."

"Can you teach us, Big Jim?" asked Michael.

"I certainly will—whenever I can."

As the boys slipped up the aisle, a woman behind James touched his shoulder. "I heard what you told those boys, sir...extraordinary! As a teacher, myself, I can tell you that never in this world will they forget what you said."

◇◇◇◇◇◇◇◇◇◇◇◇

As the train continued southwest from Topeka towards Emporia, the settled and cultivated areas began to thin out. Farming communities tended to stay within a half-day ride of some sort of a town—usually on an established trail or railroad. James, enjoying the warm air rushing past an open window, suddenly realized he saw nothing but prairie out there, stretching as far as he could see. While many Easterners were intimidated by the lonesomeness of such a vista, instinctively turning their attention inwards to the other passengers, James was excited.

Even considering the Appalachians, this was more outdoors than he had ever seen, and he wanted more. Though he was surprised and a little disappointed at the extent of eastern Kansas settlement, James remembered, the Kansas territorial government was formed the year he was born and settlers have been swarming out here ever since. Long before the railroads, even. James thought.

James found it nearly impossible to believe when Matt told him that everything the brothers would see during the next few weeks will have been discovered, invented, or developed during his twenty-six years on earth.

In fact, if today were twenty-six years ago, the entire Western world, as viewed from this point, would have seemed an endless sea of grass, some over his head as around here, and some short and bunchy as in the West. Nevertheless, the open land of the West is what the young man had been looking for—though it could use a mountain or two, James chuckled to himself, and some trees.

Fourteen years—hard to believe—but that's when James' Father joined his regiment leaving me to take care of his Mother, younger brother, and family store. As his regiment was about to leave, his Father took him in his confidence and quietly but firmly said, "James, I don't have to mention that Mother will need all the help you can give in keeping the store and house together until I come back home, but in addition, you must help with Matthew. You're older, stronger, but most of all tougher than he. You must see that he finishes high school and gets started out the right way. He's a sensitive child, you know."

The brother's Father fell at Gettysburg, while their Mother died of grief and hard work a few years later. James *did* run the store—although he had to drop out of school, himself, when Mother died—and he did keep Matthew in school. And by ultimately succumbing to his brother's relentless insistence to sell out and go West, he just might accidentally have fallen into "the right way" for Matthew to get started.

Well, I did what I promised, James reflected, but when can I start my own life? When can I cease being a tool for Matt's ambition? Father was partially right. Matthew is as sensitive as he *wants* to be and I *am* sort of tough—but not tough enough to withstand the constant nagging. "We've got to get out of here, brother. We were born after the California gold rush; we weren't old enough for Colorado's El Dorado, and now we're missing out on the greatest westward expansion of all." And on and on it went. James felt dragged out. He hadn't hunted or fished in his beloved Appalachians in over a year. His girl-friend had given up on him and he'd sold his horse in preparation for this trip. If they had to go to Colorado, why not on horseback instead of this god-awful, closed-in train?

One day James had asked, "Why Colorado? How about California?"

Knowing James' weakness, Matthew replied, "Colorado's closer and has more outdoors. Jim, you will not have lived if you fail to experience the great Colorado outdoors—much grander than your Appalachians, higher mountains, taller trees, bluer trout pools, bigger fish, and more deer. On top of that, Colorado's just starting to grow—and California is all sand dunes."

Now, how the hell could his brother say all that? Matt had never been west of Martins Ferry. And as far as "growing," all that James had seen, so far, were war vets, men pushed out of their jobs, and persons displaced by the tide of Europeans pushing in this direction. As far as that last group, James thought, there was simply nothing to stop them; anyone could come to America if he had the money for passage. Was this good or not, he wondered? Matt certainly would have no doubts. More customers and cheaper labor to make and fix things would suit Matt just fine.

As soon as he knew Matthew was serious about going West, James accepted the inevitable and started preparing himself for the trip, visiting the Carnegie Library for maps and descriptions of anything and everything about the route they would take. Maps were important in James' life. Since so much of his free time was spent hunting and fishing in the backcountry, it was imperative that he be able to find his way back from any place he might be. Given a map, a compass bearing, and a reference point he could do just that.

James could not know it, but that compass, so necessary to find one's way in the wilderness, was alike and at the same time quite unlike another kind of compass, one that was steering James into a new world of experiences, and words and reasons within that world.

Everywhere that I've been, and perhaps everywhere else as well, thought James, the rivers define the land and what it can become. All one must remember is that *water always goes downhill*, although back East, canals here and there help decide where it goes downhill *to*. When I think back to Pennsylvania, I see a gigantic water map, the Monongahela, the Allegheny, and the Ohio around Pittsburgh, flowing, ultimately, to the Gulf of Mexico, and the Susquehanna and the Delaware to the Atlantic Ocean. Here in Kansas, as though looking at such a map, I can imagine *these* rivers doing the same thing, defining the ultimate use of *this* land. Over the horizon to my right is the Platte flowing this way through Nebraska Territory to the city of Omaha on the Missouri. Dead ahead is the Kansas and its tributaries, the Blue, Republican, Saline, Solomon, and Smoky Hill all ending up at Kansas City, also on the Missouri. Off to the left the Neosho runs, heading south and east over to the Mississippi. And of most interest of all is the Arkansas River and its tributaries, rising in the Colorado Rockies and running east through the heart of Kansas ultimately turning south to the Oklahoma Territory. These rivers all rush down the mountains and then meander over the plains to the oceans.

James stayed buried in his thoughts, imagining just how the developing West would superimpose upon his imagined landscape. From beyond the southwest corner of Kansas, and mostly following the river valleys of the Purgatorie, the Cimarron, the Arkansas, and finally the Kansas River, itself, is the fabled Santa Fe Trail from the New Mexico and Colorado territories to Independence and Old Franklin on the Missouri.

In his mind's eye, James could visualize the evolution of the wagon-trail traffic, the fur trappers, and the freighters. It's easy to see how, even before the railroads, the settlement of new towns proceeded along this route, providing services and adding to the prosperity of the area.

And then came the railroads, signaling the end of the exploration and the beginning of the development—or exploitation—of the land and the people.

And my beautiful map was ruined so quickly, James lamented. Just thirteen years ago—an unlucky number—three railroads started charging across the prairie, one generally following the route of the Trail, the others the river valleys a little further north, but just as devastating.

Matthew could appreciate the role of the traders and the freighters, James knew, but might look past the flood of European humanity, men, women, and children, struggling for a piece of the West and competing against a lesser number of native people vainly trying to hold on to what they thought was their own. The younger brother was always pretty strong in mathematics, business, and everything else, except maybe history—James' only interest was geography. He loved maps.

◇◇◇◇◇◇◇◇◇◇◇◇

James also learned from the guys hanging around the livery stable back home that as the railroads moved west, they, along with the struggling towns and the enterprising developers, were extremely anxious for the countryside to become settled. They needed the cash flow to satisfy the appetites of their investors. Inducements like free or low-cost homestead or railroad land were offered. A developer, or "town puffer" as often called, would find a likely site, usually accessible by rail or trail. He would then go to some benighted area, frequently an ethnic community on the East Coast or in Europe, presenting an extravagant brochure and sales pitch. He would entice a diverse and eager group, mostly farmers, together with a preacher, some merchants, a blacksmith, and so on, to come to the land of opportunity. Sometimes it turned out to be so, but usually the work was hard and the short-term rewards scanty.

Emporia, the next stop—just coming up—had been founded as such a company town twenty years ago and there then ensued twelve difficult years before the first railroad arrived.

The community had been populated initially by Welsh immigrants, a mixed group of farmers, and a few coal miners, the former looking for some land of their own and the latter for decent working conditions. As years passed a great many family members and friends left behind in the old country followed, many settling in Emporia. It was a deeply religious group, regardless of occupation.

James also had learned that Emporia's original town agreement prohibited liquor and gambling, thus establishing the character of the town for all time. The Santa Fe construction camp, as well as the Missouri Pacific camp a year earlier, was required to be located outside of town, quite unlike almost all other railroad camps as the various lines pushed west across the prairies.

The effect of these prohibitions was evident to the Molyneaux boys and their new friends as they detrained at the station house located at the foot of Main Street, just across from the town hall. Unlike most Western settlements, Emporia did not show the scars of occupation by the rough construction crews and their appetites, most particularly the saloons, gambling rooms, dance halls, and the ubiquitous brothels of other Western settlements. The town was vigorous and obviously prosperous, not seeming to miss these entertainments. Rather than playtime revenue, Emporia enjoyed a bonanza generated by a heavy trading business—farm and dairy products, grain, and even a little coal. And this was reflected in the activity level at the railroad switchyards, warehouses, and loading docks.

In strolling through town the passengers could see a clean little place, painted storefronts, business establishments of all kinds, and three little churches on just Main Street alone. There were many shops catering to the country trade, feed stores, farm implements, and work clothes. Many persons, town folks and countryside, could be seen going in and out of stores, on the streets talking, adjusting harnesses, and all those other things going on in a busy place. All dressed in their best coveralls.

If only there were a saloon or two, I could live here, thought James.

They had a meal at the new Harvey House, the quality equaling that of the Topeka facility. The restaurant was finished much like a Palace car, dark varnished paneling, carpeted floor, cushioned chair seats, polished brass fittings where appropriate, white tablecloths and a long singles' counter masking the kitchen doorways. And young, pretty, and unmarried (it was said) waitresses.

To make conversation while sitting near Sophia, James asked, "How do you like your Philadelphia school and what are you learning?"

"To be a lovely lady," came her half-sung reply.

"You're already that—but you need a little aging, it seems to me."

"Well, that will change—and that's a fact of life."

I'll try another tack, thought James. "Seriously, what classes do you take to become a 'lovely lady'?"

"To start with, I'm learning French. That's so I can order a meal off of the menu."

"That's a good start. I'm sure you'll need that in Trinidad! But will they teach you how to order an enchilada? Since there's no French word for it, you'll have to make up your own."

"Then I'll learn to cook crow—so I can serve you."

James smiled, and thought to himself, *that* response was a little better—maybe she has a little humor inside that drawing-room uniform she's wearing. She's pretty enough and smart enough, but a little skimpy on charm, it seems to me.

They all checked in at the Kansas Hotel. Most passengers retired early to get a good night's sleep. Matthew, Leonard, and Sophia took a walk, and James went next door for a cup of coffee and a beer in a back room.

Boarding the train the next morning, in an aside to Matt, James said, "If Trinidad is as hard to understand as I'm afraid it will be; I'm coming back here to the Harvey House to find a wife. They say that Harvey girls will be populating the West."

◇◇◇◇◇◇◇◇◇◇◇◇◇

As James made his way to his seat, he was stopped by a well-dressed but somewhat disheveled man. "I'm Roger Crawford—you've met my boys."

James could understand why the man might have torn his hair a little and said so.

The man laughed. "Big Jim—that's what Peter said to call you—I have to say that I'm impressed with your novel genealogical theory as described by my son. It seems to me that you've set anthropology back by at least two centuries." He proffered a hand. "I'm happy to meet you. Are the boys bothering you?"

"Quite the contrary, Mr. Crawford—but it takes a little imagination to keep up with a couple young minds like that."

"Indeed. I sometimes wish my students would display that spark."

"You're a teacher, then?"

"Yes, I've just received an assignment as Professor of History over at Boulder."

At that moment Conductor Thomas came by. "I just overheard your boys in a very deep conversation, Dr. Crawford. It sounds like they're inventing a new kind of locomotive. I'll have to warn the engineer."

◇◇◇◇◇◇◇◇◇◇◇◇

It was in the railroads' own best interest to come through or near existing towns in order to take advantage of support facilities, hotels, rooming houses, restaurants, stage stops, stores, postal services, doctors, and the like. In addition, the workers required recreation amenities, saloons, dance halls, brothels, and gaming tables. Since some of these facilities might not exist in a particular town, the railroad would supply them, of a temporary or even permanent nature. Actual construction needs, office, shops, tool shacks, heavy equipment, and such were often mounted on flatcars, an integral element of the work train along with dormitory cars for all or part of the work force.

A construction camp was strictly temporary. When the rails moved on so did the camp, saloons, dance halls, and service people, leapfrogging the construction activity and leaving behind finished tracks, siding, water tank, and coal hopper. Some of these left-behinds would evolve into towns with branch lines radiating outward, thus establishing new settlement opportunities.

The big profit in railroad development was the near-term sale of land-grant properties adjacent to the rights-of-way followed by the natural commercial exploitation of the resulting settlements. Hence, the big push on land sales. But commerce was important as well. Where an existing flow of commodities such as hides from Mexico, furs from Colorado, or steers from Texas could be intercepted by a forthcoming railroad, so much the better.

The next town, Newton, where they would have an overnight, was a good example of such an interception. For about five very profitable years Abilene, located up north on the Kansas Pacific line from Kansas City to Denver, was the terminus of the Chisholm cattle trail from the open ranges of Texas. By establishing a temporary railroad camp at Newton, a branch line to Wichita, thirty miles south, and trailheads at both locations, the Santa Fe froze out the KP and other competition. But Chisholm Trail cattle operations lasted only three years at Newton—pushed out by farmers and local ranchers, just as Indians had pushed out weaker Indians, settlers displaced those Indians, cattle replaced buffalo, trains shoved out wagons, and so on. For hundreds of years this had been happening all over the contested prairies. James could see—but not entirely accept—that the Indians had to get out of the way. But did they have to be exiled?

Somehow, couldn't land corridors and winter quarters be provided for the nomads and something other than arid wasteland for the rest?

CHAPTER FOUR

FLAME FRONT

WITH ADDITIONAL PASSENGERS BOARDING at Topeka and Emporia, the car had, indeed, filled. In addition to the business types like Llewellyn, there were several who, judging from their conversation, were salesmen out to establish a new clientele on the frontier. Another difference from the passenger profile of the Missouri Pacific was the presence of a few family groupings, usually young adults and a few children. The men had cleaned up a bit, probably taking advantage of the tub baths at some of the barbershops at the overnights. The women, of course, had to get by with scanty sponge baths at the various hotels accommodating the flood of visitors and new residents. But the overpowering aroma of body perfumes alleviated this bathing shortcoming.

James noticed a couple of young women who might be mail-order brides. But they seemed dressed better than that. Could they be the wives hastening to rejoin their husbands who had struck it rich? Matthew was back in the smoking car or someplace; Sophia was quietly dozing; Mr. Llewellyn was absorbed with pencil and paper, probably planning some business coup—how to make more steel, perhaps.

James, half asleep himself, stared at the passing landscape. They were now beyond the settlements. All he could see was an endless expanse of grassland, the fabled man-high grass crackling in the bright sunshine. The prairie grass had now turned brown and dry. Suddenly he became aware of a dark smudge on the eastern horizon, growing and glowing before his eyes. It was fire, he knew, bending away from a steady southeast wind. He studied it as he would a fleeing deer or a soaring grouse. Only the tables were turned—he was the target. Other passengers were anxiously watching; an excited murmur echoed through the car.

Conductor Thomas entered the car. "Folks, we're watching it, also. It's a prairie fire, all right, and the flames may reach several feet above the six-foot-tall grass. No need to worry, everyone. The grass has been cleared several feet back from the tracks on both sides. As long as we're moving, the worst that can happen is a little scorched paint. These autumn grass fires occur frequently out here."

James interposed, "It would appear that our paths are converging, Mr. Thomas, but unless the flame front is very, very long, and if the wind gets no worse, we should be fine."

The conductor said, "How can you be so sure?"

"I've taken aim on a lot of running targets. And we have dry grass in Pennsylvania, too. But wait…what's that out in front of the flames?"

"It's a canvas-top wagon," someone said.

"And horses—I think two of them," another sharp-eyed person chimed in.

"That's what I make out, too," said James. "They're about one-quarter mile ahead of the flame front right now and seem to be keeping up. They can do this for a while, but their horses will tire…"

It was apparent to all that this situation could only get worse. The wagon hit a rough spot, wobbled a bit, and lost a little ground. A couple ladies gasped, some men swore, children screamed.

"My God, they'll never make it," said James. "Look, the wagon..." He stared intently for a few seconds. "Mr. Thomas, is there any chance we could slow down and pluck these people out of flame's way? Even if we misjudge a little, as you say, the fire won't hurt the train. How much distance would we need to stop from, say, half-speed?"

"About one-eighth of a mile, I think. I said that the train would be all right as long as we kept moving. But, okay, we can't lose much by trying. I'll go up to the engine to give running instructions to the engineer as you give hand signals from an open door. He'll catch on to what you're trying to do and as soon as we get closer he'll probably override you—he knows what his engine can do, how quickly he can stop, and all that..."

James and Conductor Thomas hurried to the forward vestibule. Together, they wrestled a steel floor plate away from the steps. James opened the door, preparing to lean out to make signals while the conductor proceeded forward.

"I'll help you, big guy, I'll hold your belt as you lean out the door," said a fairly large and obviously capable man a couple seats away.

"Thanks. And would a few others be ready to hop out and grab some people—if we manage to get that close?"

James made a few hand signals for speed changes, up and down, but soon realized that the engineer had quickly caught on to what they were trying to do and was anticipating his signals.

He's tracking well, thought James, and directed his attention to other aspects of the rescue. James shouted in a firm tone to his fellow passengers to stand by at vestibule doors in cars forward and to the rear.

By now, crew members not needed for train operations were getting into the action. They unlocked outside doors at the vestibules to bring rescued persons aboard and the baggage car sliding door to permit loading settlers' personal belongings if time permitted. All was as ready as could be. The fire was now plainly visible; the horses, frothing at their mouths, were still running hard but about a quarter mile from the tracks, perhaps half that much behind the train and about three or four minutes from the flame front.

James shouted to the crowd, "It looks like we'll stop about two hundred feet apart. The heat wave and flame front will be three minutes behind, and that's how much time we'll have to make one trip in and out and back to the train. Go in pairs—holding hands—take a deep breath, dive in, and pick up who and what you can and come right back. Don't get in each other's way."

Now, thought James, and as though he were mind-reading this imperative, the engineer and brakemen started applying the brakes coming to a screeching, grinding stop, just a few yards—not hundreds of feet—from the target.

"Right on, let's go," rang through the train, and a dozen passengers ran with James towards the wagon.

James said to his partner, the big man who had held him at the vestibule, "Let's go up front—I'll hold the horses while you unhitch the wagon—then I'll slip the bridles off and let the animals go." It wasn't easy. The horses, wild with fear, were neighing and whinnying and rearing upward—nearly impossible to hold.

The smoke was black and dense, the odor acrid, and the crackling noise of the burning grass intimidating—in just minutes the intense heat wave in front of the flame front would engulf the scene and moments after that, the flame itself. Rescuers held their breaths and dove into the smoke, swarming over the wagon. Fortunately, one trip in and out emptied the vehicle of passengers, crew, one dog, and a few possessions—no time to pick and choose—and rushed them to the safety of the train.

Someone yelled, "They're all out!"

James' partner said, "Wagon's unhitched!"

James was the last to leave the scene, slapping the horses' rumps with his hat and prodding them in a downwind direction. "That's the best I can do, ladies—good luck."

The train was already picking up speed as James was hauled aboard the observation platform by Matthew and a couple others. "Nice going, Brother. I'm proud. You showed us that it can be more than 'all show.'"

As they turned to glance back, the wagon exploded in a ball of flame—like the very incinerator of hell. It appeared that the horses were running free. There were thanks and congratulations all around—two adults, two children, and a yelping dog had been rescued, unhurt. But James' beautiful mustache was singed; along with the backs of his hands.

To Leonard Llewellyn, the entire incident had played itself out, back and forth before his eyes, as a performance of Macbeth on a grand stage—never completely understandable without a précis, but exciting nonetheless. The fact is, he said to himself, this young man, physically formidable, has a brain to match—when he chooses to use it.

◇◇◇◇◇◇◇◇◇◇◇◇◇

Newton was a planned overnight stop for fuel and water and to let the crew rest. Equally important, eastbound trains could pass. Cattle trains from Dodge had the highest priority.

It was a farm town—and certainly not a garden spot—located at least ten miles from the Arkansas River. First-class passengers were transported by coach past a near-dry creek bed to the Santa Fe hotel on Main Street next door to an eating place on one side and a saloon on the other, the saloon being one of only three remaining after the town's gentrification. Since the last cattle drive five years ago, the townspeople had gone all out to erase the physical evidence of the rail-camp's past even while still sharing a bit of secret pride in its checkered history. Only a few men showed holstered guns, and these seemed a little out of place.

Main Street housed most of the services expected in a thriving commercial agriculture community—much more than just a saloon and a general store. Matt headed directly to a seemingly prospering tobacco shop; James to a barber to save his singed mustache; the Llewellyns, of course, to a tea shop.

The town featured a couple restaurants but most of the passengers gravitated back to the Santa Fe Hotel for dinner. Two large tables with benches accommodated the patrons with a little spillover to nearby small sittings. Food was "wholesome Midwest"—fried chicken, mashed potatoes, corn on the cob, and lots of coffee.

A man, identifiable as the marshal by a badge on his leather vest and wearing a holstered revolver, came in. "Excuse me for interrupting, but I'm looking for the man who saved all those people today. The train crew said I couldn't miss him—he's the biggest guy in town."

All heads turned to red-faced James. "Well, according to the accounts," the marshal said, "it sounds like you done a pretty good job. I came in to tell you that the people are all fine; figured you knew that already. Some folks here in town set them up with an old wagon, a horse, and some provisions and sent them off. They're new settlers— Swedes, I think—headed for a small community about fifty miles from here on the Cottonwood River, three or four days travel. They shouldn't have been out there on the prairie all alone, but they were trying to find a shortcut from Emporia. Everybody feels you're some kind of a hero. And they're right."

"Thanks, but most everyone in this room had something to do with it, and the train crew, in particular, really pulled it off."

"They said it was your idea. How did you come up with it?"

"I'm kind of a displaced deer stalker. With or without a rifle I take aim at anything that moves."

"Anyway, the bartender next door said to tell you if you come in he'd set 'em up."

It was a good introduction to the Wild West, James decided.

The next morning, it was goodbye to Newton. The marshal was there; he was everywhere, it seemed. He spotted James and came over. "When you get over to Dodge, say hello to my good friend, Sheriff Masterson. Tell Bat I said he should buy you a drink."

James laughed. "Marshal, you'll have me falling off the back of this train.

◇◇◇◇◇◇◇◇◇◇◇◇

The ride through the heart of Kansas was beautiful, a swath of green in a world of gold and brown. And here and there some big black splotches, James noticed, recalling Tuesday's prairie fire. As the rails veered away from the near dried-up river, the land was dry and brown again. He had heard that there was a drought condition clear over to the Colorado line and this was evident.

Matthew seemed to be acting a lot like one of those "town puffers," James observed, spending all his time making the rounds of the business and political people in the first-class compartments. Well, that sort of leaves me stuck with Sophia, James thought. She's certainly a nice young woman, but she seems a little put off with my rough manner. I should try to sound and act a little more like Matt—or even Sophia's father. Like I told Matt, though, I am what I am.

Sophia leaned across the aisle, "Excuse me, James, for interrupting, but yesterday I overheard you talking about Indians. Is there any danger?"

His first thought was to give a flippant answer. But then the furrowed brow and the worried face deserved a serious response. Maybe she was feeling the uneasy loneliness that city people seemed to acquire out here.

"I don't think so. There are simply too many of us, you see. And soldiers, too. One of my friends back home explained the whole thing. The old-timer had been a trapper, a prospector, and a soldier at one time or another, had walked and ridden horseback all over the Rockies, and had even spent some time at some of the forts and trading posts along the trails. He said that things had been pretty good for many years; there was mutual respect and enough space for everyone. In fact, many of the early mountain men, trappers and traders, took Indian wives. I pray that's still the way things are."

Sophia stiffened, in shocked surprise, if not actual horror.

That's what an Eastern school will do, James thought, but went on regardless. "Some lived with the tribes. After a while, there were just too many whites, gold-seekers, settlers, and soldiers. Nomadic Indians lost their ability to move around, the buffalo were disappearing, and serious tensions and conflicts had arisen. However, that was ten years ago and the Indians are now mostly on reservations and totally subdued."

"Then who are those people out there?" She pointed a quivering finger.

James whirled to look, and quickly stood to grab his loaded Springfield from the overhead rack. Sophia moved across the aisle to the seat next to his. He sat down again. "It looks like a raiding party, all right." He pointed out the window. "See, you can count at least a dozen mounted Indians and there must be a few up front with some kind of barricade on the tracks. They're all waving rifles around but are not wearing any kind of war paint. I don't get it." The train was slowing. "We'll wait right here until we receive instructions from Conductor Thomas. He's in charge of something like this."

◇◇◇◇◇◇◇◇◇◇◇◇

Llewellyn and Matthew had been returning from the smoking car when brakes squealed and cars lurched. There were screams and shouting up ahead. As the train shuddered to a stop, the two men raced up the narrow aisle towards the Palace car, arriving just as Conductor Thomas managed to restore order. Speaking in a voice loud enough to be heard in all parts of the car, Thomas said, "We've been stopped by a rogue band of Indians—Kiowa, I think. I don't know what they want. The cavalry officers traveling with us have joined the engineer and other crew members near the front of the train in a face-off. I have to go up there right away, myself, since I'm the senior Santa Fe person around. If any of you men are armed or have weapons in the rack, be prepared, but don't join us yet, I don't want any shooting until the hostiles have shown their intentions. In any event, the best way to defend ourselves would be from inside the cars. Anyone familiar with the tribal languages is particularly welcome to join me, though."

Pointing to Leonard Llewellyn, who was still standing, he said, "Will you, sir, please carry that message to the cars behind? And will everyone else stay low—away from the windows. And you, young man," motioning to Matthew, "please take charge of this car and especially take care of the ladies. Calm them a little if you can; assure them that we train officials know what we're doing."

Finally he pointed to James. "Come with me, big fellow. I see you have a rifle—bring it, but most important bring yourself. I want these Kiowa to see a full-grown white man."

With a nod to Matthew and the Llewellyns, James followed Conductor Thomas.

◇◇◇◇◇◇◇◇◇◇◇◇

As the conductor and James neared the front of the train, the standoff was evident; the two sides had stiffened—the two soldiers were posturing—and there appeared to be no communication at all. Thomas moved to the front. In the voice and manner of a drill sergeant (and he may very well have been one a few years earlier), "Back off, soldiers," he said. "This is a railroad matter. *Put your guns down.*" The final command was laid down slow and firm.

James' arrival had caused a stir amongst the twenty or so mounted and armed Indians; he stood nearly a head above anyone else in either group. To the conductor, he said, "I know a few Shawnee words and some signs. Maybe the languages are similar. Would you like me to try?"

"Sure, go ahead. These two dismounted guys look like leaders." James stepped forward, arm raised and palm out. To his astonishment, with a trace of a smile the Indian patted the top of his own head. There was a noticeable lessening of tension. James said, pointing to himself, "Big Jim." With eyebrows raised he pointed to the leader.

The air cleared. The guttural reply sounded like, "Black Wolf."

A mix of Shawnee and sign finally got through as, "What do you want?" At least James *thought* it did.

And the reply seemed to contain within it the Shawnee word for "water." James turned to Conductor Thomas. "I don't think this group has any evil intent at all. I believe that they're thirsty and their horses are ready to drop. They seem to be saying that the river's dried up. Do we have any water that we could give them? Maybe enough to get them up to the next Santa Fe watering stop?"

"If this would defuse a dangerous situation, we certainly can. The water in the engine tender is contaminated with recovered condensate but we have extra potable water aboard."

The engine crew jumped into action to fashion and fill a trough for the animals and some containers for the Indians. Animals and men crowded in to take their fill.

"Thanks, Mr. Molyneaux," said the conductor. "Now will you use your *superb* command of Kiowa to tell them to follow the rails to the next tank, which is about a half day ahead? We'll fix up another trough there."

Most of the horsemen had dismounted and were grouped around James, cheerfully comparing him in all physical respects with their largest brave. Eventually the fractured Shawnee-Kiowa-English-sign conversation drifted to an examination of James' beautiful breach-loading Springfield hunting rifle, which he was pleased to show and demonstrate—but in his own hands. He always said that he could hit the eye of a gnat at two hundred feet. This day that "gnat" was a shiny brass button borrowed from Mr. Thomas and placed nearly beyond eyesight on a little hummock of prairie sand. James demolished the button on the first shot. A brave with a long bow then sent an arrow to the same spot, to the delight of his companions. James smiled in recognition of the fine marksmanship and then fired again, splitting the arrow in half.

As he finally broke away from his new "admirers" and turned towards the train, he overheard the cavalry lieutenant berating the conductor. "That's not the Army way to treat Indians. We have plenty fire power on this train to take the right kind of care of them."

Conductor Thomas turned away from the lieutenant in disgust. To James he said, "Thanks, Mr. Molyneaux. You have a way with these people. We should elect you president of the army."

◇◇◇◇◇◇◇◇◇◇◇◇

Back at his seat, James received the fervent congratulations of the other passengers. One of *theirs* had behaved magnificently again. But this was drowned out by the excited voices of a pair of boys. "We said you were an Indian fighter, but..." said Peter,

"...you said you weren't," Michael added.

"Well, I didn't fight them, did I?" James said defensively.

"Maybe not—but you were ready to, and when you showed them how you could shoot, they shushed up. Big Jim, will you teach us to shoot like that?"

James looked at them squarely, "Yes, I will. When you're a couple years older and if—and only if—your father agrees."

"That's a promise?"

"It's a solemn promise. I'll come up to Boulder and teach you all I know." The boys shouted, almost in unison, "Father, Father, Big Jim is going to teach us how to shoot a rifle—as soon as we're strong enough to hold one up."

◇◇◇◇◇◇◇◇◇◇◇◇

Llewellyn had observed this entire Kiowa incident with great interest. Like most senior managers, he was confident in his ability to judge the truthfulness and reliability of other men—even though that same ego sometimes didn't allow him to apply such an analysis to himself. And he was always on the lookout for potential D&RG employees— especially those who might further his own personal ambitions.

And what are those, he asked himself. That's a question behind every recommendation and decision I make. I want Pueblo Steel; and it will spin off into my lap if Palmer fails in his insane fight with Santa Fe over Raton Pass and Royal Gorge. And that's where I need James Molyneaux.

I've gotten to know this young man, possibly better than he knows himself. James is big and very strong, but easy-going, a little shy but likeable, thoroughly reliable and trustworthy, and able to take charge of a complex situation. But on top of all that, he is a little naïve—a country boy, so to speak. He wouldn't recognize a conspiracy if it were right in front of him. And he certainly wouldn't see that he was being used.

Palmer will like him. I think I can maneuver James into a position of responsibility in the gorge—an impossible situation, where *no* one could succeed. But if I'm wrong and he succeeds in the impossible, as Palmer's loyal vice president I'll get the credit. And if he fails, there's D&RG bankruptcy and Pueblo Steel—right in my lap.

Llewellyn made his way slowly back to the smoking car.

◇◇◇◇◇◇◇◇◇◇◇◇

Matthew had already returned to the lounge car; he tended to side with the lieutenant's views—we should put these people down when they step over the line. He shared this thought with Llewellyn, adding, "I remember reading that it was recognized nearly a half-century ago that 'our manifest destiny is to overspread this Providentially allocated continent.' We simply must not allow Indians, Mexicans, or Chinese to stand in our way."

CHAPTER FIVE

A WILDER WEST

DODGE CITY, THEIR NEXT STOP and overnight, had everything. Since cattle shipments were preempted from Abilene about five years before, Dodge had become the greatest cattle shipping point ever. The thousands of head passing through the massive holding and loading pens each day lent a pungent manure odor, confirming that it was more than just the hundred or so cowboys milling around that made Dodge into a cow town.

The smell of sawdust and the sight of new commercial buildings on Front Street together with new residences going up on side streets and over towards the river proved Dodge City was still a frontier town in the making. Unlike Topeka, for example, the downtown buildings were wood and largely limited to two stories. And the streets were unpaved. The distinct odor of coal smoke from the marshaling yards and repair shops over by the main line was a reminder that this was first and foremost a railroad town and destined to remain so. Bullet holes in a wall here and there proved that more than one gun had been fired in anger during Dodge's relatively short human history.

James stepped into the sheriff's office to pay his respects. "Hello, I'm..."

"Hell, we know who you are, James Molyneaux. You've been on the telegraph wires for a week now. Things seem to happen when you're around; we'll all feel easier when you get over to Colorado." The lawman smiled. "But you're welcome just the same. Have fun—we've got twenty-five saloons at last count. But don't forget to visit Boot Hill—just as a reminder to be lucky. See ya 'round."

To find a pattern of what he might want to do in Trinidad one day, James made the rounds of several of the more famous Dodge Saloons—both north and south of the infamous "deadline," or "the tracks," they would say. Most saloons featured long varnished bars, mirrored bar-back walls, oil lamps along the walls, coal-fired space heaters, entertainment facilities—piano, perhaps a small stage—tables and chairs, lots of standing room, and of course the ubiquitous gaming tables. Sometimes there would be a separate gaming room and maybe a ladies' room. There would be upstairs rooms, of course. James had made up his mind; he would have a street room for his general bar, and a separate gentlemen's club room for members and invitees. Most importantly, he would locate just this side of but as close as possible to Trinidad's "deadline," so he could draw respectable as well as not-so-respectable customers. And he would like to be as close as possible to the opera house, if they had one.

Most passengers chose the Santa Fe Hotel on the far end of North Front Street for their lodging, and meals, too, for that matter. They didn't feel too comfortable getting very far away from the heart of town. And no wonder, James thought, Front Street is a madhouse, and some of the saloons are hellholes. As Sophia and Matt made *their* rounds, Llewellyn kept Sophia very tightly corralled. And with good reason, James noted.

Knowing that his sheer size would set him up as a target for some drunken cowhand, his right hand, grasping the blackjack, was in his back pocket at all times. The evening was uneventful, possibly because there always seemed to be a sheriff's deputy no more than ten feet away. Sheriff Masterson—Bat—was going to be sure that nothing happened. Somewhat exhausted, James hit the sack early by Dodge standards.

◇◇◇◇◇◇◇◇◇◇◇◇

Sophia emerged from her room the next morning in a foul mood, thinking she might as well be in the convent, as some of the girls dubbed their Philadelphia college. She had hoped that Dodge City would be her "flowering." Surely father would be distracted enough by Front Street attractions to enable her to slip Matthew into her room. And, if not Matthew, James would do.

I've never had a man that size, she thought. Do you suppose everything is in proportion? But no, Matt's the one. Just looking at him you know he's going to be rich—richer than Father, even. And last evening Father was never more than two feet away from me. Well, here I go to play my part again—I hope breakfast is better than it was at Newton.

◇◇◇◇◇◇◇◇◇◇◇◇

Well, there goes Kansas, James thought, sitting alone at his seat in the Palace car. The balance of the day would see them following very closely to the Arkansas River, low as it was this time of the year, and within yards of the old Santa Fe Trail. It should be a nice day, and he could picture himself crawling through grass and brush hunting pheasant or perhaps some ducks. The buffalo had been slaughtered, nearly eradicated, for their hides, so his imagined hunting was limited to the little stuff. Wait until I get to the Rockies, he mused, *then* I'll dream up some real game. His daydream was disturbed...

"Do you have a minute, James?" said Llewellyn. "I'm running into a little problem that you might be willing to help with."

James, alert now, nodded.

"Briefly, two big railways—the Atchison, Topeka and Santa Fe, and the Denver and Rio Grande—are at swords' points. They have a serious dispute over passage rights through two mountain routes, Raton Pass and Royal Gorge. I imagine you know where they are even though you haven't been out here before?"

"Yes, since I'll be searching for a good spot for a little hunting cabin, I've looked at the Carnegie Library topographic maps and some surveyor's notes of the thirty-eighth and thirty-ninth parallels. I imagine you have even better topos in your files. I gather that the two companies want to run tracks through those two places where, at best, there's room for only one. Is that right? Why doesn't each company take its own route?"

Leonard smiled. "I'm afraid big business doesn't work quite that way. In any event, there's a legal standoff which will soon be in the courts. But there's a physical standoff now which is very serious. Each side has an armed work crew at each pass facing the other. Literally hundreds of men are involved. Neither side wants any shooting, but by the same token neither side can back down. Occupation by one side or the other might have an unfavorable effect upon the court's ultimate decision. You with me?"

James nodded. "So far..."

"Now, to my problem. As vice president and operating manager for D&RG's southern division, I must go back and forth encouraging my men at each location and discussing options with my Santa Fe counterparts. And I can't be out there waving a gun around. That would be deadly. So, I would like to employ you for a few months as an aide and deputy, a crisis leader as it were. You certainly have demonstrated your ability in that regard during the past several days. Also, I think that I'd have a more intimidating presence with you at my side even though we'd both be unarmed. You would be handsomely rewarded for your participation and your risk, although I honestly don't believe the danger is all that great. These men out there—on both sides—are rough and tough but they're not vicious. Next year they may be working together on the same crew. So how does that proposition sound to you?

James frowned. "I'm not sure. The risk wouldn't bother me much if we were to handle this thing in a straightforward and honest manner, but I've been wanting to get my new life together and I've lost too many years already."

"I think that I can help you with that latter concern, but what do you mean by 'straightforward and honest'?"

"That your counterpart on the other side shares the same desire that you seem to have, for a peaceful—that is, a no-shooting—stalemate until the courts decide."

"How would you propose to bring that about?"

"Maybe by prohibiting sidearms, holstered or not, requiring that rifles be secure in bedrolls, and imposing a two- or three-hundred-foot neutral zone. It might help, too, if you and the other guy agree to try to cool down your respective principals."

"I think your conditions might be acceptable to an 'honest and straightforward' man." Llewellyn smiled. "Now let me outline what we will do for you. We will pay you what a D&RG construction superintendent makes and you can have all the time off you need to find a suitable Trinidad property for a saloon, if that's what you still want to do. Furthermore, you will take additional time to scout the hills around Las Animas county for likely coal-producing properties to buy or lease—on my personal behalf and charged to my personal account. You will have a personal option to purchase the first such prospect you find. At the same time you could be on the lookout for existing privately owned producing mines whose owners might be interested in joining a wholesale consortium for effective marketing to railroads or parties other than D&RG."

"But, how would D&RG..."

Llewellyn interrupted, "They are only interested in producing coal for their own use—their own railroad and steel mill. If, in the course of my work for the General, I stumble on some other properties beyond D&RG's need, I'm free to develop them. In fact I've already formed such a consortium, the Colorado Fuel Company, and General Palmer is well aware of that fact."

Llewellyn let this sink in a little and then said, "It's a deal, then, James." He proffered his hand, and continued on as though the biggest single thing in James' life had not just happened.

"I've changed my travel plans," Llewellyn said. "I have to go up to Denver right away. I'll be in Trinidad in about a week and we can go over details of the assignment. But I don't want you taking any action until then. Fortunately, before I left for the East, I made arrangements for Sophia's maid, Isabella, her dueña, to meet us in Pueblo and travel down to Trinidad. I would appreciate your keeping your eye out for both Isabella and of course, Sophia."

James, a little stunned by the magnitude of all of this, could only nod his assent. And then to himself, I guess Matt was right. It's all show and it *worked!*

◇◇◇◇◇◇◇◇◇◇◇◇

Llewellyn left James and went back to the smoking car to find Matthew. "Oh, there you are, young Molyneaux. I thought you might have fallen off trying to hold on to that last settlement."

"Well, almost. However, I decided to have one last cigar to celebrate leaving Dodge in one piece. Would you care to join me, Mr. Llewellyn?" he said, reaching into an inside pocket.

"I would indeed." There was a companionable silence as the two men trimmed and lighted their cigars.

"This is an uncommonly good cigar, Matthew. Where do you find such quality?"

Matthew hesitated, and then said, "I sell tobacco."

"You *sell* tobacco? To whom…and where do you get the stuff to sell?"

"I've developed a market in my side of Pittsburgh, supplying saloons and tobacco shops on demand, and I get the 'stuff' through direct contacts that I've developed, in Virginia and South Carolina, where I can obtain all grades of tobacco, from the finest air-dried Burley—as are these cigars—to the rawest pipe and chewing grades. I started this back in high school to help out with family expenses. I guess you might say that I'm a tobacco trader, in a very modest way."

"How do you compete with the large wholesalers—I'm sure there are plenty of those?"

"By the simple expedient of carrying inventories of various types and grades so I can guarantee that my customers don't run out."

"But doesn't that tie up an awful lot of your capital in inventory?"

"Not as much as one might think. Especially since I've studied the market patterns and know pretty well the ordering lead time I need, how to find an alternate shipping route, and in dire straits, to be willing to substitute, on occasion, a higher quality at a lower price to get past a rough spot. In addition, I've shortened the communication lead time by utilizing coded telegraph. After all, every railroad and every train station has this vital communication link. Not only can I place and expedite orders, I can use the telegraph or Wells Fargo for bank drafts."

"In short, you're providing a service that other suppliers won't."

"Yes. I can't control the customers' needs. I can only try to analyze and understand them, and since there's no possible way to control the supply—there are hundreds of growers, large and small—I must use inventory to accommodate the uncontrollable variations in supply, growing conditions, transportation failures, and the like, and biggest of all, the customers' whims."

"Don't you ever find a situation that you can't accommodate?"

"Not often, since if I default, not only do I lose that customer forever, but others who hear of it."

"Doesn't your competition see this, also?"

Matthew laughed. "Sometimes I think that the other salesmen, who usually are peddling whiskey as well, dip into that other product too often."

"Or maybe they're not as smart as you. I have to say, Matthew, you seem to have a pretty good feel for 'supply and demand,' especially for a person not old enough to have had much experience. I haven't heard anyone talk about expediting orders or consciously using inventory control in their business." And to himself he thought, I'd better engage this young man before it's too late.

"Thank you. You said you're in railroad management now, but have you ever been in the marketing game yourself, uh…Leonard?"

"Not directly. I'm a mining engineer by training and an operations manager by happenstance. Yes, I'm with the Rio Grande, D&RG, that is. I'm Vice President of Southern Operations. As a sideline, though, for my personal future I'm just starting to develop a wholesale organization, the Colorado Coal Company, and someday I hope to branch out into steel." He smiled, then continued. "I guess we're fellow peddlers, Matthew—you tobacco, I coal."

"On a little different scale, and mine is sort of a hobby than business," smiled Matthew. But please tell me about D&RG. I know nothing about it except that it's 'narrow gauge' for some reason or other."

"Gauge is the distance between the two rails: three feet is 'narrow,' four feet eight and one-half inches is 'standard.' The narrower the gauge, the smaller and less expensive the rolling stock—freight and passenger cars and locomotives. More importantly, though, is the much lower cost of roadbed construction around sharp curves, up steep hills with a lot of switchbacks, through narrow canyons, and the like. Unfortunately, while cheaper and faster to build, operate, and maintain, narrow gauge can't carry nearly as much payload."

"So there's an optimum gauge?"

Llewellyn looked at Matthew narrowly—how many persons know how to use *that* word, he thought, either in a mathematical or even in a business sense? Then he replied, "Yes, there is—but you can't keep changing your mind. You really need a third rail to accommodate both standard- and narrow-gauge rolling stock on the same line. And your roadbed must be able to handle the heavier standard-gauge loads.

"To help you understand how complicated this is, let me refresh your Colorado railroad history a little. The D&RG is Colorado, and Colorado is the D&RG. You know, of course, that ten years ago the Central Pacific out of Sacramento and the Union Pacific out of Omaha linked at Promontory, Utah, but you might not have been aware that a year before that one of them, the Union Pacific, building west, arrived at Cheyenne. Some citizens, sensing an opportunity, constructed a branch line down to Denver. At the same time the Union Pacific Eastern Division—now called the Kansas Pacific or KP—was busily constructing a line directly across Kansas from the Kansas City vicinity. Reaching Kit Carson in Colorado ten years ago, the KP then made a fateful decision. Veering northwest toward Denver instead of Pueblo or even Trinidad and *then* north, it bypassed the Front Range altogether."

He paused to see if his listener's eyes had glazed. Not only had they not, they were boring into his as might a pair of augers. Llewellyn continued. "What you also may not know is that at the same time a retired General William Palmer, then construction superintendent for the Kansas Pacific line, was formulating his own vision of a gigantic narrow-gauge railroad from Denver to South America, by way of Mexico City. In effect, by ignoring an important segment of Colorado as well as the critical Santa Fe Trail connection, the Kansas Pacific opened up Colorado for the genesis of Palmer's railroad. The upshot was that we—Palmer's D&RG, that is—laid narrow-gauge rails from Denver to Colorado Springs in 1872, to Pueblo in 1873, and are now working towards Cañon City and Trinidad."

"How do you get coal for the engines? Clear over from Pennsylvania?"

"Good for you, Matthew. That's a question that hardly anyone besides the general thought of. The Rockies are full of coal, so potential coal-producing properties in strategic locations are developed as the rails move along. That's been my job, along with finding a way to produce good quality steel for these very same rails, which otherwise would have to be shipped from the East or from Europe. We've just started up a state-of-the-art steel mill in Pueblo. And remember the steel mills also use great quantities of soft coal in the form of coke, where the only coal is soft bituminous rather than anthracite."

"And how is the coke obtained?"

"At the mine sites, generally. Batteries of coke ovens literally roast the soft coal, driving off volatiles and impurities."

"Right into the air?"

"Yes, but that's not nearly as bad as the little petroleum distillation plant—I think that's what they call it—up at Florence, where over twenty percent of the stuff they get out of the ground is vented or flared, and it really stinks!"

"It sounds as though your D&RG plans have worked out beautifully...you're ready to roll."

"Almost. Now we have to extend south from Trinidad over the Raton Pass to intercept the wagon trails at Santa Fe, and west from Pueblo over the spine of the Rockies to the goldfields of western Colorado and the farmlands further on. And then...it's on to Mexico!"

"All clear sailing?"

"Not quite," said Llewellyn. "The large standard-gauge railroads are in the act, also. And they and we, both, have to provide a return for our bondholders as we go along. The Kansas Pacific has had the most immediate success by establishing a huge cattle-shipping point at Abilene, thus reducing the cost of getting livestock to the slaughter houses and packing plants on the Missouri and Mississippi.

"However, the Santa Fe, the line we're on, has now stolen a march on everyone. By cutting across Kansas further south, they're intercepting most of those Abilene-bound Texas trail herds. They are also serving the cattle and sheep ranches now starting to develop in western Kansas and eastern Colorado. And that's where the D&RG starts to worry. General Palmer is convinced the Santa Fe intends to drive us out of Colorado. They're messing around with our territory"

With each sentence, Llewellyn became more animated, swinging his arms around, and with that last pronouncement standing with clenched fists. "By going to Pueblo and then down to Trinidad, the AT&SF is poised to branch westward to Cañon City and through the Rockies, cutting us off at that point since there simply isn't enough room for *two* railroads to snake through the Royal Gorge. Our other worry is that the Santa Fe wants to do the same thing at Raton Pass just south of Trinidad. At the moment, we're stalemated by Santa Fe at Royal Gorge and possibly Raton Pass, as well. It'll go to the courts ultimately; no one wants a shooting war...yet. But we were hoping to get over Raton to retain that southern market we'll lose when Santa Fe pushes over from La Junta to Trinidad. We're strapped for cash as a result; La Veta construction has stopped, and we've defaulted on some La Veta bonds."

"What's La Veta?" asked Matthew.

"Oh, that's an under-construction short line over La Veta pass to the San Luis Valley, a potentially profitable agriculture area. When we open that up we'll have a comfortable cash flow and no competition in that area. Look, let me show you."

Llewellyn walked over to the little writing table in the front of the smoking car. Pointing to the table surface as though it were a map, the older man drew imaginary lines with his finger. "See, we're about here, and Pueblo is straight ahead west. Denver is up here to the right two hundred seventy miles and Trinidad nearly ninety miles south. A little more than halfway to Trinidad from Pueblo is the Cucharas River. Follow that river—and the railway tracks—about fifteen miles west and you come to the little plaza-village of La Veta. Immediately to the west, D&RG is now pushing its tracks over the ten-thousand-foot-high Cucharas Pass—the old Taos Trail—to Fort Garland and then to Alamosa."

"Ten thousand feet! That seems pretty high for a *pass*," Matthew replied with a smile and a shrug.

Llewellyn laughed. "I forget you're not a Coloradoan—yet. La Veta is at seven thousand feet and Fort Garland eight—so the climb over the pass isn't that much in either direction. Nevertheless, the railroad, when completed, will be the highest in the world...but that won't happen if we don't get the bond thing sorted out."

"I sort of remember reading in the *Pittsburg Gazette* about a railroad back East with a similar problem—poor short-term cash flow, defaulted interest payments, but with very solid future prospects. They floated an umbrella bond at a little higher interest rate, supporting their pitch with a very credible pro forma showing clearly that it was a sure-shot investment to keep the railroad out of bankruptcy.

"In other words, it was a super sales job." Matthew went on, softly and slowly in a near monotone, as though he were talking to himself. "Another approach—suppose they were to issue equity stock to the bondholders in the amount of the defaulted dividend, perhaps a little more to sweeten the pot. This would dilute the shareholders equity a little—but that could be adjusted with a little larger issue. Of course, with such a downshift in the debt-equity ratio, the shareholders should have a reduced risk of that fixed-debt debenture. This should be a saleable thing with the nearly assured increased net cash flow with the La Veta expansion—especially when the alternative is bankruptcy."

Llewellyn, in a near-catatonic shock, interjected, "Matthew, I must ask you a personal question. I know that you're a high-school graduate—nothing beyond that—and yet I hear you talking like an economics professor. What goes on here?"

Matthew stammered. "I...I guess it's the result of some inadvertent tutelage that I had, at least in that subject. My history teacher was outraged, absolutely livid, over the Pacific Railway financial scandal. With little provocation—the simplest question—she would launch into a half-hour-long tirade about the evils of railroading and railroad financing."

Matthew smiled. "Of course, one should not rely entirely upon the words of a tutor. I obtained from her some economics references, including the 1870 edition of *The Handbook of the Theories and Practice of Bond Financing*. I spent a lot of hours with that tome. I haven't had any experience but I do know the vocabulary and some of the theory."

"I imagine the General is thoroughly versed in this subject, but I'll mention your thoughts to him, anyway. By the way, I'm changing my travel plan—I'm going up to Denver from Pueblo. I'll see him then. Sophia and I are meeting Isabella, her duenna, in Pueblo. She was to accompany Sophia and me down to Trinidad. Perhaps you and your brother would see that Isabella and Sophia get back to Trinidad safely. It's only a little over eighty miles, takes a half day and you'll be met at the El Moro station."

"Most certainly."

Llewellyn stood up and peered through the observation car window at the tracks receding to the rear. He made his decision and turned back to Matthew. "Now, I have a proposition that I would like to put to you, Matt. I'll have to get Palmer's approval, and it would have to be contingent upon his getting this money squeeze worked out, but on behalf of the D&RG I would like to engage you for a few months, at least, as special auditor for the La Veta project. You would not supervise anything, but you would watch everything like a hawk, every dollar and every spike. Not only would you follow every aspect of the construction, but I would expect you to look at the commercial arrangements at the other end. As soon as the last spike is driven, I want the produce cars to start moving."

"But you know I have no construction experience."

"Of course. I understand that. But railroad construction is not only about surveying, grading, and laying track—you can find engineers and construction superintendents all over the place for that. It's all about salesmanship and money. It's about selling the job, getting the money, and doing the work. In that order! In this La Veta situation we need a super-superintendent who can see and expedite the whole picture—and he needs an auditor."

Matt nodded slowly, "Yes, I see. I think..."

"When you have completed this assignment in the manner that I know you are capable of, you will have done a fine service for me, for General Palmer, and for the D&RG. Moreover, you will be in a position to bid for your own railroad jobs—and there are going to be a lot of them."

Llewellyn turned to leave. "We'll be in Pueblo before we know it—if you will excuse me, I've some paperwork to do. You know, on second thought, I think I would like you to come up to Denver with me now so you can get your exact instructions from the General, himself. I'll ask James to look after Isabella and Sophia down to Trinidad. Isabella is very competent—she speaks English and has taken the trip several times."

Llewellyn started to say more, hesitated, and then said, "Matthew, I can't help but notice the intense interest you and Sophia seem to have in each other..." Matt stiffened apprehensively, but was quiet awaiting the blow.

"And I have to tell you, Matt," Leonard continued, "that I like what I see. However, Sophia is a little younger than you and tends to be a little flighty. So keep the pressure on and things will work out just fine. Her mother and I will most certainly approve."

Matt was in shock—and speechless to boot. To himself he exclaimed, maybe now Jim will believe me. It's all show and it *worked!*

◇◇◇◇◇◇◇◇◇◇◇◇

Conductor Thomas came by. "Just a reminder, folks. We're out of Kansas and the prairie has now given way to an area less suitable for farming but much better for cattle and sheep grazing; it's still pretty arid, but you can see off to the left a number of creek beds, mostly dry, leading to the Arkansas. We'll soon be making an overnight at La Junta. If anyone is in a hurry to get down to Trinidad, he can detrain there and take a stage rather than go into Pueblo tomorrow morning for transfer to the D&RG. Since Santa Fe will pay the stage fare, you can save time *and* money. You'll notice the huge stacks of ties and rails when we stop. These are for the Santa Fe branch line to Trinidad, which is now under construction. For the benefit of you newcomers to Colorado, at La Junta you can get your first sight of the *real Colorado.*"

It was a sight worth crossing the country to see. In a wide arc looking from left to right, the Sangre de Cristos were at left center, the Wet Mountains dead ahead and to the far right and more distant, the Front Range of the Rocky Mountains. At this moment they blocked out everything else in the world. There was no snow in evidence—after all it was only mid fall—but at the higher elevations of the eastern slopes, many small glacial deposits had survived to grow another year.

The hot dry days of Indian summer were giving way to crisp November. Across the foothills to the distant peaks, a cumulus had popped into view above the ridge, a common fall occurrence, impressive, but usually innocuous. Now, however, it appeared to have a dark horizontal base, portending an early storm, an early and cruel winter. Short days and long bitter nights.

James and Matthew were standing together; Matthew couldn't be sure, but it appeared that Jim's eyes were tearing a little. "I'm glad you made me come, Mattie. Thank you."

"Frankly, Jimmie, I'm a little overwhelmed myself. It's the most beautiful thing I've ever seen." They stood quietly for a long moment.

Then Matthew spoke again. "But on another matter, I suppose you've guessed something is up. Let me fill you in. Llewellyn made me a job offer that sounds pretty good—as special auditor for the D&RG La Veta branch line construction over to the San Luis Valley. Apparently it's in financial difficulty and there are completion delays as well."

"La Veta...La Veta? Oh, I know where that is—right at the toe of the Spanish Peaks. That's where I'll build a cabin someday." James laughed. "Do you want me to take your place as auditor? But seriously, congratulations, Mattie—Llewellyn made a good selection. You know, strangely enough, he made a job offer to me, too. But while yours sounds straightforward and believable, mine is a little quirky. He wants me to second him as leader of an armed force of some fifty D&RG toughs in a confrontation with a like force of Santa Fe combatants contesting passage at Raton Pass. Now, such a battle is quite understandable, but led by Llewellyn? He just doesn't look like a fighting man. He also made a second offer. He wants me, to his account—not D&RG's—to scout around for likely coal properties for development. It seems to me that *surely* every foot of these lower hillsides has been walked over, surveyed, and prospected for nearly ten years. What could be left that an amateur might find? It's also a little difficult to understand how General Palmer would allow this kind of thing to go on. Well, I accepted, but believe me—I'll walk very carefully."

CHAPTER SIX

THE FRONT RANGE

MATTHEW SETTLED ON A HARD BENCH on the open platform at the rear of the observation car where he could watch the land, America as he knew it, recede into nothing. It was sight that he had been looking forward to. And now and then curves in the track allowed glimpses of the magnificent Rockies ahead. His strategy had worked perfectly. But right now he had a more immediate concern to consider—James is certainly becoming more of a problem, he thought. Basically, he just wants to cut and run. And I can't have that! How can I control our grubstake without being held back by James' infernal caution? Some of their pocket money was stashed in their money belts but the larger portion was banked in Pittsburgh available by telegraphed bank draft or Wells-Fargo. Before long they would have to be making some big decisions.

Leonard returned to his seat to find his daughter seemingly deep in meditation, or perhaps it was just boredom. "Sophia, something has come up. I just received a wire from the Big Man and I must get up to Denver right away. At Pueblo I'll take D&RG to Denver. I'll be back in Trinidad in a week or two. I imagine your mother will enjoy having you to herself for a few days. You remember that Isabella will be meeting us in Pueblo. Now you and she can accompany each other home. Matt is going up to Denver with me and I've asked James to see you ladies safely home. Incidentally, I've made job offers to both of the Molyneaux boys, so we'll be seeing a lot of them."

Sophia was dismayed. Couldn't her father have arranged things so that Matt could have escorted her south from Pueblo? And without Isabella. Sophia was looking forward to Trinidad's freedom, to think and do as she pleased—especially the latter. Now she would have to wait until Matt returned from Denver, whenever *that* would be.

◇◇◇◇◇◇◇◇◇◇◇◇

The trouble with a trip is that it must end. And that it did, but not exactly at the most convenient location, necessitating a two-mile carriage ride from the Santa Fe station over to the D&RG. Disgruntled passengers were said to observe that it was beneath Santa Fe's dignity to share station facilities with a narrow-gauge railroad. But it meant a drawn-out leave-taking for the small group, father and daughter, brother and brother. Finally Leonard and Matthew took the north-bound to Denver by way of Colorado Springs and Sophia and James southbound to Trinidad by way of Walsenburg.

Sophia's dueña, Isabella, a pleasant middle-aged Mexican woman, met James and Sophia on the D&RG platform. "Buenos dias, Señora," said James, stretching his knowledge of Spanish to its limit. Isabella smiled at his effort and held out a hand in greeting.

The transfer at Pueblo from a standard-gauge Palace car to a narrow-gauge day car represented an extreme contrast in passenger discomfort. Seats were smaller, aisles narrower, and rider comfort sacrificed. However, depending upon the amount of time lost at Walsenburg, the trip to Trinidad should be just a few hours. Most of the passengers seemed to be businessmen in a hurry, or others not particularly fond of a few hours in the saddle. Some, as judged by their dress and excited manner, appeared to be visitors returning from sampling the scenic wonders and mineral waters of the Colorado Springs area. The weather, too, had changed at Pueblo. The sky had darkened and a light rain had started.

The trip south was uneventful but spectacular. There was a little grade near Pueblo but the rest of the way was relatively flat, the train seemingly picking its way through the rolling hills with the vast prairie on the left and the magnificent Sangre de Cristos on the right. It was hard to believe that they were traveling more than a mile above sea level with the Front Range abruptly rising thousands of feet above that. Just below Pueblo the rail line branched off towards Cañon City with the Royal Gorge beyond. I guess I'll soon be up there, James thought, still having a little difficulty absorbing the reality of his good fortune.

Upon arrival in Trinidad he would first locate living quarters for Matthew and himself, buy a horse, saddle, and kit, and make a preliminary assessment of Main Street saloons. Then he would go and look at a couple of local coal mines to get an idea of southern Colorado coal beds and outcrops.

If time permitted, he would go to the county courthouse and look at land records to see how much of the property of Las Animas and Huerfano counties was private, how much was federal open land for homesteading, and how much was clouded by Mexican land grants made before the Mexican war. James was a little uncertain of mining claim procedures and would have to check that out. In the course of all of this he would cautiously ride up towards Raton to see if there was anything going on, although Mr. Llewellyn specifically told him not to take any action until the two of them had met in Trinidad to make plans. Hopefully, the situations at Royal Gorge and Raton will have lightened, but he was not terribly optimistic about that.

The train paused for water and coal at Walsenburg and James could see some coal workings in the distance. It was a nice arrangement. Fuel for the train was always close by; one had only to stop and pick it up. Of course, it wasn't quite that easy; there was a distribution system to consider.

He realized that he was nearly a mile closer to the sun than in Pittsburgh, but on this day there was no sun in evidence—the rain was continuing, and starting to turn to sleet. Well, after all, winter *was* about to begin. The profile of the hills was very similar to Pennsylvania's coal-fields area. This is *coal* country, he exclaimed to himself.

James and Sophia were in desultory conversation most of the way, Isabella in the seat behind them keeping a wary eye upon her charge. As they discussed each other's likes and wishes, they soon learned that they were poles apart and the name of a third person, Matthew, seemed to come up more and more often…and in a very favorable light. Sophia pointed out the obvious. "He's really smart, isn't he?"

She leaned uncomfortably close, her hand on his arm. "But you're not so bad, yourself, Big Jim. Where did you get that nickname?" she asked, suggestively. Why not, she asked herself. Matt won't be back from Denver for a week or so.

James was having no part of this; he unobtrusively pulled away.

He then described his hunting experiences, from wild turkeys to bears. Sophia's reaction was, "Oh, Jim, do you really have to *kill* them?"

"I don't know any other way to get them to the pan," James said.

When Sophia described Trinidad's activities, her eyes glistened—with excitement, not tears. "The opera house is magnificent. Why, just last year Emma Nevada, a young soprano from San Francisco, stopped here on her way to study in Europe. And they say that Adelina Patti may stop here if she takes another American tour."

James was fascinated by her animation. "Does this happen all the time?"

"Well, no—just once in a while. Most of the time the hall is used for rowdy parties, but afternoon tea parties and card games are held many days..."

"At the opera house?"

"Of course not, at somebody's home. And Mama and I often go out for afternoon tea."

She went on. "They've brought in a new game called tennis. It's played with racquets and a small ball. The players hit the ball back and forth over a net. You'd do well, your coordination is so good. But I don't know...you're so big...chasing after a little ball..." She giggled. "And Matt might do better at something like that."

"How about the people around town?"

"Well, downtown they're mostly Mexican—they've been here a long time, fifty years, they say. But you don't have to mingle with them. Out of town, most of the people are also Mexicans, but some of the farmers are Swedes and the miners are Italians and Greeks. You get used to it. Up on 'Aristocracy Hill,' as we call it, the people are all like us. Did you know that I was the first white girl born south of the Arkansas River?" A pause, and then she went on. "Actually, I like Denver better than Trinidad. Father says we may move back there in a couple of years."

Then, with downcast eyes, "As a matter of fact, I hate Trinidad. It's dirty, filled with foreigners...you'll see when we get there."

James realized that all of this conversation was within earshot of Isabella. But Sophia seemed oblivious to that. It was as though the dueña did not even exist.

Meanwhile, the northbound Llewellyn and Matthew boarded the Denver train.

Matthew felt a strange emptiness. While he had been left behind on a countless number of James' hunting trips, never before in his life had he left James. And yet, when he was with James, all he could do was wish his brother would get out of the way.

Leonard was inordinately quiet on the train ride. He had put on his executive face, buried himself in paperwork, and used monosyllables for what had to be said. This was strictly business, his body language said.

That was all right with Matthew. He needed some quiet time to think out his future. And it would be bright, as long as he was careful. He couldn't repeat what he had done on the train—making himself look smarter than Leonard. He must hang onto LL's coattails as a loyal and obedient son-in-law should. There—I've said it—I must remember that Sophia is a necessary part of the package.

The day-trip from Pueblo to Denver followed up Fountain Creek above its confluence with the Arkansas River just south of Pueblo. The terrain was in rolling, hilly contrast with Colorado's flat, grass-covered high plains, but despite the two major rivers, the Platte and the Arkansas, and at least two creeks substantial enough to be given names, Fountain Creek and Plum Creek, the area was still classified as "arid" as opposed to the "moist" midcontinent east of the 100th meridian. The water stop was at the very small community of Monument, which happened to be at the north-south drainage divide between the Platte and Arkansas watersheds.

There was time to do some mountain-gazing. The Front Range, in Matthew's mind's eye, seemed to rise up as a giant ocean wave to crest at fourteen thousand feet—ready to break this way. But it didn't—it receded as if getting ready for the next emotional rise, the next gold rush, the next oil well, the next steel mill, the next railroad, the next coal field, the next whatever. You would have to be dead not to feel these surges and rise with them.

The day was drizzly and cold but that was Colorado at over a mile high in November, described in various accounts as "a land of perpetual sunshine with fearsome thunderstorms and occasional devastating cloudbursts." Well, he was in no hurry for those latter phenomena.

The train was D&RG, of course, but so small—hard to get used to. How do you suppose Jim is fitting into these miniature seats, Matt wondered? But the important thing is getting there; "we" can fix things later—and that was what D&RG was doing.

As they pulled into the Denver station, much of the city was laid out before them. It seemed to stretch out for a couple dozen blocks or so, in both directions, with small farmhouses dotting the surroundings. Outside of Pittsburgh, this was the only "real" city Matthew had ever seen. Downtown buildings were mostly two-storied, many three, and a few four. Concrete, brick, and stone prevailed as the building materials of choice, at least on the street side of the buildings.

Carriages and wagons of all different shapes and sizes along with saddle horses and pack-mule teams filled the streets, forcing pedestrians to the boardwalks along both sides. Altogether, it was an exciting picture for the young man. "This is *my* town," said Matthew to no one in particular. Leonard seemed to take it all in stride.

◇◇◇◇◇◇◇◇◇◇◇◇

The D&RG building was three-story but not in the least ostentatious. It sat amidst a small cluster of very similar buildings. They looked like hotels, and, indeed, turned out to be so. Llewellyn led the way to the one closest to the D&RG offices. "Here we are, Matt. I've stayed here before, and it's okay. I'll see you down here in the lobby in a few minutes, and we'll walk over to see the General."

Ten minutes later, Matthew took a seat in the reception area of the D&RG office. Llewellyn had already gone inside to talk to the General, leaving Matthew to be called. "This may take a while, Matt. Be prepared to discuss, in specific detail, how you will operate as special auditor of the La Veta project."

"Bu…" Matthew started to say. He had thought he was going to get some instructions—not give them. Llewellyn had already closed the door.

Matthew sat back. For sure he was not going to talk from notes. But he must have his thoughts sufficiently clear in his mind for a clear presentation. While he was in Denver, he would say, he would want to review every bit of paper regarding the project, maps, estimates, requisitions, bills of material, schedules, manpower estimates, names of key personnel, contracts and subcontracts—he would want to spend some time with General Palmer and staff. There…could he remember all of that? Well, most might do, if he talked with enough confidence.

This would all take two or three days and he would then travel to Trinidad to get settled and take care of some personal business. He must remember to wire James. After that he would travel up to Walsenburg or to the eastern end of the rail site, wherever the field office was located, to talk to the Superintendent. Assuming that Matt's position was known to the field people by then, he could begin his assignment.

With time on his hands, he idly looked at a basket marked "LA VETA FILE." The document on top, titled "Progress Report" and signed by the Construction Superintendent, described in some detail how the eastern slope had been cleared and rails laid up some ten miles to the summit. The several remaining papers were invoices and bills-of-lading for various materials and supplies. But there was nothing noted for cross-ties, rails, or spikes. This seemed a little strange, Matthew thought. How could they lay ten miles of track without ties or rails? I must be looking in the wrong basket, he concluded. But still…peculiar…*very* peculiar.

After an eternity, the inner door opened and Llewellyn stuck his head out. "Come on in, Matthew, and meet General Palmer."

Matt knew quite a bit about General Palmer. He'd been educated in a Friends school in Philadelphia, followed by post-graduate studies of technical and financial aspects of the European coal mining and railroad industries. Thereafter, he utilized this state-of-the-art knowledge to obtain executive assignments in American coal and railway companies.

Accounts of General Palmer had not done him justice. True, he was described fairly accurately, about forty years old, medium height, slender, with full head of light brown hair, and clean shaven except for a modest trimmed mustache. His posture reflected his military training. The officer's distinguished military career had been highlighted by the receipt of the Congressional Medal of Honor and promotion to Brigadier General in recognition of his valiant defense of Chickamauga. After the war Palmer personally conducted three trans-Colorado surveys for railway routes and then served as Construction Superintendent of the Kansas Pacific railway to Denver.

But the man standing to greet Matthew was more—very much more—than all of that. He's a five-foot, eight-inch *giant*, thought Matt. I've never seen anyone project such intelligence and competence, such boundless energy, so much control—and all before saying a word.

"So this is your financial genius, Leonard. I'm happy to meet you, young Molyneaux."

Red-faced and embarrassed, Matthew said, "As I explained to Mr. Llewellyn, sir, it's all theory and no substance—so far. But I want to learn more."

"Well, substance or not, what you suggested to Leonard was pretty much on the mark. We had already been talking to our investors about accepting revenue bonds at a little higher rate to replace the existing debentures. But we've got to get that revenue started! You said something else kind of interesting—about replacing defaulted bonds with equity stock. *That* could be exciting, but not for this job. Now, tell us how you propose to act as special auditor."

Warmed up a little, Matthew described in detail how he would examine every job-generated piece of paper, looking for the truth behind every number and representation, constantly exploring for trends in units of costs and adherence to schedule.

"Since we cannot allow the work to lag because of delays in receipt of rails and ties and other materials and equipment, either through natural occurrences or acts of the Santa Fe," he said, "I wonder if an alternate supply route from Taos to San Luis or from Santa Fe to Antonito might make sense in a supply emergency. As soon as I can get settled I'll get over to the San Luis Valley to check this out. I'll also go over to Alamosa to let it be known when the tracks will be there. I think Alamosa will be lining up to start its potatoes and stuff to Denver. The biggest potential problem, though, is the acceptance of this auditing effort by the construction people, themselves. I want the men to trust and respect the audit but not hate the auditor."

Palmer interrupted. "Do it the army way—most of these men are veterans—on both sides. They'll understand. As far as sabotage goes, you've got a good point there. The Santa Fe people will do anything. Post armed guards and insist that the workers have rifles in their bedrolls."

Matthew continued, "Another detail—I suppose there is a work train at the east end. If not, we should consider it. Primarily for some workers' amenities—we should try to keep the men out of the towns—but also to keep at the job site a larger than usual supply of ties and rails. I haven't learned yet where the ties and bridge members will come from. Rails will be from Pueblo, of course..."

Palmer suddenly stood up to signal that the meeting was over. Matthew was frozen. Well, I tried, he thought.

Almost offhandedly the General said, "Matthew, you're hired, as if you had not already guessed. And your pay will be that of a real auditor. But tell me one thing. Is 'amenities' Pennsylvania Dutch for whorehouse?"

CHAPTER SEVEN

TRINIDAD

A S JAMES HANDED Sophia down from the train to the station platform at the El Moro depot, she found herself surrounded by a crowd of greeters. The big man was nudged aside like chaff. Sophia's welcoming party included two young girls—younger sisters, James guessed—a Mexican manservant or driver, a Mexican maid, and Mama Llewellyn. The servants grabbed Sophia's luggage, the two girls held on to Sophia, and Mama led the way—eyes straight ahead—to a private two-horse carriage parked off to the side. Isabella brought up the rear; she half-smiled and nodded "adios" to James. No introductions were tendered and James faded into the background, no mean trick for one of his bulk.

James thought of Sophia, shrugged, and with a half-smile picked up his duffel bag and rifles, and headed towards the public carriages lined up to transport D&RG passengers the six miles from El Moro to Trinidad. James wasn't concerned over all this but the cold shoulder he had received was something else, again. "I guess that's that," he muttered to himself, wounded a bit, but not exactly devastated. In any event, any feeling of being unwelcome was outweighed by the nervousness of a new adventure.

◇◇◇◇◇◇◇◇◇◇◇◇

"Sophie, Sophie, what did you bring for us?" screamed the little ones.

"Here are some doll dishes from the great International Exposition in Philadelphia."

"This one's mine!"

"No, that one's yours and *this* one's mine!" said the elder one.

They squeezed into the private carriage, the Llewellyns inside on facing upholstered bench seats, the driver and Isabella up front. As they got underway, Sophia assumed her usual role of shushing up the little girls. "Quiet down, you two, you'll have your turn in a minute." Then, turning to Mrs. Llewellyn, she said, "Oh, Mama, I met the nicest man on the train. He's real good looking and very smart—he'll be rich one day and he's just my size. I'm going to marry him and I won't have to go back to that awful college again."

The little sisters giggled.

"Has he asked you, yet?"

"No, but I can handle that." This drew a nod and a knowing look from Mama.

After a pause, Mrs. Llewellyn asked, "Does this young man have a name?"

"Matthew Molyneaux."

"That sounds foreign to me."

"Oh, Mama, you worry too much. It *is* foreign, Matt told me. It's the name of a castle near Paris" Sophia said with laughter in her voice.

The carriage clip-clopped towards town at a brisk pace, and the group would arrive at the Llewellyn house in less than an hour. It entered Trinidad at the northeast end proceeding along Main Street past the crowded Commercial Street corner—Trinidad's business center—turned up Beech Street, and stopped at a large three-story home on the corner of Third Street. The house, built in what might be called "classical Southern" architectural style, stood out in a sparsely built-up, but obviously high-scale neighborhood. Four massive columns from ground to the top of a second-story portico outlined an ornately carved front door. The entrance seemed to be saying, "Welcome, everyone," and in fine print, "if you can afford the price."

◇◇◇◇◇◇◇◇◇◇◇◇◇

El Moro seemed to James to be a town looking for something to do. Plunked down on the edge of a thriving ranching area—sheep and cattle—it also had the makings of a coal town (the fledgling Engleville mine seven miles to the south) and it was a shipping terminus for the newly extended D&RG line from Pueblo and Denver. It had no history and lacked substance; maybe it needs more people living here, James thought. The nearly loaded public carriage James boarded traveled a little south of west towards Trinidad four miles away, the Purgatorie River in sight on the right most of the way. The river wasn't much to look at this time of the year, flowing placidly far inside its banks.

The surrounding plateau area was gently rolling, sloping imperceptibly eastward to the near-level plains beyond, and covered with buffalo grass, naturally dried at this time of the year. James, who had always supposed that grass was grass, had been surprised to learn that Colorado's short buffalo grass, unlike Eastern grasses, kept its nutrient value; even when it was cured naturally on the ground.

To the west and south James could see the foothills and spurs of the Sangre de Cristo Range of the Rocky Mountains, spotted here and there with groves of trees, which from this distance appeared to be cedar and piñon with pine trees further up. So that's where the D&RG and Santa Fe standoff will be, he thought. Actually, he had spent so much time looking at the topographic maps in the Carnegie

Library, to find where he would put his hunting cabin, that he could easily imagine the rail tracks zigzagging up and over Raton Pass. But whose train, he wondered, Santa Fe's or Rio Grande?

The carriages that D&RG had provided for its passengers presented a tight fit, especially after James had boarded. From the *Trinidad Chronicle* (a copy was laid on the carriage seat) James had learned the basis for the anger of the Trinidad citizens. The *Chronicle* was claiming that the D&RG was trying to pull the same stunt at Trinidad as it had done up at Colorado Springs and Pueblo. A new city, just seven miles away, was designed to replace the old one—but under D&RG control—and Trinidad was having no part of it. On top of that, the transfer of passengers and luggage added at least an hour to the travel time and the inadequately sprung carriages made the ride quite unpleasant—bumpy and noisy. Conversation of any kind was not possible.

Through actions like this, the Rio Grande—the Anglos pronounced it Rye oh Grand—had the knack of infuriating its customers and neighbors. James wondered whether either General Palmer or Leonard Llewellyn recognized this situation. Maybe D&RG would have better luck in the courts if it had better relationships with the townspeople. And he wondered if the town had reminded D&RG that because Trinidad was upstream, the Purgatorie was Trinidad's—and El Moro couldn't survive without it.

Nevertheless, at this time, there was considerable activity around both the railcar and the wagon-loading docks at El Moro. Rail shipments of agricultural products were destined for Denver, wagonloads of shearings for Independence. Cattle would be trailed up to the Santa Fe pens at Las Animas.

The grassland had been pretty well grazed down, James noted, but there were still flocks of sheep across the nearby bottomland, with cattle on the prairie to the east and on the grassy rolling hills to the north. Why hadn't the livestock been taken in, he wondered? Early snow could be expected at any time, but the heavy snows would be at least a month away. Sycamore and tamarisk could be seen in the creek beds and alongside the Purgatorie River, which was quite low. The weather was cold with a bone-chilling wind causing carriage windows to be tightly closed. The interior was stifling and unpleasant— bathing for travelers was awkward, at best. But if anyone essayed to open a window a little, response from other passengers was immediate. *"Shut the window. It's not July."*

They approached Trinidad from the northeast at a point just south of the Purgatorie River (nicknamed the "Picketwire" by Anglo residents). From this view, James thought, the town looked like the devil's workshop. It was as he had expected Kansas towns to be—but weren't, except for Dodge, that is, which was a hellhole. From Sophia's description, James could see that the carriage had entered town on the east end of Main Street. While the street itself was incredibly bad, deeply rutted from side to side and end to end, there were a few very large and very nice Eastern-style homes and a couple of sprawling haciendas for a block or two on the left side of Main Street and more up the hill.

James realized that he was looking at "Aristocracy Hill" and "Millionaire Row," as Sophia had characterized those areas. He guessed that Llewellyn's position with D&RG would have placed him about midway up the hill. Obviously, a new person in town would have to be very careful in his selection of a residence site—not too close to Main Street and not too high on the hill.

The balance of Main Street was well filled in, but mostly with older single-story adobe buildings, some not quite in line with the new city property lines. A few new buildings were under construction, mostly two- and three-story frame and board siding—some brick and stone. The town was showing signs of coming out of the '73 panic, when construction and expansion had stalled all across the country. Now there were workmen, commercial people, and customers crowding the boardwalks; wagons, buggies, carriages, and single horsemen were filling the streets; it was a bustle.

James had mixed emotions. Mentally he was excited; Matthew was right, he thought, it's evident that opportunities are everywhere. But was also apprehensive—there was a rock in the bottom of his stomach. He left peaceful Pittsburgh for this: over a month on the road, a fractious brother, an uncertain future. On the other hand, just look at those mountains! And truth be told, Pittsburgh wasn't that great anymore, either. Things were difficult after Father went off to war.

There was a near year-round flow of Santa Fe Trail wagons up Commercial and Main Streets through town. As the D&RG coach traveled west on Main Street, about to turn left down Commercial, it passed a twenty-wagon train, sixteen oxen each heading east out of town. Some wagons were coupled in tandem pairs. Off to the left coming up Commercial Street was another wagon train that looked even larger.

Trinidad, which started as a farming and sheep-raising pueblo, had become a vital trading center for livestock and agriculture because of the Santa Fe Trail, with all of its oxen. On a dry day such as today, it was still easy to imagine the kind of wintertime mess that would be made by thousands and thousands of hooves and wheels and that many more thousand tons of rainwater. Fortunately, nearly continuous board sidewalks up both sides of the two important streets gave some measure of mud control during the spring and early fall rainy seasons.

There was a commercial establishment along these streets to meet every conceivable need of a thriving community. James could make out only one saloon on the east or genteel end of Main Street, but as the carriage turned down Commercial Street, he could see at least a dozen more on West Main. And there appeared to be a saloon in every other building or so, on Commercial. What did the sheriff in Dodge say about his town—at least twenty- five saloons?

It would be expected that such a well-equipped area would be supported by a substantial and thirsty populace—and it was! Commercial Street was teeming with horses, carriages, wagons, cowhands, draymen, and nondescripts. A bright sun for shady people!

And it would be worse in the evening.

The Elm Street stage station, one block off Commercial, was a busy place, serving not only the shuttle carriages from El Moro, but the ever increasing Butterfield and Pike's Peak stage line freight and passenger traffic. There was talk that the AT&SF branch soon to be built from La Junta would also have its depot on Elm. This would cut off the bulk of the wagon traffic and establish an eastern Santa Fe Trail terminus next to the river. This was just weeks away, everyone thought.

James retrieved his gear and trudged south up Commercial, sticking his head in a few of the saloons but not stopping. He was thinking back upon what he had seen in Topeka, Emporia, and especially Newton where the townspeople had demanded clean-up, and how quickly it had occurred. Within five years one would not be able to recognize Trinidad—and soon couldn't come soon enough.

Thinking about cleanup, he could use a little of that himself. And there, a few doors up, was a shop that, through a large front window, James could see had three barbers and just four men waiting. In little time, James had bathed, had been shaved, and had picked up some information. No one seemed to know when Santa Fe would reach town—why was it taking so long to get the tracks here from La Junta? But it was a quiet anxiety. Unlike D&RG, which had built its own town of El Moro as its terminus—expected to drastically reduce the importance of Trinidad—Santa Fe was coming right into Trinidad.

Nothing having been said about the line over Raton Pass, James casually introduced that subject. "And how about Raton?" he asked.

"It'll be snowing up there pretty soon, and nothing is going on," the barber said, "but in a couple of months we should see Santa Fe construction people swarming into town. I heard that the Raton survey has already been done, which will speed things up."

It seemed no one knew more about this situation than James did, himself, and that was essentially nothing. It was curious, James felt— Llewellyn had said that D&RG and Santa Fe were squaring off for a standoff at Raton Pass, just fifteen miles away. But one would never know here in town.

Turning east on Main, James stopped at the only saloon in the first block. "The Columbian," said a stylishly lettered sign. Stepping inside, he looked around. The place was at least a cut above anything he had seen down on Commercial Street or even in Dodge, for that matter. It had a large central room, a long bar with hand-carved back-bar on one side of that room, a pool table on the other, a little office in back, and an open door leading to what appeared to be a private gaming room. Chairs and tables, some with covers, filled about half of the floor space; the balance was standing room.

Oil lamps along the walls provided more than adequate illumination. A couple of coal-burning pot-bellied stoves supplemented body heat for winter comfort. The walls were adorned with a few landscapes and flower renditions that were meant to give a certain homelike feeling to the room—but didn't quite succeed. Stairs led to at least one other floor. The place was comfortably crowded—three girls that he could see, all dressed as dance-hall girls should be, short skirts, stockinged legs, bright jewelry—but nothing like down on Commercial Street. This was all as to be expected, considering the Columbian's location on the "right" side of the Main Street deadline and just across the street from the opera house.

James stepped up to the bar and gained the attention of a bartender.

"What can I get for you?"

"Whisky, water, and directions—in that order, if you please."

The glasses were handed over and the bottle set down. "Now, where in this lovely little town would you want to go?"

"I want to buy a horse, a really good one, big, strong, and mountain-broke. And a heavy-duty saddle to match—probably custom fitted."

"I'd try Ramirez. He has a livery stable on South Walnut and a saddle shop with other supplies in front. He might have everything you need. If not, he can send you somewhere. And if you need a room, you can't beat Maude's. It's east on Main Street a couple blocks."

And then from behind came another voice, female and a little gravely. "Leaving town so soon, big man? It looks like you just got here. I haven't heard of anyone else your size in town for quite some time—and all gussied up to boot. You're sure you want to leave?"

James turned. At a little table on a platform near the door and about a foot above the floor sat a woman and her dog, the latter very large, very black, and very unfriendly in appearance and disposition, the woman indeterminate on all counts at first glance. She came down from her perch, sliding over to James. He looked at her approvingly, almost eye-to-eye. She was tall and surprisingly slender, her dress belted and her skirt split to emphasize those qualities. She had blue-green eyes, bright red hair, perhaps Nature's own shade or perhaps not. While each feature of her face was, individually, too bold, as a composition they had a pleasant balance.

"You're pretty good size yourself, Ma'am. I'd say only a couple hands shorter and much prettier, to boot."

"And at least a hundred pounds lighter. And don't call me Ma'am, I'm nearly—but not *quite*—old enough to be your mother, and my name is Lillian."

"Well, okay then, Lil."

"Not Lil nor Lily—it's Lillian."

And not very old at all, thought James.

"What's your name?"

"James—I'm called Jim."

"So you won't think I'm addressing your father?"

"Well—uh—nice place they have here."

"You're changing the subject."

"Well—uh, I was thinking that you look a little—uh—fresh for this racket."

"And just what racket is that?" She spoke quietly and slowly and with some heat.

The dog growled menacingly.

James squirmed.

But then she smiled broadly. "Oh, I see your problem. I must introduce myself. I'm the proprietor here. I keep the girls in line, and sometimes I play the piano. And I may entertain upstairs—but damn seldom."

And then to keep him completely off balance, "You're big enough, but do you live up to expectations? I think I'll start calling you 'well-uh.'"

"Well—uh—I've had no complaints." Glancing at the stairs, "We'll have to find out."

She led him up the stairs. Instead of turning right at the top of the hall where three doors in a line could be seen, she followed the hall as it made a sharp left turn to another door, out of sight from the floor below. They entered the room together.

He paused at a coin dish on a little table near the door and reached into his pocket.

"Not this time, Jim. Free introductory offer."

James glanced around. It was a large bedroom, with a moderately large sitting room, adjoining bathing, and toilet area; all in all, a rather large apartment and quite decently furnished. A couple of windows let in the daytime light. An Oriental rug lay on the polished floor and three or four paintings hung on the wall—Western scenes, probably from a client painter. But the room didn't really need such decoration. Lillian was quite enough.

"For Chris' sake, take off your boots. How long since you've had a woman, anyway?"

"Seems like forever."

"All right, now, take the rest off—everything—they're nice clothes. I'll hang them up. And stand over here right in front of me. I want to look you over—yeah, you cleaned up real good, and God knows you're well..." Her eyes lit up in appreciation.

Lillian pulled off her skirt and in two steps slipped from her underthings. He lifted her up. Holding on to his neck, she wrapped her legs around his waist and arched her back; their bodies came together, uniting with a ferocity of deprivation, the muscles of his shoulders straining, loins flexing, her nails making their own grooves in his back. They remained there body to body, breathing hard. She held on, her fingers curling in his hair, her eyes wide. Still together, they dropped slowly to their knees, then James to his back and she astride, then on to the bed.

James leaned against the foot of the bed, she against the pillows at the head. She looked at ease, not at all bothered by their nakedness. And he had never felt so comfortable with a woman before—but, to be honest about it, there really hadn't been that many. Let's see, he thought, there was that Shawnee girl up in the Alleghenies, there was

Millie in Pittsburgh, and...and then he considered Lillian again. She's sexy, intelligent, fun to talk to—and I like her.

He slid up beside her, face buried in the hollow of her breasts, tongue first on her nipples and then across her belly, and then her flank, her belly again...

They lay quietly on the bed, he on his back, half asleep, and she on her side, index finger aimlessly tracing circles in the black forest of hair on his chest and below his belly. "Where are you off to, Jim, to the gold mines, or up to the big city, or just passing through?"

He didn't answer at first. Lillian thought him asleep. Then he said, "I don't really know—but none of those. I'm looking for a moderately small town—a lot smaller than Pittsburgh. Maybe it's Trinidad. Where I can have a small business—like a saloon, a gun shop, or something—and where I can get out in the backcountry for hunting and fishing whenever I want, and where there's a big beautiful woman I can hug like this..." He pulled her to him. "Lillian, you're as much woman as I could ever want."

"And maybe more than you can handle," she challenged.

A relaxed and thoroughly satisfied James said, "I guess these are your living quarters?"

"Yes. When my husband was alive, we had a small house on the edge of town. I fixed this up to take its place."

"Among other things, you seem to be a pretty good business-woman."

"A single woman, widow or not, has to be, or go down the ditch. So, tell me, Jim, are you loaded or do you dress nice like this all for show? And how will you go about getting the gun-shop or saloon?"

James laughed. "Well, I had halfway planned to get a place about like this one, but with an adjoining members-only gentlemen's club for Trinidad's elite. Maybe I could build it right next to yours so we could share dishwashers. But to answer your question, no, I'm not loaded, but I've enough of a stake to get something started."

James stood and began pulling on his clothes. "Well Lillian, don't think it's not been fun, but I've got to go out and find lodgings for my brother and myself. I'll see you soon—real soon."

◇◇◇◇◇◇◇◇◇◇◇◇

Stepping outside, it was immediately apparent that winter was, indeed, on its way. The sky was cloudless—inconsistent with the severe cold. So his first Colorado purchase was a Mexican caballero-style poncho, waterproof and lined, suitable for horseback or afoot, on street, trail, or camp. Why didn't they have something like this in Pittsburgh?

Down Main Street a few blocks was Maude's rooming house, a large two-story frame building identified only by a small neatly lettered sign in the front-door glass pane. In response to James' knock the door opened. "Can I help you? My God, you're full size."

Maude was ample, filling the doorway so that James had to look over her head to see the large dining room—table set for ten—and behind that a pair of upholstered and a few straight-backed chairs for guests' use.

"I'd like a room for an indefinite period—at least a couple of months. And one for my brother, a little more indefinite—he should be here in a few days."

"Fine—I've got a couple of good ones, side by side. Each room has a wash basin, toilets out back. Clean sheets and towels each week. Coffee in the morning; full supper at six; nothing on Sunday. No girls in the rooms. One dollar a day, paid one week in advance. Okay?"

Dinner at Maude's was ample and acceptable; James was easy to please. Campfire dinners in the woods left a lot to be desired, except where fresh game or fish was involved. More often than not, he would have to settle for hardtack and jerky.

All day as he went from place to place in Trinidad, James had been on the lookout for any sign of Santa Fe activity. That evening, he did meet a Santa Fe chief locater who was staying at Maude's. The man, who introduced himself as Albert something-or-other, didn't seem to think that there was anything exceptional, or secret, about the fact that Santa Fe was moving all of its highest level engineering supervisors from out-of-state to Colorado—most to Pueblo. This included locating parties, teamster chiefs, bridge engineers, construction foremen, and clerks. Just waiting for the snow to melt, Albert indicated. Learning that James had just recently come through Las Animas, Albert asked whether any construction preparations could be seen.

"Only great stacks of ties and rails, lying on the ground near the station," James replied.

"Oh, yes, that would be the eighty miles or so of Kit Carson track that Union Pacific abandoned and picked up, and we purchased. That'll go a long ways on this line."

"If I might ask, why did they send you way down here, and why so near the start of winter?" asked James.

Albert hesitated, and then replied, "In a day or two, when the rest of my party arrives, we'll be confirming the UP survey data between Las Animas and Trinidad. We can do this kind of work with a few inches of snow on the ground. I'm starting at this end and another party up at the other. It was my idea to do it this way to save time, and the company bought it," he said proudly.

"In fact, they're going to do the entire job this way to save a lot of time—both ends to the middle. It's made easier by the existence of the old wagon trail, running alongside for nearly the entire distance. As far as why I'm down here so early, the company believes that a proposed railway route through the mountains, must be evaluated during the winter—something they learned in the Sierra, I guess."

"But I didn't see any mountains out at Las Animas," said James. "It's as flat as this table."

Albert hesitated, showing a little embarrassment. "I was getting ahead of myself—we'll also be getting started on the next leg over Raton Pass from Trinidad. As soon as the snow clears a little we can start clearing and grading. We don't have to wait for surveys up there—we managed to acquire field notes from another company's survey made just last year."

James said no more. He realized he had stumbled upon someone who was justifiably proud of what he was doing, and couldn't stop talking about it. James changed the subject—he had all the information he needed. He addressed the group of diners. "Can anyone tell me where I can buy a two-horse delivery wagon with a covered bed? My brother is starting a retail tobacco outlet and, with luck, he'll be making deliveries around town."

◇◇◇◇◇◇◇◇◇◇◇◇

James breakfasted at a little restaurant a couple of blocks short of the Columbian. He thought again about Lillian; his mind had been on her nearly constantly since the day before. Quite a woman and smart, he thought. She knew where she wanted to go and exactly how to get there. She said she wished I "had an older brother"— maybe I could age a little, he thought, and there really isn't that much difference in our ages, anyway, maybe five or six years.

The next couple of days were busy. After James had made a tentative choice between several horses that Ramirez had to offer, he visited the Trinidad First National at the corner of Main and Commercial to make arrangements to have his and Matthew's Pittsburgh account transferred. Then followed some shopping for more winter clothes and camping gear. The seasons had already begun to turn; fall meshing into winter at breakneck speed. A frigid wind had just started whirling down Main Street carrying a few snowflakes and promising more. And we're not even out of November.

◇◇◇◇◇◇◇◇◇◇◇◇

While waiting for Matthew to come down from Denver—a few days had already passed—and since the instructions from Llewellyn were to stay away from Raton for now, James turned his attention to the second assignment from Llewellyn, to scout for potential coal properties. He decided to ride out to the Engleville mine, a couple miles southeast of Trinidad, to see how the southern Colorado coal seams lay with respect to other identifiable strata of sandstone, shale, or clay.

James could then scout around the hills north of Trinidad to look for evidence of similar layering in various rock outcrops or eroded hillsides. It's certainly not surefire, he thought, but it's a start, and it will give me something to do while I'm waiting to see if Leonard is serious about either of these assignments. Raton certainly looks like a bust, and I have no idea what may be happening up at Royal Gorge. I'm worried about not hearing anything from Llewellyn—no instruction, no information, no nothing. Time is passing and I seriously doubt that Santa Fe is dawdling.

Thinking, again, about the coal "prospecting" assignment he was embarking upon, it still didn't make sense. It would be great to be a geologist and do this right. Maybe I should dump this Trinidad scene and go up to Golden for a few years, he thought. But it's not to be—our Pittsburgh stake won't last forever. Well, anyway, it's over to Engleville.

James relished riding again. So far, the big five-year-old black gelding purchased on approval from Ramirez appeared very good. Its normal gait was smooth, it obeyed reins and knee pressure perfectly, and seemed tireless. It appeared a little hesitant over rocks and rock-filled streams, but that might be my fault, thought James.

After all, I haven't been on a horse for a while. James named the new horse Coalfire after a similar animal he had owned in Pittsburgh. He put the horse through its paces, first into a canter, then a gallop, and finally through some cutting maneuvers—all with satisfactory results. The light snow cover was taken in stride. The saddle, custom-fitted with scabbards for his Springfield hunting rifle and his small-caliber Remington, met the big man's demanding requirements well. Coalfire was fairly heavily laden for this two-day exploratory trip with bedroll, camping gear, food, and all the maps he could lay his hands upon.

James was dressed in heavy corduroy trousers, wool shirt, poncho, and broad-brim slouch hat. A heavy Mackintosh on the pommel completed his outfit. He did not wear a holstered revolver; his Colt was in an inconspicuous saddle holster. James knew he had something to learn about a late Colorado autumn at seven thousand feet; he expected his clothing might be a little scanty this first outing.

This trip was to be out to the Engleville mine to look at any exposed strata and outcrops. Perhaps he could go into the mine portal. He would have liked to ride up towards Raton to see if anything was going on. It was very curious. Llewellyn had said that D&RG and Santa Fe were heading for a standoff at Raton. Curious or not, Jim's instructions from Llewellyn were clear—don't do anything.

Halfway to Engleville, James realized he was not entirely alone on the trail. They were about to overtake a man and a horse, both limping—the man worse. "Anything I can do to help?" James asked.

"I don't suppose so," was the reply, "unless you're a blacksmith or a doctor. My horse threw a shoe, and I twisted an ankle."

"We're less than an hour from Engleville. Let's get you up on Coalfire, here, and I'll lead both horses. I could use some honest exercise."

"That's a pretty generous offer—and the way I feel now, I'll accept with thanks. I'm Phillip Anschultz, Superintendent of the Engle mine—and responsible for the little company town just beyond."

"I'm James Molyneaux—I answer to Jim. I'm superintendent of nothing, but I'm looking around..."

Phillip mounted Coalfire and they started off. "Where did you come from, Jim?"

"Pittsburgh. And you?"

"Well, I'm from Johnstown. Did you ever work the mines?"

James smiled. "I worked a little up pit, but I was just too damn big to work the face. Some of those tunnels are only four feet high."

"Yeah, they use little children to dig out some of that coal. Isn't that the shits? That's why I left—I couldn't stomach that."

They trudged on. Finally, looming over a little hill was the tipple and just beside that the mine office, a smallish wood-plank building. The company town of Engleville lay just beyond, about fifty or sixty small houses, a building that appeared to be a stable and blacksmith shop, a much larger building that could be a general store, and yet another structure that might be a school house. A few people could be seen, but children were probably in school. About a quarter of the men were on shift in the mine—off-shift men were probably asleep.

"Here we are, Jim. I can't say how much I appreciate your help. Come on in and have a beer. You certainly deserve it. What brings you up here, anyway?"

Settling down at a table in Phillip's office, James addressed that question. "I'm on a little private assignment on behalf of Leonard Llewellyn. You probably know him. He's with your parent company. He wants me to scout the hills in this county for promising mine properties. I figured that if I could see how the coal beds lie in a couple of producing properties, it might help my search."

Phillip's pleasant smile had transformed into a dark frown. "James," he said, "let me say at the outset that I will show you the seams and everything else you want to know. Not to assist Llewellyn in any way, but because you're a good guy. You helped me a lot, today, and you certainly didn't have to"

"Thanks, Phillip. But could you tell me why you're down on Mr. Llewellyn?"

"I'd rather not say, but let me warn you that if you have any kind of agreement with Leonard Llewellyn, you had better get it in writing. Now, for your information only—and I'm sure you'll make proper use of it—our bed here is twelve foot thick and very good quality. Above us is an eight-inch layer of light gray clay and above that at least two feet of shale, gray to white and very brittle. About one foot beneath our bed is a dark red sandstone. I have no idea how thick—for all I know, down to the center of the earth. Now, the interesting thing is the consistency. We see the same pattern all around here. I understand that Walsen is about the same; farther north than Walsen the layering is similar, but fractured and upset. You have to remember that as you get closer to the real mountains, there will be more hard-rock intrusions, up-thrusts and offsets. Cañon"—he pronounced it "canyon"—"is particularly interesting. Not too far away the geologists found seepage of 'liquid coal.' I understand that's sometimes a giveaway to the real stuff. They apparently sell it—but I can't see how'n the hell they can do that. You can't store it in a pile, you know."

James said, "I notice that Engle employs a drift tunnel. Is that usual in this area?"

"Yes, because all the mines in southern Colorado are on hilly land. On flat terrain or if we have to go lower to reach another vein, we'll sink a shaft and go out horizontally from there."

"One mine I saw in Pennsylvania drove its main tunnel clear to the end of the seam and then mined backwards, letting the ceiling drop behind them."

"I've heard of that, but we really don't know where our bed might end. Also, our owner wants a quick cash flow. So, we drive in from the front in a room-and-pillar pattern and muck as much out as possible and as quickly as possible."

"Do you have ventilation problems?"

"Not yet. We have very little methane, also called firedamp out here, and no whitedamp, also called chokedamp. And, of course, never having had a fire, we have no afterdamp, which is very poisonous. You know the terms, I'm sure. Ultimately we will need ventilation shafts and tunnels—but not now."

"Yes, those are terms that I *am* familiar with. They're universal in mines."

"That's about all I should say about strategy, and maybe I've said too much already. When you leave, James, I'll take you back to the portal and you can see for yourself the strata I've described."

"Before we do that, please tell me a little about the town of Engleville."

"It isn't really a town at all—it's a coal camp. It's a good example of a new generation of such living facilities. In effect, it *is* a town with individual homes—about sixty-five now with room for a several-fold expansion—large general store, school, recreation hall, police station, saloon, offices for the mayor and other officials. In short, it's like a town with a major difference: the whole place is owned by the company, which also appoints the mayor and others, provides security, and exercises authority over everything. If a worker doesn't fit in, he and his family can be evicted. The miners pay rent and, of course, for any special services. In this way miners obtain nice uniform housing and gain a sense of unity and friendship. The company gets rental income and profit from the store."

"Do the people go into Trinidad?"

"Well, they really don't have to—everything they need is right here—and it's a long walk—hardly any of them own horses. Also, the town people aren't very friendly with the miners."

"And now for that drink I promised you." He limped over to a cupboard. "And don't forget what I told you. Protect your ass, James, and mine too, if it comes to that."

◇◇◇◇◇◇◇◇◇◇◇◇

Riding out from Engle, James was deep in thought. That unsettling conversation with Phillip Anschultz is between the two of us, he thought, and no one else, not even Matthew—he's too close to Llewellyn right now and might inadvertently say something he shouldn't. If Phillip is right in his assessment of Llewellyn, then it's possible that Matthew and I are being set up. After all, both job offers came from Llewellyn and he might have a hidden plan.

Well—my visit to Engle today never occurred. I'll watch and listen—and listen especially to that little nagging question in the back of my mind about General Palmer's willingness to let Llewellyn develop some coal properties and markets on his own. It just doesn't make sense. In the meantime, even though Leonard told me to wait for instructions, since the snow has stopped and sky is clear, I'm going to ride as far up Raton Pass as I can. I'll put off my coal exploration for a few days.

James pretty well followed the old Santa Fe Trail, south through the grassy foothills of Raton Mesa, but in truth the trail was not particularly well defined and that wasn't helped by a light dusting of snow. Double rows of wagons on the trail had become usual and with a diminished Indian threat, trail discipline was relaxed. Wagons tended to stray a little from the ruts. It's a little strange that I've neither seen nor heard any activity up ahead, James thought. I'm only about five miles from the summit now. He pulled his rifle from its scabbard, made sure there were cartridges in the magazine, and tried to act like an unsuccessful hunter as he made his way up through the brush and small trees—piñon, he thought, I wonder how they spell that word? There was an inch or so of fresh snow on the ground with clear areas under the trees. That would certainly change in a week or two as the winter storms started to come in.

Off to the right he could clearly see the flank of Mt. Raton of the Sangre de Cristos. There was less than a two-thousand-foot elevation difference between Trinidad and the top of the pass, but the grade was very steep, in some places nearly vertical. Even a landsman could see how the train tracks would have to go diagonally up this first grade and then wind around somehow to take another diagonal the other way, James reasoned. God, how I would like to be able to figure things like that out—I guess it's too late, though.

Off to the west where the Raton Mountains curved around to join the Sangre de Cristos and then the main ranges of the Rockies, the setting sun backlit the mountains, silhouetting the higher peaks and casting a rosy twilight all around. It was breathtaking, especially for one who had often viewed the *rising* sun above the *eastern* Allegheny peaks.

It's time to sack out, James decided. He threw his bedroll on a bare spot of ground near Coalfire's tether. Not wanting to attract attention with a fire, he ate a dry cold supper. Making sure there was not a cartridge in the chamber, he put his Colt in his sack with his rifle nearby.

After a cold restless night—he hadn't slept on the ground for some time and he could see that in this country he needed a heavier bedroll—he arose with the dawn and started moving cautiously up the mountainside. He tethered Coalfire again and slipped through the trees and brush for a better look to confirm that nothing was going on. Dead-on was another near-vertical face of the mountain. To his eye there was no way to get over or around it, but then he noticed over on the left where the wagon trail seemed to end, a man-and-horse trail zigzagged up the very steep slope. He and Coalfire could do it—but there's no time for that today, he thought. Off to the left a cleared path, with some heavy ropes alongside, led nearly straight up the granite face. Evidently, this was the toll road that he'd heard about in the barber shop—Dick Wooten's, they said. Stock would be unhitched and led up the zigzag, and wagons hoisted with block and tackle to the top. James guessed that Wooton's house and toll gate would be at the top of the rope hoist.

The entire area was snow-blanketed from Friday's mild storm and still untracked by man or horse. Where were Llewellyn's "hundreds of armed workers" supposedly in standoff with Santa Fe forces? Was someone giving Leonard bad field information, or was the D&RG vice president, himself, the source of it all? Leonard hadn't mentioned the toll road over Raton. Shouldn't someone from D&RG have purchased rights-of-way by now? And what kinds of permits, James wondered, are required by the Territory of New Mexico for the rail line on over to Santa Fe? Either Llewellyn has chosen not to inform me, and that's certainly his privilege, or he doesn't know what's going on, or...*or he likes it this way.* I wonder if he has some kind of a relationship with Santa Fe and is setting me up as a fall-guy as far as Palmer is concerned. Is this the reason that Leonard seemed not particularly interested in having me look around Raton just yet? In fact, Leonard specifically instructed me not to. Since I've not seen nor been seen, technically I'm following orders, so back to Trinidad. As darkness fell—about halfway to town—he camped again for a cold dinner and colder night.

He had hardly broken camp the next morning when he came face to face with another rider on the wagon trail. It was Albert, the Santa Fe locator from Maude's. In a friendly tone Albert asked, "What brings you up here this icy morning, Jim? I thought I was the only one around here without good sense."

"Just looking around," James replied, in as casual a manner as he could muster. "As soon as I get a job I'm going to build myself a hunting shack somewhere between here and Spanish Peaks—about thirty miles over that way, I think." He pointed to the northwest where a pair of snow-capped peaks could be seen.

Albert smiled. "You'd better look over there, then. Santa Fe will be running a railroad right up to where we're standing now, and you can bet that there will be more mines and towns up the Purgatorie, as well. There won't be any game for ten miles around. Tell me, James, were you far enough up the trail to see Dick Wooton? He's the toll-gate keeper, you know. I want to talk with him."

"No," said James. "I only got to the bottom of the hoist; I imagine the toll gate is up at the top, somewhere.

"I've got to get moving, Albert. See you at Maude's."

Turning back to the trail north, James considered what he had observed. Undoubtedly the Santa Fe locator was on his way to negotiate a railroad right-of-way with Dick Wooton. Another confirmation of Santa Fe's progress...

◇◇◇◇◇◇◇◇◇◇◇◇

Back in town, James stepped into the Columbian again, catching the scene just about where he left it, except this time Lillian was in her office over in the far corner of the large room.

"Jim," Lillian exclaimed. "I wasn't sure you were still around."

"Like a bear and a honey pot," said Jim, enclosing much of her in a gigantic bear-hug.

"I've been called a lot of things but never an old pot."

"I certainly didn't say old, and, anyway, I've done my arithmetic and if I assign three extra months to each of my hard-time Pittsburgh years, we come out even."

"Jim, I love the way you talk. You got any older brothers back home? No? Well, in the meantime—"

They went upstairs. Things looked the same to James with one very notable exception—the coin dish was missing.

"Would you like to sleep over, Jim?"

◇◇◇◇◇◇◇◇◇◇◇◇◇

As they lay there the next morning, Lillian turned serious. "Jim, the other day you started to mention how the railroads will affect the Santa Fe Trail. Do you think I'll be affected?"

"Yeah, I think we will very soon see some big changes around here, and from one potential businessman to a dyed-in-the-wool business-woman, there's something we *both* might think about. The Santa Fe will have its tracks in Trinidad in just a few months. This means that this will be the western terminus of the old wagon trail. For a while there will be a tremendous increase in saloon business; the wagons will be outfitting and turning around here instead of La Junta and the drovers and outriders will be camping and killing time between trips. There will be hundreds of outfitters, blacksmiths, machinists, canvas- and leather-smiths, and many more. Instead of trailing up to La Junta, cattle will be loaded here.

"So there will be more thirsty cowhands after a long Texas drive. There will be a big boom—but it will be temporary, so we shouldn't get carried away. Another couple of years and an additional railroad from the south undoubtedly will intercept the trail further west, maybe even at Santa Fe. But, while most of the Commercial Street saloons will then disappear, I think there's a future for a gentrified sa-loon and a private gentlemen's club both of which can be patronized by the 'respectable' and the 'not-so-respectable.'"

The late fall sun was already above the eastern horizon when James finished dressing,

"Lillian, I've some scouting around to do, up and around DelAgua Canyon, and I must get going. I'll be back in a couple days."

◇◇◇◇◇◇◇◇◇◇◇◇◇

Riding north from Trinidad that afternoon, James was crossing a small bridged creek about fifteen miles from town when he realized it was getting a little dark and he really needed better light to do what he wanted. He tethered Coalfire and threw out his bedroll back from the road a few dozen yards. Another cold dinner of jerky and hardtack. It didn't matter—he'd had a good lunch at Maude's but that didn't make the ground any softer.

At first light he saw that the little arroyo, carrying the creek he had crossed, came down through an opening between the hills perhaps a mile from the road—nothing at all to distinguish it from the rolling surroundings. The channel was about ten feet deep and double that distance between the steep banks.

James saddled up, rummaged in his rucksack for some more jerky and hardtack, and took off along the arroyo. At the pinch-point of the hills that he had noticed from his campsite, the arroyo and its creek took up about a quarter of the distance between the toes of the slopes, but above that point, the little valley opened up dramatically to a width of nearly a half mile, something that would not be suspected from the Walsenburg road nor from the adjacent D&RG railway. James followed up the arroyo, all the while inspecting the eroded banks for signs of outcrops, rock strata, or anything else to give an indication of the nature of what might lie below the topsoil. It was a prospector's picture book, he thought—too bad the arroyo wasn't deeper to expose more strata.

The soil itself must be pretty good, James thought. The buffalo grass, dried and frozen, obviously had been lush and a few cows here and there knew it. Why haven't they been taken in? This must be a sheltered valley, part of a Mexican land grant—but what around here isn't?

About two miles above the valley entrance, the arroyo made a sharp turn north, fashioning a somewhat smaller valley rising a little more sharply to a vanishing point at the scantily forested hills. Off to the south was a natural valley, formed by the rolling hills and running to the southern horizon. James was perplexed—a few cattle but no people. Nor was there any sign of a wagon road. Just cattle trails.

He had seen no evidence of coal in the arroyo cut, although some up-thrust sandstone looked promising. It would be necessary to scratch around these cuts; maybe he could get Phillip Anschultz up here on his day off to look at it. Phillip had told him that the land all around here was underlain by layered rocks, supporting the mat of buffalo pasture grass. To *James'* eye, the land was right—this looked like Pennsylvania coal country to him. But who owned it? Why hadn't D&RG added this to the railroad right-of-way they already held on both sides of the tracks? He answered his own question. That's why Llewellyn hired him, of course. So, off to the county land office for some very casual information seeking. He wouldn't mention minerals—just grazing rights for...for...I know, llamas, those funny-looking animals with a funnier name from South America. People would then *know* he was crazy and pay no attention.

◇◇◇◇◇◇◇◇◇◇◇◇

Returning to Trinidad, James continued west on Main Street up to the Las Animas County offices on Chestnut. After an exchange of introductions and pleasantries, James advised the land recorder, a Mr. Homer White that he and his brother were opening a business office in town and soon would be looking for residential property.

"You should register in the town directory, but you'll have to go to City Hall for that."

"Yes, I'll take care of that. But the purpose of my visit today is a little different. My brother and I are planning to introduce into Colorado an entirely different beast of burden, the llama. You've probably heard of them; they look a little like a camel, only much smaller. And they're not native to the Arabian desert but rather to the twelve-thousand-foot Altiplano of the Andes Mountains of South America. That's the elevation of Colorado's peaks, but in the Andes that's the elevation of the plateau below the peaks. You can imagine how cold it gets in July—the seasons are reversed, you know.

And, as we all know, we Anglos have brought mules into Colorado to do our heavy work, animals born in the cotton fields and transported here to the Rockies to freeze. An animal of the Andes will take Colorado in stride. So we plan to do just that. I'll be looking for grazing land for our herds of llamas.

"We need grass, of course, but I'll also look for some rough terrain—rock ledges, arroyos, and the like—so they'll feel at home. I don't want to trespass on another's property, so I would like to find out where in Las Animas County there might be some public land to purchase or some private land that we could lease for grazing."

"It's a pretty large county."

"Yes, I realize that, and I know there are some land title problems resulting from the huge land grants made by Mexico before their war with us. That's one reason leasing might make sense. I've been told that the Vigil and St. Vrain grant was for four million acres. Is my information correct?"

"Yes, but out of date. After the war, Congress reduced that grant to ninety-seven thousand acres and specified how it should be split. There are records of all of that, but we don't have them all here... and, fortunately, Congress also had the ninety-seven thousand acres surveyed. But that's still a lot of land, and most parcels have changed ownership a couple of times."

"Does that mean that the rest was public land, over three million acres?"

"Yes, but Federal land has been for sale or homestead for fifteen years and undoubtedly the good stuff is long gone. Those records are in the U.S. land office in Denver."

"Would it help if I would identify a smaller area to look at first, and then if I needed more information, I could reimburse the county for some of the clerical work? What I have in mind, for starters, is a little east-west valley about halfway between Walsenburg and Trinidad. There is a little arroyo in the middle of it."

Mr. White spread out his county map. "Do you think this is it? It's identified as DelAgua Canyon here."

"Do you suppose this is one parcel or several, and part of the grant?"

The land recorder replied, "I really don't know. I'm getting in deep water—I think I had better get our engineer to help us."

He returned in a few minutes. "This is Bill Wilcox, our chief and only engineer—Mr. James Molyneaux, a new Trinidad resident. He's asking for information about land ownership in the countryside around here, specifically DelAgua Canyon about fifteen miles north of town, for 'starters,' as he put it. Do you know it?"

The engineer, an alert-looking young man about James' age, had probably been hired about when the town was making its incorporation plans and setting up county offices the previous year.

The man also seemed eager to please. "I think I do—sort of. I've seen the arroyo from the road but I never had a reason to look around. As I remember, it isn't really a canyon at all—and quite a distance back. I think I heard somewhere that a Ramon DelAgua runs a few cattle up in those hills. But let's see if we have something in the files." He led the way back to the map room, as he called a little alcove in the back. "Here's the Trinidad plat. It's about as accurate as the

city people could make it. As you can see, town parcels are identified; the town has detailed descriptions and deeds in their files. And
here's a U.S. topographical map for the thirty-eighth parallel—it's
only good for natural features and its too far north, anyway."

He flipped a page. "Now we're getting closer—here's a Mexican
land-grant map. I've not looked at this before. It shows the boundaries of all of these grants in southern Colorado. Look at the Vigil
and St. Vrain grant. It takes in almost all of Las Animas County. It's
coming back to me now. I have to apologize, sir, but I haven't had
occasion to think about this since I was up at Boulder. After the
Mexican War and, of course, the Taos uprising, Congress reduced
that extraordinarily large grant to a 'mere' ninety-seven thousand
acres. But that was in direct violation of the provisions of the Treaty
of Guadalupe Hidalgo which ended that war about ten years ago.
The Senate ordered the grant surveyed and specified the split between grantees. I believe that there's still some dispute over the al-
location; there are dozens of claimants."

"Do you have county maps?" asked James.

"Not really—only this incomplete one here. We're putting together a revised map now. Of course, the county lines, major roads,
railways, bridges and the like are already well defined and we're surveying the Purgatorie and its tributaries for better data now. As we
build new county roads and other structures, surveys will be run
and maps made. But we're a long way from any kind of a plat of individual parcels. They're described on tax rolls, but that's all. Frankly,
I had forgotten about the Vigil and St. Vrain survey—that's probably
because we don't seem to have it. I'll look in the bottoms of all our
boxes. If I can't find it, I'll ask Denver. We need it. I'll superimpose
the data upon our own work in progress. It will be very useful—and
will help you, too—but not immediately."

"In the meantime, can we have a look at what land documents we have for the DelAgua area?" This was addressed to Mr. White.

"We can do that for you, Mr. Molyneaux. Bill will fit the descriptions to the terrain as best he can."

"Yes, I'll do that," said Wilcox, "but we must remember that most old deeds or claims use some natural land feature as a base. Sometimes it's only a stake or other monument, and that's a problem. We'll see. Maybe you and I could ride up there some day soon, Mr. Molyneaux, and search for stakes."

And outcrops, said James to himself.

◇◇◇◇◇◇◇◇◇◇◇◇◇

On his way from the county offices James dropped in at the livery stable to finalize not only his purchase of Coalfire, but also to buy a pair of road-trained horses and a canvas-covered carriage. There was a telegram at Maude's—Matt would be in this afternoon. James cleaned up a bit and took the carriage out to El Moro to meet the late-afternoon D&RG train. Matthew and he had a lot to talk about. Without exposing Phillip Anschultz, James had to warn Matthew about Llewellyn. And without admitting that he had looked around Raton without Llewellyn's instructions, he had to find out what mischief was in the air—and who the target was. As James had learned in poker games back home, if after one hand you don't know who the mark is—it's *you*.

◇◇◇◇◇◇◇◇◇◇◇◇◇

Leonard and Matthew were on the afternoon train from Pueblo— they had stayed overnight in order for Llewellyn to talk to some of his Southern Division people. This was the first undisturbed chance for the two of them to discuss Matt's upcoming assignment at La Veta.

"Matt," Llewellyn said, "I'm sorry there wasn't much time for you to be with Palmer this week, but he wants me to assure you that your assignment as La Veta auditor has not changed. You will still be counting spikes and rails, schedules and man-hours, and all the rest, and you will report to me through the construction superintendent. It's very important to lay track quickly, at least over the pass, and commence rail shipments from Garland. This will appease the investors a little.

"But there's more at stake over there than a railroad over the mountain. Former Colorado Governor Hunter has purchased thousands of acres of Mexican land-grant properties in the San Luis Valley as has General Palmer, himself. Their plan is to sell selected parcels to D&RG for construction of company-owned towns along the railroad. For example, La Veta is a company town next to Francisco Plaza. Garland will be such a town near Fort Garland, and Alamosa will be across the Rio Grande from an existing Alamosa. D&RG will control the shipments out of the entire valley and the political control of all towns along the way. A couple years of that will be worth more than the La Veta trunk line. So, of necessity Hunter's wishes will supersede D&RG's apparent interests even though the railroad construction may be disrupted. To make this work, most of each town must have been built before the railroad arrives. So from time to time D&RG resources, men, and equipment will be diverted to Hunter's work." Llewellyn continued, "Obviously, Palmer's name will not come up. Field decisions will be made by Hunter and Superintendent Oswald. You will have nothing to do with it—except to turn your head the other way."

Matthew was visibly shaken, and speechless. He had not expected anything like this.

Llewellyn noticed Matthew's dismay. "That's just the way it works in railroading, Matt. I'm sure you'll get used to it."

It was an introduction to big business—no ethics whatsoever? But, at least Leonard isn't part of it—he's just a messenger, thought Matthew. Leonard had already turned back to some business papers he had picked up at Pueblo; Matt tried to immerse himself in the passing scenery but beautiful as it was, he couldn't get out of his mind the words, *"That's just the way it works..."*

As the D&RG pulled into El Moro, it was easy to pick out James standing a head above anyone else. It was sort of comforting.

◇◇◇◇◇◇◇◇◇◇◇◇

James was surprised to see both Matthew and Llewellyn detrain. He thought that Leonard would have gathered his strike team together, ready to effect a standoff with Santa Fe. Instead, here is my fearless leader still in business suit and tie.

There were greetings all around, but a little strained, James sensed.

"I'm surprised to see you here, Jimmie," said Matt. "I thought a couple of weeks would find you with your own saloon."

James wasn't sure whether his brother was being cute or snide, so he let it go by.

Leonard was still silent. James broke the quiet. "I've a carriage over at the rack. Pick up your things and let's go to town."

"Nice rig, Jimmie," said Matthew when they reached the carriage, breaking the silence again.

"Glad you approve, Mattie," James replied. "This is community property. It has springs up front so it can comfortably carry people as well as stuff. Your house, Leonard?"

"No, let's stop for a drink. I've some things to talk over with you both."

James pulled up at the Columbian.

"Back so soon, Big Jim?" Lillian asked.

"Not quite, Lillian, I've some guests." He nodded to a table in the back.

The big dog, Mike, nuzzled James but was aloof with the others.

"I guess you're a regular customer, Jimmie," noted Matthew.

"It helps to get along with the bouncer."

They made their way to the private table and sat down. By now, Llewellyn was ready to unload—something was obviously bothering him. "Matthew, I have a private message for James from General Palmer. Would you mind leaving us alone for a few minutes?"

Matt rose. "Sure. I'll be over at the bar."

A bar girl came up with some glasses and a bottle of whisky. "Compliments of the house," she said in a voice tinged with wariness.

A quick sip and Llewellyn came right to the point. "I have to tell you, James, our 'deal' is off. I'm on thin ice with Palmer. He almost sacked me, and it's your fault. First, his lawyers told him that Santa Fe had applied to the State of New Mexico for a charter from the state line to New Marcial. The ruling is due in February. He also found out that Santa Fe's Trinidad charter has been extended over Raton Pass. And then someone told him that Santa Fe has about fifty miles of rails and ties sitting on the ground at La Junta waiting to be laid.

"The General wants to know why you haven't come up with all of this information, yourself. He knew, of course, that I had hired you on a provisional basis and what you were charged to do. I tried to explain to him that you were new out here and couldn't be faulted for letting Santa Fe outsmart you—after all, they're old hands at this. But he said you're through and he won't pay you for the time you've wasted."

"This is horse shit, Leonard. You told me specifically to do absolutely nothing, don't go anywhere, don't talk to anybody, until you arrived in Trinidad. And that's today! I've been sitting around here for a week, doing nothing. I actually picked up that same information a week ago from a Santa Fe locator at Maude's, and a lot more besides—but I had no way to get hold of you.

"Your wife refused to talk to me, the Denver telegrapher replied to my wire saying you already had left for Pueblo, and the steel plant had not seen you at all. The other information that I wanted to pass on to you is that Santa Fe is moving all of its top-level out-of-state engineering personnel to Colorado, has obtained Union Pacific's survey data for the La Junta section, has probably secured a right-of-way at Wooton's toll-gate, has ties and rails acquired from Kansas Pacific on the ground at La Junta, and has acquired D&RG survey data for Raton. Did you hear me, Leonard? Denver and Rio Grande data for Raton," James half-yelled to the boss man, as his hands began to cinch.

"That's nonsense. In D&RG we have strict rules that all instructions are confirmed in writing. I would never have given you unwritten orders. So where are these so-called orders telling you to stay in Trinidad and do nothing? You can't produce them, can you? That's because they don't exist. And as far as not being able to communicate with me, I distinctly told you I would be up at the Mining Department at Golden. And about giving me this new 'information,' it's just as well you didn't. I've never heard such unfounded garbage in my life."

A white-faced James was frozen. "Protect your ass!" Phillip had said.

Llewellyn went on, "The other thing that bothers the General is a bald-faced lie that's going around. Fortunately, it's so blatant that Palmer can't believe it, either. But someone—and it could only be you—is saying that I am engaged in a private coal acquisition program in competition with Palmer's Colorado Coal and Iron Company. Believe me when I say I'm going to bury you for this."

James started to defend himself point for point. "To start with, Leonard, I haven't seen a written order or any other kind of written communication since I first heard of D&RG—and as far as the next thing…oh, to hell with it…" James stood to his full height. "Someone told me once not to get in a pissing contest with a skunk—you can't possibly win."

Mike also stood, hackles up, growling and staring intently at Llewellyn, who spun around and left.

Matthew came back to join James at the table. "What happened, Jimmie?"

James responded, "He sacked me, Mattie, for 'doing nothing' and 'not doing anything.' So, that's that. But how about you, Matt? You don't look too happy, yourself."

"I still have the job—but now I'm not sure I want it. I can hardly believe what Leonard said in a matter-of-fact way. Railroading's not about laying track over prairies and mountains, he said. It's about land. *Stolen land,* or nearly so, to sell off when the railroad is finished, and private towns to be exploited forever. And conned folks thinking they have a real investment by pyramiding mortgages. This is like Crédit Mobilier, only smaller scale. Just business as usual, I guess—no ethics at all. But on the other hand, he seems so sincere. I don't know..."

James was silent for a long moment, "Matthew, I think you should take the job. It's still your opportunity for a really big future. And it's the superintendent who will be playing games. As auditor, you need have nothing to do with it. You're just supposed to count spikes and things. And anyway, Llewellyn's quarrel is with me, not you."

Lillian came around to the table. "You boys look like you've come a cropper," she said.

"Just about," came the reply. Lillian, this is my brother, Matthew."

James nodded to Matthew. "Lillian is the proprietor of this establishment, and Mike, whom you've met, is head peacemaker and bouncer."

"Hello, Matthew. And what do you two want from the bar? Sit still, I'll get it."

"Whisky," they said in unison, as they sat back down.

The brothers looked at each other without speaking. James reached over and touched Matthew lightly on the shoulder. "Mattie, we have to do some serious thinking. As far as Raton is concerned, Llewellyn is lying through his teeth on all counts. What's he trying to do? And what does he have to gain?"

"Maybe it's as simple as trying to save his job—and you would be the straw man," said Matthew. "But Leonard is a really nice person. I simply can't believe he would do that. Is there any chance that you misunderstood his instructions?"

"I suppose it's possible, or maybe we're *both* being set up for something; and maybe not by Llewellyn, alone. It could be that Palmer is saving his own hide with his investors. Now, other than my natural disinclination to be the butt of anything or anybody, it really doesn't matter to me whether I work for D&RG or not. As you well know, I have an entirely different plan for my life."

They sat quietly for a few moments, sipping their whiskeys. Then James continued. "I'm confident that you're smart enough to handle these corporate shenanigans—just don't let yourself become too emotionally involved. So, I repeat. Take the job, Mattie, and outsmart the bastards. Like Mom used to say, don't get your dander up.

"But, I worry a little about your personal safety. You will be out in the backcountry where everyone will hate you—or at least we'd better assume so."

"Jimmie, La Veta isn't exactly backcountry. Some of these little Spanish pueblo towns were founded before you were."

"Nevertheless," James said, "You've got to protect yourself. Let's check you back into Maude's and then head downtown to outfit you for a potentially dangerous situation."

CHAPTER EIGHT

A PARCEL, LOST (BUT FOUND)

MATTHEW AND JAMES HAD GROWN APART a little with their diverse interests and seemed to have less and less to talk about. Finally, one quiet day, James broke the nervous silence, "Let me tell you about what I've been doing with *my* time while you've been up in Denver with all those big operators. I'm a coal prospector."

"You're a what?"

"Yeah, that's right—a what. I'm on the trail of some very good-looking land north of Trinidad. Obviously, my deal with Llewellyn is dead, but I'm going to follow *this* up on my own. If my hunch is right and it *is* potential coal property, we'll have to find someone who might be interested in developing it. Of course we'll need big money for that—like hundreds of thousands of dollars."

Matthew, eyebrows raised, said nothing. His interest was mild, at best. His thoughts switched to Sophia, whom he hadn't seen for nearly two weeks. But that last incident with Leonard at the saloon left him wondering whether he was still welcome at the Llewellyn household.

◇◇◇◇◇◇◇◇◇◇◇◇

Responding to a note left at Maude's, James met Bill Wilcox at the county office. Unrolling a map, the engineer said, "I've found some of what you need. Here's the map—I've marked in some additional information like the Purgatorie River channel and the little village of Aguilar below Walsenburg. And most important, the major land-holdings of D&RG on both sides of the railroad—about a mile on each side in many places, but closer to a half-mile through DelAgua. That's pretty good grazing land through there, and probably more than D&RG would pay for undeveloped potential coal property.

"Now here's the interesting part," Wilcox continued. "I've super-imposed the outline of the revised Vigil and St. Vrain land grant on this map. Not the individual plots—I haven't dug them out, yet. You notice that the eastern edge of the grant, for convenience referred to as the 'Las Animas Grant,' comes down through DelAgua Canyon and then turns southwesterly to the Purgatorie. In fact, it seems to come right down the centerline of the east-west extension of Del-Agua Arroyo."

"I see. But why is nothing lined up north and south, east and west?" James asked.

"That's because cartographers nowadays all orient to the me-ridian system, degrees east or west of Greenwich and degrees north or south of the equator, but mapmakers of old Mexico used point-to-point surveying without reference to absolute latitude or longitude or compass direction.

"So, while it looks strange on a meridian-oriented map, the orig-inal Mexican land grant description, as revised, is perfectly valid as long as there is a fixed reference point. In this case, that point is described as 'Las Animas Corner Number One, near Trinidad, one league below the Purgatorie.' I guess all you need to know at this time is the identification of the holder, or holders, of this part of the Las Animas grant?"

James nodded agreement; he had only been half-listening to Bill's little geography lesson. His mind was occupied with what appeared to be a little wedge of nothing between D&RG's western edge and the Las Animas' eastern. They didn't quite come together. Is that a tiny plot, he thought? It looks like a few sections at most, a piece of Federal land that fell into a cartographer's crack, overlooked and forgotten...and now possibly available at essentially no cost, as homestead grants or mining claims as I've heard them described around the cracker barrel.

"Does this give you what you need, Mr. Molyneaux?"

"Yes—this should do it—with the addition of parcel-holders' names, of course. You surveyors really amaze me. Is it possible, for example, to locate these boundaries in the field?"

Wilcox looked at James a little sideways and with a hint of a smile. "Oh, yes, sightings could be made up from the railway straight along the arroyo to establish the location on the ground, very precisely. What you do is this..." He went on in great detail exactly how the field orientation would be made...and on...and on...

"I know a land man in town who could do the job. Here's his name, Jack Meadows." He handed James a scrap of paper.

James pondered the situation. Meadows' name had already been written on that paper, and Wilcox knew very well that *now* it didn't matter who owned the Las Animas Grant. Wilcox saw that wedge of land, too—and probably yesterday. James knew he had to talk to Matt immediately—he's better than a lawyer for this sort of thing.

"Could I borrow this map? I'd like to take it to DelAgua the next time I'm up that way. And thanks very much for your help. Please drop me a note when you have those landowners' names."

"Take it, it's a copy. No thanks are necessary—it's part of my job," Wilcox replied.

◇◇◇◇◇◇◇◇◇◇◇◇◇

Early the next day, James and Matthew were sitting a semi-private table at Lillian's. "And that's the story, Matt. Undoubtedly, there is a small strip of land between the Las Animas Mexican land grant and the D&RG property, and we may be the only ones who know it. If so, I believe it would be U.S. Government open land and hence subject to homestead or mining claims, which under the current laws incur little or no cost to the applicant..."

Matthew interrupted, "That's all very well, but what in the world could we use it for?"

"For a coal mine, of course! Consider this—it's very close to the D&RG main line for convenient shipping of the produced coal, not to mention D&RG's own use; it's exactly on a north-south line between the producing mines at Engle and Walsen, and just a little off-line from Cañon City; and from my own observation, it's *coal country*, Mattie—a little piece of Pennsylvania.

I've spent hundreds and hundreds of hours hiking over that kind of land back home, and I know what coal properties look like. Of course, you can't be absolutely sure. Coal is where you find it, not necessarily where you want it to be."

"Why hasn't D&RG caught on," asked Matthew?

"It's understandable," James replied. "D&RG has vast acreage along its rights-of-way and may not be actively looking for more potential coal properties just now. Remember, Matt, Llewellyn told us that himself, suggesting that there is room for one or more new suppliers since D&RG is interested in producing coal for its own use only—

fuel for its engines and coke for its steel manufacture. Furthermore, DelAgua Canyon is nearly shielded from view from the railroad and adjacent road. I stumbled on it only by accident."

Up to this point, Matthew was just making idle conversation, but had begun to focus in on what James was talking about. "Are you saying, Jimmie, that you're the only one that knows about this possibility?"

"I don't know, but it doesn't seem possible that the county engineer, Bill Wilcox, could miss something that was so obvious to me. Wilcox may not be on the 'take,' but you would certainly expect him to try to personally benefit from a legal and ethical opportunity—as *we* would do. That 'surveyor friend' may be his brother-in-law."

"You say he looked kind of funny when he gave you the surveyor's name?"

"It was a 'sly' look if I ever saw one. Now, Mattie, all I know about federal land that has been opened up is that one of two laws applies, the Mining Law and the Oil and Coal Law. And maybe the Homestead Act may fit as well. And its mineral value could be determined with little more than a couple of core samples."

Matthew asked, "How big a parcel is this"

"I couldn't ask; that would have been a giveaway. I would guess a thousand acres or so—not tens of thousands; otherwise it would have been conspicuous. If you and I were to take a fifty-foot piece of rope up there we could get a pretty good idea of where the Las Animas line would lie with respect to the terrain."

"No, that's a waste of time. I think you should talk to this surveyor immediately, and I'll find a good lawyer. We can be pretty sure that there truly is some unclaimed open land there. I think it was a surprise to Wilcox—he probably caught on about the same time as you. So, since as a county employee he probably can't make a claim, himself, he may be using this very good surveyor friend as a way to get a piece of the action. That shouldn't bother us—we're not doing anything wrong, but we must be careful not to compromise either one of them by deed or even implication. So far, Wilcox probably is thinking we're looking at homesteading for grazing or farming—not coal mining. We have to keep it that way."

"I agree on all counts, little brother. So what's next?"

"I'll find a lawyer this afternoon. Maybe Mr. Hepplewhite can recommend one; maybe Lillian can. The main thing is to get the paperwork started for whatever course of action the lawyer suggests." Matthew's voice grew louder with each word. He was clearly on a roll. "To save time, I'll take applications up to the Denver Federal Land Office, myself, if necessary, and you can stand by the telegraph office to send me more information as I ask for it. Okay?"

"Sounds good," James replied. "This afternoon I'll feel out the surveyor. See what Wilcox has told him. I'll listen between the lines to see if he is expecting a kickback—and how big. Also, I'll ask him if he knows anything about grazing claims—that might keep him off balance," he added.

Jack Meadows, that's the surveyor, and I should go to the field as soon as possible, hopefully early tomorrow." James continued, "I imagine he will take two bearings, a chain or two apart, from the railway along the arroyo up the canyon. Knowing the real distance from the railway to the Las Animas line, a point on that line can be located in the field. A northeasterly compass sighting from that point would indicate the position of the extended Las Animas bound.

"If it looks to be in a favorable location with respect to the canyon floor, the arroyo, and the hillsides—which is what we really want—we'll pace off quarter-mile frontages for several parcels. No stakes or markers quite yet, but I'll see if we can somehow identify the surveyed point with a permanent buried monument or, better, with sightings on fixed terrain features."

"Christ, Jimmie, you sound like a surveyor yourself."

"What was it that you said the other day, 'All theory and no substance.'? I thought I'd never get away from the County engineer. He seemed determined to teach me the science of civil engineering—or else he was trying to show me how much he knows. And I think it's plenty."

◇◇◇◇◇◇◇◇◇◇◇◇

Walking east on Main Street from Maude's, James and Matthew were mentally cataloging the existing establishments on this, the "right" end of Main, each with his own needs in mind. As a minimum, they needed a place to hang their hats and receive their mail. Matthew suggested they try to find a small building with bachelor quarters above and an office and storage room on the street floor. There was no room at Maude's, and they couldn't continue imposing upon Lillian so much. There could be a hitching rail in front of the building, and a water trough in back. Commercial stables would be used for overnights. They could still take their meals at Maude's or perhaps at one of the small restaurants on Main Street. Matthew had already mentally composed the sign for the front door and graphically described it for his brother with his forefinger on the very dusty glass pane of the first unoccupied building meeting their requirements.

JAMES & MATTHEW MOLYNEAUX
COUNSELORS

James could hardly contain himself, "Counselors of what? Dog-catching?

"We'll think of something. Remember, Jim, *it's all show.*"

Matthew was pleased that there was not a single specialty tobacco shop to be seen, and looked in vain for the sort of deluxe saloon that he knew Jim had in mind. Even the Columbian fell short of that.

"It looks to me, Jimmie, that there's no competition for what we may want to do. It's wide open."

Coming up to the Commercial Street intersection, the brothers could see some clearing activity on the southeast corner. James said, "I saw this yesterday. It's the site of a new three-story hotel, The Grand Union. The barber told me that it will have a fancy entrance and lobby on the Commercial Street side—the rest of the ground floor space along Commercial and Main streets has not been assigned, yet."

Matthew excitedly grabbed his brother's arm. "There's your saloon, Jimmie, my tobacco shop, a lavish restaurant, a gentlemen's club, and who-knows-what upstairs and down."

Caught up in Matthew's excitement, James put in, "We could pull this off, a few working girls on the second floor and an elite ladies' tearoom on the third. Something for everyone."

Still laughing, they crossed over to the Columbian. Mike barked a welcome and Lillian added, "What's with you guys? Your ship come in?"

"Carried away, Lillian," said a sobering James. "Just a little happy dreaming about taking over the bottom floor of the new hotel."

"Perhaps not a dream," said a dead-serious Matthew, spacing his words as he usually did when thinking and talking at the same time. "Maybe the owner would like to have someone else develop that street floor; we could raise some money and leverage our stake and find some investors, like D&RG or Santa Fe..."

"Count me in," Lillian said, surprising even herself. "We could gussy it up and move the Columbian right across the street. I rent the property, but the furnishings are mine. And I have a little stake, too." She added some more energy to the conversation. "On the house— whiskey for all? And by the way, the owner over there is a friend of mine, Matthew. Let me know when you want to talk to him."

"I have a lot of spare time the next few weeks," said Matt. "I'll run some numbers on this. At the same time I'll set up my old tobacco contacts. Most of it, actual orders, prices, delivery dates, payments, and the like will be by coded telegraph just like I did in Pittsburgh. The big trick is establishing the retail outlets."

"How do you get people to change from their current supplier to you?" asked Lillian.

"Quality and reliability." Matthew said, looking upward with fingers crossed behind his back.

"Not price?" Lillian questioned.

"I like to think I can get an even higher price as long as the other two factors are truly better. Reliability is guaranteed if I carry sufficient inventory. My retailers never—*never* run out. Quality is quite another thing. But I have a feeling that no one in Trinidad has ever had a good cigar. I base that on Llewellyn's reaction to one of mine. Leonard Llewellyn, whom you met, is a top Denver and Rio Grande executive."

"You boys interested in another drink?'

"No, thanks," said Matthew, standing and turning to leave. "I have to go over to the bank."

"And you, Jim?" Her hand, as if by accident, brushed his leg lightly.

He grabbed her hand and held it. "How about I sleep over tonight, Lillian?"

◇◇◇◇◇◇◇◇◇◇◇◇

The next morning, James met with Jack Meadows, the surveyor acquaintance (or perhaps very good friend) of Bill Wilcox, at the new Molyneaux office in town. James had already brought the buggy around, and they planned to drive up to DelAgua together. Jack was about the same age, size, and coloring as his friend Bill Wilcox, but a little sharper, at first glance. I'll have trouble fooling *him* with this llama story, thought James.

It was a clear sunny day but very cold in the shade. A brisk wind made them very happy for the partial protection of a covered buggy.

The road was good, the trip taking a little more than two hours. At the outset James stressed the need for confidentiality. "I realize that we may be concerned here with public lands, and everything we do is ultimately in the public domain. But at the same time, we most definitely will be dealing with private land owners on the Las Animas grant. So that's why we can't say much at this point—I guess Wilcox told you about the llama-grazing possibility.

"Well, that's the plan," James continued. And we've been told that these particular animals thrive best where the terrain is a little rough—unlike cows that like lush meadows. As soon as you and I locate the Las Animas grant line out there we'll know whether to go for a homestead application or go after the purchase of grazing rights from the Las Animas people."

"Do you know anything about surveying, Jim?"

"Only some terms that I picked up from Bill Wilcox. He seems like a very competent person. Have you known him long?"

"We knew each other, slightly, at Boulder, but that's about it."

With a broad smile, James said casually, "So you didn't marry sisters?"

Jack reddened. "Well, yes, as a matter of fact we did."

"Oh, I'm sorry, Jack, I didn't mean to be so damned inquisitive. Now to the survey..."

Jack said, "In this survey, we're only interested in one dimension, from here for thirty thousand, five hundred and twenty yards, which is the distance scaled from the U.S. Las Animas survey map—straight back through the canyon. You'll take the rod and move back as I direct with hand signals. I'll take a shot, move a chain length over and take a second shot. When a tree gets in the way, we'll use it for the target and move on. There's our first triangle. We'll do that until we've marked off the thirty-five hundred yards, and that's our intercept and our master corner marker." Jack's idea made sense.

"We won't know the elevation but we don't care," he continued. "That's all you need for a property description to the accuracy of the county plat. We know the true geographic direction of the Las Animas line so we convert that to magnetic north, which will allow you to look as far as you can see, north or south, from the surveyed corner to evaluate the terrain. For example, you can identify any size parcel using the real Las Animas line and this corner in your description. You should erect a monument at this point but it might be prudent to bury it a couple of feet deep or locate it with reference to two natural terrain features—but I can't see any. Let's make the measurements. We'll conduct additional surveys will be needed to locate specific parcels."

It was mid-afternoon before they were finished. The calculations showed that the line would fall approximately in the middle of the canyon—plenty of room for error, and plenty of hillside for shale examination.

"Looks good." James spoke slowly. "How far up and down would you guess this nearly flat grassland runs?"

"We don't have a topo for this, but from the plat it looks like a mile in each direction. Let's take the buggy up a ways and see. We have a couple hours before we have to start back. Remember, James, it doesn't really matter what we measure today. The true lines are portrayed on the map and its coordinates. What we're trying to do is see what the land as so portrayed actually looks like—what it might it be used for. And that goes for both sides of the Las Animas line. Right? And while I think of it, you'd make a pretty good apprentice surveyor—you looking for work?"

James laughed. "No, thanks—there's too much climbing up and down hills for my taste."

The land, both north and south of the surveyed marker, looked much the same, fairly level grassland up to the toe of the hills on each side, more grass over the hills to the west, and to the east grass and quite a few rock outcrops. Both sides were dotted with shrubs and piñon pines. The entire area, being at an elevation over six thousand feet, would have snowfall and, in fact, there were a few patches still remaining from the last light storm. The arroyo, shallower up here, ran more or less up the middle of the pasture.

Jack packed his equipment for the return to Trinidad. "How do you know that those llamas will like this grass? It's called buffalo grass, you know." Jack half-smiled and seemed to stare clear through James.

For the first time all day the big man was caught flat-footed. Trying to meet Jack's steady gaze, he said, "Well...well, you see, the grass on the Altiplano isn't all that great, either...and, that is...oh, hell! Look, my brother and I and a couple other partners are in on this—whatever it is—and you're in, too, if you want, and maybe your sister-in-law, as well. I'll insist on it. Matt and I will talk to you tomorrow."

◇◇◇◇◇◇◇◇◇◇◇◇

James and Matthew had much to discuss that evening in their new and barely furnished office. "I think you handled that just fine, Jim. And you sure got a lot of information. I'll have you survey my first house. Here's what I learned from the lawyer. He says we're not breaking any law—but we'll have to talk to him about giving Bill Wilcox an indirect interest through his wife, since Wilcox is a county employee. He says there's a couple ways we could go. We could homestead a number of one-hundred-sixty-acre parcels and then form some kind of an association. But that's risky and worse than that, each homestead must be proved, or lose it. We could go over the Las Animas line and purchase or lease land or rights, but that would be expensive. And from what you tell me about the survey, east of the line is just as good."

"And possibly a better chance for coal beds."

"The lawyer said that the Mining Act of 1872 doesn't apply to coal or oil—it's been supplanted by the 1873 Coal Act. That new law does permit purchases under some circumstances, but the government prefers a 'lease-royalty' arrangement. The royalty is one-eighth and the lease is good as long as there is some kind of mining or exploration going on."

"That has my vote," James indicated with a smile.

"Yeah, now, how many parcels... You and me and Lillian as stakeholders. Jack Meadows because we need a surveyor, and Jack's sister-in-law because Bill Wilcox probably has guessed what we're thinking of doing—we don't want any claim-jumping. That's five. Any others?

"I'd like to ask Phillip Anschultz over at Engle. He's a mining engineer and knows mining inside out."

Matt fished in his pocket for his calculation pad. "Okay. That would be six parcels, seventeen hundred and sixty foot each on the frontage line—one half to the north of our surveyed marker and the other half to the south. I'll give this to the lawyer tomorrow. I'll ask him to go up to Denver to present the applications in person."

◇◇◇◇◇◇◇◇◇◇◇◇

James left the office for a nightcap—or more—at the Columbian. He was tired after hours in the buggy, hikes up and down DelAgua, and all followed by an exhausting business discussion with Matthew. Something new caught his eye as he entered the saloon—a decorated piñon tree, colored ribbons, some candy, some tinsel... James hadn't seen a single Christmas Tree since before Mother died.

"Merry Christmas, Darling," said Lillian, throwing her arms nearly around him. James couldn't reply—the big man held back tears.

"Good to see you, Jim. You look a little tired. How you can ride hours on end in that little box with wheels you call a buggy is beyond me."

"It's better than a bar stool, but it does bump up and down and weaves around a bit."

"You talk so good, Jim, how'd you learn to do that?"

"I guess I learned to speak listening to Matthew—he used to read a lot and talk even more—and Mother had been a school teacher, for little kids. I'm glad you're with us, Lillian. You'll be the glue that holds us together."

"That does it! I've been called everything else but that before. How do you get it off your hands?"

"Haven't you heard about becoming 'unglued'? That's how."

◇◇◇◇◇◇◇◇◇◇◇◇

James returned to Maude's to find two messages on the entry table; one was a transcribed telegram, addressed to James:

WESTERN UNION

JAMES MOLYNEAUX TRINIDAD DEC 27

MEET ME GRAND PALACE PUEBLO FRIDAY WILLIAM PALMER

"What do you suppose this is all about?" said James. "He can't fire me—he's already done that. Well, on the off chance that he's playing this straight, I'll go on up to Pueblo tomorrow."

Matt wasn't listening. He was busily engaged in opening the perfumed letter addressed to him, written in an obviously feminine hand scripted in perfect Spencerian style.

December 27

Dear Matthew,

I am taking the unprecedented step of writing this letter because I feel there have been a couple of terrible misunderstandings. Firstly, I am afraid I treated James so very shabbily at El Moro. All I can say to that is that he is so big and strong it is easy to forget that he may have sensitivities like the rest of us. Secondly, I don't know why there was such a sudden rift between my father and you and James. I do think he is sorry, but won't admit it. Men are so obdurate in such situations.

I make bold to ask you, Matt, you being the younger, to call upon my father in his office to search for a better relationship. It will help us all.

Your very good friend,
Sophia Llewellyn

In his excitement, Matt showed the letter to his brother. "Look at this, Jimmie, could it be confirming that my La Veta deal is still alive?"

James, the big brother, couldn't hold back an unsolicited observation. "Are you sure, Mattie, that Llewellyn isn't using Sophia to get control over *you?*"

"Oh no, Jimmie, Leonard wouldn't do anything like that."

◇◇◇◇◇◇◇◇◇◇◇◇

Matt hastened to catch Leonard Llewellyn in his office. "Come in Matthew, it's good to see you. I have wanted to talk about your La Veta assignment"

"I don't want to take up much of your time. I'm sure you have a lot of catching up to do after the last few weeks."

"My time is your time, Matt," Leonard said, proffering a cigar. "And thinking of cigars, have you initiated your tobacco wholesaling business yet?"

"I've reconnected with my suppliers and have considered how this Trinidad market can be penetrated. Up to this point I've made no headway in convincing users that a better quality tobacco is something worth having. I'm fear Colorado palates have been seared by rotten whisky and worse tobacco; I have an education problem on my hands."

"I suppose that a Trinidad gentrification must establish a mood and a need for better things," said Llewellyn. "But that's for the future—right now I rather imagine you're concentrating on the La Veta assignment?"

"Yes—but I have no idea of what to expect," replied Matt.

"All I can say is that the superintendent's a drunk, Matt. Everyone knows it. I don't know why Palmer puts up with it. Maybe because of his war experience—they say that the generals were drunk half the time but still did a good job. And Oswald will do exactly what Palmer wants. There will be no problems with priority at La Veta. My advice to you is to clearly assert your authority as an independent auditor right off the bat. Don't let him get the upper hand."

Matthew was a little taken aback. No mention of the intense scene at the Columbian and not a word about compromising D&RG's interests for the mysterious Mr. Hunter. But more important to Matthew at the moment was the invitation to dinner at the Llewellyn's the next Saturday evening.

◇◇◇◇◇◇◇◇◇◇◇◇

At the appointed hour, Matthew arrived at the Llewellyn home on Aristocracy Hill three blocks up Beech Street. He was driving a one-horse Boston chaise hired without driver from Ramirez. The Llewellyn house was new—somewhat larger than its neighbors— three stories and an attic above a full basement. The recessed front porch with double doors was outlined by a pair of Grecian-style columns, an altogether pleasing arrangement—not too ostentatious but appropriate for a midlevel executive.

The butler—who doubled as a driver—answered the door. "May I help you, Sir?"

"My name is Molyneaux. I have an engagement with the Llewellyns," said Matthew.

"Please come in, Mr. Molyneaux. You are expected."

Matt stepped into a marble-floored front hall. To the right were a stairway to floors above and entries to a library and sitting room. To the left was a dining room with pantry and kitchen behind. Servants' quarters, he presumed, were off the pantry. All walls were paneled with red cedar, highlighted here and there with hand-carved picture frames displaying ancestors' portraits.

He was led into the beamed, high-ceiling sitting room, furnished with imported furniture in a new trend-setting style, described as "Victorian." Several upholstered chairs were grouped around a gigantic stone fireplace. Complementing the marble entry, this room had a polished hardwood floor covered with woven area rugs.

Upon receipt of the dinner invitation, Matthew had hurried to find a tailor to be fitted in a suit suitable for a proper drawing-room function. What can I expect today, he wondered. Of one thing he was certain—it would not be a boisterous affair.

Leonard rose from where he had been sitting with Mrs. Llewellyn. "Come in, Matthew." He half-turned towards the woman and addressed her saying, "Agnes, I'd like you to meet Matthew Molyneaux, Sophia's very good friend. Sit down, both of you, if you please, Sophia should be down in a minute."

Mrs. Llewellyn wasted no time. "So—just what are your intentions with Sophia, Mr. Molyneaux?"

Matt took this in stride. "I hope to marry her—and with her father's permission I will propose to her."

As if on cue, Sophia entered.

Leonard beckoned to Manuel. "Please see what everyone wants as an aperitif—some sparkling wine perhaps?"

Then, standing, "A toast—to Sophia and Matthew."

This transpired so quickly Matt wasn't sure what had happened.

◇◇◇◇◇◇◇◇◇◇◇◇

Two days later as she left her house, Agnes Llewellyn had some last words for Sophia. "Your Matthew will be here soon—his card said two o'clock—so Manuel is driving Isabella and me downtown and around for a few hours." Then, in a conspiratorial whisper, "He was wavering a bit the other evening so *clinch it*—he's going to be an important man."

Sophia had some thoughts on how to do just that.

Matthew found the front door ajar. Perplexed, he slipped inside, announcing his presence by means of a small bell sitting on the entry side-table.

A voice called from upstairs, "I'm running late—come on up."

Nervously, he did just that, entering an open room near the top of the stairs. Sophia, wearing only an unbuttoned chemise, rose and turned from her dressing table.

"Oh, Mrs.—oh, Matthew! I thought it was Mama's friend, Mrs. Armstrong." Matthew was transfixed, some five feet away, unable to move. Sophia said resignedly, "Well, come on in, Matt. You've seen all of me, now. What's the matter—haven't you ever seen a woman before?"

Matthew thought, well yes, but not quite like this. He felt himself harden, even as he stood there. As he moved towards her, he tried to casually adjust himself and his trousers, to no avail. No matter; without the conscious intent of either, they had come together. Her undergarment pressed again—hard, and again, and once more, and then a deep breath and a relaxed smile. She leaned back, guiding his hand. "Up a little...there..."

His fingers searched; she pressed hard on his hand; her breath shortened.

With his other hand he felt the beating of her heart, at least as rapidly as his own; her nipples were still hard, her face a little flushed. Still holding his hand securely in place she raised her mouth to his, her tongue slipping between his lips. He opened his mouth, tongue to tongue, in and around, his hand still engaged, bodies still pressing, a new and delicious sensation—something to be said for these Eastern schools.

"That's called a French kiss," she murmured, as she led him over to the bed. "I told you and James that I was studying French."

"I can see that education sometimes goes beyond the class-room."

"Very much further," she said in a voice like velvet.

She took forever to undress him—she wouldn't let him help. It was one hand for the buttons and the other for stroking. This, too, is the French way, Matthew figured, every nerve fiber afire, every touch of her hand, her tongue triggering a reflective spasm...then, "Oh, God, Sophia, *now.*"

Sophia lay back, pulled his head down, "Now for me, again, Matt, that's it—yes."

They were sitting on the love-seat. "That was just for starters, Matthew. Won't it be wonderful when we're married? Then we can do it the other way, although I sometimes think this is better—I could do it over and over again all night, every night. Do you suppose you could? Mama won't be home for a couple of hours and my sisters are in school—and it's my room, anyway."

CHAPTER NINE

CRISIS MANAGEMENT

J AMES ARRIVED IN PUEBLO late Friday afternoon as requested by General Palmer, having left Trinidad at first light. It was an easy half-day ride. He might not even have come except for his remembering something Father had said, "You don't say 'no' to a general." But James was being pulled away from what *really* excited him, and by his nature, he was never very excited—nor very distressed, either, for that matter. Perhaps his "excitement," at this time, was more a comfortable satisfaction that for the first time since he left Pittsburgh things were starting to come together for him.

Foremost there was Lillian—as he told her, "You're as much woman as I would ever want." Then there was the saloon project— it was shaping up to be much more, even, than he had hoped for. And DelAgua coal—it's a gamble, he thought, but what isn't when you can't see or touch what you're talking about? Win or lose, it will be intriguing, that's for sure. Whatever General Palmer has in mind can't possibly hold a candle to these other things, but unfortunately, I can't always say no when I should, James admitted to himself. His present reluctant mood had not been conveyed to Coalfire; the big black was high stepping like a yearling.

The weather along the Front Range was generally unpredictable in January. But James was lucky. The well-traveled road was dry—only a little dusty—and the weather clear and bright. The snow level was down to seven thousand feet, creating a spectacular contrast with the winter-brown slopes below. Scattered pine and piñon punctuated the picture. Coalfire was packed in full-winter mode—double bedroll, poncho, duffel bag, tarp, rifles, water, and emergency rations.

I should have stayed to help Matt with the Grand Union Hotel thing and to hell with the General, he thought. I don't know how to build a railroad, let alone run one, and I couldn't care less. As soon as I finish up here I'll head back south—I can be back in Trinidad by Monday. I can do a lot of the legwork while Matt does the money side. This is my big hope come true—or almost—and Matt pulled it right out of the clear blue sky. On the other hand, this squabbling over railroad rights-of-way and strategy is something I can do as well as the next guy, and the salary for a few months would be useful as the New Columbian project plays out. Unsettled thoughts continued to scatter through James' mind.

With all of that settled in his mind, James turned his attention to finding the Vail hotel. But first he had to find quarters for Coalfire. Both tasks were quickly accomplished and James found himself at General Palmer's door. James was dressed in his "backcountry best," but the long ride had mussed him up a bit. He dusted himself off as best he could. The hotel was fairly new. But then, most everything in Pueblo was fairly new. Not plush—the best that could be said was utilitarian. Palmer's Pueblo office was that—and no more—a desk and chair, a pair of occasional chairs, and a map table. Perhaps the Denver head office was a little fancier, imagined James, but clearly, the Pueblo office of the Denver and Rio Grande was not for show.

Palmer invited James in while dismissing an aide. "Thanks for coming up, Mr. Molyneaux, but I really thought you'd have taken the train—we're in that business, you know." With that light remark, the General tried to smile but didn't quite succeed.

He was an average-sized man, slender, clean shaven except for a small trimmed mustache, with a full head of reddish hair. He had a commanding presence, causing James to have an irrelevant thought: Does a man with a commanding presence become a general—or does a general adopt such a stance after he becomes such?

James tried to put a little banter into the conversation. "No offense intended, sir, but it is said in some quarters that a train that runs twice a week is often beaten by a horse that runs every day."

"We'll have to find a way, young man, to disabuse you of that old-fashioned notion. But the business we're here for..."

"First, sir, if I may bring up something that needs clarification," James spoke with a diffident tone.

Palmer nodded.

"Matthew and I are a little confused after meeting with Mr. Llewellyn a couple weeks ago. I can speak for myself, but Matt would like to know whether his arrangement with you and D&RG still stands."

Palmer called his aide back in, "If the lines are working, send 'PROCEED AS DISCUSSED' to Matthew Molyneaux in Trinidad. Otherwise, send a courier immediately."

Turning to James he said, "Now to the business at hand. I had you come up here to discuss why Santa Fe is getting ahead of us on every turn. We can't run a railroad if our competitors are smarter and quicker than we. I've obtained Raton Pass information from outside sources that I *should have received from you,* and much sooner. I expected you to be my eyes and ears in Trinidad—and I find you deaf and blind. I expected an armed task force at Raton—and find that if there any task force at all, it's Santa Fe's. Furthermore..."

James interrupted, speaking quietly, "But, General, I have had nothing to do with it. I don't work for D&RG and I don't think that I ever did. Llewellyn engaged me for two jobs but I never had any kind of an employment contract for either. I never received any salary or expenses—I didn't even know how much I was *supposed* to make nor what my job title would be."

He paused—General Palmer's frown suggested that the explanation wasn't going over too well but there was nothing to do but to push on. "The only instruction I had—and that was back in Kansas a month ago—was to shepherd Mr. Llewellyn's daughter and dueña to Trinidad and wait there for him. I was not to take any action, even so much as looking around to see what was going on at Raton. Apparently, he didn't want to risk stirring things up. Regarding Royal Gorge, nothing at all was said.

"So he fired me from a job I didn't have—for doing nothing *either* right or wrong. It's the easiest and shortest job I've never had—and the lowest paid." Then, to himself, There—I've said it and to hell with the consequences.

"Then, why did you come up here today?"

"I received your wire, sir, and as a courtesy to you, acted upon it. Also, to close the books, so to speak, I wanted to report to you, first hand, what I saw up at Raton Pass. But I'm not pleading a case—it would be no use. It's my word against Llewellyn—and he's your vice president. I'd like to see Llewellyn boil in hell, but that will happen sooner or later, regardless of what you or I think or do."

James rose to leave.

"Just a minute, if you please. What were those two assignments from Leonard, as you understood them?"

Still standing, James replied, "In the first I was to be his 'crisis leader,' as he put it. I would stand beside him as his lieutenant in nonviolent standoffs with Santa Fe at both Raton and Royal Gorge. He seemed to think I would add some stature to his position." James smiled. "I guess we can both agree, sir that I have stature to spare."

Palmer said, "And..."

"In the other assignment, on his behalf, I would spot and evaluate likely coal prospects in Las Animas County. This would include small producing properties that might want to join a wholesaling consortium that he said he had already founded—with your knowledge. As a 'finder's fee' I would receive a first option on my choice of properties."

"Please sit down, Mr. Molyneaux. For that second assignment, what qualifications do you bring?"

James smiled ruefully. "Not many, General, but I've worked in a couple of coal fields and I've walked and ridden over or around almost every coal mine in western Pennsylvania. I know what coal country looks like."

"Let me tell you, James Molyneaux, it takes a helluva lot more than that. Why, I have an entire staff whose *only* mission is to locate such properties."

"I understand that, sir, and I wondered, myself, why Llewellyn would have picked me for that job. Finally, it dawned on me that his interest might not be so much in *potential* properties, but rather in little one-pick private mines. He could use an unknown person, or persons, to scout around and recruit independent producers for his wholesale consortium, which could remain secret until the entire deal was put together. It doesn't take a geologist or Golden graduate to recognize an outcrop or some mine workings, so 'qualifications' may not be much of an issue."

James noted that as he talked on, the more intense was the General's concentration and the deeper his frown.

"I know I'm probably naïve, sir, but if I'm not looking for a lump of coal, I'll be looking for the rabbit hiding behind that lump. I intend spending a lot of my waking hours over the next half century hunting for anything that runs, swims, or flies. So you see, General, I have nothing to lose. I love mountains and I'll be in them—whether or not I'm looking for coal."

General Palmer was thinking that this conversation was not going at all like he expected. He had intended to call a junior employee on the carpet for a good ass-chewing for not doing his job of scouting Raton. That's how you made good older employees—and officers. Now, he was being asked to believe that this man was not an employee at all—never had been, may not want to be, and may not have done anything wrong, anyway. My whole life has been spent sifting fact from fiction, Palmer thought, judging whether I am hearing the truth. It's not particularly important whether Molyneaux is lying or not, but whether my trusted vice president is *still* to be trusted.

To change the atmosphere a bit, Palmer lightened his tone. "James—may I call you that?—tell me something about yourself. I guess you were a little young for the war?"

"Yes, a little, but pretty big for my age and I might have gotten in. But to nip that possibility, when Father joined his regiment, he made me promise to take care of Matthew and Mother. Father fell at Little Round Top—Eighty-third Pennsylvania."

"That was a terrible battle—but it won the war…" The General paused, looking out the window as though assessing the costs of those victories…and the losses.

Palmer continued. "So you did what he wanted?"

"Yes, and it wasn't too bad. Mother wasn't helpless—she worked the counter of our general store and I did the heavy lifting. By the time Matt was fifteen he did the books, watched inventories, and re-ordered stocks. In fact, by the time he got out of high school Matt was running a little wholesale tobacco business on the side. Having met him, you can understand that."

"You two brothers seem so unlike."

"Yes, we're physically at opposite ends, and Matt's a lot smarter. But he didn't have a father when it would have counted. I regret, now, that I simply didn't have the patience to teach him to hunt, to fish, and to fight—like Father taught *me*. On the other hand, he had a lot of time to study things way beyond what he got in school."

"It sounds like you did hold things together."

"It was my job. Anyway, after Mother passed away, Matt and I agreed to sell the store for our stake in the West." And not for the first time, James thought about Matt's actions and attitude since that date. Most of the time he was just as a brother should be—companionable, supportive, and all the rest. At other times he was off in a world of his own, one James didn't always like.

Palmer got up, paced back and forth a few times. He liked this man, finding him believable. But believing him was to condemn Leonard, who had done a lot of good work for D&RG for a long time. The General took a deep breath and sat down again.

"Now, second things first. I remain totally unconvinced that you have any particular qualifications for coal prospecting. But every-thing else aside, if in your wanderings over these mountains that you profess to like so much, you stumble upon a valid and transferable homestead or mining claim, I'll give you a fair price."

James remained sitting. Palmer was warming up.

"James Molyneaux, I called you up here to give you a good ass-chewing for not properly reporting Santa Fe's activities. But finding that you're not an employee and possibly not guilty as charged, anyway,

I'm robbed of that pleasure. Therefore, I propose to hire you as *my* crisis manager and *then* chew you out. Is that satisfactory with you?"

James nodded his agreement to this unusual job offer.

General Palmer was pleased with himself. Just like Solomon, he thought; we'll keep this big hulk of a young man on our side—and he may prove out to be a good one. We'll still keep Leonard—and he may be able to regain our trust. Llewellyn's capable enough. We need him in the boardroom where he shines, but he's got to be straightened out. I'm just the one to do that sort of thing.

"And now, about Raton—what do you suppose is going on down there?" General Palmer asked.

James replied without hesitation, "I think I *know* most of what is 'going on.' I can assure you, though, that there is no field activity...yet. Last month, tired of waiting for Llewellyn to show up, I violated his specific instructions, saddled up, and rode up the northeast flank of the Cristos." James stopped to make a point. "You see, sir, there can be no question—a horse is somewhat superior to a train without tracks."

Palmer showed the hint of a smile. "Noted for the record... Please proceed."

"First, I should say that back in Pittsburgh, long before I even heard of D&RG, I studied the Carnegie Library's meager map rack—particularly topos—for the Sangre de Cristos. As a consequence, I have a fairly good idea of the terrain from Trinidad to Cucharas Pass, and on up to the Spanish Peaks, for that matter..."

General Palmer interrupted, "What'n hell did you do that for?"

"I had a plan—and still do—to build a hunting shack somewhere in the Cristos." James smiled in recollection, "Anyway, as soon as Llewellyn described the Raton controversy and before I even arrived in Colorado, I was sure that it would be very easy to grade and clear a roadbed from the Purgatorie River at Trinidad up the northern slope at least to the toll road near the top.

"Mr. Llewellyn had indicated that he would have D&RG armed construction forces effect a standoff at that point. I didn't feel that I was in a position to ask a critical question, namely, what if Santa Fe arrived first? Nor did I ask another question that still nags at me, that is, isn't there any kind of law in Colorado to keep individuals and companies from taking violent and even lethal action—from taking the law into their own hands? And what is meant by armed resistance?"

"Yes, there are plenty of laws—territorial, state, city and town," General Palmer responded. "But not enough enforcers. The vast stretch of plains, deserts, and mountains west of the Mississippi supports a folklore of outlaws, Indians, cowboys, prospectors, and a whole society operating just outside the law. And an unwritten law has evolved that permits a man to defend himself in any manner possible. If he is incapable of doing that, a local sheriff may step in to help—but generally too late. As areas such as Denver or Pueblo build up, lawful enforcement follows. In the larger picture, local courts together with U.S. district, circuit, and federal courts have jurisdiction over major issues such as land, civil unrest, and Indian matters. But in many disputes the courts seem to be overly per-suaded by 'status quo.'"

"So with rights-of-way, for example, he who occupies, ultimately wins?"

"Exactly," replied Palmer. "But a physical standoff is frequently enough. You have to remember, our work force *is* our army. Most of the workers are adept with rifles—some are war veterans—but they're not killers. And almost all are very uncomfortable with hand guns. But anyone can swing a brake club. And that's how we can ef-fect a defensive standoff. So each worker is provided with a cudgel and a rifle, the former at hand and the latter in saddle sheath or bedroll."

"We're always reacting—not acting?" James added.

"Well...a certain amount of interpretation is always in order..." hedged the General, "and with the first shot from either side, all restraints are off."

After letting that information sink in a little, James continued. "Then I rode over to where I thought the tracks will probably go, hoping to find some D&RG stakes to prove you had been there first, but there's too much snow. The slope is absolutely free of activity: there is no sign of any work parties."

"We must remember, it *is* winter," interjected Palmer.

James went on, "In the barber shop, a source of information usually only slightly better than the Commercial Street bars, I overheard that Santa Fe had purchased Union Pacific's survey data for the La Junta to Trinidad branch line."

"Yes, I know about that; I still have Union Pacific *and* Kansas Pacific contacts."

"Coincidently, that same evening I talked to a man who had just moved in at Maude's. He mistook me for another big guy he had met on a job over in Missouri a couple years ago. He called me Sam and said something to the effect that he was a little surprised that 'they' were bringing the Missouri engineers over here as well as those from Utah and Kansas. By the time we got the identity thing straightened out, he had dropped the additional information that Santa Fe has two rush projects in Colorado that would need every surveyor, locator, bridge engineer, and teamster crew chief in the SF system.

"I asked, in my innocence, why they would need so many. His reply was to the effect that anyone familiar with railroad construction would recognize that with the Santa Fe Trail so close to both of the track sections, they could triple or quadruple the crews, working both ends towards the middle, and vice versa, so to speak, and this would apply to the New Mexico side as well. In other words, with the ability to enter the survey line at multiple spots, all crews could be working at full speed all of the time."

James then continued, "And, he also said that Santa Fe had obtained D&RG's survey, General—*D&RG's survey*—for Raton Pass. He indicated that this would speed the Raton job since they could almost immediately start clearing and grading."

James paused for effect, and there was plenty. General Palmer had gotten to his feet as if ready to repel the charge at Chickamauga.

"A little more… When we passed through Las Animas in November, alongside the tracks were large stacks of rails and ties. The conductor, who seemed know everything, told us that Santa Fe had obtained these from Union Pacific. Apparently this was the eighty miles or so of trackage salvaged from UP's abandoned Kit Carson to Las Animas line. You've looked at the mileage from La Junta to Raton, I'm sure, but I'll add my own observation. This is supposition, of course, but why hasn't Santa Fe pushed through to Trinidad? They were supposed to have done that over two months ago. They blame the weather, naturally. But could it be that most of that work—at least the locating, and perhaps the clearing and grading out in the middle, has been completed and they don't want to call attention to that fact until they make a quick push for Raton? Once started, Santa Fe could throw tracks over Raton Pass before D&RG was even aware what was happening. They'd be in Las Vegas or Santa Fe in just a few months— and there goes Trinidad as a D&RG shipping center."

"That makes sense, James, I'll have to talk to some of my people, but offhand it sounds that we would literally need an army to create any kind of resistance. But, go on with your report."

"While I didn't see any Santa Fe action last week, neither have I heard of any by D&RG. So, my guess is that Santa Fe is already up at Wooton's toll road and maybe they've already *bought* passage rights from him. If true, where does that leave them? As I said, the topo maps suggest a totally defensible spot just below the summit on the Trinidad side, but I don't know—I've not been up that far. I would wager, though, that even as we speak, Santa Fe is bringing an armed construction group around from the New Mexico side, the old Cimarron Cutoff. At least that's what I would do in their shoes. In the unlikely event a D&RG force has beaten Santa Fe to the bottom of the toll road, for example, a Cimarron party could shred it from the rear."

They were both silent for a moment, then James asked, "What would it take to prove in court that D&RG was there first, or would that make any difference, anyway?"

Palmer picked up a humidor on his desk. "Cigar, James?"

They prepared and trimmed their cigars in quiet anticipation.

"Occupation would be the best and maybe the only thing," said General Palmer. "Beyond that, it would help a little to prove we had surveyed the route earlier and would help even more to show that Santa Fe had used the D&RG survey. But you can be sure that the first thing Santa Fe will do is replace our survey stakes with theirs. The only thing we'll have left would be our surveyors' notes."

"Could a surveyor in the field and using those notes find out whether Santa Fe is following D&RG's exact line?"

"I'm sure he could, at least I could have when I was doing that kind of work—and that may be our only recourse, weak as it may be. I'll see if one of the locators who did our survey will be available in about a month or whenever Santa Fe starts charging up the mountain. You could go with him and protect his back."

"I'd be glad to do that. This kind of talk is good to hear, General. Sitting in Trinidad the past couple of months, I was beginning to wonder whether D&RG *wanted* to win at Raton."

A flushed General Palmer stiffened. "My army can be expected to lose a battle now and then, but it doesn't give the war away. They whipped us, pure and simple, in this skirmish. It's clear that we should have moved our clearing crews and track layers into the field last summer when we finished the survey. Now let's talk about Royal Gorge."

"I've not been there, yet. I'm anxious to see it."

"It's quite a sight. The main part of the gorge is about ten miles long with walls on both sides as much as a thousand feet—straight up. In many places the Arkansas has carved a channel down in the bottom just wide enough for itself. We'll have to cut a shelf above the water for much of our roadbed. A bridge expert from Kansas City told us that in one place he would have to hang a bridge from the sidewalls, somehow. I would like you to go up there tomorrow. Try to see where we might locate a campsite for the workers—I don't want them down in Cañon City—also, space for material storage and grazing for horses and mules. And, most important, how would we guard them? How many riflemen would we need? I'll stay in Pueblo until you get back. I'd go with you except I don't want to show my face and tip off our plan."

"But let me ask—why not go around the gorge instead of through it?"

"Several reasons: In the first place, it's much shorter. There's a feasible route south of the gorge, up Hardscrabble or even Grape Creek—in fact, I surveyed it myself a few years ago—but it's a very rugged thousand-foot rise ending up considerably south of where we want to go. A northern route might be even more difficult. The climb is even higher, much longer, more mountainous, and a lot of it is through gigantic sand dunes. It's tough to build a roadbed on that kind of stuff."

"I'm convinced. How often does the train to Cañon City run?"

"Once a day, each way. But you would be less visible if you went by horseback. You decide, but be prepared for ice however you get there."

"All understood. I'll be back in three or four days."

◇◇◇◇◇◇◇◇◇◇◇◇

There actually were two railways to Cañon City, one dedicated to coal and coke shipments, the other and newer one to general commercial traffic. James took neither; he chose horseback. One pleasant day in the saddle beats a day on the train and in the station house, anytime, he felt. He followed the broad channel of the Arkansas River as it meandered comfortably over this part of Colorado's Piedmont with an elevation drop less than seven hundred feet from Cañon City to Pueblo. The river was resting, James fanaticized—its work was done. Now there was only the long but easy run to the Mississippi. But up-hill from Cañon City it had been something else altogether. The river had clawed and chewed its way through seven thousand feet of all the hard rock in sight, finishing with the excavation of the Grand Canyon of the Arkansas, itself. It deserved to sit out its time.

The weather was cold—clear skies, but temperatures in the teens. Where eddies had caused quiet backwater, ice was forming.

Although on average nearly flat, the area sandwiched between the mountain foothills and the high plains to the east was dimpled with small hills curved one upon another and cut by feeder streams to the Arkansas River. It showed the effects of the drought followed by low snowfall, but beautiful to James' eye. It was the kind of country that Pennsylvania only promised—*Colorado delivered.* The terrain was irregular with year-round ground cover and trees along the river channel—tamarisk, poplar, cottonwood, and another broadleaf tree he didn't recognize along the banks, and stands of piñon and juniper further back. It was suitable habitat for all kinds of small game. The land seemed to flatten out as he approached the foothills and became more arid. Cultivation here would need irrigation, but water was readily available from the Arkansas. Near Cañon City an eroded cliff along the river channel had exposed a layer of sandstone much like he had seen in Engle.

He slipped between the new oil town of Florence—oil had been discovered there only ten years before—and the outskirts of the very old Cañon City, which, in turn, had been an Indian campsite, a mining community, and then a railroad town. Was it the railroad that finally made it a city or the State Penitentiary that came along after the oil? This oil thing is kind of interesting, James thought; you just drill a hole and then wait for the "liquid coal" to come out, put it in a tub and carry it away—then another tub, and another. No pick or shovel, no blasting powder, no roof supports, no firedamp or afterdamp, no mules—beats the hell out of a coal mine.

James veered back to the Arkansas and followed the undeveloped road up to the entrance of the Royal Gorge. There was no mistaking it. A stream—James guessed it was Grape Creek and possibly a branch of the Hardscrabble—joined the Arkansas just outside the portal. The passage into the gorge was guarded by a vertical five-hundred-foot granite up-thrust on the north side of the river and a somewhat less imposing ridge on the south. The Arkansas dog-legged out of sight at that point, giving a first impression that the traveler was about to enter a bottomless chasm. It was comforting to know that countless others had entered this dark abyss before, presumably to come out someplace at the other end.

Moving past the portal he could be see there was reasonably good foot access through and over the jumble of rocks along both sides of the river, as well as passage for horse or mule and travois. Generations of Indians, trappers, traders, and gold seekers had made it through one way or another. Not wishing to risk injury to Coalfire, James removed saddle and gear and tethered the horse in the portal meadow. In four months or so, when construction workers could move in, there would be plenty of good fresh grass for grazing this side of the portal, he knew. Grass would pop up so quickly after the snow melt, one would almost see it grow. At the outset, this year's dried grass on the ground, being short-stem buffalo variety, would have retained much of its nutrient value. That's how the nomadic Indians had gotten along.

But this would not be a place to make a stand. We could put snipers on the forested ridge to the left, James thought, and build a rock wall with firing slots in front of the portal, but that position could be easily overrun. And it would take an army to defend a larger fortification closer to Cañon City. The only hope would be to have heavily armed breastworks and sniper's nests back in the gorge, itself.

James moved up canyon on the right side. It was wide enough to accommodate rails at this exact point but it was evident that there would still have to be an enormous amount of rock removal, shelving, bridging, and filling. It was also apparent that considerable hand grading had been done over the decades as predecessors tried to improve their footpath. But this was not his concern; his only interest lay in how to protect the people doing the new work. As he hiked and scrambled up the north bank, he noticed that access along the south side had become severely limited—he had chosen the correct path, it seemed.

The river's roar was overwhelming, with spray laying down ice on the rocks, suggesting what was in store in the next month. This led to a disturbing thought. The mighty fast-moving Arkansas would be, at the same time, a help and a hindrance. It made construction between those towering walls much more difficult, but it improved defenses against attack. With the river frozen over, things would be profoundly different—even reversed. This could lead to twelve-month construction activity.

James noticed along both sides of the gorge a number of clefts worn by tributary creeks and streams. These suggested that the sheer canyon walls were indeed scalable in some locations, but not by James—another promise to himself. At one point about five miles above the portal, a sizeable side canyon on the north side caught his eye. This might be accessible from the rear by swinging in a wide loop on the high plateau north and west of Cañon City, he thought. If so, and we were busily laying track from the east end of the portal, we could be blindsided. Santa Fe could leapfrog around us.

Visibility at the bottom of the gorge at this point was not good. As James moved on, the canyon walls grew higher and steeper, and increasingly intimidating, The footing was more difficult as ice built up on the rocks. Twice he slipped, once going down to his knees, the other flat on his face. He had to crawl over one particularly glassy stretch. And then, he went into the icy water almost to his waist. Fortunately it was in an eddy pool and he pulled himself out, albeit with extreme difficulty. At that point he concluded that no man should ever be alone in the gorge, either winter or summer. They must be roped together, in pairs.

As James returned down canyon, shivering almost uncontrollably, he reviewed in his mind how he would summarize this for the General. The area outside the portal was an excellent staging area in many respects. Equipment materials—rails, ties, and other supplies—could be stockpiled, and horses and mules tethered. A workers' campsite could be provided. There was room for all of this in the meadow but it would be essentially indefensible.

So, at the outset of the job it would be necessary to take all materials and supplies back into the gorge, finding room wherever. At the onset of an assault, the workers would pull back into the gorge covered by guards at the portal fortification and from the hills south of the river. The portal guards would be reinforced and construction could continue—with considerable difficulty. Construction forces could be resupplied by means of an armored train pulling over newly laid rails right into the gorge portal. Mounted groups could harass the attackers around the outside of the portal and additional guards would patrol up and down the gorge to avoid surprises. Armed guards would be posted to watch the canyon rim. Off-duty workers and guards would sleep in the numerous nooks and sand deposits back in the gorge. Spring runoff would create additional problems in this regard. The commissary would have to stretch its imagination to provide food under such irregular conditions. It's too bad the General himself couldn't look at this, James thought. He must have had the same problems of strategy and logistics during the war.

Back at the meadow, James built a warming fire, changed into some dry clothes he had in his rucksack, and saddled up. Some hardtack and jerky was the best he could do to substitute for a dinner at Maude's.

On the way back downriver, James branched out to be sure he wasn't missing something. He passed near the railhead at Cañon City and then followed the tracks themselves for a few miles. At one point he was again in sight of the oil facilities at Florence. Nowhere was there any sign of Santa Fe activity. Based on Santa Fe's prompt action at Raton, D&RG should get surveyors and construction crews up here right away. That would be his recommendation to General Palmer.

At dusk he was still some distance from Pueblo so the tarp and bedroll were laid out on the frozen ground. James had to laugh at himself. As much as he proclaimed aloud how he liked to roam around the hills and do nothing, in truth he sort of liked this high pressure and the rough conditions.

◇◇◇◇◇◇◇◇◇◇◇◇

General Palmer listened attentively to James' report the next afternoon, breaking in repeatedly for clarification, always cautioning himself to remember that the young man was neither a soldier nor an engineer but had proved to be a keen observer of terrain. That's what Llewellyn had noticed about him as they came across Kansas.

At the conclusion of James's presentation, General Palmer leaned back. "Now the big question, James. Suppose we're as late at Royal Gorge as we seem to be at Raton. And suppose Santa Fe does about what you just outlined D&RG should do. How should we react?"

James had to shift his rudder to the other tack and hope things would come around. What had been a construction offense, suddenly would have to be a defensive mode. "I think we should put the same kind of pressure on them at the portal that we would expect them to exert—with one big difference." James paused.

Palmer frowned and cleared his throat. "I'm listening."

James took a new breath and continued. "With all the resources that it has, Santa Fe would simply bring up another and larger group behind us. I don't think we could possibly drive such a force out of the meadow and into the gorge."

"Well, hell, James, you think we should quit?"

James was taken aback. He considered what he was doing—*giving a topography lesson* to a man who had personally clambered over the passes and surveyed much of Colorado—telling a Medal of Honor recipient *how to fight*. But it was too late to turn back.

"No, not at all, sir," he said. "I think you might consider a 'hit and run' tactic in the meadow, trying to make Santa Fe nervous and off balance, but also trying not to kill or be killed. Let's keep the sheriff out of it. At the same time, you might try to harass the workers— roll rocks down from the rim, shoot a few mules or horses, bring up a tub or two of that 'liquid coal' from Florence and try to start a fire—and above all, go for the jugular, *go to court*. Show that D&RG was here first."

"Is that all?" A bit of skepticism in the tone.

"Not quite, sir. A couple additional actions to consider. First, send a small exploratory party into the hills all along the north rim of the gorge. Maybe you can find a couple old trappers in Cañon City who know those hills, but pick ones who happen to be favorable to D&RG's cause. Try to find spots where snipers or rock throwers might be effective and, better yet, find a place or two where a leap-frogging construction team might enter the gorge. You might send a similar party to the south rim."

James was getting worked up, throwing all parts of himself into his description. "Then, this afternoon—it should have been yesterday—send a work train with a locating party and a clearing team up to the rail end at Cañon City. Put them to work preparing to lay track to the gorge to reinforce your 'first here' legal position. Include a couple of snipers. And then the big thing…"

"I can hardly wait."

"Somehow or other, General, get a locating party and clearing team over to Cotopaxi and up as close as they can get to the western portal, if there is one. I have no idea how to get over there. Would it be north from Walsenburg or east from Texas Creek? But make noise that you are coming in from that end to meet the D&RG track layers at the middle of the gorge. Again, the 'first here' angle."

"James, I think you've lost your mind, but just on the off chance I've missed something sensible, go over the whole thing again."

"Yes, sir, but first I'd like to add, maybe you might follow that first work train with an armored one the next day. What I'm trying to say is…drive your fortified position right up to the front door, sir."

James went back and forth over the basis and logic for his recommendations. Finally General Palmer stood. "Thank you, James," he said. A dismissal.

James stood as well. "With your permission, sir, I'll go back to Trinidad and wait for Santa Fe's action at Raton. As soon as they're far enough up the mountain that their exact line is committed, I'll request your surveyor to come down. That should be very soon, I think."

General Palmer nodded. Other business was pressing, two hundred and fifty miles of operating railroad, one hundred miles more under construction, a steel mill at Minnequa, coal mines at Cañon City, Walsenburg, and Engle, investors to placate, and politicians to pander.

CHAPTER TEN

RATON PASS

HAD HE BEEN GONE A YEAR? James asked himself in disbelief. No, just a week—a very busy week. Trinidad was still the not-so-little frontier town that James had left but something was missing. And then he realized that there were no wagon trains on Main Street, or cattle in the pens on Elm Street. No wranglers or drovers in the Commercial Street saloons. And he didn't have to wait for a shave and haircut. Winter was here and Trinidad had hunkered down.

He left Coalfire with Ramirez and checked in at Maude's. There was a note from Matt saying that the Grand Union Hotel project had heated up and that he, Matt, had gone up to Denver to see some bankers. James should go see Lillian—as if that would be a problem—and she would fill him in. As an afterthought Matt had added the information that their office lease was approved and Lillian was taking care of the furnishings.

◇◇◇◇◇◇◇◇◇◇◇◇

"Ah—my beautiful little doll," he said, grabbing Lillian while keeping Mike at bay.

She finally broke loose. "You've only been gone a week. Do I look so different?"

"No—just lovely, as usual."

"You've been drinking"

James shook his head.

"Then how about something to drink, now?"

"I don't think so. I'm kind of beat and I've some chores to do this afternoon."

"Why don't you go over to my office? I have a nice little settee and you can relax a bit. I'll come in for a little while after I catch up here."

"Come as soon as you can—being tired is not my only problem."

Lillian came in quietly. James was sitting with head back and legs stretched out ahead, sleeping like a baby. Sitting down beside him she slipped a hand under his shirt, exploring gently. As if by magic, his belt buckle came unfastened—a button came undone, and then another. Her hand kept searching and searching and then finding. James stirred and started to turn towards her. She gently pushed him back. "Stay right where you are. Try to relax. This one's on me." She dropped to her knees.

◇◇◇◇◇◇◇◇◇◇◇◇

Winter was holding on. And it's just started, thought James. Fortunately, Matt was back from Denver—with plenty of indoors things to talk about. He and James were having breakfast at a little place downtown.

"Let me fill you in on where we are. Lillian introduced me to a Mr. Hepplewhite, the managing partner of a group of five investors who are building the new Grand Union Hotel. After introductions and preliminary conversation, she left and Mr. Hepplewhite and I talked serious details. The hotel will have two stories above ground level, one hundred guest rooms, and a large ornate lobby opening on Commercial Street. The lobby plus support facilities, office, and storage rooms will cover about one-third to one-half of the ground floor. I told him that we would propose to develop and operate the balance of that floor with an upscale saloon and dining room, gentlemen's smoking room, ladies retiring room, gaming room, barber shop, and tobacco store. I said we would provide all of the furnishings for the facilities we'd be leasing."

"How about future development?"

"I emphasized that we would propose to develop the street floor not taken up with hotel lobby and support. And if we needed more space we would consider developing the basement for a gentlemen's club. I suggested that the architect take into consideration the future need for basement light and ventilation, whether we immediately develop it or not. We would be interested in a long lease with appropriate cost index adjustments."

"Where do we stand now?"

"I didn't say anything about our thoughts of encircling two sides of our saloon with a balcony of roomettes. He's a businessman—we can talk about that later. He then asked me to go up to Denver and meet his partners. That's where I've been the past few days. I suspect that no one else has come up with such a comprehensive proposition. I'll spend the next couple weeks working out details of just what we'll need in the way of furnishings and how much they'll cost, how many employees we'll require, and other operating costs including fuel for heating and lighting. I'll also find out what are typical lease rates for Trinidad buildings. With all of this, we can make a firm proposal to Mr. Hepplewhite and Partners in a week or two."

Matthew continued, "I made a rough cost analysis of this and it looked very good. And it will take little more than half of our stake. I have a question, Jim—do we still want Lillian in as a partner? Do we know enough about her? What would she bring to the enterprise? After talking to the new Grand Union Hotel owner and his bankers, I don't think we really need her money."

James was silent for a long moment. What was Matt trying to say?

James then raised his voice a little. "I think she would be a very good addition. She's the only one of us who has actually run a saloon—and by present Trinidad standards, it's a pretty good one. She's most certainly the only one who can run the girls, but we probably should gentrify that activity a little—as we heard all across Kansas. I'm sure she can operate to any standard we all agree to."

"And the hotel would insist upon that. Do you think she would be acceptable to all kinds of people—from the members of the elite men's club to the ladies at the tearoom's afternoon festivities? Not to mention the blue-collar guys at the bar?"

"I think so, as long as they have separate entrances. One other thing about Lillian: I like her."

Matthew hesitated a long moment. "All right—I'll go along with you, Jim. I can see that you're pretty positive about this. I think, though, that we should include an escape clause designed for fair and equal treatment of each party, should we not all get along. Shall we offer Lillian up to one-quarter interest or whatever she can afford?"

James quickly replied, "I want to see her with a full one-third interest regardless of how much she puts in."

Matt hesitated. "Okay, then. I'll write a 'letter of intent' for the three of us to sign, and get it over to Hepplewhite. In about a month we'll have to sit down with the architect to work out details of the interior partitions, windows, and the like. Lillian will do a lot of that."

James nodded assent.

"Okay, but now for a couple other pieces of business. As we agreed, I found and purchased two building lots up on Aristocracy Hill, actually on fifth street near Chestnut. They're about two blocks apart—we can flip a coin. Then I took the liberty of buying a third lot, a big one on Second Street for investment purposes. That's in both our names. All okay?"

"Sure. And the other thing?"

"The General left word with his staff that I was to go up to La Veta on that auditing assignment about the first of February; that's in three weeks. Will you help me put some things together, Jimmie?"

"Sure. I suggest you take our wagon. I think you should have a four-horse team instead of two, but you're a better driver than I, so it's your choice. You can ask Ramirez—he knows this country and I think he's honest. Across from the livery stable is the Pioneer Store. You can pick up clothing and a lot of supplies, food and water, and whatever. And a couple bags of oats to tide the horses over.

I've got my little 'pop' gun—will that be enough?'

"Hell no! I'll help you pick out a short-barreled scatter gun and a Colt revolver. Not that you'll ever need them, but you might have to run a bluff. I suggest you keep them hidden in the wagon, but out of sight. You had better take a day or two to practice a little. You don't really aim with either weapon—just point and shoot. If you're close, you can't miss. Let's face the fact that you're the auditor from Denver—they'll hate your guts, at least at first. Be careful with the superintendent; he'll set the tone at the outset. Tromp on him if you have to."

"Do it 'the army way,' as Palmer would say?"

"Yeah. If I were you, I would sleep in the wagon out on the job." In addition to the driver's and passengers' seats up front, the wagon had a covered bed about six feet long with thirty-inch sideboards and a tail gate. "It's cleaner, drier, and more comfortable than the ground, and you'll look more like the Inspector General that Palmer has dubbed you. Another thing I would throw in the wagon is a stout pick handle—to kill snakes, of course."

◇◇◇◇◇◇◇◇◇◇◇◇

Matt had hired from Ramirez a closed-top buggy, without driver, for a picnic drive up the Purgatorie to the south fork. The weather was clear and cold but Sophia and Matt hardly noticed. They stopped at a knoll several yards back from the slow moving river, wasting no time in humdrum conversation—a very pleasant experience, thought Matt.

Sophia slipped back into her chemise. "You must think me an awfully loose woman, Matt. I seem to be taking these things off and putting them back on every time we turn around."

"No, I think you're lovely and I love you for it," said Matt

He leaned back against the grassy knoll and spoke dreamily. "Tell me, Sophia, how do you expect to spend your next several years, or longer?"

Sophia answered, "I want to live in a big house, like Daddy's, furnished and decorated with items that you and I will have acquired abroad, from England, France, and maybe...Egypt."

"No, I mean when you're alone in that big house. Remember, I'll often be away on business, just like your father."

"Well, I'll travel extensively and when I'm home I'll entertain a lot—important people, of course. And I really don't expect you to be away too much; you can delegate most everything to your subordinates. After all, that's what they're for."

"And do you want children?"

"Oh yes, I'll work that in someplace.

◇◇◇◇◇◇◇◇◇◇◇◇

Between Maude's dinner table, the barber shop waiting room, and an occasional ride around the town's perimeter, James hoped to have an early warning of Santa Fe's dash for Raton. Finally, two weeks after Matthew's departure for La Veta, Commercial Street was jumping, seemingly overnight, and Maude's was filled to capacity—usually two or more to a room—with Santa Fe construction personnel. Two dinner sittings were necessary. Talk was loose and James quickly learned more than he wanted to know.

Since it would take the D&RG surveyor at least a week to get down here, James thought it prudent to get a wire off to General Palmer right away. An exchange of telegrams followed:

WESTERN UNION

GENERAL W PALMER GRAND PALACE PUEBLO JAN 20

HORSES ARE RUNNING JAMES

WESTERN UNION

JAMES MOLYNEAUX TRINIDAD JAN 22

ACKNOWLEDGE STOP ALAN WILL WIRE STOP PALMER

WESTERN UNION

JAMES MOLYNEAUX TRINIDAD JAN 28

ARRIVE TUES ALAN

◇◇◇◇◇◇◇◇◇◇◇◇◇

"I'm Alan Matthews," a smallish, somewhat weather-beaten man introduced himself, "and you have to be James Molyneaux—you seem to be the only one left. I have a whole sack of things to show you. Where can we spread them out?"

"Let's take my buggy into town. We can use our new office. An introductory occasion, so to speak."

Alan said, "General Palmer told me what you're after. I think I can help. But whether the lawyers can make anything out of it is another thing." They spread the papers out on the table in the office.

"Jim—if I can call you that. Do you know anything about surveying?"

"Yes—to the first—and no, but I'll try to follow you as you explain."

"This is my field notebook. As we 'run a line,' the elevation at each station and the horizontal angle to the next one are recorded.

The 'line' may change direction at each station or conversely, a line might be run in an unchanging direction and successive stations established in that set direction. The terrain will determine which method to be used.

"It must be possible from each station to see, with the leveling telescope, the target on the rod at the next." As he talked, Alan pointed out the sliding target on the rod and the gradations marking its position. "The surveyor can sight the target with his leveling telescope and read the gradations. He calls out or signals his rod-man to slide the target up or down. Thus the difference in elevation between the transit and the surveyed point is determined. And obviously the change in elevation from one station to the other must be less than the length of the rod. That sets the maximum distance between stations." Alan went on to explain how the direction of the line is thus established between the base station—the transit—and the newly surveyed point.

"We have a 'chain,' an actual chain of known length," he said, "which we use to determine the real distance between near stations. And then with the known angles from each to the far station, we can calculate that distance—I carry a little handbook of angles and distances. And I should mention that there are at least two persons involved, the surveyor with the level or transit and an assistant on the rod. Are you with me, so far?"

James gave a tentative nod. Alan accepted that.

"We must know where we're starting. That is our 'bench mark.' We must know its position on the map and its elevation. If we don't have an established point from which to start, our beginning point is our bench mark."

"Surveying has two similar but opposite functions. First to determine, for purpose of mapping, the exact position and elevation of every point on our desired field to the accuracy desired. In an uneven field, we make multiple observations to portray the contours.

"Second, to establish marks to control construction or to indicate land boundaries. Construction control is our concern here.

"To start, we have a map of the area, very accurate with respect to land boundaries, very exact as to starting and ending points and elevations of those points—hopefully showing descriptions and locations of enduring landmarks—but very inexact with respect to intervening elevations. In other words, we have only an approximate topographic representation.

"So, we run a first approximate line based on that approximate topography and staying within our grade and boundary limitations. We determine the probable number and location of switchbacks. In our survey, then, we are correcting the topographic map to the extent deemed necessary and superimposing upon it our final line. As we modify our map, or plat, we prepare a profile of the line. This enables us to check on the reasonableness of our grade and the switchbacks. It enables us to make minor adjustments to our line. Got it?"

"It's sort of a 'trial and error' approach?"

"Not bad. You've got it. We also call it 'metes and bounds.' It's highly unlikely that two surveyors would come up with the same exact line. Therefore, not only can we prove with our handwritten and dated field notes that D&RG was there first, if we find that the lines are identical, we have a very good case that our data were stolen, somehow."

"That sounds pretty good. Do you think you can do that?"

Alan shrugged. "We'll see. I've got my transit in my bag and you can be my rod-man and we'll try. On top of that, you'll learn to be a surveyor."

"That'll be the day," said James.

They left the office and drove down to the livery stable to arrange for horse and saddle for Alan. The surveyor kept a tight grip on notes and maps, all wrapped for weather protection.

"Are you comfortable riding?" asked James.

"So-so," said Alan with a self-deprecating shrug.

"Well, no matter. I can help you over the rough parts. It'll be a little more difficult than just a ride in the woods. We'll have to try to be inconspicuous. And now to Maude's."

◇◇◇◇◇◇◇◇◇◇◇◇

Maude gave them an early breakfast and packed a dry lunch. "Will you two be here for supper?"

"Don't think so, Maude. We fixed up a bedroll for Alan. We probably won't be back until tomorrow. I've a lot of dry food we can keep alive on."

As they left the boarding house, James explained the care they would have to take. "I haven't seen any indication yet of Santa Fe bringing in any ties or rails, but they undoubtedly are well along with clearing and grading. So we'll have to be careful not to show ourselves."

The men slipped out of town taking the trail for about an hour and then veering southwest towards the toe of the Sangre de Cristos. There were more snow patches than they really wanted to see. James could see Alan nervously watching the ground—his horsemanship really wasn't adequate and the patches of snow didn't help. The mountains were ghostly in this early half-light, adding to Alan's uncertainty.

Suddenly, and surprisingly, Alan shouted, "Aces and aces, we found it! I guess they picked up my line further along—at least, I hope so. But here is part of our evidence, anyway. Jim, look carefully at this stake and memorize what's written on it. Note that it shows 'D&RG' and a station identification. Someone, very recently, has scraped it clear of snow. You may be a witness."

James asked, "Can we drive it a little further into the ground? And cover it with snow?"

"Sure, and I'll make a field note. Now, I need my level, and I'll pick up my old line from my notes." Alan set up his folding tripod and sent James off with rod in the indicated direction. "Farther...farther... left...there." Arm signals accompanied the voice. "Can you see a stake anywhere?"

"I'm looking... Alan, come here. There's a stake—a new one—but it's not ours!"

Alan hurried to James' side.

"You're right. Take the rod off in the same direction while I set up the transit again."

James followed Alan's instructions.

"Back...back...to the left...too much...right a little...back a little... there. See anything?"

"I sure do! Stay there, I'll come back to you."

James came up. "Alan, we've come to fresh grading and gravel. Let's get back out of sight."

"James, I think we've proved our case. But one more..." He examined the old map and looked up at the hill. "Our survey had a switchback about a mile ahead. Let's ride up and see if that checks. I wonder if we can find any fixed landmarks. Let's go see."

Back with the tethered horses, James said, "Put your level and stuff out of sight. Wrap it up in this tarp. Take this small bore rifle and shove the barrel under your thigh—there are cartridges in the magazine but not in the chamber. I'll do the same with my hunting rifle. There—we're a couple of unsuccessful hunters. Follow me."

They proceeded slowly up the steep slope paralleling the new railway cut on the flank of the Cristos until they had traveled about one mile. As Alan had predicted, they then reached the clearing for the first switchback.

"Anything else, Alan?" asked James

"I'd like to set up and take a few bearings from a fixed bench. There is this switchback, one more in sight farther up the hill, and a cleft up above that shows on the map. Do you see a cleft? Oh, there it is…just as described."

Alan had just finished putting his stuff out of sight again when a shot echoed through the canyon.

A voice rang out, "What'n hell you guys doing? This is private property."

They looked in the direction of the sound; about two hundred yards up the slope a man carrying a rifle was making his way towards them.

"Getting ready to fix some lunch," shouted James.

"I mean what are you doing up here on the mountain? I thought I saw one of you with a telescope."

"That's to look for deer, friend—that's one of those animals with horns on their heads that run around in the trees."

"I'm coming down to run you out of here"

"I don't *think* so. I told you we're deer hunters, and we're hunting on public land. This rifle is pointed at the center of your forehead. Now, leave us alone and let us eat our lunch."

"I'm coming down."

"But not with your hat." James fired. The hat flew and the man took off in the other direction.

James and Alan packed up and headed back down the mountain. All in all, a very satisfactory outing.

"Thanks, Jim. You covered my back pretty well. That was quite a shot—weren't you afraid you'd nick him?"

"Well, I was relaxed—I didn't care much whether I hit him or not. That warning shot he fired asked for it. By all the rules, it was an invitation. Alan, it was a pleasure to watch you work. Someday I'd like to learn to do it."

"Surveying itself isn't very difficult. For example, it's using the survey information in order to locate the tracks to eliminate or minimize switchbacks—that's the sort of thing that takes some experience. And when you have to locate both ends of a tunnel that's supposed to meet in the middle, extreme precision is needed. But, it's never cold and snowy like this—I've never had to clear the snow so I could set up my tripod."

As they parted, James asked, "What's your conclusion, Alan? Did Santa Fe steal D&RG's survey?"

"They used it without a question. Their profile as built exactly matches our design profile. That simply cannot happen by chance. But whether they stole it or bought it, I can't say."

CHAPTER ELEVEN

A RAILROAD ABOVE
THE CLOUDS

THE MIDDLE OF FEBRUARY had arrived. Time to get started to La Veta, Matt thought. It had been a winter of low snowfall so far and only patches high in the mountains remained. He was uneasy over the discrepancy between the field progress report and the rail and ties bills-of-lading he had read in Denver. It didn't really matter if winter conditions were still hanging on and even worsening, Matt assured himself. He could start a field audit and at least get the record-searching underway.

Matt had decided for a two-horse team for the small "quartermaster wagon," leading a spare and his saddle horse. The wagon bed held a sleeping pad, bedroll, and a large wooden box for personal gear and clothing. This, with chair, would serve as a field desk. A short-barreled, small-gauge shotgun and a revolver were tucked away out of sight. And, of course—Matthew had to smile—the pick handle that Jim had insisted upon. Emergency water and rations for himself and the four horses completed the mix.

Matthew felt good. It had been a wonderful two weeks in Trinidad and good weather was only the smallest part of it. The high point, Matthew happily recalled, was the visit to the Llewellyn home where, surprisingly, he had found Sophia unattended. I'm going to marry that girl—maybe I'll *have* to, Matt smiled to himself. What a week!

In the days prior to his departure, Matthew had been diligent in obtaining information about Walsenburg, La Veta, and Raton. Meeting in the Molyneaux Main Street office with Jim's surveyor friend, Matthew had received a geography lesson.

"You have a choice of routes up there, Matt," Jack Meadows had said, pulling a map from his notecase. He explained, "You see here, you can go up to Walsenburg and then up the Cucharas River Valley all the way up to La Veta—the town is right on the river as you might imagine. You can take a train, a 'sometimes' stagecoach, or go up by wagon or horseback. Another choice—and perhaps less time consuming—would be to go by horseback west from Trinidad along the Purgatorie to the Sangre de Cristo foothills, and then turn north over Cucharas Pass." He stopped, temporarily out of words.

"You sound like a town promoter, Jack, but keep it up," Matt said. "It kind of dispels some of my reservations. Frankly, I'm a little nervous about this assignment. I really am short of background."

"Don't worry about it, Matt. You'll learn that Colorado is half bluff."

A tentative smile. "And the other half?"

"Guts and grit. Now, back to the map—another idea would be to take a stage to Taos, get a horse there, and go through the San Luis Valley to San Luis, then to Fort Garland and over La Veta Pass. I wouldn't recommend that route but it's not a bad way to San Luis if all you want is to get to the county seat."

"As a matter of fact, I'll have to go over to the San Luis Valley and to all of the individual towns. Part of my job will be to build relationships with the officials in these locations—but not quite yet. Before you put that map away, please show me where the rails are—or will be."

"I can't really tell, since I don't what the locater has in mind. You can be certain, though, that the total rail distance can be more than double a straight line over the top." Folding his map, first one way and then the other until it was finally flat, Meadows continued, "Once in the San Luis Valley you might be as surprised as I was to learn how much land in addition to that around Trinidad and up to the Arkansas was included in the Spanish-Mexican land grants and how strong is the Mexican heritage. The older man had begun to slow down his words.

"I understand that the grants out West were Spanish, were much smaller, and were generally awarded to New Spain nationals. In this area, most of the grants were made after Mexico's independence in 1821, and given to foreign as well as Mexican nationals, providing that the recipients pledge to defend Mexico against American expansion westward." Meadows now spoke even slower.

"And some of the parcels are huge. Over four million acres were originally included in the Vigil and St. Vrain grant alone, more or less bounded by the Purgatorie, Arkansas, and Huerfano rivers, and over one million acres in the Lee and Beaubien grant, mostly in the San Luis Valley. This was Spain's and then Mexico's incentives for settlement of New Spain and the northern properties. But in the long run it didn't work—the land-hungry northern neighbor took it all as the spoils of war."

Taking most of Meadows' monologue in, Matthew interjected, "Not much different from the promises of our country's Railroad, Homestead, and Mining Acts, currently being fulfilled. Land ownership is the driving force of all time."

"Helped a bit by gold, we should add. You're amused, Matt. What struck you?"

"Right now, we're talking about millions of acres of land being parceled out…and just a few weeks ago, my brother, you, and I were scheming how we could latch onto just a few hundred 'lost' acres of some Mexican land grant that might have fallen into a crack."

"How is that project working out, Matt?"

"Quite well, I think. Our lease applications are in Denver and our attorney is drawing up the partnership agreement. My guess is we'll be discussing partnership details in about six months. But, remember, Jack, we don't really know that there's coal down there."

"It's fun dreaming."

"Yes, but right now I have to get to La Veta. Thanks for your help. I feel a lot more comfortable now."

◇◇◇◇◇◇◇◇◇◇◇◇

Matthew chose the Cucharas route, arriving in Walsenburg before noon. It was an easy drive, his matched pair stepping out prettily. He had been there once before—it was a water and coal stop on the D&RG Pueblo Line. Now he needed neither, but still had to stop at the railroad station to pick up a La Veta construction payroll bag left there for him. Then back past the Walsen coal mine about a mile west of town. Walsenburg seemed quite a bit larger than Engle, and so was the mine itself.

Another two or three hours, he estimated, but easy going all the way along both the railroad and the Cucharas River. A lovely spot; this ride was like driving out of Pittsburgh for a Sunday picnic. To the south and southwest the snow-covered Sangre de Cristos curled off majestically with its sister peaks, as if it wanted nothing to do with the lesser mountains. Matt had seen the other side of the Spanish Peaks while in Trinidad, but only from this angle could he view gigantic ridges of rock radiating outwards like spokes of a wheel from the peak—volcanic intrusions, as he had heard such geologic forma-tions described.

Francisco Plaza, lying on the banks of the cottonwood-lined Cucharas River, was a picturesque sight, but flawed. What had been an adobe-walled Mexican-styled village, sleepy-eyed, they would say, had been desecrated by the removal of an important part of that wall for some railroad tracks right to Francisco plaza. And worse than that, where the wall had been, there stood an untidy row of new structures and tents—a saloon, billiards parlor, livery stable, and tobacco shop.

The city hall and other offices remained in their original location in the center of Francisco Plaza, but all civic functions and physical facilities were placed under the new name, La Veta. And even more unsightly, along the tracks stood an untidy row of what appeared to be personal-use tents, presumably for construction employees. It was difficult for Matt to accept that a D&RG construction camp could be so disorderly.

With suspension of the La Veta Pass project, the Cucharas leg ended at this point, but the finished and usable rails tying into the D&RG main line back near Walsenburg were sufficient to spark a commercial development around La Veta. Farming increased to the limit of the tillable soil, livestock grazing was expanded, and an area north of the rails was platted for commercial and residential town lots.

Matt could see where construction had recently resumed after nearly two idle years. The new track had been extended out of sight towards the mountains to the west and a small depot was being built. A work train—engine, tender, day car, three-tiered dormitory car, and three flatcars were on the section of new track. It did not ap-pear that the engine had steam up. Matthew drove over to the largest of the group of tents, one that appeared to be the construction of-fice. He didn't have an opportunity to bring his team to a stop—the bridles were grabbed by a couple of workmen under the orders of a large heavily bearded man heading toward the wagon, weaving a bit and waving a revolver.

Stepping down from the wagon and walking back to the rear tailgate, Matthew was thinking fast and furiously—this must be the superintendent, and he's dangerously drunk. And why are all these men, at least twenty that I can see, not working? Are the rest in the cantina?

"Get the hell outta here, little man, you're trespassing."

Matthew, standing at the tailgate, hoped his quivering didn't show in the shadows. "My name is Matthew Molyneaux, sir. Are you Superintendent Oswald?"

"I know who you are, shit face, we got a letter from Palmer, but we don't need you here. We don't want you here." He pointed his pistol. "Now dance your way out of here...*dance...I* say." A bullet hit perilously close to Matthew's right foot, then one to the left.

"Now please listen, Mr. Oswald. I'm here on General Palmer's orders, as you are. I'm only here to help you out. I'm not a construction superintendent..." another shot and another bullet—this time between Matthew's feet. There was no reaction from the on-lookers—they seemed frozen in disbelief.

"Okay, okay, I'll leave, but first let me give you the payroll bag." Matthew reached into the wagon and pulled out the bag, tossing it a little off-line to Oswald. The superintendent turned and reached to catch the bag. Then, with a move that James had insisted his brother practice over and over, Matthew pulled the pick handle out of the wagon and, with a roundhouse swing clubbed Oswald on the side of the head—probably a little harder than intended. It sounded a little like an overripe watermelon falling off a wagon. Oswald crumpled to the ground, not making a sound. Oddly, there was still no reaction from the watchers.

"Assume the worst, Matt," Jim had said. "Assume the men will support the superintendent. So that's when you pull out the loaded shotgun."

Matthew did just that. But the men still held back, neither threatening nor supporting. A few more came out of town, perhaps from the cantina.

"Come on over, men," said Matthew, desperately speaking as slowly and calmly as he could. "Let's talk about this situation. But first, will a couple of you please run into town and get the marshal—and maybe the coroner, too." The others moved in, forming a half circle facing Matt, some standing but most sitting on the ground.

Matthew set the shotgun against the wagon wheel, took a couple deep breaths—he hoped inconspicuously—then turned and faced the group as it quieted. "First, let me say that I'm sorry that my meeting with Oswald had to turn out this way. I came over from Denver to help him, not to replace him. But there's something about dancing at gun-point that just doesn't sit well with me. Let's hope he's all right."

"He don't look too good right now," one of the men said with a matter-of-fact tone.

Matthew continued, "Now, as you probably all know, I'm the assigned D&RG auditor to help expedite this job, keep track of construction material, get it to the job site on time, make sure there is no lost time, place future long delivery orders, approve the field purchases, and help work out scheduling and sequences. In short, to do the things that you would want done if you were the owner, and don't like to do yourself. Now with Oswald out of it, and since I'm the senior D&RG person here, I have the responsibility to keep this job going until Denver sends another supe over. Okay?"

"Not okay," shouted one man, and a couple others nodded. "We'll just sit here until that replacement arrives."

"That's all right," said Matthew, picking up the shotgun. "But you can't stay right here. You'll have to leave camp right now—return to Walsenburg or wherever. Your pay stops. Your rations stop. And you are invited to leave this meeting. It's your choice. But if you stay, you work." No one moved away.

Matt paused. "Please relax and be comfortable." Matt pulled his own chair out of the wagon; those men still standing sat on the ground. "First, will all foremen come up front. Are all foremen here or out on the job?" With Matt's last remark came laughter and a few comments, "There hasn't been anyone out on the job for over a week—Oswald's been drunk for twice that long."

Matthew could sense the group relaxing—no one seemed particularly concerned that their superintendent was on the ground, probably dead. It appeared to Matt that they were looking for leadership, any *kind* of leadership.

"Do we have a chief locator and any subordinate locators?"

"I'm Chief Locator George Stevenson. We have two locators. Also we have instrument men, rodmen, chainmen, and three engineers."

"Teamsters?"

"Teamster Chief Thompson here. We have eight clearing and grading teams and eight wagons, mostly mule drawn."

"Ballast placement?"

"Smith, here, with four labor pushers and twenty-five roughnecks."

"Setting ties and rails?" Christ—what do they call those guys who pound the spikes? Matt asked himself.

"Johnson here. We have four foremen, welders, blacksmiths, carpenters, skilled laborers, and spike men. Forty men altogether."

"Purchasing?"

"I'm Clarence Cameron. I have three buyers, an expediter, and a clerk. Everything is okay—all purchases of materials and supplies have been made and deliveries arranged for—except for one major item, cut ties. Just today Kansas Pacific advised us that the ties available from the dismantled Kit Carson to La Junta short line, which we had arranged to buy, are no longer available. They've been picked up by Santa Fe and freighted to Raton. I've sent inquiry wires to other suppliers with only negative results. It would appear that Santa Fe has bought up the tie output of all the mills south of the Arkansas. I'm concerned about rails, spikes, and other steel products. We buy these all through Colorado Coal and Iron, although I think that most, if not all, of the rails are transshipped from Eastern mills. That would seem safe enough, but would Santa Fe stoop to seizing shipments coming this way?"

"Well taken, Cameron. I'll look into the security question."

Matt continued, "Financial, payments and the like?"

"Cameron again. I have one timekeeper-paymaster, one disbursement clerk, and two supply clerks. Each week we receive cash from Denver by way of train to Walsenburg in response to our disbursement requests, which will have been checked against budget and special authorizations. We have no problems now, but as we get over the pass we'll have these functions in two places."

"Next, how about bridges? Bridges, anyone?"

"I can speak to that." It was Stevenson, his voice raised. "The four small bridges over creeks on this side of the mountain—Johnson's people will build those. The larger bridge over the Sangre de Cristo River near Fort Garland has been contracted to an outfit out of San Luis."

"Stevenson, a question or two, please. First, what is your experience?"

"I was a locator for the Santa Fe Emporia and UP Cheyenne lines, and engineer for the D&RG Pueblo line, sir. I have also been a teamster foreman for the Pueblo-Cañon City line."

He looked to be in his mid-fifties, Matt judged. A big man, weather-beaten but energetic, immediately likeable. You would think that a man with his experience, and above all his bearing, would command at least a superintendent's rank. I wonder what happened? "Okay, Mr. Stevenson." Matt said, "I want you to take Oswald's place, temporarily, until we get a supe from Denver."

Stevenson nodded, showing no particular emotion.

"Now, everyone," said Matt, "pick up where you left off. New rules: work dawn to dusk, seven day week, pay for hours worked, keep moving the dormitory car ahead and make camp each night at track's end—not in town. Foremen, look at the materials you will need for the next two weeks. After that, I will be asking you to look farther ahead at materials from outside."

A pause for emphasis, then, *"Men, let's lay track."*

It was not exactly a roar of approval and enthusiasm, but rather a buzz of interest, at least.

Matthew took Stevenson aside. "Stevenson—can I call you George?—I'm sure you've guessed by now that I don't know deuces about building a railroad. But I'm what you're stuck with. On the other hand, I do know about money and how to deal with Denver, and I've reviewed all the paperwork on this particular operation. And, above all, I know how Palmer feels about this job; how desperately he needs the revenue from the San Luis Valley."

Matthew took a moment to adjust to a different subject. "Now, a couple of questions. First, do we have enough men?"

"I think so," said Stevenson. "Remember, the rail spur from Walsenburg to La Veta was finished almost two years ago and then the project shut down for lack of money. We've had a skeleton crew here since November doing some clearing and grading on the flat over to the mountains and waiting winter out. About two miles of track are in. Meanwhile, we've been building up our crews. We may be short of spikers. But we can move some roughnecks over. They learn pretty fast—after you hit your toe a couple of times, you start to catch on how to hit the spike." With eyebrows raised and a hint of a smile, he added, "Maybe *you* could teach them how to swing a sledge, Boss."

Stevenson accepted the cigar proffered by Matthew. After a few companionable puffs, Matthew said, "George, what are your two most important problems?"

"First, a drunken superintendent—but you've certainly taken care of *that*. Next on the list is a hauling contractor out of a gravel quarry near Walsenburg, who has been two weeks late on all deliveries since we resumed construction. And you've just heard about ties and rails. Other than materials, then, the big problem is elbow room. This mountain is just too tight. We'll too often have to stop laying track to let the grading crews and wagons get by."

"Why not work both ends towards the middle?"

"Huh?"

"Up from Fort Garland with clearing and grading crews, and maybe even ballast and ties to meet this group at the top? Not rails, I wouldn't think, because they all come from or through Pueblo. But everything else? Is the surveying and locating sufficiently accurate to permit this?"

"Locating is. But we would have to continuously resurvey as the two headings approach each other. I know leapfrogging has been done elsewhere on the flat, and it might work here since we're running nearly alongside one branch of the old Taos Trail. The only disadvantage is that we can't have a work train on the other side. But we're used to working in rain and a little snow and in any event the weather should get better pretty soon. Another good thing about this idea, it will give us a base for the next leg of the line over to Alamosa.

"I should also mention, though, that our destination on the other side of the pass is not Fort Garland, but rather Garland City, at the edge of the fort's six-mile buffer zone and outside its jurisdiction. A couple months before our project was shut down, about a dozen small buildings from a abandoned railroad camp near Aguilar were dismantled and put on flatcars, loaded onto wagons here at La Veta, and taken over the Taos Trail to the new Garland City site. This past January, when we were setting up to resume work, I rode over to see what, if anything, was left of Garland City. I found it booming. Most of the surrounding land was under cultivation and a few permanent buildings erected. Civil activities, including the mayor's office, had been transferred out of the Fort Garland premises."

"Okay, then, George. Work out how you'll split the crews. Get started on moving a second crew to the other side of the mountain as soon as possible. I know you've surveyed over to Fort Garland; is the old trail suitable to work from and travel over? I want to go over there myself to talk to the bridge contractor, and most important, I want to send a procurement team to Garland to fan out through the valley and find some tie cutters. Actually, we need a procurement office over there for the second half of the job, anyway."

"Yeah, the old Taos Trail is all right. It carried wagons once in a while but block and tackle was needed in a few places. And they got those Garland City shacks over, somehow. You can get over the trail by horseback, but you might have to get off and lead in a couple places. That sort of depends how good you and your animal are together. I'd like to suggest you take Dan Douglas along as a guide; he surveyed that area. We don't want to lose you your first day."

"Fine," Matthew replied. "We're all set, then. And I'll straighten out that Walsenburg hauling contractor tomorrow—that's in my line of work. The next day, Douglas and I will go over the pass to Fort Garland. Cameron and a couple of buyers will go over independently in the following day or two."

Matthew started to leave, then hesitated. "George, how are our relationships with the officials and people of La Veta?"

"Not very good," he replied. "In fact, terrible. Everybody hates D&RG, except possibly the cantina owner."

"Is this just a normal 'Mexican-gringo' thing?"

"I don't think so. The Mexicans up here have taken so much shit from Americans crowding in on their territory for the last thirty years since the end of the Mexican War, that they shrug most of it away, now.

"When D&RG's tracks arrived three years ago, La Veta, then called Francisco's Plaza, was a pretty little pueblo town, with a plaza in the center and an adobe wall enclosing everything. It wasn't a particularly old town, only about seventeen years, but Mexican as anything can be. Now look at what Oswald has done to it. Those rails didn't have to go right up to the Plaza. At about the start of our war of secession, a retired Mexican officer, Colonel Francisco, bought a very large parcel of land from the Vigil and St. Vrain Mexican land grant, built a large house for himself, constructed Francisco Plaza as a 'shelter' from the Indians, and leased the balance of the land to a bunch of farmers and ranchers. It was a happy little place. I know—because I married a little Mexican schoolteacher from Taos and we settled here, she to teach and I to run some cattle. And then Superintendent Oswald arrived with his railroad. And fast talking land-grabbers."

"So it adds up to hard feelings?"

"Part of the reason but not the big thing. Oswald was accompanied by former Governor Hunter of the Colorado Territory, who started laying out streets and town lots for this new town he named

La Veta, adjacent to the old Fort Francisco. With both the Cucharas and San Luis valleys being opened for development with the coming of the railroad, these 'hot' properties quickly sold directly to individuals or to other land investors.

"While Hunter and the other speculators *owned* the property they were busily selling was not an issue nor was the fact, not even mentioned, that the second phase of the project—the continuation of construction over the pass to the San Luis Valley—was likely to be suspended indefinitely because of the fallout from the seventy-three panic. As soon as the La Veta transactions were completed, Hunter went over the pass to do the same thing with the fledgling Garland City.

"In the process, some original Mexican settlers and farmers were displaced, raising a little heat in all quarters. Louisa and I were among those evicted."

"Incidentally, is this ex-governor Hunter giving you any trouble now?"

"He's a pain in the ass—he thinks he owns D&RG. But we'll handle him one way or another."

"So you and your wife were losers in the war, just like the Mexicans?"

"Yeah, that's true, but the treaty of Hidalgo ending the Mexican War in 1848 had guaranteed property ownership, including land grants and successive owners. So Louisa and I feel we were victims, not losers, and not of the treaty makers but of the former governor of Colorado who was ignoring the conditions of that agreement."

"Do you have any idea of what that war was all about?"

"I never heard any two people give the same reason. Some said a land grab—to validate the annexation of Texas—some said it was to get more slavery votes in Congress, and many argued that this was simply a fulfillment of America's Manifest Destiny; whatever that means. Some even said that a border incident had been staged, or at least incited, to provide a cause for war. Apparently the president changed his *own* story a couple of times—so maybe he didn't know, either."

"Or maybe the public didn't need to know. After all, this 'Manifest Destiny' stuff is pretty difficult for us ordinary people to understand, let alone accept. But back to the present—did Oswald take any kind of a stand against the speculators grabbing La Veta land?"

"Not that I ever heard. But Oswald was disgustingly drunk most of the time and a buddy of the ex-governor, to boot. And who can argue with a fast-talking land-grabber, anyway? But Louisa and I are getting along okay. We moved over to Trinidad and started all over, she teaching and I with a few head of cattle to care for when I'm not on railroad jobs."

"Well, at least the farmers will use the 'hated' D&RG to ship their produce," said Matt. "A few bad feelings will stop neither progress nor commerce." Matt didn't add that in while up in Denver going over D&RG material, he had seen several references to ex-Governor Hunter, apparently a personal friend of General Palmer, one of the original incorporators and directors of D&RG, and Colorado territorial governor just ten years before.

"George, something else is bothering me a little. When I was looking at the paperwork before coming down here, I saw a comment in the last field progress report to the effect that 'fortunately we were able to finish all clearing and grading on the eastern slope before the big snow dump.' That doesn't seem to jibe with what I just heard from the men, and when I was down in Trinidad no one said anything about a 'big snow dump' anyplace."

"That's exactly right. This has been a remarkably low snowfall year. The progress report that went to Denver showed what *should* have happened. We have a good experienced crew, good foremen, good engineers," said George, "but they need leadership. Someone has to say 'go,' and Oswald was drunk for a couple of months. Nothing got done. Field reports go to the vice president who forwards them to General Palmer. I guess Llewellyn felt he had to make the report look better."

Sometimes judgments are made with insufficient evidence, Matthew thought. There's no way Leonard would do that. Besides, he was involved with the Bessemer steel mill about then.

◇◇◇◇◇◇◇◇◇◇◇◇

Matthew's two-hour horseback trip to Walsenburg was short and sweet. Entering the quarry office he said, "Good morning, Mr. Davenport, my name is Matthew Molyneaux of D&RG. I should like to discuss the late gravel deliveries to La Veta."

Still sitting and hardly raising his eyes from the papers on his desk, Davenport said, "I will talk only to Mr. Oswald, not some snot-nosed kid. So good day."

Patiently, Matt said, "Snot-nosed kid or not, I've taken Mr. Oswald's place, if you please."

"I do not 'please.' So good day."

"Then I must advise you, Mr. Davenport, that I am the only person authorized to approve contractor payments on this job, and without that approval no payment will be made on any invoice. After the first one-week delay on any delivery I will defer my signature one month. After the second week, it will be two months, and after the third week delay, there will be no approval—and hence no payment whatsoever. So take your chances, sir—it's your choice. And I assure you that we have an alternate supplier lined up."

There was a long pause. Slowly Davenport rose. "I think there has been a misunderstanding, Mr. Molyneaux. Our shipping clerk gave me no indication that timely deliveries were a D&RG imperative. You can be very sure that this situation will be corrected."

"Thank you. I've enjoyed this little chat. Is it Fred? Yes, I've enjoyed this little chat, Fred."

◇◇◇◇◇◇◇◇◇◇◇◇

Another loose end was quickly disposed of with a short visit to La Veta's town offices located in the center of the old plaza. The marshal and the mayor were together when Matthew arrived. "I'm glad you came in," said the marshal, "I've received statements from two of the railroad workers, who said that Mr. Oswald was *shooting* at you and somehow or other you hit him with a *pick handle.* That seems incredible—it takes only seconds to point and shoot a revolver."

"Well, he was pretty drunk—and I pretty desperate."

The mayor added his view. "It sounds pretty clear to me, Marshal. It was justifiable self-defense."

"Of course," the marshal said, "and so be it."

As Matt turned to leave, the mayor said, "Your Mr. Stevenson came in. I was pleased to learn that you had ordered the tracks moved a little, the adobe walls repaired, and a new station house built at a location of the town's choosing."

Reflecting upon this, Matthew concluded that this was an example of amicable Western law. The two town officials also acceded to Matthew's request for protection against any unlawful actions of the Santa Fe, especially when assured that costs of extra deputies would be borne by D&RG.

◇◇◇◇◇◇◇◇◇◇◇◇

Matthew prepared a short message to General Palmer. U.S. Mail pickup at La Veta was two days hence, so Matt dispatched a courier. He felt it inadvisable to use the insecure public telegraph in La Veta.

Feb 21

General William Palmer
Denver & Rio Grande Railroad
Denver, Colorado
Sir:

I am pleased to report that the eastern end of the La Veta project is proceeding satisfactorily despite the loss of Mr. Oswald. Mr. George Stevenson, Chief Locator, a very competent person, has been appointed temporary Superintendent, and I have assumed the temporary position of General Superintendent and Auditor. Please advise if you disagree with this action. Crews will soon be going over the pass from two directions simultaneously, La Veta and Fort Garland.

The bad news is cross-ties. We learn that Santa Fe has preempted not only the salvaged ties from the abandoned Kit Carson to Las Animas line, which you had arranged to purchase, but has bought all of the ties south of the Arkansas. I will dispatch a procurement team to Fort Garland to scour the San Luis Valley for an alternate source.

This all causes me to be concerned with the security of rail shipments from CCI. I would suggest that armed guards accompany all shipments.

Sincerely,
Matthew Molyneaux

◊◊◊◊◊◊◊◊◊◊◊◊

"So it's an office in Garland City we need, as I see it, Clarence. Do you agree?"

Matthew had dropped in to the purchasing manager's office to describe the proposed activities on the western side of the mountain.

"I most certainly do—I've wanted this for a while. I'll leave two buyers here and take one with me to Garland City. I'll try to pick up a couple men over there that know the area, find office space, equip it, and hire some kind of a wagon. Something like yours, I guess. You know, if you want to get yours over the grade, we've got teamsters who could drag it over the top." Clarence Cameron got up, walked over to a file box on the floor, and picked up a piece of paper.

He said to Matt, "Here's a note from Jim Smith—he's labor foreman, you know. The note says he has ties for only about ten miles of track. It's a pretty desperate situation."

Matt replied, "No question—it's our top priority."

"I'll see if I can *borrow* some from around here to keep us going," Cameron said. "Then I'll head over to Garland City in the morning. I'm afraid we'll still need two offices, one in Garland City because it's closer to the job, and one in La Veta because it has D&RG telegraph service and faster U.S. Mail."

"That's fine, Clarence. I'm particularly interested in reconciling bills-of-lading with requisitions and progress reports. Please spend a couple hours with me later today to go over your cost summaries. Then in two or three weeks, when we're both back in La Veta, we can hit your books in more detail. I told General Palmer that we would be counting every spike, and that's what we'll do."

◇◇◇◇◇◇◇◇◇◇◇◇

The next morning, Stevenson rode with Matthew up towards the railhead where they picked up Dan Douglas. The engineer was supervising construction of the first Middle Creek bridge. His part pretty well finished, he could be spared for a few days.

"Got your bedroll and heavy clothes?" he asked Matt. "We'll have to spend two cold nights on the mountain—over nine-thousand feet."

"Sure do. I've enough for the arctic, if it should come to that."

As they rode on, George explained to Matthew a little of the location strategy employed in laying out a railroad. "You see, the first leg goes straight across the level until the break at the first foothill where it will have to start traversing left or right up the hill. The locator, standing there the first time, doesn't know which, nor does he know where the line should best meet the toe of the hill. He will guess. Does that shock you a little, Mr. Molyneaux?"

"It's Matthew, George. What if he's wrong?"

"He'll do it over. It's a trial-and-error thing—mixed in with a lot of gut feeling. And a little help from the surveying party out front."

"Oh, so *that's* how you use all that stuff we send you," chimed in Dan, with a *now I understand* pretension.

"Yes, and God help you if your metes don't meet your bounds."

"Over by that little piñon, Matthew, you can see the cleared but not yet graded roadbed heading up the hill to the south. So, that's where the locator—that's me—decided to start the traverses," said Stevenson. "In this case I selected a conservative two-percent grade to give me leeway to make corrections, and kept going until I ran out of mountain. At that point I had the roadbed take a great sweeping curve to start a traverse in the opposite direction, and so on until I reached the top—on paper, that is. Had there not been terrain to take all these curves, I could have used switchbacks, but that would have been considered a locating failure."

They came up upon the work train at the railhead, an engine, two flatcars, and a dormitory car. Some rails had already been unloaded on the ground for immediate placement. Others were being loaded onto mule-drawn wagons to be carried ahead along the cleared, graded, and ballasted roadbed. Some hundred yards ahead cross-ties were being embedded and leveled into place in the gravel ballast, and yet farther ahead and nearly out of sight, gravel was being spread on the graded bed. Graders out ahead a half-mile or so could not be seen. Still on the flat immediately ahead, the most difficult work—placing, leveling, and spiking the steel rails—was underway. This operation might be repeated two hundred times today, and tomorrow, and…so on.

The work train was inching along on the completed rails. Railhead camp would be made at dusk. "Here's where I leave you," said Stevenson. "You're in Dan's hands."

"Thanks, George. While I'm over in San Luis valley, will you please pay particular attention to security? I'm a little worried about what Santa Fe might do. If anything happens, send a courier over the pass to tell me—and bring the La Veta marshal into the act; he's the law around here."

Matt and Dan moved on, passing the grading crew. Grading, filling, and leveling was a combination of hand labor and mule-drawn scrapers. A surveying party constantly established grades and placed stakes.

Even a construction novice like Matthew could appreciate the degree of coordination required for an operation like this. Each work element other than surveying was simple enough in concept and execution, but had to move like a well-wound clock—time spent by one element waiting for another to catch up was time lost forever. And as Stevenson had noted, "Someone has to say, 'go.'" That had been missing for a couple of months.

The semiarid flatland, grass and some irrigated farmland, gave way to a series of foothills, sparsely covered with brush and stunted piñon. At the toe of the closest mountain slope the cleared railroad path swung into a southward heading traverse, rising at a gradual slope.

"Just before the rails go out of our sight on this leg, the tracks will be doubled—a 'wye,' we call it. It will permit the heavier laden trains to be double-headed," Dan said.

"Double-headed?" asked Matt.

"Two engines," said Dan patiently. "Lighter trains will go about two miles farther uphill to another 'wye' before being double-headed to the summit, and maybe with a pusher, to boot. As part of this maneuver, the assist engines must be turned around—thus the need for the extra track. At each 'wye' there will be a little station—telegraph and crew shelter."

"Would this be called a 'switchback'?"

"Not quite. A switchback permits an entire train to be reversed. Where there is no other way for a train to turn around—when it has run out of mountain, so to speak, it can reverse itself on the switchback and continue uphill on an opposite traverse. In other words, it can zigzag up a hill like a man or horse trail can. But, it's very time consuming. In a way, it represents a locator's failure. He has been unable to find a path weaving back and forth through the slopes—always ascending and never exceeding a curvature of about ten percent and a grade of about four.

"On this route we were able to avoid even a single switchback but we had to weave a considerable distance from a 'bird's flight' path. It's about ten miles from La Veta to the summit with a railroad weave of five miles to the north. From the summit to Fort Garland, it's about seventeen miles bird flight with a three-mile weave. And a few loops and whip lashes in between. So the total railroad distance will be at least double the distance the little sparrow would fly."

"And that's the essence of locating?"

Dan looked at Matt narrowly. "Not really. That's the 'art' part. Every slope to be traversed must be examined for feasibility—since it's usually necessary either to build or to carve a shelf, perhaps twenty feet wide or more, for a single track. Cantilevering out over the void is generally not sensible, so that leaves carving. What is the stability of the slope above the shelf? How much soil and rock must be shaved or removed? What bridging is required, what fill is needed? Should we cut and fill to balance?"

Here in the field, Matt could see that what would be a garble of words in the office—carving, cantilevering, bridging—took life where the spatial relationships were evident. Looking above, he could see a void where *something* would have to be done. This is why I aspire to be a financial person—not an engineer, he thought.

Dan went on, "Finally, given a seemingly sensible route with no identifiable serious construction obstacles, the engineers develop a profile of the projected route, adjusting grades and exact routing to match the terrain, construction limitations, and roadbed specifications."

"Today, will we use the old Taos Trail or the new roadbed to go over the mountain?" asked Matt.

"Generally the trail—it's shorter. Remember what I said about switchbacks. However, wherever the trail is close to our line, we'll veer over to take a look. You'll find our most difficult part of the trip starting just ahead and for the next two hours. We'll be on a narrow trail ledge most of the time except when we're going straight up."

As they started their ascent through rabbit-brush and gnarled cedar and junipers, there was an awe-inspiring view of the Spanish Peaks to the south, standing majestically alone above the Sangre de Cristos. "Twin Sisters," some called them. To the Indians they were "Breasts of the Earth"—in Comanche, of course. That's where Jim will be, thought Matthew, as soon as he gets D&RG off his back. I sometimes think he'd rather be an Indian than a white man. Those are the wonderful mountains I promised him—I really didn't think they would look *this* good. Most people would call this a breathtaking view, Matt thought. I'd call it very beautiful, and save 'breathtaking' for my first sight last month of Aristocracy Hill and the Llewellyn home. I could get used to living like that.

◇◇◇◇◇◇◇◇◇◇◇◇

Behind and to the left stretched the great prairie all the way to the horizon—from this distance it looked featureless, but Matt had been there and he knew differently. He took only a peek in that direction, partly because that was where he came from and he never wanted to return, but mostly because the trail seemed a mile above nowhere, a long way down—*straight down* for at least a thousand feet. Of course, after the first hundred feet it wouldn't make much difference.

They continued upwards, the path steadily steepening and worsening. Dan led. "That's so your horse will know where to go," he said. Matt was paralyzed. It would be bad enough to stand on this ledge, but perched up here on a little leather seat five feet above the ground was indescribably unsettling. With every sway of the saddle he was sure he would be catapulted over the edge.

And then came some advice from Dan. "Give him his head. He has four feet and he'll balance for both of you if you let him. Remember, he doesn't want to go over the edge any more than you do!"

Finally, Matthew took a deep breath, calmed himself, loosened his grip on the reins, and forced himself to look down. He could see graders on the cleared roadbed below and ahead—he and Dan were already a hundred feet higher because of the zigzag climb the trail took. Looking down again as they zagged, he had a clear view of the work below. Two mules, a scraper blade, a mule skinner, and four men with hand tools all jammed onto that ledge. How do they do that, he thought—and why? There was certainly something to be said for not "working with the tools," he thought—for the thousandth time.

"Well, you did it—you climbed the hardest part of the Taos Branch of the Santa Fe Trail. And it took but three hours out of your life."

"Seemed much longer, somehow," came the reply.

"We're at the summit, nearly two miles high. You can see why the Mountain Branch over Raton Pass and the Cimarron Cutoff through New Mexico got all of the traffic. Only trappers and Indians would have used *this* route with any frequency. In recent years the need to transport wagonloads of ores to smelters near Pueblo brought about the fashioning of a wagon road some miles to the north of here."

"I rather imagine you were up here a few times on the original survey?"

"At least twenty times—I wasn't counting, but I know this area better than my own back yard. Going down will be easy, but it *will* take time. Since we don't want to enter Fort Garland—I should say Garland City—in the dark, I'd suggest we sack out here and enjoy sunset over the Continental Divide—that is, if the snow holds off a little while longer."

Just a hundred yards farther on, a natural clearing opened upon a Western world. A forest of struggling piñon and spruce seemed to have won out over an underbrush of chaparral in the ages-old battle for a little soil and moisture. The trail looked down, nearly vertically it seemed from here, to the wide-open expanse of the San Luis Valley. Immediately to the west beyond the horizon of the valley floor were the thirteen-thousand-foot snow-covered peaks of the San Juan Mountains, but even closer loomed Blanca Peak, a fourteener. And beyond was the setting western sun, its beams pouring between the peaks.

◇◇◇◇◇◇◇◇◇◇◇◇

For several hours Matt had given no thought to Trinidad, but now he could think of nothing but Sophia. And just the thought produced a nearly unbearable tingling in his loins. It's the saddle, too, he thought.

Trinidad's not too far away, he thought, about a day each way. After a few weeks, if things are going right, I'll be able to get away for two or three days. Maybe Jim will be there, unless he's tied up with the General's locator on the Raton problem.

And that started Matt thinking about his spotty relationship with his brother. It wasn't because of the vast difference in their physical characteristics nor in their interests—they'd adjusted to those things years ago. Matt loved his brother, who had practically raised him, protected him, and kept him on a straight and narrow path—and it worked. But now he guessed it was a "Llewellyn" thing that threatened to separate them. Matthew concluded that Leonard, like every other highly successful business manager or political aspirant, kept his eye on his objective, no matter what, and if he had to step on an impediment now and then, so be it. And that's where I'm going, Matthew thought—holding on to Llewellyn's coattails.

◇◇◇◇◇◇◇◇◇◇◇◇

It was a dry dinner—dried beef, dried hardtack, and coffee brewed with the little bit of water they carried. And a few raw carrots that they had stuffed into their packs at La Veta. But they still made out better than their horses, who had to get by with the very scanty forage at nine thousand feet. They faced a cold night, a little below freezing, but this was expected and they had clothing and bedrolls to suit.

"Where did you learn your surveying, Dan?" asked Matt, the two of them toasting their front halves before a crackling fire.

"I went to college in a western Iowa town for a year until I ran out of money. Then I came out to Kansas and worked on the railroad—picked up some basics of surveying as a rod-man and bought a big thick book for the rest. Then I came here, lied a little bit—representing myself as an engineer—and got on with the D&RG. At the end of this La Veta job I'll have enough saved to go up to Golden or Boulder for a real education."

"Civil engineering?"

"They call it mining engineering. It's sort of a new field and folks in the field say Golden is one of the best."

◇◇◇◇◇◇◇◇◇◇◇◇

Day two was a little easier; they traveled north on a good trail through a mixed piñon-and-spruce forest along the spine of the Sangre de Cristos. Finally in mid-afternoon the trail turned west and south and *down* the western slope—the arid side of the Cristos. At dusk Dan called a halt as the forest thinned out and underbrush nearly disappeared. "We're about three hours from Fort Garland," he said. "Actually, our destination is Garland City, just outside of the six-mile buffer zone around the fort. Everything inside that zone is subject to military approval and control.

"When our project shut down, ex-Governor Hunter selected this site for a company town, platted it, and hauled in all of the amenities for an end-of-track town even though the track was still on the other side of the mountain. Empty buildings in Cucharas Junction and La Veta were dismantled, hauled in by wagon, and tacked up at the Garland City site. These included a small hotel, barber shop, blacksmith, general store, saloon, and town office. But even this meager commercial arrangement was an improvement over the settler's store at Fort Garland and drew customers from the myriad of small plaza settlements dotting the valley. With the company's approval, mayor, hell, a whole town government, were selected and a post office established. I understand that Garland City has many new town buildings and residences, but I haven't seen any of this since our construction was suspended."

"I've heard a little about company towns," Matthew said. "Where it's not possible to obtain federal land grants along proposed railroads as was done on the Pacific railway, bonds are sold, rights-of-way obtained, cheap land purchased along the ROW, company towns built, and lots and farm plots sold for profit—*big* profit. The company owns the town and can do what it wants.

"D&RG has done it a few times already, most notably at Colorado Springs and El Moro, where town people were outraged by D&RG's arrogance."

"That's exactly what was done here," said Dan, "except the fort couldn't care less."

Another cold dinner, but just getting out here away from everything made it all worthwhile, Matt thought. Sitting with Dan before another campfire, he asked, "You mentioned 'small plaza settlements dotting the valley.' I didn't know anything was out here. I'd like to get your slant on an area so different than where I came from."

"Well, the early Spanish explorers were first but they backed off. Maybe this vastness was just too much for a European to comprehend. Of course, the Indians were always here but they were fighting each other too much to be a dominant factor—the last big push into southern Colorado was by the Cheyenne, active traders and great horseback warriors. But pretty soon there were too many whites, too much gold, and too many homesteaders. The Sand Creek massacre fifteen years ago marked the end of the Indians as our fathers had known them." He paused. "We'd better hit the sack, Matt—we've a big day tomorrow."

While saddling up the next morning, Dan took up the topic again. "It's important to remember, especially right here in the San Luis Valley, that Mexican settlers—mostly mixed Spanish and Indian descent—started gravitating in small numbers from the Rio Grande Valley more than seventy years ago. But they had only limited support from New Spain, who actually banned even *trade* with the Americans, since that might have helped the French as well. And there was no military help at all to keep the violent Indians in line. With Mexican independence thirty years ago, everything changed."

As they rode along Dan continued, "Mexico was very aggressive in its expansion, and made massive land grants to Mexicans and non-Mexicans alike, anyone who would promise to settle the land and defend against American expansion. In this state alone, about ten million acres were so granted. Land around La Veta and up to the Huerfano River was included in one four-million-acre grant and most of San Luis Valley up to Alamosa in another; the U.S. guaranteed to honor all of these land grants. But as you've seen in La Veta and in Trinidad, as well, this guarantee hasn't always worked."

"The developers moved in?"

"Did they ever! I think I'd call them land grabbers and speculators. And watch them follow *this* railroad into the valley in the next few months. Some Colorado territorial political figures did pretty well in grabbing up much of this land. Many Mexican landholders were deemed 'squatters' and displaced. I know of at least twenty farmers around La Veta alone who have been thrown off land they'd had for twenty-five years, or more. I guess that started about five years ago."

"How can you feel so sorry for them, considering the thousands of Americans who have died defending *their* land against the Indians for the last hundred-plus years—from the Atlantic to the Pacific oceans?" asked Matt.

"For one thing, no one counts dead Mexicans or *any* dead enemy, for that matter. We don't know how many really died on their own frontier. Hell, down in Texas they're not even considered people," protested Dan.

◇◇◇◇◇◇◇◇◇◇◇◇

It was an intrinsically beautiful sight as the mountain slope started to open out to San Luis Park, undulating from the Sangre de Cristos on this side, to the San Juans, poking their heads above the horizon to the west. And there, less than a hundred miles away was the Continental Divide. All of San Luis Valley was this side of the Divide and in the Rio Grande watershed. As far as Matt could see, the valley was dotted with little plaza communities with a moderate amount of agricultural development. And where do they get their water? Matt answered his own question—from the Rio Grande and tributary creeks, of course. This is what General Palmer envisioned, the purpose for his "railroad above the clouds."

Garland City was not as Matt expected, not the cluster of shacks as was the La Veta addition. True, there were a dozen or so temporary buildings along Sangre de Cristo Creek, but the main part of Garland City was up back from the creek, with new one- and two-story adobe and frame buildings along Main Street, and one-story residences beyond.

Barlow and Sanderson had established a stage stop already.

"Here we are," said Dan, "I'll lead the way to the town offices. There's a hitching rail right in front."

The mayor's and other offices were located on the second floor of a new two-story adobe building with clay tile roof; public offices were on the lower floor. Matthew introduced himself to the striking brown-haired and brown-eyed receptionist. She's a beauty, thought Matt, but hands off, I'm here on sensitive business. He noticed the nameplate on her desk, "Estrella de Cielo."

"Miss de Cielo, my name is Matthew Molyneaux of the Denver and Rio Grande Railroad. My engineer and I would like to have a few words with the mayor, at his convenience."

"Si, Señor...Moly - nix. I'll see if el Alcalde Dominguez can meet with you *ahora*...now."

She went through an open door to an inner office. A smallish, extremely energetic man came to the door. "Come in, gentlemen. I'm

Euardo Dominguez, Alcalde." He was obviously comfortable in English, only slightly accented.

"I'm Matthew Molyneaux, auditor and acting general superintendent for D&RG. And this is my locator and engineer, Daniel Douglas."

"Please be seated. Cigars are in the box—help yourselves. And what brings you to our little town? I have to tell you—we don't see many outsiders. Most business is conducted over in San Luis."

"Well, you soon will, Señor Alcalde. As you undoubtedly know, the poor economic conditions following the seventy-three panic forced D&RG to postpone the La Veta to Alamosa leg of our railroad. We've resumed construction, and at the moment are laying track west of La Veta and up towards the pass."

"So we'll see you pretty soon, then?"

"Yes, in fact, in order to meet shipping requirements of this year's harvest, within a week or two we'll have a second construction crew building up the west side of the mountain from here to meet the first crew at the top. And, as soon as possible, we'll start from here to the terminus at Alamosa."

"Our farmers and ranchers are anxious to see this come about. As you may have guessed, ours is a hardscrabble existence. It simply costs too much to ship wagonloads of produce to Denver or Taos markets. We trade back and forth with each other, but that can go on for just so long. How can we help you?"

"Thank you, Mr. Mayor. First, Mr. Douglas will want to meet with your people as soon as possible to pick a location for a passenger station, freight, produce, and livestock storage and loading areas, and trackage in and out. Next, in a couple of days our purchasing manager Clarence Cameron will be here to set up a procurement office. He'll have a couple buyers in residence here for the duration of the job. Very soon a paymaster and other office services will be added. The most immediate problem for this new office will be to find a source for wooden railroad ties—sleepers, some call them—for all trackage on this side of the mountain. And that's a lot of trees. We'll appreciate any help you can give us in locating sources."

"Yes, we can help in that. There are forested areas over in the San Juans and in the Rio Grande River valley. A little farther north there are sawmills that now provide large timbers for the mines up at Salida."

Matt continued, "This leads us to a potential problem that we hope will not materialize. The reason we have a ties supply problem is that the Santa Fe railroad bunch has cut us off from our expected source of supply over east. They don't want this D&RG line built. They want to service San Luis Valley from Taos—they'll have tracks to Taos in a year or two. Now, a competitor in Taos is fine for your shippers—it keeps everyone on his toes. But you wouldn't want to have to depend upon the Santa Fe railroad, alone. Nor D&RG alone, for that matter. The problem with Santa Fe is that they've proved at Raton and Royal Gorge that they'll use any means at all to shut D&RG out. Frankly, we're afraid of unlawful physical violence on their part."

"Let me assure you, Mr. Molyneaux, that we will maintain law and order in our jurisdiction. I think you should also talk to county authorities in San Luis and Alamosa, and of course Walsenburg."

"We were sure you would feel this way." Matthew stood. "One last thing. You know that some railroad workers are pretty rough and tough characters. Other than the office people and a few foremen, everyone will camp at the railhead as it moves along. But a few may slip away now and then to your cantinas and cause a problem for your marshal. If this starts to get out of hand, please get hold of me as soon as you can."

◇◇◇◇◇◇◇◇◇◇◇◇

Matt and Dan checked in at the El Fuerte Hotel just as a courier was arriving with a message for Matthew.

Feb 25 Via Courier

To Matthew Molyneaux

El Fuerte Hotel, Garland City

From George Stevenson

Matt, a rail shipment (three flatcars) has arrived from Pueblo by way of Walsenburg. Crew reports they were stopped by a barricade on the tracks about five miles this side of Walsenburg. About a dozen armed toughs came up upon the engine. Of course, they didn't know that the engine was armored and manned with four armed guards plus the crew. None of the train guards or crew was injured as they quickly dispatched the invaders, but I'm afraid there probably were some serious casualties on the other side. The engine has been decoupled here and the crew given instructions to pause in Walsenburg long enough to report the attack to the county sheriff and then to return to Pueblo to report to the D&RG offices. I have posted armed sentries about two miles up-track from here and have told the La Veta marshal about this incident.

Feb 26 Via Courier

To George Stevenson

D&RG, La Veta

From Matt

Good work, George.

You might ride over to Walsenburg, to talk with the county sheriff yourself. I'm going over to San Luis and to Alamosa to alert the sheriffs of those two counties to the kind of stunts Santa Fe might pull. At the same time I'll engage a lawyer in each of those towns to be ready to

petition the respective courts for injunctions at the first
hint of Santa Fe interference. George, please forward
this message, along with a copy of your message to me,
by courier to General Palmer in Denver.

◇◇◇◇◇◇◇◇◇◇◇◇

With Garland City business pretty well in hand, Matthew was ready to go down to the county seat.

"Dan, I'm going to take the stage down to San Luis and then over to Alamosa to alert officials about possible Santa Fe interference. It'll take about a week for each of the two visits. After you've found a station site and trackage routing that the town officials will approve, please go over to the fort and talk to the commandant. Tell him we're going to run our rails along his northern six-mile property line and are willing to run a spur over to the fort to any location he might want. All we need is approval and an easement.

"Also, Dan, please think about what will be needed to start clearing and setting cross-ties up the western slope. If we could find or fabricate some scrapers and other heavy tools somewhere around here, it would be a great help to our working men."

◇◇◇◇◇◇◇◇◇◇◇◇

A coach, even with hard wooden benches, was kind of nice after more horseback in three days than all his life put together, Matt decided. This wasn't what he really expected from the West—he considered himself more of a financial type. It was ironic—and maybe amusing—that he and James, neither of whom had even ridden a train before last fall, were both employed by the same railroad company, James by happenstance and Matt by design—but not my design, he reminded himself. And neither of us is entirely sure of his responsibility and where he's going from here. What is clear is that D&RG will try to stand up to Santa Fe on the ground—at Raton, San Luis Valley, and Royal Gorge—in the courtroom, and in the boardroom. And between us, Jim and I will have a piece of most of the action. And the pay is good.

◇◇◇◇◇◇◇◇◇◇◇◇

The Barlow and Sanderson stage coach ride to San Luis was comfortable and interesting. The ranching and agricultural value of the San Luis Valley was evident. At seven thousand feet, the growing season was short but the soil was rich, Matthew had learned, and irrigation water was available from streams emerging from the encircling mountains. It was a matter of local cultural pride that there had been Hispanic settlements around San Luis nearly forty years before, and the town itself was the oldest in Colorado. The town had been built in "plaza style," single-story adobe structures surrounded by a rock-and-adobe wall to achieve some sort of protection against the very hostile Indians. While the town had managed to maintain its Mexican plaza flavor for some twenty-five years, and it was now surrounded by numerous farming and ranching enclaves. San Luis was the economic and political capital of the valley.

The San Luis town offices were but steps away from the stage stop. "Good morning, Mayor Alvarez. Thank you for seeing me."

"The thanks are ours, Mr. Molyneaux. San Luis is very happy that the La Veta railroad is alive again, although we're still sad that it won't be routed here."

"Yes," Matt said, "But as I understand the D&RG plan, San Luis may very well be better off with rail access to Santa Fe, by way of Garland City and Alamosa, rather than Taos, even though it will require wagon shipments from here to Garland City. It's likely that Taos will be always be a commercial dead-end because of the mountains. D&RG plans to go south by way of Antonito to Santa Fe very soon." Matt paused. There was no reaction from His Honor.

"In the meantime," he continued, "Garland City should be ready for shipments to Denver by July or August. Our construction crews will be gone by then and there will be a clear track to Pueblo and Denver; farmers can send their wagonloads of produce to Garland City instead of Taos." Still no response from the Mayor.

"In about a month we'll have a shipping expert over here to talk to your farmers and ranchers to work out what we'll need in the way of rolling stock for the longer term." At last Alvarez replied with the words Matt had hoped to hear.

"That is good news, indeed!" the Mayor exclaimed. "I imagine that diversions will be a little slow, at first. Some of our farmers have de-livery contracts with Taos merchants and consumers."

"We recognize that, of course, and it's the wrong time of the year for new plantings." Matthew responded.

"There is a new factor, too, that could upset this timetable. Santa Fe Railway people, who desire above everything else to drive D&RG out of Colorado, may take aggressive steps to stop our work. Just last week they put up a barricade and stopped one of the trains carrying steel rails to our worksite at La Veta. Fortunately, we had foreseen this possibility by armoring the engine and providing armed guards. The attackers were easily driven off. We're a little afraid that Santa Fe will become even more aggressive—perhaps on this side of the mountain."

"I agree that it would be very bad for San Luis Valley should Santa Fe prevail. Is there anything we can do to help?"

"Perhaps." One word was Matt's economical retort. "Last Friday we filed a complaint in Huerfano County, where the attack occurred. We may be requesting an injunction over there as well—I don't know. It would be helpful if similar action were to be taken in Costilla County at the first sign of unlawful activity."

"Absolutely, Mr. Molyneaux. We won't tolerate unlawful actions, even from mighty Santa Fe. And I might suggest you bring to the at-tention of the D&RG legal staff the possibility of utilizing the Costilla

County Circuit Court for petitions as soon as you have a presence over here. You might find them more reasonable than the Denver courts." To Matt's great satisfaction, the Mayor offered him his hand.

◇◇◇◇◇◇◇◇◇◇◇

Matthew's timing was fortunate; he managed to catch the weekly Barlow and Sanderson stage to Alamosa, arriving at the new hotel on the nearly new Front Street after crossing the Rio Grande on the Alamosa ferry just south of town. This has been a good trip, he thought, especially since I can work in all three Valley towns in one circuit. It's very important for D&RG to get some shipping people over here right away. I'll work on that, but first, a cool beer and a little information.

Two doors down from the stage stop was the ubiquitous saloon.

"A tall beer, if you please."

"I'd recommend you stick with whisky, stranger," said the bartender. "Our beer's a lot like dishwater just now."

"Well, okay. But tell me, where are the town offices?"

"Sam White, the barber, is down Front Street about a half block. He knows all about town matters."

A couple of patrons overhearing these directions broke into unrestrained laughter. "Save plenty of time, Mister, to talk with Sam..." and, "Better borrow his razor and shave yourself, if that's what you're after..."

Before braving that fearsome shop, Matt looked around at the cluster of buildings and tents on both sides of the Rio Grande flowing southeast from its headwaters. Most of the tents—about twenty or so—were on the far or northeastern side of the river. On the near side were permanent structures lined up in some kind of order. Obviously this was Front Street. We should bring our rails to the northeastern side, Matt decided. That way we could avoid building a bridge and we wouldn't bother the permanent residents.

Entering the shop he said to the barber, "I was told over at the saloon to come to the barber shop if I wanted to talk to someone about town matters. Are you the person?"

"I guess so. I'm Sam White. Do you want a shave while we talk?"

A nervous reply. "I suppose—but not too close."

"Well, last year a bunch of people around here got together and said we should have a real name—not just 'Tent City'—and elect a mayor and sheriff. So it was decided to call it Alamosa. Someone said that's the name of a tree but someone else said it was the name of the sister of the wife of a bartender we had last year. I think it's a pretty name, regardless. At the same time, we laid out a new main street over on this side of the river. We call it Front Street. Gradually this last year the tents on the other side have been replaced on this street with..."

"Ouch—easy does it."

"...with wood and 'dobe brick. There are a couple of saloons on Front Street, a doctor's office, a livery stable, and sort of a hotel. Actually, that's a stop for the stage that comes through each way once a week. The Sanderson people wanted a hotel with more than two rooms, but we told them that if six people could fit in a stage, they surely could fit into two rooms. It was especially good to have a substantial structure for the mercantile store where the flour and stuff won't get wet. By the way, I was voted mayor—they said that was because I talked more than any ten people put together—and Ed Biggs, the blacksmith, is sheriff. He hasn't arrested anyone yet because we don't have a judge..."

"I think that's just fine, Sam, let's stop now."

"...nor a jail. Okay—I'm about finished on this side, anyway. Have a cup of coffee, stranger. I didn't get your name."

Matt, nodding, replying, "Yes, I would like that, thanks. My name is Matthew. And please tell me more about your town, Mr. Mayor."

"It's a nice little place, cottonwood trees all around, being right on the Rio Grande as it is. But the folks are all pretty poor. There are quite a few small farms and ranches around—mostly Mexican. The soil is real good, and there's water from the river. But about all they can do is trade with each other since it costs so much to send potatoes to Taos by wagon."

"But you have to have a lot of supplies shipped in, don't you?"

"Yes, and we have to ship at least that many potatoes out in order to break even. There've been some rumors that a train is going to come in—we can hardly believe it—but a guy named Hunter from Denver came through here two months ago and said it was so. In fact, he was laying out a bunch of town lots up from Front Street. He said he was going to put them up for sale although he realized that not many of us could afford to buy them.

"All of us along Front Street will be allowed to keep ours free. I asked him about all of the small farms and ranches around here. At that point he mentioned that he had formerly been governor of Colorado and that as a consequence he should be addressed as Governor. Anyway, he said that he didn't have anything to do with the land outside of town—that property all belongs to another ex-governor. And it's two bits for the shave."

Matthew put on his most convincing manner. "Well, Mayor White, I don't know anything about the ex-governor and the lots he's selling, but I do know about the railroad—it *is* coming in. I know, because I'm building it. You'll see surveyors here in a couple of months and tracks soon after that. You can expect to be able to ship your potatoes and whatever to Denver and anywhere else before Christmas. Actually, a little sooner than that. By July your farmers can start sending wagonloads of produce to Garland City for transshipment to Pueblo and Denver."

Matthew stood to leave. Proffering a hand, he said, "I'll have a D&RG commercial representative over here in month or so to discuss shipping arrangements and rates with as many farmers and townspeople as he can find. Thanks for your time, Mr. Mayor."

◇◇◇◇◇◇◇◇◇◇◇◇◇

Matthew managed another stage connection back to Garland City, immediately setting up a meeting with most of his people. First he barked a question to Clarence Cameron, his procurement officer. "What's with the ties? That's been nagging at me for the last week."

"We've located and signed up about half our needs. We'll have to go a little farther north for the rest but that shouldn't be a problem. The price is right and delivery might cost a little less. With the help of Dan, our office is set up, we have three scrapers being fabricated right now, and we've acquired most of the wagons, mules, and work horses we'll need." With a half smile he continued, "We found some gravel ballast, also—he's the brother-in-law of that guy over in Walsenburg."

Matt turned to his engineer, "Dan, what can you add to Cameron's report?"

"The mayor and council have agreed with our station location and trackage routing. At first, they thought we were taking too much ground, especially around the station. But I made some track layout sketches to show how much side trackage was needed to switch cars and engines around and storage tracks for partly loaded cars. I also showed them how we would have to build maintenance facilities in the future—perhaps even a round house."

"And temporary sidings for wagonloads from Alamosa and San Luis?" Matt wondered out loud.

"I didn't think of that—I'll add it to my layout. And you'll be glad to know that George sent one surveying party and two clearing and grading crews over the hill. They arrived yesterday and are setting up now. George sent a note telling me to stay here and start things going—but not to worry, we'll send a guide back over with you."

"Dan, while I think of it, when you start locating facilities around Alamosa, bring the tracks in to the eastern side of the river. That's the site of the old 'Tent City'; the town has been moved to the west. You probably know about an ex- governor who has laid out and is selling town lots at La Veta?"

"Yeah, I know about it. It looked sort of fishy, but Oswald didn't seem to care."

A resigned expression. "Well, the same 'ex' has been in Alamosa and is doing it again. I learned secondhand that he's planning to put houses and buildings on flatcars at Garland City and bring them over to Alamosa. It sounded like the 'hell-on-wheels' operation that the Union Pacific conducted across Kansas. But it might be a quicker way to get this area developed—we need farmers to grow some crops that we can ship, and that's what counts. Furthermore, by our bringing the tracks over to the eastern side, the portable stuff won't mess up the new town.

"Anything else, Dan?"

"Yeah, something I have to toss back to you. Our friend the ex-governor came in just this morning and told me...*told me* to arrange for some flatcars, and to send about twenty men over to dismantle some more buildings—this time at Cucharas Junction—and send them over here as soon as our leg over the mountain is completed. Then he'll get them over to Alamosa. When I replied that I didn't have authority to do that, he blew his boiler and said that if I were an *experienced and capable* supervisor I would know that this is how things are done. Anyway, he's still in town and if you like I'll send one of our men out to find him and tell him you're here if he wants to talk about it."

"Fine, please do that. And I want you here so together we can dismantle *him*."

◇◇◇◇◇◇◇◇◇◇◇◇

"So you're finally back, Molyneaux. Have you straightened this clerk out yet?"

"I'm here to listen, Mr. Hunter."

"It's *Governor* Hunter, Molyneaux."

"And it's *Mr.* Molyneaux, Hunter. Dan has told me what you want. This is what we'll do: First our Mr. Cameron will help you set up a drawing account with Denver for payroll and other expenses. Then as soon as you've been funded you can hire any of our people who are idle, but you might find it easier to meet your requirements in Walsenburg—I don't condone much idleness. You'll find my supervisors very cooperative, but unwilling to let anything endanger their schedule or productivity. You'll find Mr. Cameron very helpful, but unwilling to jeopardize his budget. You'll find me extremely understanding, but not willing to let anything disrupt the main track usage schedule. Our priorities are *first*, railroad construction, *second*, produce shipments, *third*, supplies, and *fourth*, anything else. We will provide sidings for your flatcars at La Veta, Garland City, and Alamosa, and fourth-level rail service at no charge."

Matt stood up. "Thanks for coming in, Alex." Hunter stormed out.

Well, Matthew thought, that wasn't exactly what Leonard had in mind. But I was an auditor candidate then, and now I'm the top D&RG person this side of Walsenburg and I simply won't bow down to pressure from someone like Hunter, no matter what his connection to Denver might be. I've a hundred men out here who are busting their asses for me and I won't let them down.

◇◇◇◇◇◇◇◇◇◇◇◇

The second time over the pass wasn't a bit easier, Matthew decided. In fact, going down the steep part was even worse than going up. The rider was perched up there to take a nose-dive over the horse's head. I suppose, in time, I'll get used to it—but I'm not sure I want to, he said to himself. It offers an incentive to finish this job and get the hell out of here.

As he approached La Veta, he could see that railhead had made great progress in less than a month. It's amazing, he thought; it's gotten to the point that everything I think of to ask them to do, they've already started. Somehow or other every man on the job has been stimulated. They weren't the sullen group that had met him a month ago. Coming down the trail at points where it paralleled the track construction, he passed working groups that quite obviously knew the boss was on his way—it was almost as if they had smoke signals or something. Work didn't stop, but there were a few nods, or perhaps a hand raised in recognition—and George came out to meet him partway up the slope.

"Remarkable progress, George. I imagine that even as we speak your west-side grading is well underway. I heartily approve of your selection of Dan to handle that side of the mountain. I think that Cameron has his part well in hand, also. I'm anxious to hear from him how we're doing on budget."

"I can't speak for Clarence; he's been off on his mission to San Luis Valley. He'll be back in a couple of days and we three can look at every 'spike,' as you put it. I can say this, however—a project that's ahead of schedule will generally be just fine on budget. And *we're ahead of schedule.* Matt, I've never had such a crew. They call themselves 'the pick-handle team.'"

"Well, whatever! Let's compose a status report for the General."

April 7 Via Courier
To: General Palmer, Denver, Colorado
From: Matthew Molyneaux
Subject: Status Report, La Veta

Track laid to six-mile mark on east slope. Cleared and graded to eight-mile (Fir). Ties are immediately behind the graders. Up from Gardner City, where the terrain is easier, graders are halfway up with ballast placement just behind. I expect graders from the two sides of the mountain will meet about at Fir and ballasted ties two weeks later. Graders will then start at Garland City towards Alamosa. Rails will be laid east to west about as fast as mills can turn them out. Garland City, San Luis, and Alamosa officials have been alerted to availability of shipping out of Garland City by July.

I would suggest having D&RG commercial reps over to those places as soon as possible.

"Any questions, George? No? Well, let's go lay track!"

◇◇◇◇◇◇◇◇◇◇◇◇

Matthew and Stevenson were so busy the next few days that they hardly had time to digest General Palmer's last transcribed telegraph message. In fact, it probably hung on the hook in the telegraph station for at least two days. No matter—the La Veta was well under control. Palmer's north-south vision was evolving—with an east-west component.

WESTERN UNION

MATTHEW MOLYNEAUX LA VETA MAR 30

DIDNT ANSWER YOUR FEB 23 MESSAGE FIGURED

WOULD LET YOU STRAIGHTEN THINGS OUT STOP
NOW REPLYING BOTH MESSAGES STOP WHAT
HAPPENED TO OSWALD STOP APPOINTMENT OF
STEVENSON AS SUPERINTENDENT APPROVED STOP
OTHER ORGANIZATION CHANGES IMPLICIT WITH
APPOINTMENT ALSO APPROVED EXCEPT YOU AS
GENERAL SUPERINTENDENT NOT APPROVED STOP
YOU ACCOMPLISHED WHAT SENT TO DO VERY WELL
DONE NEED YOU IN DENVER AS SENIOR FINANCIAL
AIDE STOP TURN EVERYTHING OVER TO STEVENSON
BY MIDJUNE TAKE THREE WEEKS FOR PERSONAL
BUSINESS AND REPORT TO DENVER STOP SOMEONE
ONCE TOLD ME QUOTE WILLIAM YOU DO GOOD
WORK BUT YOU LEAVE A LOT OF HAMMER MARKS
END QUOTE STOP SIMULTANEOUS EAST WEST WEST
EAST OVER PASS MAGNIFICENT STOP I DID THAT KIT
CARSON DENVER LINE STOP OF COURSE YOU HAD A
MOUNTAIN SO HALF YOUR WORK WAS DOWNHILL
WHICH IS EASIER STOP PALMER

That message had hardly been read than a second one arrived.

WESTERN UNION
MATTHEW MOLYNEAUX LA VETA APR 7
JUST TALKED TO MUTUAL AQUAINTANCE WHO
SUGGESTS YOU ARE STUBBORN AND UNCOOPERATIVE
STOP HAD SIMILAR TALK WITH SAME PERSON TEN
YEARS AGO NOW GOOD FRIENDS STOP KEEP UP GOOD
WORK STOP PALMER

◇◇◇◇◇◇◇◇◇◇◇◇

"My congratulations, *Superintendent* Stevenson."

"You did it Matt, and I thank you. I'm not sure that Louisa will be quite so pleased, though. She kind of likes me around to fix things."

"Well, with a supe's salary and bonus you can buy two of everything so nothing will need fixing."

"Anyway, thanks—and what's next?"

"For starters, it's time to tour the territory again. I'd like you with me this time to meet the mayors and to use your keen eye to see what may need fixing out there."

CHAPTER TWELVE

THE ROYAL GORGE

I T HAD BEEN A SLOW TWO MONTHS since Matt had left for
La Veta. James reflected that the only thing happening of real
significance was his and Alan Matthews' ride up the flank of
Mt. Raton to look for evidence of Santa Fe's activities. I'm glad we
got the Raton survey work out of the way, he thought, but I can't see
how it will do much good. I'd better not mention this to the General,
but I know in my gut that Santa Fe outsmarted us at Raton Pass. The
D&RG simply isn't capable of acting quickly enough.

So it was a surprise to receive a telegram from Denver *before*
something happened. Pueblo seemed to be acting—not re-acting—
this time.

WESTERN UNION

JAMES MOLYNEAUX TRINIDAD APR 10

NEED YOU FOR COUPLE MONTHS IN GORGE STOP

MEET IN PUEBLO APRIL 18 STOP PALMER

This a pretty good time for this summons, peremptory as it might
be, thought James. He was satisfied with how things were going in
Trinidad: the Columbian owners had approved the saloon lease; Lil-

lian and the architect were busy working out saloon and restaurant floor-space details; the DelAgua land lease application had been submitted; and the tobacco shop was getting a start, albeit a little shaky.

Alan would have reported to Palmer by now—maybe that was the reason for this latest telegraphed summons. I guess things are warming up at the gorge, James concluded. At least he had a few days to get ready—a half-day for unfinished business and another half to put his gear together, leaving the balance of the time to say goodbye to Lillian. He headed to the Columbian, finding that Lillian had not yet returned from a meeting with the architect, but Mike was on guard and…and sitting alone at a table was Sophia Llewellyn. James walked over and sat down, saying nothing.

"Oh, James," Sophia said, "have you heard anything from Matthew? I know I shouldn't be in a place like this, but I miss him so much."

James didn't reply—he was shocked at her presence without escort in a saloon. Sophia managed a tight smile, paused, and said, "Well, I'm with *you* so I guess it's all right. And, anyway, I'd like to know you better." Under the table her leg pressed against his.

He pulled back a little and signaled the bartender. "Mario, will you do me a personal favor? Please escort Miss Llewellyn to the cab stand out front and help her engage a carriage to take her anywhere she should desire."

◇◇◇◇◇◇◇◇◇◇◇◇

Business and pleasure behind, James could look ahead. This time he would be taking the train to Pueblo, being reluctant to expose Coalfire to errant gunfire as well as to the rocky footing up in the chasm. The heavy downpour all along the Front Range meant snow a few hundred feet higher, but it wouldn't stay on the ground long at these elevations—this being the second week of April. But no problem, he was wearing heavy clothes, corduroy trousers, cotton pullover shirt, soft leather jacket and Stetson hat; he had plenty of winter and rain gear as well as dry clothes in his kitbag and a tarpaulin for his double-thickness bed roll. He carried his rifle and had his revolver tucked away out of sight. A watch and compass in his pocket and an oil-skin-wrapped Fremont County map in his greatcoat provided the finishing touches.

James compressed himself into the undersized D&RG seat on the Pueblo train, seizing the opportunity to nap—or at least day-dream. He hated leaving Trinidad, Lillian being the main reason, but between running her own saloon and working with the archi-tect for the New Columbian, she found herself having to squeeze in time for James. On top of that, Palmer paid very well for hours worked—and for traveling hours as well—and so far it was an enjoy-able activity that James felt comfortable with. Hard to call this work, he thought before drifting off into a light sleep.

A little less than an hour out of Trinidad they crossed the wooden bridge over the freshening DelAgua Creek. Wouldn't it be funny if that venture should pan out? A now awake James asked himself. Of course, coal is where you *find* it—not where everybody thinks it *should* be.

A water stop at Walsenburg about halfway up to Pueblo caused James' thoughts to drift to Matthew, probably deeply embroiled in construction by now—just a few miles west of here. James was a little worried. Of all the things suiting Matt's experience and ap-titude, railroad construction has to be pretty far down the list. Of course he's an auditor, not a track layer, so maybe...

There was a hint of green on the hillsides all covered with rem-nants of the native grasses of the previous growing season and dotted with juniper and piñon trees. Beyond in the higher canyons and valleys could be seen the stands of cedar, spruce, and yellow pine. The coming of spring in the Colorado Rockies—the season he'd been waiting for.

◇◇◇◇◇◇◇◇◇◇◇◇

It was late afternoon when James was ushered into the General's office, a scantily furnished "away-from-Denver" facility for the ever traveling D&RG chairman. Seeing Leonard Llewellyn seated there, James was momentarily taken aback. But Palmer was not about to allow an awkward dead-time to occur; he stood to shake hands, his modest-sized frame seeming to fill the room. "Thanks for coming up, James. Are you prepared to stay awhile as I requested?"

James nodded. The general preferred as few words as possible.

"Now I'll tell you, James, exactly what I told Leonard before you arrived. I need both of you to help save my railroad. What's passed between you two is past and I won't hear more of it, *period.* Can you live with that, James? Do you think you can work with Leonard?" His tone was intense, almost chilling.

James half turned to Llewellyn, an unspoken question.

Leonard rose, proffering a hand. "We can do it, General."

James, already standing, hesitated briefly and then accepted Leonard's peace gesture. What a turnaround, James thought. Llewellyn certainly has an emotional problem. He was so defensive that day in Trinidad. It could only be that he had really fucked up Raton. Both men sat down.

Palmer squared away. "Now, here's where we are. We've reviewed your recommendation, James—my staff and I, and Leonard, as well. We agree that the defensive position that you submitted as a contingent plan is the more likely to succeed. As you and I talked last month, I gathered that you were leaning that way yourself?"

James nodded understanding and agreement. "I came to see that Santa Fe's too strong for us. Since we're in the right—as *we* see it, at least—our best chance is in the courts, and, as you explained to me, a 'prior presence' carries a lot of weight."

"Yes, strategically," said Palmer. "But tactically I'd like to combine the defensive posture with an offensive maneuver right at the outset."

It seemed to James that Llewellyn was taken aback by what might be a shift in strategy. What favors Llewellyn's personal ambitions more, offense or defense? By delaying everything at Raton, *nothing more* was needed. D&RG lost without a fight.

Palmer continued, "I want Leonard, centered here in Pueblo, to have overall control of the Royal Gorge operation as well as his other duties at the steel mill in Bessemer. I would like you, James, to head up a strike force, mostly skilled riflemen, to stop Santa Fe in its tracks." He half smiled—it was an accidental word-play.

"Keep them off balance some distance inside the East Portal, and, having accomplished that, you'll provide security for a leapfrogging D&RG construction crew to start laying track upriver from the Santa Fe position. Leonard, will you take it from there and give us the details?" The General then sat back. It was his custom to give a subordinate an assignment and then step back out of the way.

"Since you were up here, Jim, we've acted on a couple of your suggestions," Leonard said. "First, we're laying track from the end of our line at Cañon City towards the East Portal; we have a small but fully complete construction company—about fifty men altogether—up in Cañon City extending our line towards the West Portal of the gorge. And I almost forgot to include the dozen snipers perched on the high ground at the portal to cover the workers. We're nearly to Grape Creek now. We have a work train at track's end with engine and armored dormitory cars we run out each morning and back to town at dusk. Santa Fe hasn't interfered with us yet, and we see no activity in the area. Should Santa Fe attack, we'll retreat into the work cars and back to Cañon City. Even if we're driven out by a superior Santa Fe force, we will have demonstrated to neutral parties that we have been actively engaged in construction and have established prior rights."

"And peaceful, to boot?" James interjected. A dumb question, he thought, even as he spoke the words. If you have guns, someone will shoot.

"Yes. Don't forget, we want to be perceived as the aggrieved party. And that leads into our second endeavor. Our lawyers are prepared to file immediately for an injunction on the basis that we have prior rights, not only here but at Raton as well. For our Royal Gorge petition we will be presenting the data and engineers' notes for the Cañon City/Texas Creek survey we made six years ago—right through the gorge."

Leonard stared James down for a moment and continued to talk, and talk! "Eyewitness accounts describing Santa Fe's current aggression will be most useful—especially as we maintain our posture as the aggrieved party," he continued. "We will also present the Raton Pass evidence that you and Alan Matthews put together that strongly suggests Santa Fe's improper use of the D&RG grading profile for the Raton slope and, of course, there is Santa Fe's overaggressive attitude, in general. This probably won't cause Santa Fe to vacate Raton Pass, but it may influence the court as it considers the gorge issue."

James was thinking that this sounded a lot like the waiting around that occurred at Raton. If D&RG had gotten in the field early, a handful of riflemen could have held the toll road from the south and possibly the Cimarron side as well. But as it was, Santa Fe walked in like going on a Sunday picnic. Why can't Palmer see this?

"What if the court rules against us?" James asked.

"We do what they say, of course, but slowly and reluctantly. Remember, we really don't expect much out of the District Court. They'll try to make both parties happy and duck the real issue—

'prior right' versus 'might is right.' They'll issue an injunction quickly enough—they're good at that—but it probably will be drafted to allow the strong guy on the ground more time to assert his 'might.' If it goes that way, we'll appeal to the Supreme Court as soon as possible. We've already done most of the paperwork and witness preparation to see this through."

James spoke up. "And while we're waiting...with all due respect, Leonard, and I realize that it isn't a simple thing to stand up to mighty Santa Fe, but why aren't we already in position? Paperwork and witness preparation can't do much for us in the field."

I've got to shut up, thought James, or the General will throw me out. It's plain to see that what I've said hasn't gotten across at all. What kind of a hold does Llewellyn have over him? Can it be that Llewellyn is really the indispensable man, the only one in the organization who understands modern steel making, or for that matter, coal mining and coking?

"That's where you come in, Jim. We won't be waiting. A scout has just returned from the high ground north of the Arkansas. He located the side canyon that you identified down in the gorge on your scouting trip the first of the year. We'll talk to him as soon as we finish here."

James interrupted. "But, Leonard, scouting is fine when you have time, but we already know a lot about the gorge and I don't think we have time to confirm that knowledge. In fact, we even have the D&RG survey of the gorge at river level.

"As I recall, that side canyon—which almost surely provides some kind of entrance to the gorge—may be perfect for defensive purposes, much better than anyplace downriver. Just past the fairly narrow East Portal the gorge opens up a little—it has five-hundred-foot cliffs on each side—and the river occupies only a very small part of the canyon bottom. However, I think it would be nearly impossible to stop Santa

Fe at that location—it would take an army. Just above that wide spot, the side walls, a thousand feet high at that point, really start to close in, coming nearly together down at the river level in about five miles. At that point, called the 'Narrows,' about a quarter of a mile long, there is no access at all along the south bank and barely enough on the north to accommodate a very small wagon or perhaps a travois," James paused and waited for Leonard's reply.

There was only silence as James continued, "I've been told that the gorge has been a horse and foot trail for trappers for many years and for Indians before that, so a certain amount of trail improvement has been made from time to time. About a quarter-mile upstream of the Narrows is where I saw the side canyon that we're talking about." James paused. "And there's nothing new about any of this."

Leonard seemed to ignore this attack upon his strategy as if it had not been made at all.

"James," he said, "I've assembled twenty expert riflemen for the plateau operation—at least they so represent themselves—plus two wranglers, a cook, a carpenter, a blacksmith, a commissary wagon, and a scout, too. This is your strike force." Leonard said firmly.

"You know, you might want to include a few 'roughnecks'—heavy-duty guys who can grade, clear, and blast away, if needed. These extra men could follow the mounted troop by foot or you might want to have another quartermaster wagon for transport. It's your call."

"Sounds like something the general might set up," suggested James, "shades of Chickamauga." He looked at Palmer, who smiled; not many people were aware of that high point in the general's military life.

Without reacting to that interchange, Leonard resumed. "Jim, your mission is to circle around two or three miles to the north of the East Portal—far enough away to stay out of sight of anyone around Cañon City. You will go north on Sand Creek and then veer west and upwards when the terrain permits. It will be up nearly a thousand feet to the plateau, so it's a pretty good trudge. About three miles west and parallel to the canyon rim, with luck you should come upon the side canyon we've been talking about—a dry or perhaps even an ancient river bed that may afford access to the gorge. Of course, you will have traversed up a thousand feet or so, up to the plateau, so you will have to descend a like amount at the side canyon. This may require a considerable amount of doubling back and forth. Our scout—Luke's his name—said it's passable, but he wasn't pulling a wagon. I hope you and he are talking about the same side canyon. When you get over there you will be able to gauge things a lot better and you have full authority to use your men any way you feel is advantageous. I've asked Luke to scout the entire gorge rim and find a way to advise you of any other access points."

Now I'm seeing the picture, thought James. By devising a detailed plan—workable or not—Llewellyn is throwing the general off-guard, and then may simply find some way to avoid executing it until Santa Fe has moved ahead of us. A plan without action! And he has already squandered two action weeks; most of the gorge ice melted at least that long ago. But why...why would he want to favor Santa Fe as a preferential customer for his developing coal company?

Anyway, I've already said all I can—and perhaps too much—since I have no proof, just intuition. Without question, Llewellyn has stacked the deck. I should simply back out of this whole thing, but my competitive spirit has been aroused. If I play my own hand correctly, I'll beat that son-of-a-bitch.

James was quiet for another moment, and then continued on a different tack. "Leonard, since you already have a small construction party almost in the gorge, you might consider *immediately* taking a scraper crew, a couple mules, and a dozen workmen, and push ahead of track's end right past what they call the 'Gate.' Your snipers could provide security. In this way you would really establish a prior occupancy. When Santa Fe attacks, as they most certainly will do, most of your construction people and animals could retreat in the work train back to Cañon City as now planned. But leave the point group and riflemen in the gorge to retreat upriver in loose engagement, as pressed by Santa Fe, until they meet my people coming into the gorge from our entry—if there is one. We'll have food and reinforcements and together we'll give Santa Fe a 'surprise party.'"

This caught the general's attention. "Do it, Leonard, like to-morrow.

James continued, assuming the tone of a good subordinate. "From your description and my dead reckoning, Leonard, I think there's a very good chance that Luke and I are talking about the same side canyon. But, do you suppose that we would be better off with a mule train than the wagons? Although I must confess that I've had no ex-perience with that kind of transport."

"I really don't know. Let's press the scout pretty hard on this point. Just exactly how does one get a wagon up a very steep hill, we should ask. And something else to learn from the scout, what's the water sit-uation on the plateau? I imagine it's pretty grim."

"Block and tackle for the wagons, I imagine he'll say; that's what they do at Raton. As far as water—we can take two or three barrels with us. We can dump them if we have to."

James then posed a new question for consideration. "I think a substantial part of our force must be assigned to protect our out-of-canyon rear. We don't want to lose either our horses or our food."

"Yes," said Leonard, "that's important. At this end we'll set up a watch between Cañon City and the East Portal to look out for someone trying to come up on your rear. In fact, you might ask Luke to do just that once he has steered your group in the right direction. We must assume that Santa Fe will soon know you're in the canyon. And above all, remember, this is an operation of intimidation—a standoff. We'd rather not kill anyone, but if an 'accident' *should* occur, don't make too much of a thing about it. Neither side wants to report casualties—the respective shareholders would be very upset."

"Might I suggest an exception?" said James. "Mercenary would-be gunslingers will be wearing gun belts—easy to spot."

"I suppose so...but roll their bodies into the river—nobody will count them and they'll wash home to Kansas."

"And how long do we stay?"

"I believe just a couple weeks or so, until the court rules on our request for injunctive relief. But if we lose this first court battle, your strike force should hold its ground as long as safely possible, harassing Santa Fe at every step and retreating only as necessary, preferably up the gorge to maintain a 'prior presence.' Otherwise, go along the high ground to the north, stopping near or at the West Portal to take a breather. There's a high valley—they call it a 'park' out here—with a few Mexican farmers and ranchers who have been here since shortly after Mexico separated from Spain. For some reason it's called Parkdale—one of the few names that have been Anglicized around here. Maybe you can buy some fresh meat and other foodstuffs from them. If not, we'll need to develop a supply line upriver to Texas Creek."

Leonard continued his monologue. "The Arkansas River canyon continues on for about ten or fifteen miles but that part is not nearly as deep or rugged as Royal Gorge. About ten miles above Parkdale you should meet a D&RG construction party which is now leaving Walsenburg to work along the old Taos Trail, cutting north to Texas Creek where they'll start clearing and grading upriver towards the town of North Arkansas. It's not a very large party—there again, designed to assert 'prior rights' in the eyes of the court, just as your presence in the gorge will have done.

"The Taos party will include about a dozen more rifles to reinforce your strike force. Your enlarged group will then create a Santa Fe standoff at or before Texas Creek and provide security for the upstream construction work, as well. All clear?" Leonard's mouth closed at last!

"Yes, but I'm mostly concerned with our supplies while we're still in the gorge—possibly backing up under Santa Fe pressure. I don't like to think we'd have to hand carry supplies along the rocky Arkansas River trail; it's a tough five miles from the Narrows to Parkdale— and we don't really know whether we can purchase anything there, anyway. Once we're at the West Portal, though, I think a fifteen-mile supply line to Texas Creek is manageable."

"Remember, too, Jim," Leonard put in, "supply wagons out of Cañon City would be awfully conspicuous; they could lead Santa Fe to your exact position."

"You're right, there," acknowledged James. "So, we'll cram our wagon with staples—flour, tobacco, coffee, eggs, bacon, and the like, send out hunting parties for fresh meat, and set up a supply line for fruits and vegetables from Parkdale or Texas Creek. We'll have to give a lot of thought to our horses—twenty-five or so. Grazing may be a little spare up on the plateau; the herd will have to be moved around."

Llewellyn added, "Actually, it's been proved, you know, that a man can live on meat alone—even horsemeat—for a considerable period. So—anything else?"

James was silent as he tried to make sense of what sounded like a "fasting" suggestion. Exactly what did Leonard mean by that, James wondered. He *said* two weeks or so. The "or so" sounds pretty flexible, it seems to me. I had better think months—not weeks.

Aloud, he observed, "It seems to me that another major problem will be communications. How will we know what everyone else is doing, like the word on necessary changes in plans?" For all his talk, I know Llewellyn hasn't given me the full story. I'm not going to take a fall if I can help it. Like Phillip said, "Protect your ass."

Llewellyn responded, "You're right, Jim. And communications is a big thing we missed. We'll need a few couriers, all knowledgeable of the area. They'll have to be coming and going constantly. I imagine there's U.S. Mail service to Texas Creek, but I'll have to check that out."

"We'll pick a spot on the plateau above Sand Creek to meet the couriers and exchange messages," James replied. He wasn't about to let *anyone* know his exact position in or above the Royal Gorge.

"Anything else?" Llewellyn asked in a tone bordering on a command.

"Well, I need a horse—I left Coalfire in Trinidad—and we should have a few spares, as well. And I think we'll need some workmen in the party right at the beginning. Perhaps a dozen—with some tools, ropes, pulleys, dynamite, and whatever else necessary to clear our way through to the gorge and perhaps build some firing shelters after we get there.

"Every man, whether he can swim or not, should carry a twenty-foot lifeline and, since we may have *some* combat without bullets, we'll need some pick handles, brake clubs, or whatever is available. We'll need some spare rifles. And I think a scraper team and mules to make a pretense, at least, of roadbed grading. It would strengthen our position of 'prior occupancy.'"

James paused to frame his thoughts. "The riflemen should be mounted and hopefully the workmen as well, but if not, there's wagon transport. So, the second wagon is a must—and both equipped with cooking equipment. And the more horses we have, the more feed we must carry—we can't rely entirely on natural forage, although the native cover up there is probably buffalo grass, and will make good feed even after having been covered with snow." James was now weary from their long conversation. Or rather, Leonard's way of using too many words to avoid unpleasant possibilities.

Time to wrap it up, James thought before he spoke. "And, another thing, I don't want anyone wearing or otherwise showing a handgun—only a rifle. Revolvers can be put in saddlebags or bedrolls—but not in holsters. I want to avoid this becoming a shoot-from-the-hip gunslingers' holiday. Oh...one other thing. Could you obtain for me a small bottle of red paint and a brush? I may want to post some signs or messages."

"Consider all that done," promised Llewellyn.

James went on, "And I'd like to meet my team right away—we have some 'getting acquainted' to do, but for the most part, we'll do that as we go along."

"I'll take care of my end while you're doing that," said Leonard. "And, Jim—I have to tell you—I was dead wrong down in Trinidad."

With a full smile James replied, "Like the General said, Leonard, 'past is past—period.'" But not beyond memory, he said to himself. Remember Phillip's words.

"Let's talk timing," James said. "First, I'd like to meet the leader of the East Portal riflemen. We'll have to get our signals straight so we don't start shooting each other when we meet in the gorge. Where can I find him?"

"He's here in Pueblo; I asked him to come down from Cañon City just to meet you. His name is Andy Devalle—probably hanging out with your men. We can have him here Monday, James."

Speaking softly and slowly, James said, "Leonard, it will be very difficult to keep this operation secret for one day, let alone four. I'll give you odds that Santa Fe is planning their move into the gorge for tomorrow or Friday, latest. I'd like to go tonight. I want to get my guys, their horses, and everything else on a special train—about midnight—so we can detrain and be ready to start up Sand Creek by first light."

"James, there's no way I can put together a special train so quickly."

"How about two trains—the first for my people and horses, the other for the wagons and supplies?"

Palmer broke in. "Just do it, Leonard."

The general stood as though signaling an end to the meeting, but then stopped and said, "In summary, I don't want to see a 'fire and fall back' mentality around here until it's time to disengage. James, your job is to stop Santa Fe cold. And Leonard, yours is to give James every resource he needs."

James again pondered the reason for his doing this—why was he involved at all? *I guess I can't help admiring General Palmer. I'm impressed with his "grand vision," but it seems evident that his vision and D&RG, to boot, will go down the drain if Santa Fe can't be stopped at the Royal Gorge.*

James wouldn't dream of telling Matthew, but it felt good to be part of something important—*to be a difference.*

◇◇◇◇◇◇◇◇◇◇◇◇

During the night, men, horses, and wagons were transported the nearly fifty miles from Pueblo to Cañon City by a special train made up for the purpose. Detraining in the darkness, a mile from the D&RG station house, James's strike force slipped away by ones and twos and moved away from the tracks towards an assembly area behind and west of the hogback ridge hiding Sand Creek from Cañon City. At breaking dawn James assembled his party at the base of the hills and out of sight of the town; it was not really very cold, but the darkness, the unfamiliar terrain, and the very strange mission, itself clothed in secrecy, all led to some chattering of words and teeth and some churning of innards.

James had a few last words with the Portal riflemen squad leader, who was preparing to ride south to Cañon City. He seemed to be a copy of James—a shock of black hair, a handlebar mustache, a deep voice, and a very serious mien—but a little smaller in all dimensions. And as leader of the Portal security detail he'd shown he wasn't overawed by the AT&SF.

"I guess Leonard's filled you in to what he wants you to do, Andrew. It *is* Andrew, isn't it?" James asked.

"Yes, or Andy, or 'you there.' This assignment sounds good to me. We've been getting pretty nervous, standing around waiting for something to happen. It's tough to keep focused when you're not busy. I can't see why they haven't sent us in sooner; it'll be a lot harder when Santa Fe comes in full force. I understand you're going up Sand Creek and then up to the plateau."

"You know the area?"

"Not very well. I went hunting up there once. I remember that you have to stay with Sand Creek itself longer than you'd think you should. Finally, in about three or four miles the creek bed, or maybe it's a tributary, veers northwest up through what they call 'Devil's Gap'—which I wouldn't call a gap at all. My horse and I made it and I'm sure you can, too. But it'll be tough getting the wagons up; I see you have a couple of them."

"I'm glad to get your view on this. We have a lot of manpower with ropes and pulleys, and that'll help. And Llewellyn has arranged a guide for us—a former fur trapper named Luke."

"Oh, Luke—that guy. Well, lots of luck..."

"So it's like that—well, we're stuck with him until we're on the plateau. I'll watch him carefully and make sure he doesn't know what we're *really* thinking or doing. Anyway, back to our job. Llewellyn's told you what he wants?"

"Yes. I'll have a dozen rifles and half that many workmen—and I'll try to have a scraper and a couple mules. I understand that you'll have extra horses and saddles for us up at your end. We'll hike upriver till you find us. We'll have *some* rations, but I imagine we'll be pretty hungry by the time we meet."

"That should be sometime Friday—Saturday at the latest. And with luck it'll be just about at the Narrows—that's about midway between the east and west ends of the gorge. I don't have to describe it—you'll recognize it at first sight. But you'll have to get over to the north side of the river before you get to the Narrows. There's absolutely no passage on the south at that point. Since we'll know where we are, and you won't, it will be up to us to find you. One other thing—have everyone tie a highly visible white rag on his arm. We'll do the same—we don't want to be shooting each other. I suppose you're pretty handy with a rifle yourself, Andy?"

"Pretty good with deer and bears, but not much experience with humans."

"Are you married, Andy?"

"Not yet. I've a girlfriend in Cañon City and we're pretty close."

James then casually pulled Andrew aside, out of earshot of the others. "Andy, you won't actually be reporting to me until we meet again in the gorge, so you have to make up your own mind about this operation, about its objective and how we plan to carry it out—whether you want to be a part of it. First, let me say that I admire General Palmer and accept that his grand D&RG vision is worth striving for. But he's told me and I've told my men that this is not to be a killing mission—our weapon is intimidation. We will fire with deadly aim only after demonstrating to Santa Fe the strength of our firepower at a particular location. Of course, the general says that all bets are off if they fire upon us first or, for that matter, if they start waving revolvers around."

James went on, "But, I'm not sure that this same attitude prevails in Denver. I sometimes think that the Denver and Pueblo people, a level or two below Palmer, would like to see a little bloodshed to strengthen their legal position. So I'll do my damnedest to stop Santa Fe in the gorge, but no one in Denver or Pueblo will know exactly how my forces are deployed, nor precisely where. And I'll keep a back door always open for our safe exit up the gorge or over the plateau."

Sensing some puzzlement, James continued, "What I'm trying to say—in a roundabout way—is I'd very much like to have you join my group, but whether you make your way up canyon or not, and how, is *your* decision."

"James, you sound like you're expecting trouble."

"I suppose I am. Santa Fe has made a habit of beating us at the mark—sometimes they seem to know what we'll be doing before we know ourselves. I think there's a good chance there will be hundreds of them waiting at the East Portal when your work train shows up this morning."

"Do you have any advice?"

"No advice—but a little information. The Santa Fe forces should be on the north side of the river—that's the trail side of the gorge and where the tracks will be laid. I'm sure you know that the river is very wide near the portal; the south side of the gorge is wooded and very passable for at least a couple of miles from the entrance, but then it becomes increasingly difficult—I've been up there. Further up, at the Narrows, there's no foot trail on the south side at all, so you'll have to be already on the north bank. I don't know if the river is fordable anywhere but it certainly can be crossed if you have rope and guts. Remember, that water is *cold*—it melted yesterday." James thought to himself, here's a man I can count on. Almost anything can go wrong, and he'll be awfully close to the enemy. He'll do, judged James.

"Okay—thanks for the ad...no...suggestions. See you in a couple of days."

"That's Friday or Saturday. If you're in the gorge, I guarantee we'll find you, Andy."

◇◇◇◇◇◇◇◇◇◇◇◇

Andrew Devalle arrived at the Cañon City depot after a half-hour's ride from Sand Creek. Riding along, he had mulled over his conversation with James; without coming right out and saying so, James let it be known that he didn't like or trust the Pueblo connection but he was proceeding anyway, Andy thought. And he told me that I should carefully consider the situation before I joined his strike force. Hell, as soon as James Molyneaux opened his mouth I signed on. I've a gut feeling that he would be a pretty good guy to serve under.

The armored work train was being readied for the short run up to track's end near the eastern end of the gorge. Andrew's presence was acknowledged by the construction superintendent standing on the station platform checking the roster and late coded instructions telegraphed from Pueblo. The engine crew had topped off the water and coal tenders and had fired off the boiler.

"We'll be leaving in an hour," the superintendent said. "I suppose you and your men will go up on horseback as usual?"

"Yes, and we'll cover you, also as usual. But there might be a change later in the day; there's some worry that Santa Fe may be preparing to drive us out. In fact, there's thought that they may beat us up there this morning. I know you have a whistle signal that will summon everyone back on board. I've seen you drilling on that. Whatever happens, we'll cover you until you're safely withdrawing back to Cañon City. I've been ordered to split at that point and try to slip up the gorge, ahead of Santa Fe, with my riflemen and some workmen—a show of prior presence.

"I'd like to have some extra rations for each man, if possible, and a couple dozen bags of oats for the horses. Can you do that? And have you seen any unusual activity around here this morning?"

"No—but it was still dark when I arrived. Come to think about it, I heard a little commotion down Main Street but there are a bunch of saloons around there and I didn't pay any particular attention. I'll lay out some extra jerky and hardtack for your guys to pick up and send a wagon down to the feed store for some oats."

"Thanks. And Supe, you might be extra cautious this morning—be ready to reverse in an instant."

A puzzled superintendent replied, "In that case, I'll ride up in the cab. We'll go a little slower than usual and keep a sharp lookout. I'll explain all of this to the construction people as soon as they come in—oh, they're starting to arrive now."

"I'll have one outrider up front," said Andrew. "The rest of us will stay in position to cover your retreat if it comes to that."

Andrew found his men huddled around a small fire pit in the open area behind the station, all saddled and ready. "We're going on up the gorge today, so bring your bedroll, kit bag, and everything you own. We'll try to take the horses, but we may have to send them back and go on foot. Wind your rope around your waist—we may go for a swim, later. Tie a white rag around your arm. Is everyone here? All of your equipment?

"Today and for the next few days we'll do things differently than we have been doing—we half expect Santa Fe to show up, maybe ahead of us. Each day we'll start out escorting the work train to track's end, as usual. As long as Santa Fe is not there, we'll split up, half of us providing guard duty, but I'll take the other six and a scraper gang upriver—on the north side—a little ahead of the main construction party. We'll do a little preliminary clearing to help the engineers who will be following immediately behind. When Santa Fe attacks—and they most certainly will within just a few days—all of the construction workers will retreat to the armored work train and be escorted back to Cañon City.

"Our in-canyon group of rifles and workmen will then make its way up gorge until it meets up with a larger D&RG force now entering the canyon from the high ground to the north. Santa Fe will probably soon be aware of our presence and may press us. If so, we'll go into a fire-and-fall-back mode until we get up to the Narrows. Our workmen with their mules and scraper will be able to build firing walls, and of course everyone, riflemen and workmen alike, will be armed—rifles and brake clubs. I don't mean that you can't shoot—but fire to miss close on the first couple of shots. As you pack your gear, keep in mind that we may have to abandon our horses at some point. We'll probably be up there for a couple months, all of the time showing neutral observers that D&RG has been there, which our lawyers say will be very convincing to the court."

"And if Santa Fe doesn't attack?" asked Albert. He was one of the boldest of the snipers as long as he had a rifle in hand, but didn't promise much with a brake club.

"Then we win—the railroad war is over. But I'm afraid that simply won't happen; more likely, we'll find in an hour or so that Santa Fe is already ahead of us at the East Portal, and in force. All twelve of us, including you, Albert, will then escort the work train as it returns to Cañon City. As soon as we can safely withdraw this protection, our entire group—rifles, workmen, teamsters, horses, and mules—will cross the river at the ford just west of town and try to slip unnoticed through the trees and brush into the south side of the East Portal and travel upriver as quickly as we can.

"Now, do you all have saddle bags? Stuff them with jerky and hardtack and anything else you can find in the commissary. The one thing we don't have to carry is water—the Arkansas has plenty left. We'll need oats for the livestock, so put a couple sacks on each horse. And don't forget the ropes, fifty feet for each horse and twenty for each man. That's right—tie one end to the pommel.

"Rifles—please listen up. Some of our construction companions may not have done this before, so give them a hand collecting the gear they'll need and help them find horses... Hey, buddy, that's a mule not a horse... Make sure they've got life ropes, lots of food, and spare dry clothes. Each should have a brake club. No revolvers—but rifles if they know how to use them. Okay, have something to eat and then we'll be off."

◇◇◇◇◇◇◇◇◇◇◇◇

Andrew and his riflemen were fanned out on both sides of the work train as it crept out of the station yard heading for track's end, a little less than two miles away. The scraper, six workmen, and a pair of mules were on a separate flatcar at train's rear, arranged with an exit ramp for quick detraining. One of the outriders out about one hundred yards in the front of the D&RG engine came racing back. "Santa Fe is *there*—a couple hundred of them," he yelled to anyone who would listen. "I don't see anybody on horseback, just a confused mob milling around, some with rifles, some with shovels, and a few with whisky bottles shared with their buddies." The engine recall whistle blew as the train made a screeching reversal.

Andrew came up, and could see that disorganized or not, Santa Fe quite effectively plugged the north side of the East Portal. The D&RG work train retreated. Andrew and his dozen riflemen and the scraper team had no trouble slipping past on the wooded south side not noticed in the breaking dawn. The river drowned out any noise created by the men and animals.

An hour into the gorge the traveling became more tortuous—over the years nearly all horse and foot traffic had been along the somewhat improved trail on the other side of the river. The south-side path had become nearly nonexistent and it was frequently necessary to lead the horses around the rocks and gullies. And it was freezing cold.

"Any of you men know anything about rivers? We've got to get across to where the going is easier."

"I've been in and out of a lot of them." This from George, one of the older riders. "And I think right here might be as good as anyplace. See, the river is a little wider, which makes it shallower, and there's no white water. Tie another couple lengths to the rope around my waist and I'll try to wade and swim across. The river may pull me a little downstream, so have plenty rope at hand. And, *please,* tie this end to a tree."

Stripped of his boots and outer clothing, George waded into the icy water to nearly midstream until he had to swim—with all of the grace of a yearling steer—until he was again able to wade to the far bank. He walked upstream until he found a scrub tamarisk for the rope's end. "I-I-I- think the horses can h-h-handle this," he shouted, shivering from the cold. "But be sure to stay upstream of the r-r-rope. And for Christ's sake bring me a b-b-b-blanket."

Horses were first across, one by one, a swimmer leading and a nonswimmer riding, each with one hand on the pilot rope. Lastly the scraper and stores were roped across. A successful but very wet and cold operation—the results couldn't have pleased Andrew more.

He deployed a couple men as rear guard, while the rest built a rock firing ledge in a strategic location, suitable for retreat into and out of to river-level without exposure. Andy kept looking back downstream, expecting Santa Fe at any moment. How could they not have seen us, he wondered.

"This is how we built them at Antietam," said one self-appointed fort-builder. "It worked just fine until the Rebs brought up their field pieces."

Even deep in the gorge there was daylight left so Andrew pushed on upstream a couple of hours, stopping at another little beach nestled between the sheer granite cliffs. It was suitable for men and animals and they made camp, although the roaring waters and chilling cold intensified the combined discomfort of wet clothes and a nervousness about Santa Fe's whereabouts. He posted two rearguards a half mile back and two pair of forward scouts to go upstream to look around. The rest did a little more "fort" building and conducted a firewood search to keep a bone-warming campfire going.

They all settled down to a cold dinner and hot coffee with Andrew's admonition in mind, "I don't want anyone to take an unexpected nighttime swim, so go in pairs to piss, roped together." One pair of roped-together scouts returned, reporting a clear trail up to what appeared to be the Narrows.

Andrew said, "That means we can reach the meeting place by next noon. It's up to James now."

The early morning view of the Narrows was truly extraordinary—not entirely for the scenic beauty, but as a logistical barrier. Between the thousand-foot near-vertical granite walls, the mighty Arkansas was crowded into a chute just thirty feet across, leaving no more than ten feet for man and animal, the water velocity measured in feet per second—not miles per hour. How do they expect to get a train through there, Andrew wondered. But of more immediate importance, it was evident that James had picked a nearly unassailable defense location. The narrower the opening, the easier the defense.

◇◇◇◇◇◇◇◇◇◇◇◇

In the half-light James' party—men, horses, and quartermaster wagons—moved up the Sand Creek trail, ghostlike shadows, creaking saddles, rattling spurs, and an occasional cough, a sneeze, a fart, and an expletive or two, "Shit, I've stubbed my fucking toe."

James' plan was to go northwards along Sand Creek for about three hours and then, as the slopes started to flatten out a bit, to turn a little south of west and zigzag up to the plateau. The party would then head towards the rim in as straight a line as permitted by the terrain. The only problem was that Luke and Andrew seemed to have vastly different ideas of where to turn west from Sand Creek. I'll just have to wait until we get farther up the creek and then I'll decide, said James to himself.

The flat area north of the Royal Gorge formed a transition between the Front Range on the north and the Wet Mountains on the south. Even down on Sand Creek—aptly named, since there was so much more sand than water—it was apparent that the going would be rough up to the higher ground. On the right the hogback had disappeared and to the left the impassable slope had been replaced with hills that *looked* like hills, but still with precipitous slopes that could not be traversed even by judicious zigzagging. There were a few spots of spring-green grass showing between the rocks.

After two hours riding along Sand Creek at a comfortable "all day" pace, James was getting impatient—just as Andrew had suggested might occur. Finally, "This is it," said Luke confidently, but pointing a little vaguely. "Right up there."

It was clearly evident that the Sand Creek bed had veered to the northwest, as Andy had described the turnoff, but there sure as hell was no Devil's Gap in sight. Luke's the guide, thought James, a little knot in his belly. And so up they went—"rough going" was an understatement, at best. If the devil had created a "gap" up here somewhere, this slope was where he had dumped the refuse. At times the horses had to be led; sometimes the wagons were unloaded, sometimes double teamed. And frequently block and tackle was employed. James was happy they had opted for more laborers. The mules and wranglers dragged the scraper to the top. Even so, it was well after noon before they were out of the rocks and onto the plateau. Not exactly a platter, thought James, but rather an unforgiving landscape of rocky rolling hills as far as he could see, stretching north to the snow-topped Front Range and west out of sight. Since everything was relative compared with the Front Range, in truth, this *was* a tableland.

Immediately gratifying was the sight of the four hogsheads of water that they had managed to carry up with them—although more than once they had been tempted to lighten their load. James was upset over the strange behavior of the guide. Luke had been little help in selecting the best turnoff from Sand Creek up to the plateau—it was as though he had never been here before. And by the time the party reached the top, he had disappeared. Mistake number one, I should have listened to Andy. Even though it would reduce the strength of his strike force, James decided to dispatch a warning message back to Pueblo immediately—Luke was not to be relied upon, incompetent, or worse.

James had divided his plateau party into two squads of approximately the same complement, each with a commissary wagon, cook, workmen, riflemen, outriders, and rearguard. Attached to the first squad was a paymaster clerk with full gear and rifle, differing in appearance from anyone else only by the money satchel chained around his waist. Two men in the group, Sam Alexander and Pete Warren, seemed to stand out in stature, manner, and from the questions they raised. In addition to Andrew Devalle, these would be his squad leaders.

"As much as possible, I want you two squads to proceed independently a little west of south heading for the canyon rim, and always with outriders in visual contact. If we get to a side canyon, I'll go in with Sam's squad while Pete keeps moving westerly along the top. If my guess is correct, we'll be able to find a campsite, and send scouts in. Unless Santa Fe has beaten us, we'll take up defensive positions in the gorge, send a party downriver to find Andrew, and dispatch a rider up the plateau to catch up with Pete's group.

"Pete, your job is the tougher since you really don't know what to expect. If in about one mile you haven't found a decent entry point, you should make a temporary camp, send one man back with that information to me, and put two scouts out forward until they find something."

"What if we're too late; what if Santa Fe is already there?" That was from Sam, a lanky bearded rifleman, always thinking and questioning.

"Sam, then we'll back out and catch up with Pete. That's why I said that he has the more difficult job. By the time we catch up, he will have had to make some decisions without knowing what we might have encountered. But don't forget, our very first responsibility is to hook up with Andrew. Okay?"

"Just asking..."

James mused, Sam's testing me, just as I'm testing him; he's a good man—a good choice. "Where did you come from, Sam? You seem to know this land like you were born here."

"I practically was. Pa brought his family—I was ten then—out to Cherry Creek. He had a small strike but when it started playing out he went over to Silverado, for silver, of course. About ten years of backcountry and I decided to come to the city—Pueblo, that is. Pa's still over there scrabbling it out. I'm saving everything I can—and this job pays pretty well—for a stake to get into a business. I'd like to get some kind of a little shop. And that's all there is."

That's not so different from my situation, James thought. But Father left Matt and me in a lot better shape. We've got to be sure not to throw it away. But right now I'd better think about what I'm doing. I'm responsible for a bunch of men who are looking to me for guidance.

"Any questions, anybody?" he asked. "No? Well, as I see it, this will be just the first leapfrog of several we'll make in the next few weeks. Even in the canyon we'll fall back in this manner, always staying aware of what the others are doing. We've got to keep thinking all the time. Now, I've said it before but I'll repeat myself. We're not out here to kill or be killed. *It's not worth it.* You all know that. Hell, next year we may all be on the same side fighting XYZ railroad company. Shoot to frighten—not hit anyone—and in short range, use your brake clubs. And leave your side arms in your bedrolls."

Sam was a little upset at this restriction. "What if the bastards start shooting at us?"

"If they hit one of us or act as though they are *really* trying to do so, we'll stop playing games. So keep your heads down and your rifles ready—or as we used to say, 'keep your powder dry.'"

The day before, when James first realized that he was being asked to lead a group of armed horsemen up Sand Creek in the darkness, he was momentarily taken aback until he recalled that it was the *other* Sand Creek, the *infamous* one, about two or three days east of here that had been the site of the massacre by the U.S. cavalry of nearly five hundred Cheyenne, mostly women and children. James clearly remembered the *Gazette's* screaming headlines. He had been sensitized to tragedy by his father's death at Gettysburg just the year before and the Sand Creek incident had hit him particularly hard. Most others had said, "They're *Indians.* They're hostiles and deserve it." Matt, too, seemed to share that opinion.

The afternoon shadows exaggerated a nearby landscape of rocky outcrops against a backdrop of sparsely grass-covered hills in all directions. The surface was marked by rugged outcrops, evidence of subsurface folding from Day One. There were no volcanic structures anywhere around, nor did it appear that the rocks had been waterborne. Most of the surface was sand and gravel—semiarid country supporting scrub pines and cedar here and there, scattered dwarf brush and cactus, and a few native grasses. Off to the north and west James could make out some forested ridges—that's where the last of the moisture is squeezed out of the storm clouds coming eastward, he reasoned. And that's where some game would be found. The area was cut by a few small and seemingly dry arroyos and ravines, but James knew that nature was capable of producing a surprise now and then—when it rained up here it really came down all at once. It was difficult to know for certain which direction the water would flow when it *did* come, but James was sure it would ultimately have to flow to the Arkansas River and that was south. Picking a direction was simple, and from experience he knew how fast he could travel, afoot or on horseback. However, he could only guess whether he was gaining or losing elevation. And it was important not to do either until there was a sure and clear descent to the river. If he went down too much, he would have to find a way back up.

Shortly after turning south, his forward rider—it should have been Luke if things had worked out better—sighted a depression crossing their line of travel in a direction a little south of west. Since the Arkansas ran in a southeasterly direction, this might very well lead to the side canyon he wanted.

The party pulled up at what turned out to be a shallow wash or arroyo—about five feet deep and nearly fifty feet at the bottom, about one-third occupied by a snow-fed fast-flowing tributary creek—heading southwest with a fall of about ten percent. James' dead reckoning, reinforced by the opinions of several of his men, led him to feel that this, indeed, led to the side canyon they were looking for and it should meet the gorge about midway between Cañon City and the West Portal.

"Sam, please take a couple riders along the north bank of this creek. I'll follow with the rest of your squad for about an hour and then make an overnight. Try to find the best, or maybe the only place for us to get the wagon down into the wash since that may be the only way down to the river. Please wait there for the rest of us but send your riders ahead to locate any problem spots. Ask them to go as far as they can on horseback, tether the horses, and continue on foot. If they get to or near the river, have one man come back to guide us. The other should take some kind of cover and keep watch downriver. Remember, if Santa Fe is already there, retreat as fast as you can. Got it?"

◇◇◇◇◇◇◇◇◇◇◇◇

Sam Alexander and his two scouts, brothers Miguel and Raimondo, rode along the northern edge of the channel. In about an hour Sam noticed that the arroyo bottom was falling off a little faster than the plateau, thus deepening as they went along, but still in what seemed the right direction. Travel along the rim of the ravine was reasonable, but it became evident than the ravine itself had become too rocky for the wagon—they might have to use the scraper team earlier than intended. About a third of the bottom was occupied by a small freshening stream. They could hear water flow, which meant they were close to the river or perhaps there was a waterfall in the creek entrance to the gorge. By this time it was growing much too dark for exploration, so they tethered the horses and threw their bedrolls to the ground. Hardtack and jerky made up their dinner.

At first light they had breakfast—remarkably like yesterday's dinner.

Sam gave instructions to the brothers. "Raimondo, while it's still possible, will you please climb down into the ravine and move ahead, and you, Miguel, stay on the rim and follow along. Be sure you can see and hear each other as you both move towards the river. Leave your horses here with me."

Sam waited anxiously as his scouts disappeared out of sight. Why is it taking this long, he wondered? *The River has to be close—I can hear it.* Finally, there was Miguel, alone, running towards him. *"Señor Sam, socorro…socorro, Raimondo ha caido, socorro…"*

"In English, Miguel, in English, *por favor!*"

After some tortured mixed English and Spanish, Sam began to get the picture. As the men had progressed down alongside the ravine as they had been told to do, they'd come upon an eroded spot and Raimondo had slid down into the ravine—about twenty feet, Miguel thought. Both had then started for the gorge, Miguel at plateau level and Raimondo down below. Pretty soon the ravine became shallower, so their paths had met and together they'd proceeded down towards the river. Finally they were just one step away—the noise was overpowering—but that step was twenty feet. A twenty-foot hard-rock cliff with massive boulders stood in their way; water was falling over about eight feet of the twenty-foot ledge. They tied two leather belts and a short piece of rope together and Miguel lowered his smaller brother over the edge. There was still about ten feet to go, so Raimondo bumped and scraped the rest of the way down. He wasn't bleeding much, he told Miguel. It was an easy climb down the balance of the way to a sand gravel beach and the Arkansas River. But it wasn't quite so easy going back, and at the cliff, impossible. The improvised climbing rope simply wasn't long enough. Miguel started on a run back towards Sam and the horses.

"My God, I don't have any rope either," said Sam. "I'll get back to main camp as quickly as I can, Miguel. In the meantime please go stay near Raimondo and assure him that help is coming—*comprende?*"

"Sí, *apresure…*er…hurry!"

Sam was more than a little disturbed that he hadn't properly prepared himself for this. *Not a decent length of rope on a little scouting trip. Jim should really chew me out.*

◇◇◇◇◇◇◇◇◇◇◇◇

Having broken camp, Pete, the other appointed squad leader, awaited his orders. A clean-shaven sandy-haired man, he was not as ferocious looking as Sam, but he was a shade larger and exuded confidence from every pore. Pete was a veteran of the war of secession, having served in the 7th Michigan Cavalry. He was heartily sick of the "brother versus brother" fighting. What had been accomplished, he wondered? He had come West as soon as he could to get away from it—but wasn't what he was doing now nearly the same thing?

James turned towards him. "Pete, I'd like you to split now. Take your squad to probe for a possible gorge entry about one or two miles up canyon from this one, assuming that this actually *is* a way in. Take your wagon, of course, and all of your people. Keep sending out pairs of forward scouts; every couple of hours send someone back here to report. The objective is to have a backup or support camp that would also serve as an emergency retreat route. Watch the

"Now, everyone—early nightfall up here. Don't lose anyone—okay?—before we split. We'll try to start out with two plateau camps, a mile or two apart, accessible overland to each other, each handy to the river but set up for quick and easy retreat, with rear-guard protection. When Andy joins us we'll start thinking about a third camp nearer the West Portal. Down in the gorge we'll want to set up a series of about twenty rock forts—from a quarter mile below this entry, if possible, and up past Pete's spot, wherever that may be. Our job will be to harass Santa Fe from every firing position—from every nook and cranny, and from river's edge to canyon rim. We'll fall back as we're pressed—but as slowly as possible and always covered. We'll have to do some clearing along the river bank so we can move around. The rest we'll work out as we go along. And lastly—no shooting at people—yet."

◇◇◇◇◇◇◇◇◇◇◇◇

Pete Warren moved out with his party in a westerly direction. The going was easy and in less than an hour a forward rider came back. "Pete, we've come up to a ravine much like the one the main party took south towards the rim. A small stream in the bottom suggests that this also may be a feeder stream for the Arkansas. The other forward riders are waiting there for you."

Pete pushed on, all the time thinking about the possibilities. This might turn out to be a fork of James' creek and would be useless. On the other hand, it might be an independent tributary and hence very significant. Pete sent scouts down the ravine, a messenger back to James, and turned his main party towards what he hoped would be the Royal Gorge of the Arkansas River, surely no more than a half hour away.

The gorge entry was a magnificent sight. It was guarded by a pile of massive boulders, each at least the size of the cook wagon. The creek took the easier path down to the left (and why shouldn't it—it was softer over there) while the remnants of an ancient footpath took a tortuous course to the right. The trail and creek bed played tag with each other zigzagging a hundred feet or more down to the Arkansas. Halfway down the slope they came upon a level grassy meadow, large enough for the cook wagon—if they could get it there—and a couple dozen bedrolls. Horses would have to be tethered at the rim. This is totally defensible from top or bottom, Pete concluded. Tomorrow we'll try to move the wagon—or at least its contents—to the middle site.

Back in the temporary camp at the rim, Pete let his mind ramble. Why was he doing this? He didn't care if either or neither of the companies ran a railroad through the Royal Gorge. Well, the pay was good and…the pay was good. And Big Jim Molyneaux would keep his men as safe as possible. Just thinking of Jim made Pete's blood start to quicken. Now, there's a guy you can like and respect. Look out, Pete, he told himself. If you're not careful you'll start to get excited about this mission…er…this job.

◇◇◇◇◇◇◇◇◇◇◇◇

The main party moved on, following the ravine in a southwesterly direction. Finally, with the sun starting to set as though it were following Pete's tracks, James called a halt.

"This is it for tonight," he said. "I need three volunteers to ride back about a half mile to keep watch. Spread out a little but stay within shouting distance of each other. We'll spell you in a couple of hours. You others form a large half circle in front of the wagon—and tether your horses behind. I'd recommend you sack out while you can—I'm certainly going to. And Cookie—cold supper tonight, no fires, maybe a tiny smokeless fire for coffee."

While the men were arranging themselves according to James' orders, a couple of youngish men came up to him. "I was on your train out there on the prairie the other side of Dodge when you handled them Indians," one said. "It makes me feel pretty good about serving under you on this job."

"Yeah, and word gets around," said the other. "They say you even stopped a prairie fire in its tracks."

James laughed. "Well, thanks—and keep spreading the word. Maybe we can *talk* the shit out of that Santa Fe bunch."

In a little over an hour one of Pete's men came riding in. "We come on a pretty good-looking ditch—maybe better'n this 'un. Pete's goin' on in towards the river. He's planning to go on till dark. He told me to tell you that he thought that's what you would want him to do. And say—how about a cuppa coffee?"

There were only hoots from the men gathered around. "You come to the wrong damn restaurant, Robert. This here's a workin' man's camp."

"Robert," said James, "since you gave us such a cheerful report, you can hang around. We'll send you out with a message for Pete first thing in the morning. Make yourself comfortable—throw your bedroll down anywhere you like. And go see Cookie over behind that tarp—I imagine he has a little coffee over there somewhere. And some supper, too, if you like."

"Say Cap'n, this is excitin'—kinda like the army."

James said, mostly to himself, "God, I hope not."

To most everyone's surprise, Cookie managed a halfway decent fireless breakfast. Camp stirred, fresh rear guards sent out, Robert dispatched westward, and personal gear stashed away. James was not so optimistic as to believe that they could come upon the tributary channel to the gorge quite so easily. Consequently, he was working out an alternative strategy. If they didn't come upon Sam pretty soon, he thought, he would have to start considering turning west to find Pete. Then coming towards them in a fast trot was an obviously excited Sam.

"We did it! We're in the gorge, Jim," Sam shouted. Then, sobering a little, "But we've got to hurry—I've got two men down near the river without a way out."

"Easy does it, Sam. Tell me all about it as we ride."

Sam took a deep breath. "As we rode along, the ravine kept getting deeper and deeper than this high ground—we could see that it was much too rugged for the wagon, and maybe the horses, as well. But then we noticed that the high ground was dipping sharply, too—and perhaps even more than the ditch. We could hear the river, so we knew we were close, but we couldn't see any kind of a break in the canyon wall. So I sent my men ahead on foot. They're brothers, by the way, Raimondo and Miguel Dominguez. In a little while Miguel came back to find me; he was so excited he was nearly incoherent. Raimondo is in the gorge; he managed to get down a steep embankment, I think he said. And Santa Fe was not there yet. So, except for one small detail, it looks like our scouting trip was successful."

"And the 'one small detail,'" asked James, "Raimondo can't get back up?"

"Yes—and if it wasn't so damned serious it would be almost funny. If Santa Fe should come around the corner, he would be chopped meat. So, we have to get down there with ropes and riflemen right away."

And they did. Raimondo was hoisted up to the mixed congratulations and gibes of his mates. Someone proclaimed, "It'll be 'Raimondo's Cliff House' from now on." That rescue was hardly accomplished than a half dozen riflemen were dispatched down canyon to meet Andrew.

◇◇◇◇◇◇◇◇◇◇◇◇

Sam and James were exulting over their good fortune. "Look at the down-canyon field of fire. The way this little ledge sticks out almost to the river gives us command of nearly two hundred feet of river and trail.

"We can quickly build a firing wall on top of the ledge—leaving room for the creek. Can you imagine how this looks with a full head of water in the ravine? But that's unlikely with this year's light snowfall," said Sam.

"The carpenter is fashioning a rope ladder now. With it pulled up, this becomes a near-impregnable fortress. We can hold off a downriver army and if we *must* withdraw, two or three sharpshooters on this wall would give all the cover we would need. Palmer would go nuts if he could see this," James commented. "Did you see a good spot for our base campsite?"

"Not too good, at first glance. The cook wagon has to stay on the plateau, but Cookie and every off-duty person will sleep and hang around down in the ravine. In short, it's not too defensible from the plateau side."

"Sam, finish up here, if you will, and then get someone started on improving access in and out of the ravine. That will be our plateau base camp to start with. While you're up there, please see that our rear guards are set up properly for both day and night protection. And I'd like you to send a messenger overland to Pete's camp. If they have made access to the gorge, I want them to send someone down-river to our entry to see that it's a clear trail all of the way.

"While you're doing that, I'm going downriver to meet Andy."

◇◇◇◇◇◇◇◇◇◇◇◇

James had hardly gotten down to the gorge trail before shouts and laughter reverberating in the canyon wall announced the arrival of Andrew's group and the "greeters."

"Welcome, Andy. It's only been two days but it seems like two weeks since we talked. Please bring me up to date, but first"—he turned to a nearby rifleman—"Harry, will you grab a buddy and the two of you go up to Camp B and ask Pete to come down? Now, Andy..."

"You were right to be concerned, Jim," said Andrew. "On Thursday morning, as usual, we escorted the work train to track's end only to find that Santa Fe had made a predawn push into the East Portal. It looked like at least a hundred men, some genuine construction workers, some guards, but mostly town drunks probably picked up in a saloon sweep.

"The work train backed safely away and we split just out of sight of the people at the portal. Santa Fe, with their surprise move to plug the north side of the canyon, destroyed our original plan to escort a small construction party into the gorge upstream of the entrance. So I decided to sneak a larger force up the south side of the canyon and move upriver to the first defensible place and send scouts forward to meet up with you. We kept our horses—they could carry more supplies—and added some workmen and a small scraper and mule team, just to make us look like a construction party. And here we are. We haven't fired a shot and we had a little swim, to boot, but we couldn't find a truly defensible location. So we pushed on."

"Good decision, Andy. I see the workmen, the mules and scraper, and eight rifles... That's a nice addition to our company."

"And there's four more riflemen. They're on rear guard, about a half mile back."

"We'll relieve them with some fresh men right now," said James. "Andy, lead your boys up that rope ladder over there to the Camp kitchen. Later, you can take your horses along the gorge trail up to Camp B where there's a good exit to the plateau for the horses."

A little after noon the next day James met with his lieutenants on the little sandy area below Camp A—an informal war council.

"So you're telling me, Pete, that you think the B site is better than this one—better access to the river, and better suited for plateau rear-guard protection. That's fine; our mission is to stop Santa Fe construction somewhere in the gorge. It doesn't matter where—so let's consider the entire picture."

James picked up a little stick to draw a map on a smoothed-out area of sand. "Here's Cañon City with Sand Creek running to the north and then northeast for several miles. About here is where we roped up through Devil's Gap to the tableland, I guess you would call it."

"Should we put out some markers for the courier to follow? Asked Sam.

"I don't think so," James responded. "For our own protection we don't want anybody to know exactly where we are. We may be able to pass on some disinformation from time to time if we're clever. We'll have to send the first message to Pueblo by way of Cañon City. We'll use one of our own men until we *want* to let Pueblo know where we are. It's lonesome duty, but I think we'll establish a courier message center with a couple of our men over near the gap above Sand Creek."

"That will also serve as a rear-guard warning post," suggested Pete. "Our men, mounted of course, and knowing the way, could get back here long before an attacking force could make it."

"Exactly," said James, "and we'll have to have a few more outposts here and there on the plateau. But now, back to the map...here's the Arkansas, a weaving, snakelike line from Parkdale at the West Portal in a southeasterly direction for ten miles to the east entrance called the Gate. Here's the Narrows, halfway through, and here are Camps A and B about a mile and a half apart and both north of the river.

"Now here's the thing that strikes me, and perhaps you other three as well. The Royal Gorge is not just a clean slice through a big mountain—like a knife through a block of cheese—but rather a cut of varying width through a whole bunch of mountains. As a consequence, the two rims are not really rims at all, nor are the walls really walls as we would normally think of it. Both are irregular and discontinuous. The great Arkansas River is the only thing that makes sense at all. It had only two rules to follow—first, always go downhill, and second, find a crack or the softest stuff around to go through."

James paused. "Now, Andy, please fill us in on how you got here."

"I'm not much of a mapmaker," said Andrew, "but I'll try—and at least I can talk a blue streak. When we came up on Santa Fe blocking the north side of the portal, right where I'm pointing, we faded back accompanying the work train to a place about halfway to town—

about here—where we unloaded the scraper, mules, and workmen and moved through the trees and brush to the south side of the river. Santa Fe either didn't see us or didn't care. We forded the Arkansas in about two hours, getting everything across by noon. Let me tell you, that water is *cold*, and well it might be—there's actually some ice remaining around the edges here and there." Andrew stepped back to view his marks in the sand—like reading what he had written—and then continued. "We spent the afternoon drying out, warming up, and making our way upriver to a big bend with a sandy beach about two hours south of here. We built a firing wall—a bend like that makes for a fairly good downstream field of fire—but we didn't have to use it. When we arrived at the eastern edge of the Narrows, we stopped to let one of our riders, a kid named Frederic, make some sketches. He's pretty good and you might find them useful, James."

"You next, Sam. What's your take on this?"

"Well, Jim, we've all seen parts of the Royal Gorge. It's mean—mean for Santa Fe but good for us." Picking up the stick, he addressed the sand map. "Let's assume we can stop them here at the Narrows—we certainly can put together enough firepower to do that. I think a firing wall large enough for about a dozen riflemen and loaders and located here—about three hundred feet upriver—should do it." Sam paused to study the sand picture.

"But an over-the-plateau attack coming down this Camp-A arroyo worries me."

"Wouldn't a firing wall at the Cliff House do it?" asked James.

"Only if they come in with a small party. If they start swarming, we'll have to get out—right now," Sam answered.

"That's where our covering snipers can come into the picture," said Andy. "We need three or four sniper's forts positioned to cover both Cliff House and the Narrows fort—to cover a disengagement upriver. Camp A becomes expendable—we really can't protect it."

"What you're suggesting," said James, "is that essentially all of our riflemen must be used in the event of an attack at either of the identified locations. Fortunately, it's highly unlikely that a night operation would be attempted, and we'll have plateau rear guards to avoid a surprise. So we can have skeleton staffing at each location."

"Sounds good," Andy put in. "Every single person must know his exact post in case of an alarm. And since we're envisioning a 'fire and fall back' disengagement, this applies to all of the upstream sniper's forts and camps."

"I certainly agree," chimed in Pete. "I think, though, after you all see Camp B you'll agree that it's much better than A in that regard—not good, but better. There are a couple places where access down from the plateau can be fairly effectively blocked. I have rear guards posted there, now."

"Andy," said James, "you've seen the lower part of the gorge. What can you add?"

"I'm not sure how far we want to stretch ourselves, but there are two places down there that offer good defensive possibilities; in fact, on our way up we built a couple of rock ledges with this in mind."

The four of them sat quietly thinking. Finally, James spoke. "Let's arrive at some tentative conclusions based upon all this. I don't like A site either. But, located as it is just one-half mile from the narrows, it's useful as long we're up at this end of the gorge. And make no doubt about it, that's where we'll try to keep Santa Fe from taking over. The further west we allow them to go, the less valuable is our 'prior presence.' And there's no reason I can see that they should get past us here. A dozen rifles with back-up loaders can stop anything at that narrow slice in the rock. But let me suggest that we keep an abandoned Camp A as a very active decoy. Keep one cook wagon and a couple of horses here, along with some bedrolls, a few tools, and some camp debris. Rotate a couple men here in nearby sentry pits—not in camp and not asleep—with a quick escape route down the rope ladder. Couriers would not even see our real main camp, and even Pueblo would think that's where we are. In our communications, we'll mention 'the camp,' only. Do you have any comments, Sam?"

"Don't completely write off Camp A for defensive purposes, Jim. I know it's not as unassailable as the Narrows, but it wouldn't be too bad if we built *another* firing wall on the ledge but facing backwards towards the plateau—maybe a two-step wall to double the fire power," said Sam. "And we could cover defenders at the ledge with snipers near the river."

"That sounds good to me," interjected Pete. "We should do the same at B and C. There's a big difference, though. The rifles at the Narrows and at Camp A are to stop Santa Fe; those at B and C and at the sniper's walls are to protect us—to get all of us out of the gorge alive."

"Your ideas, Andy?" James asked.

"I like Pete's thoughts about the purposes of these camps, or sites. As I see it, Camps A and B are only about a mile apart in the gorge, but how far apart are their respective plateau-level ravines or creek beds? Wouldn't that determine how the plateau defenses should be arranged? And also our plateau escape routes, for that matter? We should make sure that Camp B has two exit routes—one into the gorge and then upstream, the other over the plateau to a new Camp C—near the West Portal. And we should select that new C site with easy access to the gorge and protected escape to a new Camp D near the portal in mind."

There was no disagreement, so James continued. "Andrew, will you take on the job of locating and developing the new Camp C? And start a training activity so that each one of us knows what to do if Santa Fe starts swarming.

"Pete, I'd like you to finish developing the B site and its defenses and escape route. Sam, since you're left without a camp, will you to coordinate our *offensive actions*—after all, that's why we're here. We want to harass Santa Fe every daylight hour from all directions—and that generally means a 'fire and fall back' action using a series of protected firing walls all the way to the West Portal, each located to give covering fire to the one downriver." James paused. "Also, that the very existence of these 'forts' gives nearly permanent evidence of D&RG's prior occupancy."

James continued. "A major question is how far downstream should we start. Andy, do you think we can do an effective harassing job back where you built those two firing walls, or should we really start at the Narrows?"

Andy thought for a few seconds, then replied, "The trail on the north side of the river is fairly clear all the way—about four miles— from the Gate up to the Narrows, at which point it's only about thirty feet wide at water level, for at least a quarter-mile stretch. The granite gorge walls are essentially sheer and come nearly together at places. They're a thousand, and maybe two thousand feet high—really intimidating, I'll tell you. I think it will take Santa Fe at least a month to scrape and grade a roadbed up to the Narrows, but they will have scouts and engineers way out in front. We can irritate and even impede the efforts of these forward people where the gorge starts to weave back and forth a bit and gives a good field of fire. That's about halfway between the Narrows and the East Portal, but I think we will be most effective where the gorge is restricted since we can stop them cold with a defense line on this side of that narrow stretch, and do it without exposing ourselves unduly. Can you imagine the devastation that could be caused by a group of twelve rifles firing into a fifteen-foot-wide tunnel? What I can't see, though, is how *either* Santa Fe or D&RG will run tracks along that scanty path at the Narrows."

"I agree with all that," said James. "I think we should have those dozen rifles trained on that slit every waking hour. But I think, too, that a little bluffing may be in order. We might show our presence a little sooner—maybe create a little nervousness in their Denver office. Sam, let's send a couple rifle teams downriver as far as Andy's forts, but back off just after the first few shots. Make a lot of noise, perhaps some smoke, and see what reaction we get. As far as the building of the railway, that's Palmer's job, ours is to protect the site."

James continued, "And Pete, I'd like you to take a half-dozen laborers and a couple of snipers over to do some nuisance work at the rim. If you can get above the Gate somehow, you can roll some boulders over the edge. Keep that up for a couple of hours and it will give the construction people something to think about. Have your snipers fire a few near-misses *but don't hit anybody*."

"All of this may drive them up Sand Creek after us," said Sam.

"Hell, they'll be up Sand Creek sooner or later, anyway," replied James. "And this way we'll have time to make our preparations. Remember, we don't want to kill or be killed. And I have to believe that Santa Fe feels the same way. So that's where we demonstrate—we must, in some way or other, make them think that we really *might* kill, and the price to them would be more than they can stomach. Maybe the Narrows is the place for that demonstration. And, you know, there's something else we might consider. We talked about making Camp A, a decoy—Santa Fe will most certainly send a strike force up Sand Creek, and it would be my guess that this will occur very soon. Why not go a little further and make Camp A a *trap*—and a demonstration?"

"That would work," exclaimed Sam. "The terrain is a natural. We could lure them into the ravine that's blocked at one end by Cliff House, and surround them from the ravine sides. They would be at our mercy."

"We're not supposed to kill anyone—unless they ask for it," said James. "So we disarm them, take their horses, and let them walk back to Cañon City."

"You'll never catch me playing poker with *you*, James Molyneaux," said Pete. His grin belied these words.

◇◇◇◇◇◇◇◇◇◇◇◇

"Sam, I need the help of a couple of your men down in the gorge," said James. "Here's what I aim to put at our defense line." James pulled from his rucksack a hand-painted sign:

DEADLINE
ANYBODY PASSING THIS POINT WILL BE SHOT

"Where'n hell did you get that?" said an astonished Sam.

"I made it myself."

James and two workmen made their way to a point near to and easily visible from the canyon slit. "Please plant that stake right here in the sand. Good, that will do it. Those bright red letters really stand out against the gray rock. Lets go back to the sniper's pit and see if we can stir something up."

They waited there at the lowest sniper's wall to wait for Sam—his squad hadn't returned from a little down-canyon harassment. A few shots broke out and finally Sam and his men came into sight and backed into the sniper's nest. A minute or two after they were clear, James fired a couple of shots down canyon just to rouse Santa Fe's curiosity. Sure enough, two guys came tip-toeing up that skinny trail through the Narrows. They saw the sign right away but couldn't read it through the spray until they were about twenty feet away. That's when Jim 'punctuated' the three 'O's' in the bottom line of the sign. They'll have to clean themselves up, after that." Sam said, laughing nearly uncontrollably. "Jim, I didn't know you could shoot like that."

"That's the one thing I can do in this world—shoot a rifle. I can hit a rat's ass at one hundred yards."

"While standing still?" This comment from some wise guy in the rear of the sniper's nest.

◇◇◇◇◇◇◇◇◇◇◇◇

It was not until early afternoon two weeks later that the camp preparations were completed. At that point the two new Plateau camps had been established, each laid out for quick exit. Decoy Camp A arrangements were finalized. Horses were tethered at each location to take advantage of the small amount of natural fodder. The wagon horses were unhitched but kept in harness. Raimondo's Cliff House and six canyon sniper's walls were manned. In addition, other riflemen were deployed as perimeter guards around the camps and as scouts downriver, just below the Narrows.

That evening James received the first message from Llewellyn, hand typed with plenty of errors, three weeks after James' note regarding Luke's defection. So we can think three weeks for an exchange of messages, James decided. Is this another bit of Llewellyn's stalling strategy?

```
          Tues May 7 via courier
Pueblo/Royal Gorge
To Jamed Nolyneaux From Leonard L.,
    Received your mesasge re: Luke. Too
Bad. Received your April 20 Status
report. Good work. I imaginw you are in
the canyon by now. Please advise status
of the east portal group. At this end
as expexted SF moved in ahead of us
at the protal, but as not expected
they used town people. They must have
emptied every saloon in Canon City.
```

```
Heard today that they are now bring-
ingf in constrution forces. By the time
you receive this they may be in full
swing. How do you like this message? I
did it on a new Remington typewriter.
It's slowr than hand wtriing but a lot
easier to raed. Burn this message and
all others.
```

◇◇◇◇◇◇◇◇◇◇◇◇◇

James decided to ride over the plateau to assess the vulnerability of Camps B and C. The big gray that he had ridden up from Sand Creek was tethered with a few other horses behind Camp A. This is as good a time as any to move my bedroll and personal gear down to Camp B, he thought, and my horse with the upstream horse herd.

The rolling terrain between the two camps was a little more hospitable than the area closer to Devil's Gap. It was still arid, but not quite as rocky and forbidding, dotted as it was with small groves of pine and spruce and sparsely covered with native grasses. An easy hour's ride brought James to the stream winding down to Camp B. James judged that a horse could handle the steep and poorly marked trail following the stream but decided to tether the animal and proceed by foot. Out of the corner of his eye he picked up a little movement in the brush and what he thought was a glint of reflected sunlight. A minute or two later two shots followed by a pause and a third shot—obviously a signal—echoed between the narrow canyon walls. Another hundred feet and James were joined by a pair of riflemen who led him a few feet off the trail to Camp B.

"Everything here look all right to you?" asked Pete.

"It certainly does. I especially like the way you've protected your rear from a plateau assault."

James answered, "It works out nice. The side arroyo does not make a straight line from plateau to river—it zigzags all over the place, presenting several good defensive positions."

"Passing by I noticed that they're manned," said James.

Pete nodded his head in agreement, "Yes, three of them, dawn to dusk. And how did you like the signaling device? One of our guys was with the U.S. Cavalry down in New Mexico and learned about these things. The soldiers on the plains used them a lot—called them heliographs. He cobbled up this one from some little mirrors and one of Cookie's tin pots. At night we'll rely on three sentry posts up on the top. How about a cup of coffee?"

James and Pete had their coffee at this newly established camp. The level site itself was barely large enough to accommodate the cook wagon, a campfire, and a dozen or so bedrolls.

"To answer the question you haven't asked yet," said Pete, "we lowered the wagon down with ropes. We'll use the same ones to haul it back up, if we have time—otherwise it stays."

"Anything to make Cookie happy." James laughed. "Especially since this is becoming our main camp. In the meantime, you might send someone over to Camp A for the last of their supplies. By the way, how are the daily hunting parties for fresh game working out?"

"Pretty well for meat—deer, bear, and such—but not for water fowl. The horses seem to be finding enough grass; we're not getting into our reserve oats, yet."

"Another thing, Pete. I think that you might look at a couple more firing walls between here and Camp A. I expect we'll be firing and falling back to this point when we're finally pushed back from the Narrows, so we want both good coverage and good communication. In that connection, the river noise makes shouting pretty difficult so we should have eye contact."

"We'll get on that right away."

"Have you seen Camp C yet, Pete? What's the best way over?"

"Yes, I have—it's a good site but not nearly as defensible as this one. The plateau exit at C will be particularly useful to get our horses and stuff out when we leave. I've talked to Andy about it—and we could do it today if we had to, but there are some improvements we should make. Mostly, they involve providing covering fire. The river route is the quicker route for foot traffic."

"I'll take the long way today. I want to see what Andy's rear guard looks like. So long, Pete. We'll have a leaders' meeting tomorrow noon. See you then."

Camp C had an easy access from the gorge, for men or animals. Unfortunately, the plateau side was nearly indefensible. An ancient streambed led nearly all the way down to the Arkansas. The best that could be said is that with some well-placed sniper's pits, Camp C would be a good withdrawal point.

James discussed all of this with Andy, who added a couple more points of weakness. Both agreed that an additional exit position, maybe two miles up canyon, would be desirable for a "last stand" in case the plateau exits were blocked.

"And I don't mean stand and die," emphasized James. "I mean stand long enough for every one to get out and away. I want each firing wall to be located for fall-back cover for the next downstream position. This may or not be what Denver wants—but it's what they're going to get. So, I'd like you to locate that next position—we'll call it Camp D—and improve it. And if it looks to you that two up-canyon exit positions might make sense, that's okay, too. And as part of it, please map out our best and second-best land escape routes from both C and D. You might have to send scouts clear to Texas Creek."

"It'll probably be Parkdale from either C or D. I don't think Texas Creek from there is any problem, at all. How much longer long do you think this whole operation will take, Big Jim?" Andy questioned.

"Who knows? But I'm not making any personal plans for the next three months." James replied.

As in most of the rest of the gorge, the countless years of Indian and trapper traffic on the trail had cleared out many of the natural obstacles. Clearing and grading for the rail bed will go pretty fast, James thought. It took him a little more than an hour to get back to the main camp.

◇◇◇◇◇◇◇◇◇◇◇◇

James arrived at Camp B just as a courier message was delivered.

> *Wed May 30 Via Courier*
>
> *Pueblo/Royal Gorge*
>
> *To James Molyneaux from Leonard L*
>
> *Your end sounds good. Today we petitioned the District Court to enjoin Santa Fe. But no action yet. I think Santa Fe is a little worried. I heard today that they have hired our Kansas City engineer to design a bridge for the canyon narrows. But let them. They are taking a big risk. We see no indication of SF coming in behind you. Interesting that you have found no other entry points to the gorge. So does that mean you have all of your forces at that location?*

"Hey Sam," called James, "Pueblo isn't worried about anyone coming in behind, so you'd better double the rear guard." This drew a smile.

James had interrupted one of the men around the campfire regaling his companions with another tall tale about the near-legendary Big Jim. "...three quick shots and he popped the centers out of those three 'O's' like with a paring knife. It was beautiful, I tell you. The Santa Fe guys..."

"But seriously, Sam, we really have to watch it now. They undoubtedly will probe with a stronger force up the Narrows. I want a dozen rifles sighted low at the opening. At the instant they come in view I want a volley above their heads and then a second round at their feet, and if that hasn't stopped them—raise your sights. Got it, Sam?"

Sam smiled and nodded. "First thing in the morning. As soon as we're set up, we'll send a rifle team through the Narrows and try to tease them to advance. I think they'll bite since they're probably pissed off about the sign."

James then continued, "I don't think Santa Fe will be very aggressive. They want to live, too, and when we demonstrate that we can knock them off one at a time—all day if we want—that's a higher price than they might want to pay. But they may try a siege tactic. I've read about it. They could fashion some kind of a movable steel shield to stay behind. If they do that, we'll have to get serious and pour a hail of fire at them, do a little damage, fall back to the Cliff House, if Raimondo will let us…" This drew a laugh. With the ladder up, Santa Fe will then have to bypass Cliff House as they engage B squad, James thought. It was clear that Cliff House could then rake them to little pieces with flanking fire. He didn't think that Santa Fe would have stomach for that and he didn't either, for that matter.

The next morning, spectators (including James) and relief riflemen watched from the Cliff House as their stratagem played out in the gorge below. It was nearly noon before Santa Fe's advance contingent crept out of the shadows from the Narrows to the wider beach. James could hardly contain himself—nearly a dozen Santa Fe scouts were clearly in sight. He begged, inaudibly, "Now, Sam, fire now"— then finally a volley, then another. The noise was deafening, reverberating in the narrow gorge, as though the rock walls were trying to convey what it must have been like at Creation. When the smoke cleared, there was no sign of Santa Fe. Who knows if there were any casualties?

In his next dispatch to Llewellyn, without giving away camp locations other than A, James described a nearly impregnable defense that the Canyon team had put together. He suggested that Leonard meet with the most senior Santa Fe person he could find to discuss a standoff ceasefire at the deadline. Then they could all stand easy until the final Supreme Court decision. "Otherwise," he wrote, "we will defend the Narrows and our camp until it looks hopeless. Then we will engage in a fire-and-fall-back action until they wake up and come in from behind us. At that point we will pack up and run. We may have some casualties, but because of our protective strategy, the Santa Fe losses will be horrendous. Who *really* has the stomach for this?"

Fri June 15 Via Courier

Pueblo/Royal Gorge

To James Molyneaux from Leonard L

No agreement with Santa Fe yet re deadline. But I think you scared the piss out of them. So hang tough. The District Court enjoined SF from interfering with us. But it was weakly written and SF ignored it. The court then issued the same injunction against D&RG so we'll take the same nonaction. We have done a little harassing at the portal. The armored work train is very useful. As I understand from your accounts it would seem that your camp is very vulnerable from the arroyo. Does that mean you would have almost all individuals go into fall-back mode if attacked from that direction?

◇◇◇◇◇◇◇◇◇◇◇◇

"Big Jim," Sam reported, "I've doubled the rearguard. Actually, I've doubled the number of men but we're alternating stand-downs to keep them fresh. Same thing at the lower firing posts. I've talked with the men over and over about how to execute a fall-back cover and how to get everyone up the ladder in a hurry."

"And up the arroyo to the camp?" James asked.

"Yes, that too. And the big thing to report, Camp A decoy is ready. The fake camp is about two hundred yards up the arroyo from Cliff House where a double firing wall has been built—one facing the gorge and the other up the arroyo. There's enough space between the walls where the defenders on 'stand down' can relax and sack out. They can return to their posts along the rims of the arroyo in less than two minutes. The 'camp' itself has a twenty-four-hour campfire, a cook tent, bedrolls on the ground, a few stacked rifles, and some camp debris. If you agree, the wagon, Cookie and all, will be driven to Camp B, and the empty wagon brought back here to strengthen the appearance of occupancy."

"That sounds perfect," said James. "That means, of course, that B becomes our main camp right away."

"Yes, and we'll have to set up rotation, relief, and meal schedules for everybody. Standing guard is damned tedious work."

"What's to induce Santa Fe to come down into the arroyo trap?" asked James.

"Our riflemen are stationed in sentry pits about a hundred feet from the arroyo edge and not visible. Last week's rain washed out the footprints and wagon marks—including where Pete's group took off from the Camp A party. So we've made new wagon ruts and footprints where we want them. And we'll have a smoky camp-fire all of the time. Short of sending them an invitation—that's all I can think of to do," said Sam.

"You might think about having a couple of roving sentries up on the plateau near the Sand Creek turnoff. Catching sight of an advancing force, they could retreat down the arroyo, always keeping the intruders in sight and drawing them in."

"Good idea. We'll do it."

"Well done, Sam. I imagine you'll have to wait here for a week—maybe more—but they'll come. I guarantee it."

Going into the third week, James still nervously awaited word from Sam, pacing back and forth and generally upsetting everyone else in the main camp. Pete approached. "One of Andy's men, a guy named Henry, has brought you a message. He'll be over in a couple minutes. He's getting some coffee. They like ours better than their own. Oh, here he is."

"Hello, Henry," said James. "Thanks for coming down. Did you find the trail okay? And what do you have for me?"

"No problem with the canyon, Big Jim. Andy don't like writing messages so he made me memorize it. He says that his scouts have found a really good spot for Camp D a couple miles up from C. The north-side canyon wall seems to disappear and the plateau slopes gently—that's what he said, 'gently'—down nearly to the river. We'll need rope ladders for a short distance but Andy said he thought you'd like that cause it would be a good fall-back—better, even, than camp C."

"Fine. When you get back, please remind Andy that we're having a leaders' meeting up here in the morning."

"Yes sir. And...I almost forgot...Andy also said he sent out two pair of horsemen to look for routes up out of the canyon and to the west. He thought it would take them a couple of days. They'll also see if we can buy supplies over at Parkdale."

After returning to Cliff House, James decided to go down canyon to the deadline to appraise Santa Fe's progress. He took two snipers for cover—he intended getting just around the next corner from the farthest fire wall. James hadn't looked around much when he set up the warning sign, and back in March when he had walked through the gorge, it was wet and cold and it was all he could do to plant one foot after the other on the slippery rocks.

The scene he now beheld, as though seeing it for the first time, was almost his undoing. Sheer canyon walls towered to what seemed to him at least a thousand feet—and perhaps double that—on both sides of the tumbling and roaring river. The cliffs seemed to come nearly together at the narrowest point, about two hundred feet downriver from where he stood. It was, truly, an awe-inspiring sight and sound. He was transfixed, at first, his mind frozen in time, not cognizant of some workmen suspended some fifty feet above the river and just in sight in the narrows, busily drilling and splitting the granite sidewall. Obviously they were creating ledges to support some kind of structure—like a bridge, was his instant thought as he backed away. He had not been seen; they were too absorbed in their hazardous task.

James was deeply troubled. If the workers could go up the wall fifty feet, why not a hundred? And the most bothersome thought— what if they were lowered from the canyon rim to split off troublesome and dangerous rock ledges? That could bring hundreds of men up on both gorge rims, thus compromising our back door.

He later thought that he must have had a mysterious foresight of what was about to happen, for he had barely reached the top of the Cliff House ladder than some random shots rang out—then a volley. He scrambled to the arroyo edge in time to hear Sam call out, "Once more I'll say it, 'you're surrounded, drop your guns.' Riflemen, take aim at every other man...ready...aim..."

"Wait—we give up—don't shoot," from several voices below.

"Why in hell shouldn't we? It looks like there are about twenty or thirty of you trespassing on our camp and cook tent, and firing into our bedrolls. You were trying to murder us in our sleep."

At that instant James came upon the scene, rifle in hand; "Let me take the first shot, Sam." There were a couple of the attackers wearing holsters and cartridge belts and waving revolvers around. Mercenaries, James decided. Fair game. Two quick head shots were followed by the clatter of rifles and revolvers hitting the ground.

"Sam," James said, speaking very loudly so he could be heard down in the ravine, "the way they shot up this camp, obviously with murder in mind, causes me to order you to not only disarm them and take their names, but also take their horses *and their shoes*, and escort the lot of them to the top of Sand Creek. If anyone gives the slightest trouble or complaint, or if he has tried to conceal a weapon or give a false name, you will shoot him and the group leader on the spot. And, let them know that if we see any one of them trespassing again we will shoot to kill. We have long memories for faces. Please drag those two mercenary bodies down to the river, and roll them in. That will get them back to Kansas in a hurry." To himself, he added, and avoid a body count by the Colorado authorities.

A little later, "By the way, Sam, I liked that little twist you added to the removal of the would-be marauders' shoes—taking their trousers, too—that's beautiful."

◇◇◇◇◇◇◇◇◇◇◇◇

It was midsummer—the best time of the year on the high plateaus. Things were quiet—disturbingly so. "Sam," said James, "It looks like we've discouraged Santa Fe on the plateau—no sign of them in over a month."

"Yeah, but if they were to make a wide sweep with a hundred men or so, coming into the gorge farther upstream? We wouldn't be able to stop them. They'd come in at B or C and cut off our gorge people."

Sam went on, "On the Narrows front, we've managed to repel their forays so far, but they're getting more active every day. We've exchanged fire three times today already, and we've inflicted a few leg wounds, I'm afraid."

"Yes, you can't keep playing with guns without someone getting hurt. Let's try something else to shake them up a bit. You know that case of dynamite sticks we brought along in case we had to blast our way through to the gorge? Under covering fire, do you think one of us could get close enough to the Narrows to toss a few sticks down through the crack?"

"Sure, we could. And we have a few men who have worked in the mines, where they play with dynamite every day. Let's do it today," replied Sam. After a brief pause, the enthusiasm in the men's voice was replaced with slow and somber reflection, as Sam tried to believe his next neat set of words was indeed true. "People might be killed...but you know...it's sort of impersonal, not like shooting someone."

"Something else occurs to me," suggested James. "You might try floating slow-fuse dynamite sticks on little rafts down the river. That would be upsetting at the very least."

Turning to leave, James added, "Back to what started this little diversion, and when you've had your fun with the dynamite—and you might as well use it all up—I would like you to start backing off. Don't disengage, but reduce your exposure. Clear out the decoy Camp A. If attack comes from the plateau, be ready to evacuate Cliff House and your forts up the gorge trail. If they push through the Narrows, fire and fall back up the gorge or over the plateau or both.

"We've done our job already. Three months' standoff with Santa Fe and a disengagement might take at least a month more. That's construction time totally lost. And what's more, we have absolute proof of 'prior occupancy.'" Like a prosecuting attorney confident of victory, James rested his case and walked out into the heat and dust of the high afternoon.

◇◇◇◇◇◇◇◇◇◇◇◇

Sun July 15 Via Courier

Pueblo/Royal Gorge

To James Molyneaux from Leonard L

Bad news. Both companies took the issue to Federal Court. Tentative ruling permits Santa Fe to resume grading, bridging, etc. But no tracks. So back off a little until there is no contact. Your observation re Santa Fe apparently trying to get through the narrows by hanging a bridge from the sheer side walls is interesting. But if it can hold up an SF engine, it will hold up one of ours. Your warning of possible Santa Fe rim activities is well taken. We'll have spotters down here and also keep a lookout for large quantities of rope or cable being brought in.

A lighter note—I'm told that about two dozen half-naked Santa Fe roughnecks came limping into Cañon City a few days ago and took the first train out—back to Kansas, I hope. This sounds like something you might have had a hand in.

◇◇◇◇◇◇◇◇◇◇◇◇

Nearly another month passed. James was getting more than a little nervous, his anxiety only made worse by his inactivity. The big man had taken to prowling around, up and down canyon, around the camps, giving advice to those who needed it least, that is, his three lieutenants. He even walked all the way to the Camps C and D sites and found the changes to his liking.

Finally James rode up to the wooded area at the northern foothills and bagged a nice four-pointer. Jesus, this is what I came to Colorado for—not to play soldier. After dressing the animal, James' asked himself the same old questions, "And I'd like to see what we might do up in Berwind Canyon. And what will be the floor plan of our saloon? I'll bet Lillian is having a ball with the architect. And how the hell is Matt making out?"

He brought himself up short. Christ, if I keep canoodling he would soon find himself riding over the rim. So he *did* ride to camp, and they all *did* have some fresh venison.

◇◇◇◇◇◇◇◇◇◇◇◇

Tues Aug 1 Via Courier

Pueblo/Royal Gorge

To James Molyneaux from Leonard L

No change. We are producing more arguments to the Federal Court. Not that these will change the ruling, but it may be a good way to emphasize our position to the U.S. Supreme Court. We will appeal the lower-court ruling at next sitting of the Supremes in August. We are arguing prior occupancy by virtue of our 1871 and 1872 survey, our constructed lineup to the portal, our ongoing construction activity at that point until being forcibly driven out, and our current occupation of over half of the gorge. I'm disturbed over the comment in your last dispatch about fighting complacency in your men. Does that mean your rear-guard surveillance is a little weak?

James, I saw a message from Matthew to the general. It was signed Superintendent, La Veta. What do you suppose happened down there? I understand construction is moving right along, but what's with Matt?

I was thinking about Matt a few hours ago, and then this message arrived. James' anxiety was now painted over by strains of good old fashioned anger.

A deluge of thoughts now gripped James' mind. *Leonard writes as if he doesn't know what's going on at La Veta,* he thought. *I wouldn't tell him, even if I knew. Let him sweat it out.*

But if Matt said "superintendent," that's what he is. I don't know how, I thought supes are all a bunch of old men. But Matt has been a step and a half ahead of me since the day he was born. When Father left for the war, Matt became my responsibility—and I was only three years older. I did the best I could, and we were closer, even, than most brothers. He's smart and quick—but sometimes kind of blind. He can't see in his future father-in-law what is so very clear to me. Leonard Llewellyn is a scheming, lying son-of-a-bitch, and he's using Matthew for some reason I can't fathom. And there's nothing I can do about it. James felt his mood grow darker.

Reading between the lines of this latest message made James think that the time had come at last. He was afraid that Pueblo has its collective head up its ass, or maybe Llewellyn wanted more shooting. James had already cleared everything out of the A site. Today he would finish moving Camp B over to C site, leaving the kitchen and part of the commissary behind. His idea would be to fall back when the time came, by way of the canyon trail to Camps C and D and then to Parkdale. James figured most of the men and all horses and wagons will go overland from there. Finally, a few men would retreat along the river to maintain prior presence.

◇◇◇◇◇◇◇◇◇◇◇◇

Tues Sept 1 Via Courier

Pueblo/Royal Gorge
To James Molyneaux from Leonard L

   It appears from what you tell me about gorge activities that Santa Fe is tacitly accepting the concept of a cease-fire standoff at the deadline. I guess it's hard for them to admit that we have stopped them in the gorge.

You have quite literally stopped them in their tracks,
but they're not going to come right out and say so.

I wish there were some way for you to use your six-
and-three-quarter-foot persona to convince the District
Court to do the right thing. How do you look in a black
suit, white shirt, and tie, Jim?

Seriously, I share your nervousness. These guys
aren't dummies, even though sometimes they seem
like it. I think consolidation of your support group at
the narrows is a good idea. It will give you maximum
strength where it counts most.

James was only too happy that Leonard appeared to believe what
he wanted him to think that Camps A and B were already abandoned.
James knew however he would have to require keep all sniper's forts
manned until he and his men were present. However, we'll keep all
sniper's forts manned until we're pressured.

While James knew it was a long hike from Camps C or D to
Parkdale, he also felt deep down that he had more than enough men
for relief and supply. In fact, James was thinking of ways to devise
some activities to keep people busy. Sitting around is dangerous.
Marksmanship contests and wrestling matches might start things
rolling. Other ideas will come along, he felt.

James had a gut feeling that this thing would come to an end soon.
Thinking realistically, he knew that there was no question about Santa
Fe's ultimate ability to overrun the strike force. Surely they can see, he
believed, that a hundred-man force could come right across the pla-
teau—the one they sent was neither large enough nor smart enough.
Maybe the disinformation he sent to Llewellyn threw them off—at
least, that's what he had tried to do. James thought that maybe Santa
Fe now wanted a legal solution—it probably had a couple judges in

its pocket. The situation strengthened his resolve not to lose a single man.

And then, all his rationalization about Santa Fe's intentions proved wrong. As he and Sam were inspecting the remaining Camp A and Narrows rear-guard posts, a plateau sentry came riding down the arroyo and clambered down from the ledge firing wall. "They're coming, they're coming—at least a hundred of them, maybe double that, right down the arroyo, some at the rim, some on the bottom. It looks like they're stopping at the Camp A site, kinda confused. The Cliff House snipers—six of them—are standing firm."

"Yes, under the withdrawal plan if they're asked to surrender, they are to fire one volley to warn—not kill—and then immediately disengage down the rope ladder and up the trail. If there is no call to surrender, they will do the same thing—but first shoot to disable. In either event, they will receive covering fire from sniper Post 1, which will be covered by Post 2 and so on up the canyon," said James. "I want you to go up canyon *now* and warn each sniper post from here to Camp C that the withdrawal plan is being executed. And point out that we have full-moon conditions tonight, which makes our job much more difficult.

"Sam, let's help out at this end a little. I'll join the snipers at Post 1 and you take Post 2. I'll see you at Camp C, but if Santa Fe is pressing too hard, we'll go on to the Portal."

After the single volley, the six Cliff House riflemen retreated down the rope ladder and up the river trail; they were not pressed and in any event Post 1 was already providing firing cover. "Cease fire," said James. "We'll wait for Santa Fe to make a move. If they try to come over the ledge one by one, we'll pick them off—I'll take care of that to start with." James took down the first two would-be rope climbers with shots to their legs. The third ducked behind the wall.

"If they swarm some way or other, we'll fire one volley and *immediately* fall back to Post 2, which will be providing fire cover for our retreat," James said. So far, Santa Fe had not fired a shot. James guessed that when this swarming multitude failed to find sleeping targets, and for that matter no evidence of any camp at all, its personnel would be furiously critical of the leadership—and that is not the way to run a war.

Some minutes later, receiving no more fire from the canyon, about twenty Santa Fe men very cautiously climbed down the ladder to the river trail. They split at that point, half downriver to the Narrows the others even more cautiously up the trail. These were immediately under fire from Post 2. Several received leg wounds—some serious, all disabling—and were helped back to the ledge by their companions. All was then quiet; so far Santa Fe had not had a single target to shoot at.

"Okay guys, let's go," said Sam.

"But Sam, we could do this again," complained one of the riflemen.

"We're executing the withdrawal plan. And a plan is a plan," Sam replied sternly. "We'll go over to Post 3 now and boost its manning. They're in skeleton mode—just enough guns to cover us. It's a larger fort and has a much greater field of downriver fire. Our combined group—we're up to ten now—will make a stand at Post 3 until we get a report that Camp C has cleared to Camp D and the horse herd has been moved. The final step is a little uncertain and depends some on Santa Fe's actions. We'll stay in the gorge at or near Camp D as long as we can, but at some point all rifleman not needed to cover withdrawal to Texas City will scatter out on both sides of the river, find shelter, and give Santa Fe flanking fire all the way to the West Portal."

◇◇◇◇◇◇◇◇◇◇◇◇

Wed Sept 15 Via Courier

Pueblo/Royal Gorge

To James Molyneaux from Leonard L

Disaster! Final ruling from District Court. Santa Fe given right to build through canyon, D&RG enjoined from interfering. D&RG must back off to twenty miles from Cañon City Portal. So please effect an orderly withdrawal to Texas Creek.

The interesting thing is the effective date, September 15. You had no way of knowing that, of course, but Santa Fe did. In the course of a conversation I had with a senior Santa Fe official, he let drop the fact that Santa Fe had suffered so much embarrassment over their failed try a couple of months ago that they were mounting a massive attack to flatten D&RG for all time. They made their strike five days before the effective date of the court order. I have no idea of what could have happened, but street talk put SF losses at 20 percent. Of course this could not be reported to the authorities or to the newspapers. Santa Fe investors would be outraged over such ineptness.

D&RG construction of rail line to south Arkansas from Texas Creek will continue. Any of your men may join the construction party, including at least a dozen riflemen. The others should return to Pueblo for discharge and pay when you finish at Texas Creek. Palmer says there is a continuing role for you as this thing plays out in the courts. I would like you to come to Pueblo to talk about it.

> *General Palmer wishes me to convey his thanks to*
> *you and your crew for stopping Santa Fe at the narrows.*
> *He says, "Another Chickamauga, but we'll return again."*
> *I'm not sure I know what he means. But of course there's*
> *still the Supremes to be heard from in a few months. I'm*
> *optimistic.*
>
> *Your observation that only penguins dress that way*
> *is taken under advisement.*

Well, we pretty well had that figured out, James said to himself. It's kind of sad, in a way. But like I told the men, "We did the job we came to do. We stopped Santa Fe at the Narrows! And we're all alive to celebrate that fact."

The Canyon men insisted they pause long enough for a marksmanship postscript. James was challenged by the winner of the "Big-Jim Shoot-Out-the'O's' Tournament." He knew that it wasn't politic to compete against your men—but, as he was heard to say, "I'm not one to turn away from any kind of a match, be it checkers or man to man behind the barroom."

James' final words that day were mixed, "Nice score, Freddie, but let me tell you, you hold too long on-target."

They split up the next day, Sam and James on the river trail, picking up men at the sniper positions on the way; Andrew and Pete with the balance of the strike force, horses, and wagons, over the plateau to Parkdale and thence upriver towards Texas Creek.

"You know, Jim," said Sam at one point, "I've an empty feeling, deep down. We won—and we lost. We stopped their construction cold at the Narrows for at least four or five months and, while ultimately we might have had to retreat, we could have inflicted heavy casualties at Cliff House and again at Camp C. I think we could have lasted until spring."

James replied, "I feel the same way—sort of defeated through no fault of our own. On the other hand, look at it this way—we demonstrated our resolve and ability to effect a 'prior presence' in the disputed Grand Canyon of the Arkansas and maybe in so doing helped force the matter into the highest court of the land. What are your plans, now, Sam?"

"Pete and I are joining the South Arkansas construction party. I don't know after that. We've talked about settling down and starting some kind of a business—but all we know anything about is guns. Andrew says he's off to Cañon City—probably a woman."

Riding along with the balance of the strike force, Andrew and Pete were summing up the Royal Gorge experience in much the same vein. Andrew said, "I kinda feel that James thought all along that Denver would cave in just as it did."

Pete answered, "Yeah, and that's why he was so determined that there be no bloodshed on our side, at least. But now, not knowing exactly what's going on in Denver, it seems a shame to be pulling out of such a fine defensive position. We had them licked."

◇◇◇◇◇◇◇◇◇◇◇◇

Fri Oct 11 Via U.S. Mail

Pueblo/Texas Creek

To James Molyneaux from Leonard L

Another disaster, and maybe the last one, I fear. D&RG bond holders have instructed General Palmer to lease all of D&RG lines to Santa Fe. In return SF abandons the Arkansas Canyon lines, and D&RG builds its narrow gauge to Leadville. SF continues to build over Raton. D&RG gets 43 percent of the gross of leased lines. I don't know how the Supreme Court petition will play out with this development.

For the next two months until the lease has been

*signed, hold your position in Texas Creek with as many
men as you have left after some have joined the South
Arkansas construction party. So then it will be back to
Pueblo Steel for me and Trinidad for you I guess. But
come by and see me either at Pueblo or Trinidad. I
might be interested in your potential coal property in
DelAgua Canyon.*

Best personal regards,

Leonard

James was angry; Christ almighty, couldn't they at least have waited for the Supreme Court ruling? This makes our whole six-month effort meaningless—railroad war, my ass. And "personal regards," the same. And how'n hell did Leonard learn about DelAgua?

The resulting idle months created the usual problems only partially obviated by "make work" recreational activities of every stripe. James was relieved in the first week of December to learn that the lease agreement had been signed and he could disband the balance of his force. But how could Palmer have been so foolish as to give in this way—was this whole enterprise worthwhile, or was the General bluffing and got called?

James cooled off a bit after a little more than the usual rounds of leave taking and "good wishes." After all, these men had been together under difficult circumstances for over half a year and the bottle had been passed around more than a few times. He was sitting with Sam at a small table off to the side.

"Level with me, Jim," Sam said. "Have you been having a problem with Leonard Llewellyn the past few months? It seems to me that you two have been somewhat disconnected in your communications with each other, and you've been particularly obsessed that no one—including Llewellyn—should know exactly where we were."

After a long moment of silence James replied, "Well, Sam, I'm somewhat in my cups or I probably wouldn't be saying anything... but I will tell you this. I'm not accusing—and I can't prove anything, anyway. But since the beginning of this year I've had serious and growing reservations about Llewellyn's loyalties and personal aspirations. He delayed at Raton, and D&RG lost. He tried to delay at Royal Gorge, and D&RG almost lost. He has formed a coal-buying consortium—a conflict of interest. He's the only one at D&RG who knows anything about coal and steel—and he's keeping it that way. General Palmer doesn't seem to see any of this, I suppose because he's a railroad man."

"I don't see the connection between D&RG and Llewellyn's interests."

"If D&RG could be driven to bankruptcy and breakup, its steel and coal assets would be ripe for plucking—by someone like Leonard Llewellyn. And his good friend Santa Fe would love to buy his coal."

And to himself James said, and Llewellyn's apparent interest in DelAgua scares the shit out of me.

◇◇◇◇◇◇◇◇◇◇◇◇

As he left Texas Creek heading for Walsenburg and Trinidad, riding up the dusty road that passed as Texas Creek's Main Street, James couldn't resist the temptation of the town's single cantina—not that he needed more alcoholic stimulation, but to be inside a saloon again, even a cantina. His way towards the bar was blocked by an unkempt bearded man waving a revolver.

"*Tú! Gringo! Bastardo! Voy a matarte... donde está tu pistola? Tire!*"

"*No tengo pistola,*" said James, dropping his hands to his sides, palms forward. "*Soy amigo.*"

"*No importa, gringo.*" The man started to level his revolver, his actions as slurred as his speech.

James' right hand, only inches from his hip pocket, had already extracted his "enforcer." One step forward with a simultaneous forehand blow to the head—the man dropped like a felled steer.

"He wouldn't of had time to shoot you, Jim," a deep voice came from behind. "We both had beads on him."

It was Henry and a man named Frank, both Canyon riflemen. "He had only a heartbeat to live. I think you saved his life—if he *is* alive, that is. And he don't look too good right now. What'n hell did you hit him with?"

"That's my 'enforcer,'" said James. "It seems that you're my guardian angels,"

"Not really angels. Me and Frank are only saints—Mormons, that is."

"More like Jack Mormons—we ain't good enough to be real Mormons."

"Whatever—thanks."

"That's not all, Boss," said a voice from the other side of the room. Three more Canyons were standing, guns in hand, "You don't think we'd let a drunken cowboy gun down one of us Canyon guys, do ya?"

CHAPTER THIRTEEN

AS A CONSEQUENCE

I T WAS MIDSUMMER IN THE ROCKIES. Days were bright—hot, but dry—and nights delightfully cool. A high elevation chill might be expected before dawn. A more mature and confident Matthew (actually matching the veneer he had adopted these last several months) drove his two-horse carriage at a brisk rate over the Walsenburg road. Not that he needed to travel so fast—he had time to kill in Trinidad and he knew exactly how he would do that. His top priority—after Sophia, of course—was DelAgua Partners. Josephson should have all of the land-office paperwork finished by now and be ready to draw up a partnership agreement.

Matt's expectations for the coal mine development were modest, the entire project a bit of a nuisance in light of the really exciting and potentially fruitful work ahead of him in Denver. Even the New Columbian Saloon, a sure thing, was more up Jim's alley and of only minimal interest to Matt. Just thinking of his brother piqued his curiosity. What in the world could Jim be doing? Matt knew that he was in the Royal Gorge with a strike force trying to effect a standoff with Santa Fe—he'd obtained that information indirectly from a Denver source. But what was he *really* doing, and was this connected with D&RG's ever growing financial mess, the rumored takeover by Santa Fe? Well, he thought, I'll soon know, its three weeks' leave in Trinidad and then up to Head Office where it's all happening.

Crossing the freshening DelAgua Creek, Matt paused, as he had the last time he was on this road. It's certainly a pretty little valley, he thought, bounded by two creeks, barely a mile apart, each making a tortuous passage through the rolling hills. Leonard didn't hold out much hope, though, for a producing mine in this location. Maybe Jim was on the right track with his fictitious llamas.

After a bath and haircut in town and a change of clothes at Maude's, Matt drove up the hill to the Llewellyn's. He had telegraphed from Walsenburg so his mid-afternoon arrival would not be a surprise. And, perhaps, it should not have been a surprise for Matt to find Sophia answering the door.

"Oh, Matt," she said, "I'm so glad to see you." She leaned into him and kissed him long and deep. "So you haven't forgotten the French variation, have you?"

"That's not all I haven't forgotten." Matthew smiled.

"Come on in, Matthew, Mama's in town for a couple of hours. She said if she's not back before you arrive, I should invite you for dinner. Father's up in Pueblo—he'll be back this weekend."

Matthew was amused. Mrs. Llewellyn seemed to take these trips to town at very convenient times.

◇◇◇◇◇◇◇◇◇◇◇◇

The trial shipment of tobacco had arrived, all cigars of the very finest air-dried burley. As far as James and Matthew had been able to determine back when they placed the order, nothing of this quality was to be had anywhere in Trinidad. And why not, they had asked themselves.

The answer, quite simply, was the price of this tobacco—significantly more expensive, and of superior quality to the "sage brush" smoked out West by all but the very wealthy. The Molyneaux brothers' original thought was to set up a wholesale business, as Matt had done in the much more sophisticated Pittsburgh, serving the myriad of more refined saloons that existed. It seemed, now, they would have to concentrate more on retailing until the Trinidad saloons would become more gentrified. They would have a tobacco shop in the new hotel, and perhaps cigar counters at the various restaurants.

Above all, they would have to find a way to cultivate good tobacco appreciation in the younger generation. For starters, Matthew made the rounds of the better Trinidad saloons, leaving cigar samples for trial—he had already set up telegraph ordering and money-transfer connections similar to those he had in Pittsburgh. But most of his efforts went towards procuring sandwich boards to promote the new hotel cigar shop. They would want to hit the streets a month or so before the hotel opening.

Matt dropped in on Lillian to show her how the ordering could be done in case both he and James should be out of town at the same time that early orders materialized.

"How's the New Columbian coming along?" Matthew asked.

"Much better than we—or at least I—expected," Lillian replied. "The Grand Union people are providing more than we asked for and for less cost, but it'll still be more than a year away. This facility—saloon, restaurant, and tobacco shop—will be magnificent, Matthew. I can't describe how beautiful they will be. And the mezzanine rooms will be splendid—the girls will never have seen the like."

"So the owners didn't balk at this detail?"

"Heavens, no. Mr. Hepplewhite suggested it, himself."

◇◇◇◇◇◇◇◇◇◇◇◇

The land attorney Jacobsen had nothing to report—DelAgua lease applications had not yet been approved. "I'll start drawing up a partnership agreement as soon as we receive them, Matthew. Are the provisions we talked about still what you want?"

"Yes. And particularly the participation by Colorado Coal Company. I've talked with Leonard Llewellyn and this is what he wants, also."

"And how about your brother?"

"Oh, he'll go along with it—he's not interested in these kinds of details."

With loose ends pretty well taken care of, and his leave about up, Matt still had time for Sophia. And Mrs. Llewellyn had a couple more of those mysterious afternoons in town.

◇◇◇◇◇◇◇◇◇◇◇◇

Arriving in Denver, Matt expected to be greeted with fervent congratulations. He had, after all, cleaned up the La Veta mess in just four months. But that, apparently, was yesterday. Today was the start of an intense top-to-bottom analysis of D&RG's internal financial matters. He was a schoolboy again but still a quick learner. Squeezing six months' study into three, by September he was judged fit to join operating managers in their strategy sessions only to find that there really was no strategy at all to solve an imminent bondholders' foreclosure. Finally, a bondholders' committee let it be known that it was either that or acceptance of a Santa Fe offer to lease and operate all of D&RG's lines, sharing revenues of those lines leased.

Matthew never thought he would see General Palmer so low—a beaten man. And with good reason. "My God, Matt, the damn fools—the D&RG bondholders, that is—wouldn't listen to me, they were entranced by Santa Fe's offer of a long-term lease of our operating facilities for a modest fixed fee plus part of the revenue generated by these leased lines. And worse, they were blind to the fact that nothing could stop Santa Fe from setting tariffs and arranging shipping schedules and routes to their own benefit."

"How much of our system did they take over?"

"All of it—except La Veta. You hadn't quite finished that. And, of course, Royal Gorge isn't operating yet."

"So…we're not dead yet?"

"We might as well be. There goes the El Paso vision."

"Suppose, General, I set up a little team of clerks and accountants to monitor every smallest action of Santa Fe—look for lease violations and every unfair practice, maybe build a case for breaking the lease?"

"Go ahead, but the thing goes a lot deeper than that. We need outside money."

"What's changed?"

"The ground rules. Matt, you know that the transcontinental railway was financed by the federal land grants along both sides of the route. Union and Central Pacific sold the land to home-seekers and had plenty to build the railway and line a few pockets as well." There was a trace of a rueful smile.

The General continued, "But we couldn't do that here in Colorado. Instead, we sold some revenue and even some fixed-rate bonds. That worked for the Cheyenne-to-Denver line, but with La Veta we ran into trouble. The bondholders got pretty jumpy when we missed some interest payments, but we quieted them down with some revenue promises and some long-term certificates. And fortunately— with your good work—produce shipments started even before the line reached Alamosa." A rare full smile flashed across the General's face.

He went on, "Looking back a few years, on the line south from Denver we took a different approach. Land companies were formed to found new towns near to but independent of established towns, notably Pueblo, Colorado Springs, and Trinidad. Stock in the land companies was given to the subscribers of railroad bonds as an incentive."

"So that's why the old towns are so mad at us?"

"Well, you can't please everyone, Matthew," he said with a sly smile. "But now we need a new gambit, I'm afraid." General Palmer had brightened—he was his old self for a moment. "Matt, you break that goddamn lease and I'll get the money."

◇◇◇◇◇◇◇◇◇◇◇◇◇

It wasn't difficult for Matthew and his assistants to find evidence of foul play—at least from D&RG's viewpoint. Denver merchants were in an uproar. By the end of January, the second month of Santa Fe operation, Matt's investigators had compiled an impressive dossier of lease violations, bookkeeping errors, and unfair practices.

"With every day, the list gets longer and the file thicker," said Matt. "Do you want to start proceedings with what we have?"

"Yes, I think we should," replied Palmer. "I'll give this to our legal team today, and we'll see what happens."

It was a couple days—nervous ones for Matt—until the D&RG chief counsel caught Matt in the hallway. "It worked, Matthew. The bondholders bought it and the D&RG board has authorized General Palmer to take action to break the lease. So pack your bag, we're heading for San Luis Valley, tomorrow."

◇◇◇◇◇◇◇◇◇◇◇◇◇

It was with special pleasure that Matthew, in company with the D&RG legal team, took his own—his *very* own—railway over the snow-capped La Veta Pass to Garland City. "See those rails winding up the mountain—the highest in the world? I built them," was the response he was ready to make to anyone who might ask almost any question, apropos or not. But nobody did; the lawyers took something like this for granted.

Following courtesy calls to the Garland City mayor, Eduardo Dominguez, and the Fort Garland commandant, the D&RG team hired a rig to travel the three hours down to San Luis, calling upon Mayor Alvarez as the first order of business. The mayor and his town attorney offered enthusiastic support of the legal mission. "The train was built over the mountain just like you said it would be, Mr. Molyneaux; you made it happen."

Mayor Alvarez turned to the D&RG chief counsel. "As you can see, Señor Abogado Jefe, we have great confidence in what Señor Molyneaux says. I'm sure that Circuit Judge Bowen will be receptive to your arguments.

"You might not be aware that just yesterday another action involving AT&SF was initiated in Alamosa District Court by the Colorado Attorney General. It will also be heard here in San Luis by Judge Bowen. That suit will inquire into the legality of Santa Fe's presence in Colorado *at all*. Colorado's law requires any corporation operating in the state to have a certain minimum capitalization or, in other words, muscle. This action holds that Santa Fe, by operating in the name of a subsidiary that, in itself, fails that minimum, is in violation of state law.

"It would seem, gentlemen, that the D&RG railroad has brought San Luis Valley into the Colorado mainstream. I think that is a good thing."

D&RG's plea to vacate the Santa Fe lease was a huge success in San Luis District Court, or so it appeared. Matthew had armed the D&RG team with more facts and arguments relating to Santa Fe's breach of contract than that small court had ever seen. The court bought all of the breach argument, appointed a receiver to protect

D&RG's bondholders, and took the minimum capitalization issue under study for decision at the next court session in April.

◇◇◇◇◇◇◇◇◇◇◇◇

James had left Texas Creek on a clear and crisp early December morning riding upstream alongside the town's namesake creek. Early snows, even at nearly seven thousand feet, had prematurely melted—except on the higher Rocky Mountain elevations. The high plateau, or "park" as they called them out here, had obviously been grazed upon. The buffalo grass, not high at best, was now just a stubble; at the moment, with winter setting in, stock had undoubtedly been taken either to shelter or to market, wherever that may be. He looked back over the gently rolling hills—sparsely studded with stunted pine and spruce, groves of Aspen, and a variety of sage brushes—to a rocky spot on the Arkansas that marked the town of Texas Creek, and noted little activity. There was the stage-stop with eatery and minimal lodging, the stable and blacksmith, the small general store, and the cantina, of course.

The cantina. It felt good, James thought, to have that kind of support from the "Canyon Guys."

Short-lived as it had been, the standoff at the Royal Gorge was the most important nine months of James' life. It was the first time he had led a group of men in any kind of an endeavor, and what a group it was! They were all in their early thirties, mostly war veterans—both sides—mustered out knowing nothing but war, and now competing for the lowest kind of job with hordes of European immigrants pressing west from the eastern seaboard. His men were not farmers, and had no inclination in that way. They couldn't all be fur trappers and the only Indian fighters were in the army. They all understood discipline and how to handle a rifle. But they seemed to lack a sense of purpose—now, five years after the war, they'd still not found their direction. And James had learned something about himself. He felt comfortable as a leader—but unfortunately, what was the direction?

James felt that he had allowed himself to become distracted from what he thought was *his* direction—all he wanted was a saloon in town and a hunting cabin in the mountains—and he'd found himself playing soldier for a railway company he hardly knew. I'm in nearly as bad a shape as the war veterans, he lamented, but now it's finished.

About an hour south of town James' path joined an established wagon road, rutted and dusty, the route taken by ore wagons to the Pueblo smelters from the mines north of the Arkansas River Canyon. The wagons crossed that river at Cotopaxi, then turned south and finally east over the Wet Mountains and the diminishing Front Range. This had been the route of the construction and support force from Pueblo to the eastern portal of the Royal Gorge. Regardless of who wins the behind-the-scenes Royal Gorge court battle, James thought, the Wet Mountains and San Luis valleys are in for some drastic changes. While in Pueblo, James had heard stories of scouting and surveying trips taken back in 1870 by General Palmer, accompanied by several friends and political and financial advisors, to find a rail route to the south. He was amused that a two-star general would become first a surveyor for Kansas Pacific, and then a freelance locator and visionary in the middle of the Colorado Rockies. It occurred to James that it must have been during this survey that the General decided that Colorado could, and should, become the commercial pathway connecting the eastern seaboard with Santa Fe and El Paso and on to Mexico City.

It was nice to be on the move again, James thought. It had been kind of exciting being responsible for so many men up on the plateau, but nothing much really happened and the occupation became a little tedious. Perhaps "nothing happened" because the containment of Santa Fe at the gorge had been crafted so well—undoubtedly Santa Fe could see that their losses pushing through the gorge would be so high their cause would be better served by going up on the plateau behind the D&RG strike force. James' carefully planned and timed withdrawal strategy took this into account; the trap at Camp A and the successful fire-and-fall-back mode must have been very disquieting to Santa Fe. On the other hand, judged by D&RG's pull-back without a whimper, perhaps the gorge defense wasn't supposed to work out so peaceably. Maybe Denver really wanted a firefight, with more than a few casualties, to strengthen its court case. Without question, Llewellyn had not had the plateau scouted as promised, nor had he suggested any task strategy at all—particularly withdrawal. Well, if bloodshed is what they desired, they certainly didn't get it from me—and if I had to do it all over, they still wouldn't.

Not for the first time, James reviewed in his mind Leonard Llewellyn's actions since day one in Colorado. Without a doubt—and Palmer's opinion to the contrary—the Raton thing had been botched. At the very least, Llewellyn had gone to sleep. And *someone* had given Santa Fe the D&RG survey. Also, James said to himself, Llewellyn *did* proposition me about secret coal prospecting—I'm not imagining *that*. And there was that oblique reference to DelAgua in his letter to me in Texas Creek. How does he know about that venture? Maybe it was our land lawyer, Josephson, with the loose lips. I can't believe that Matthew would let even his near father-in-law in on this. But Llewellyn undoubtedly found out about our lease application some way or other. It's terrible that someone would be able to do this. On the other hand, Leonard is probably a shrewd judge of coal properties and his interest has to be encouraging, albeit threatening.

Phillip Anschultz's words, "Protect your ass, Jim," kept slipping back into James' consciousness.

Soon the magnificent scenery—the rugged Wet Mountains on the left and the towering Sangre de Cristos on the right—cleansed his mind of these disturbing thoughts. Travel was easy on his horse—a big gray—seeming to welcome the exercise after the idle time on the Royal Gorge plateau. A good horse, he had decided; not quite like Coalfire, but I'll keep her. The animal was fairly heavily laden, double-thick bedroll, tarps, duffel bag, goatskin water bags, two rifles, and emergency rations for both horse and rider. To give both himself and his horse a break, James dismounted and walked about a quarter of the way each day.

All day he had traveled up along the ore-wagon road following Texas Creek, crossing over several dry (or nearly so) tributary creeks. In mid-afternoon the main creek bed veered right, up the slope, towards its source, leaving the road to pick its own route south. James veered a little himself, spotting a likely grouse thicket up the slope. Three birds richer, he rejoiced in being able to postpone dried meat a day or two.

In late afternoon when he was about to make camp, he came upon a small community that he had not expected to still exist. As James had heard the story from General Palmer, a large and industrious group of German settlers out of Chicago built the town of Colfax on Grape Creek near the toe of the Sangre de Cristo Mountains. It was good fertile land, semiarid, but laced with creeks that were easily ditched to the fields. The colonists soon found, however, that it was very difficult to get by without a means of shipping their produce. And, just when it appeared that things were getting a little better, an accidental but devastating explosion of a dynamite cache in the back room of the general store decimated the town, killed some settlers of the failing colony, and discouraged most of the rest. Some scattered to eke out a living on the land; others returned to Chicago. It was a case of the colony being ten years too early, or General Palmer's "vision" that much too late.

Riding into town, James observed it to be it to be a functioning entity, a store, a blacksmith, and surprisingly a barber. But not surprising, a saloon. The latter was just a place—four walls, roof, dirt floor, and small bar. The proprietor of that enterprise was several years past his prime—in fact, time may have stood still for him since the explosion—but friendly and helpful to a fault.

"Yes, big guy, we have beer—and here it is—not very cold, but us Germans like it warm. And yes, we ain't very busy, but times are getting better. And no, the town doesn't have a name yet. Some are calling it Silvercliffe—did you see that silver mine over on the rock outcrop next to town? I hear they're down about twenty feet and assaying pretty good. We get supplies in here and to the store about once a week—it was once a month a while ago. And do I know anything about the trails around here? Yes, I do—but I've never taken any. Where did you say you wanted to go?"

"Trinidad." Seeing no immediate comprehension, James continued, "It's a little pueblo town down below the Spanish Peaks."

"Oh, yes, I remember now. We, the Colfax Colonization Company, two hundred fifty strong, come out to Fort Lyons in fifty-nine. That's pretty close to Trinidad. We come by train that far, then switched to covered wagons, six mules each, up Hardscrabble Canyon through the Wets and over near here. Military escort the whole way— the damned Indians, you know. If we coulda kept them mules and wagons we might have done all right. But we couldn't get supplies in nor products out and the frost was like somethin' we never seen, even in Chicago..."

"And the trails over to Trinidad?" James tried to keep on subject.

"Here's a guy who can really help." The barkeep beckoned to a work-hardened youngish man who had just come in. "Hey, David, come over and give some directions to this gent. By the way, how'd the diggin' go today?"

"Pretty good. We're going to get an ore wagon out of here this week. Where'd you like to go, mister?"

"Somewhere around Trinidad. Do you know the country?"

"Hell, yes. Like the back of my hand. I can't say I've taken *every* trail, though. I've worked the mines all the way from Oro City to Engle—from gold to coal, and believe me, I know the difference. They can shove that black stuff up all their asses for all I care. You're an old man at thirty and dead at forty—that is, if you're not in an explosion before then.

"The quickest route, and I don't know it well, goes south from here about thirty or forty miles to the Huerfano River. This time of year you should have no trouble fording it. Then you bend southeast to the Cucharas River and on over to Walsenburg. They say there's good hunting around the Huerfano. Right now there's no snow, but if you go that way watch the sky."

James wished these guys would take a breath now and then, but maybe you get this way when you never see anyone from outside. He waited for an opening and quickly said, "For my money, any kind of hunting is 'good hunting.'"

"You've got my vote there, big guy, so—good hunting."

◇◇◇◇◇◇◇◇◇◇◇◇

Opting for what sounded like the fastest route to Trinidad, James headed south for the Huerfano. Seeing Lillian after an absence of seven months was uppermost in his mind and the status of the saloon project a poor second. He had every confidence that Lillian could hold her own with the Grand Union people, but nevertheless...he also thought that something should be forthcoming from the Lands Department with respect to the DelAgua leases.

The ride was not difficult, the terrain rising to the divide between the Arkansas and Huerfano watersheds. The trail at that point was nearly invisible. As predicted by the hard-rock miner at Silvercliffe, the forested Huerfano river valley was truly a small-game paradise.

He had hardly forded the river than he encountered a small hunting party—possibly Kiowa and an apparently frustrated one at that. The half-dozen braves gathered around the gigantic white man, admiring his equipment and his haul. Prudently certain that the Kiowa needed his saddle-load of game greater than he, James used his mixed Kiowa and sign to offer his entire bag—less one bird for dinner. All gratefully and peaceably received.

At the Cucharas River he came upon the D&RG tracks leading westward. The rails were shiny enough to suggest recent travel on the La Veta route, either with construction materials west or produce east. Either way it was good news, he thought, and encouraging enough to get him to turn towards Walsenburg and the station telegraph. More good news—there_was freight and passenger service to and from Fort Garland and completion to Alamosa was no more than a couple months away.

"They're still sending steel rails west," the station master said, "and about two trains a week bring potatoes and apples and such stuff this way from the Cucharas and San Luis Valleys. And, say, is your name James? You answer the description. Here's a letter for you from Mr. Molyneaux. He left it when he passed through last July."

So it's *Mister*, marveled James.

In deciding on the Walsenburg route, James at first thought he might drop over to La Veta to check on Matt but now that was no longer necessary. Obviously, things went well. He opened the letter.

July 5

Dear Bro,

    I'm finished at La Veta. General Palmer wants me to do some financial things in Denver. I'm on my way there, now, after spending a few days in Trinidad to drop off our wagon and pick up some city clothes.

    The La Veta job went well. The first day I got everyone's attention. To his misfortune, the superintendent got in the way of the pick handle that you insisted I have at hand. I guess I hit him too hard. Anyway, it inspired the track-layers to really put out—they called themselves the "Pick-handle Gang" after that.

    You'll see in the stuff on our desk in Trinidad that we've started moving on the tobacco wholesaling thing. We'll get our first small trial shipment next month. Whichever one of us is around can try to find some buyers. I guess DelAgua is coming along, but have you given a thought as to how we will finance digging a mine?

Matthew

◇◇◇◇◇◇◇◇◇◇◇◇

Like a magnet, the closer James got to Trinidad, the greater the pull. He would spend some time with Lillian—and then some more time with Lillian, part of which to go over the saloon project.

Passing DelAgua Canyon he rode up far enough to see that nothing was going on—at least superficially. The corner marker that he and Jack Meadows had placed seemed to be undisturbed. So far, so good, James concluded.

Trinidad looked bigger, somehow. After the better part of a year in the backcountry it seemed a city, in fact. A bath, shave, trim, and change of clothes made James a new man. He made a beeline to the Columbian, first meeting Mike who seemed a little standoffish, but finally produced a little bark. Where have you been for eight months, the big animal seemed to be asking, and do you know how many years that is in dog time? But Lillian wasn't standoffish at all. In fact, had James been a normal mortal he would have had a crushed ribcage.

"I'm glad to see you, too, Lil." He ducked the bar-rag shied at his head. Mike growled.

"Damn, it's good to be back where things are normal." This time James grabbed *her*. "I really did miss you, Lillian. Things are pretty lonesome out there on the plateau. Say, I think you've gotten prettier—and certainly livelier." One hand had worked its way up her split skirt only to find itself imprisoned by her tightening thighs.

"This is all very well, James, but my customers haven't paid for this extra entertainment. If you think you can pull yourself away, let's go in the office, I've got a million things to go over with you."

"That, too."

"Now back to where we were," he said, as they entered the office.

"Not there yet...not quite...*there*. Oh, James, I'm so glad you're back."

"So—you've been working things out with the architect?" He moved behind her and pulled off her blouse.

"Yes, and with Mr. Hepplewhite, as well. The architect's kind of tough but Gregory's a cream puff. You're not listening, Jim." She turned and pulled off his shirt.

James arched his eyebrows. "So it's 'Gregory,' is it?" Off went her skirt and that French thing underneath.

"Of course—and we've got most everything we want. And it's not going to cost nearly what we thought. The Grand Union will do all of the insides except specialties and built-ins."

Down went his trousers.

"Here we are, bare-assed naked again, Jim. You're so predictable." Lillian leaned back, appreciating James in all his unclothed glory. "Well, what are you waiting for?"

◇◇◇◇◇◇◇◇◇◇◇◇

"As I started to say before that pleasant interruption, it sounds good," a satiated James said. "Matt and I knew that you were the one to do the negotiating. What's the status? Coming in I noticed a lot of construction work over there.

"Do you plan to put some clothes on, Lillian? Although I could sit here and look at your beautiful body all day."

"I have a pretty good picture of the hotel project from spending hours with the architects. I could almost do it myself. I now know the difference between a threshold and a lintel, between a joist and a rafter, between a plinth block and a...oh, whatever that was—and much more. Anyway, the building will take up all of that corner. It will have three stories but the bottom floor will be double height to accommodate mezzanines in both the hotel lobby and the saloon-restaurant areas. The lobby and restaurant will face on Commercial Street and the saloon on Main. There will be doors between the lobby and restaurant, saloon and restaurant, and lobby and saloon, a gentlemen's club, and more."

"When will all of this happen?"

"Gregory—that is, Mr. Hepplewhite—says it'll take a few more months. He also says they may put in an elevator off of the lobby. He said the first lift for passengers was installed in New York twenty years ago and they've improved a lot since then. Wouldn't it be great to beat Denver with the first elevator in Colorado?

"You're not listening again, James—God, you're as randy as an old goat.

"Oh, and I almost forgot. Your brother was here a couple months ago. He dropped in—but didn't even get past Mike. For some unknown reason that dog has taken an enormous dislike to him. Matthew didn't have time for a drink and wasn't a whit interested in our saloon project. He was in a hurry to get over to see his girlfriend, Sophia. You know, James, that 'girl' is a little older than she looks and has had a lot more experience than she lets on."

"What makes you think that?"

"Women, and especially those in my former profession, just *know* those kinds of things, Jim. She wasn't put in an Eastern 'finishing school' for nothing, you can be sure. I'm told it's the next closest thing to a chastity belt. I heard—and you know we hear a lot in this place—that she was getting involved with one of the 'locals,'" this with a knowing smile.

"So Matt's buying into a set-up, you're suggesting?"

"You can call it anything you want, but to me it's clear that the Llewellyns see in Matt a happy solution to a problem. I don't imagine they spent much time positioning you as a suitor."

With a puzzled frown James said, "I'm not sure how to take that."

She pulled him over towards her, "Just joking, you big lunker."

"By the way, can you ride a horse?" James asked.

"This is a helluva time to ask that—but yes, I can, sort of."

"Try to get someone to watch the bar sometime next week, or the week after. I want to take you up to see your coal mine."

"My what? Oh, never mind. We can talk about that later. Now, do I leave them off or put them on? Say, Jim, if I move to one of those islands where they don't wear anything at all—would you follow me?"

"Follow you? Hell, I'll go first and check it out. Now, just lie back and do nothing—this one's on me."

◇◇◇◇◇◇◇◇◇◇◇◇◇

They were lying there, talking softly about mixing business with pleasure and pleasure with business, when James said, "I'm sure, Lillian, that you think I'm only interested in sex…"

"So what's worse to think about—sex or business?"

"When I'm out on the prairie I think of you, my saloon business partner and how we'll build it up together…"

"That's business."

"But then I get excited."

"What's 'excited'?"

"You know…"

"Oh, *that*. Well, I guess that's sex."

"And then I think of you, my saloon partner, and how we'll develop it together…"

"That certainly is business, but I guess you get 'excited'? The picture is starting to come together."

"But strangest of all, I think of real estate and I see us, you and me, buying a house together…and…"

There was no reply. Lillian had slipped on her clothes and with a tear running down her cheek, turned towards the door.

"Lillian, wait a minute. What did I say to hurt you? I wouldn't do that for the world, honestly."

"Nothing. Nothing at all—it's just I can't joke about some things. Good night."

James took both her hands in his. "Lillian, my darling, now I get it. I was being flippant about a matter that is very important to you. And let me tell you that it is important to me, too."

"No, Jim, it's all right, I was just tired."

"Please let me finish. Lillian, I think about you all day, every day, and dream about you every night. You are part of my very being—the very biggest part. I need you; I want to share my life with you forever. I want to love you forever, but wanting is not committing. Love is committing and it is all consuming." He kissed the palms of both her hands, "I beg you, please wait for me until I've resolved a few last distractions."

"James Molyneaux, I will wait forever—if I have to."

◇◇◇◇◇◇◇◇◇◇◇◇

After dropping in on Mr. Hepplewhite—mostly to find out if he really *did* look like a cream puff—James crossed Main Street to see Frederick Josephson, Matt's land lawyer.

"I'm happy to meet you, Mr. Molyneaux. Your timing is extraordinary. The approved DelAgua Canyon lease applications just came in today."

"All six?"

"Actually, seven. The extra one will contain, in addition to a potential mine site, the common facilities like screening, cleaning, and classification facilities, rail spurs, office, shops, workers' houses, and so on. It will be in the middle of the other six parcels, two to the north and the other four south.

"A partnership agreement and resolution will be required. Your brother liked CCC as lessee of parcel seven and I'm drafting these documents accordingly.

"And here are the individual lease applications, each with one hundred thirty-eight acres, one-thousand-foot frontage, five-thousand-foot depth, and subsurface rights to the east. They are for you, your brother, Mrs. Lillian Wilson, Mr. Jack Meadows, Mrs. William Wilcox, and Mr. Phillip Anschultz. Is this correct?"

"Well...so far. Will you tell me what each leaseholder is to do, now?"

Speaking with authority, Josephson said, "Matthew was here just a few weeks ago and we discussed the leases and the partnership agreement that I am in the process of preparing. He understands it all."

"But I don't. So will you please outline for me your thoughts relating to the partnership agreement, as well as what the leaseholders must do now. And should they be told what's going on?"

"I really don't think that should be necessary, nor is a detailed discussion at this time. But, if you insist, I can give you a general idea of the provisions that your brother and I discussed."

"I *insist*—so please do."

"Well, each of the seven leases, once registered, can be sold or transferred only with great difficulty—that's the law. The specific parcel for each leaseholder was determined by lot for each one before submitting the applications. There will be six partners, plus the holder of the seventh parcel, each with equal rights and responsibilities, and each obliged to sell all of his produced coal to the partnership at the very minimal value of one dollar a ton—adjustable with majority vote—less the one-eighth share government royalty. The partnership will pay equal dividends—after expenses—to each partner regardless of the production from his individual holding, even though there may be none at all.

"The partnership will name the 'Colorado Coal Company' as shareholder, and developer of Parcel Seven and recipient of four-eights of the proceeds of the enterprise. The first shaft will be named the 'El Sobrante Mine.'" Josephson stood, closing his notepad to signify the end of the discussion.

James continued sitting, clearly indicating that he had something to say. "As I understand what you are saying, each leaseholder has applied for and received a DelAgua Canyon lease—admittedly with your help—and certain rights. It is not up to the rest of us to restrict those rights. At the outset, each leaseholder, including me, should have the choice to join the partnership or not. If not, he should be able to sell any raw coal that he will have produced independently, to the partnership at an agreed-to price, or crush and size it himself for sale on the open market.

"Most important, I'm not willing to blindly give Colorado Coal Company—and that's wholly owned by Leonard Llewellyn—or anyone else, one-half of our enterprise without knowing exactly what we're getting, and when. After the partnership has been formed it can pass a resolution to invite CCC or anyone else to submit a development proposal. Maybe we can find someone who will do it for two-eights or even nothing at all. And as unthinkable as it may seem to you, some of the leaseholders might prefer to go it alone. So it is up to you to draft an agreement that benefits everyone. Will you please add wording that will do all this."

"I don't know that I should. Your brother saw and approved the outline I described."

James stood to his full height with eyebrows in a tight "V." "Well, I didn't and I don't. Just add these provisions, *if you please!*"

◇◇◇◇◇◇◇◇◇◇◇◇

Eight weeks and as many storms, rain, sleet, and snow passed. A ride in the country for a picnic luncheon was always a fine attraction, and combined with an opportunity to view some properties, this one was an irresistible invitation enthusiastically accepted by the invitee. It was a nice day, a little cold, with a few fluffy clouds in sight over the Spanish Peaks, those lofty twins named Huajatolla or Two Breasts by the Indians. Nothing threatening, though—the next storm would be at least a couple days away. James rode Coalfire up Main Street towards the Columbian, with the big gray he had ridden down from Texas Creek on lead. He had fashioned a nosegay of juniper berries, a mistletoe sprig, and red ribbon and tied it to the pommel of the gray—about the only materials available in early winter.

Lillian was waiting, dressed, like James, for an active day but with some heavy outerwear to tie behind the saddle.

"All I could find this morning is a Western-style saddle," said James. "Can you handle that?"

"No problem. I'm wearing a divided skirt—you know the one, Jim—and winter-weight bloomers."

318

She swung into the saddle, jostling the "bouquet" a little. "What's this?"

"A belated Merry Christmas, darling. "This big gray mare is yours to keep"

Lillian could hardly breathe or speak for a few seconds. "This is the nicest gift I've ever received, James. Thank you—she's beautiful. What's her name?"

"She's yours to name."

"She's not really gray—she's closer to silver. I'll call her Silver Trove, my treasure."

After a couple of hours at a brisk pace, they turned into DelAgua Canyon, following the creek westward for about a mile before dismounting to stretch and eat the lunch that Maude had prepared. "Lillian," James said, "we're sitting just about where the coal-processing facilities will be located. The individual parcels stretch along the creek, two on the creek line eastward towards the railroad. The other four are on that same line westward, but the creek starts to curve a little bit north of west..."

Lillian interrupted, "I see how it is. So at each parcel, where the hillside comes down to the flat..."

James put in, "That's called the 'toe' of the hill."

"If that's so, where's the heel?...but anyway...at that point they dig?"

"What they do is drive a tunnel straight in or dig a shaft straight down. If the coal bed down there has folded upward with the rest of the rock and overburden, the tunnel will reach it sooner or later—but if the coal bed is still down there, lying level like when it was made, the shaft will reach it and then they'll drive tunnels out from there."

"But how do you know there's any coal there?" asked a curious but perplexed Lillian.

"We don't. Anyway, your parcel is the second one over—it starts from where you can see the big rocks and stretches over about a thousand feet."

"James, you're crazy as a loon. If you don't know whether there's coal here or not, why not dig down in the basement of the Columbian? It would be easier—there're no rocks in the way. Or at least dig a small hole out here to see what's down below."

"Lillian, you're wonderful—how do you know all this? You should have been a geologist. Or at least a cesspool locator. As soon as we finish the paperwork, we'll follow your advice to a tee. But don't bet your dowry on it. At this point it's only wishful thinking."

"And what 'dowry' is that?"

"Just an imaginary object—sort of like a sweet young thing waiting for her knight errant. Seriously, though, I hope you're enjoying this little outing."

"Seriously, I am. It's the first date I've had in a spell."

"You ride quite well, I'm glad to see. As they say in horse circles, you have a nice seat."

"You mean, a hard butt? Okay, I've seen the mine site—it's exciting enough but I'll put my 'dowry' thing on the New Columbian. I don't have to dig a hole to find out how thirsty and lecherous men can be."

◇◇◇◇◇◇◇◇◇◇◇◇

Walking over to the offices of Molyneaux and Molyneaux, Counselors, James was deeply disturbed over the DelAgua situation. How'n hell did Llewellyn's Colorado Coal Company get in on the act, and essentially as a leaseholder, no less? At the very most they might be identified as a potential development contractor—not a leaseholder. And what else is there about this that I don't know? What's Matt up to? Shit, he's marrying the whole Llewellyn family. His wife will manage his life and his father-in-law the business.

Well, all I can do, he thought, is to insist on a fair partnership agreement. I'll talk to my potential allies and get some opinions. What I would really like to do, though, is take Phillip up to DelAgua and poke around a little—maybe see if this whole thing is worth worrying about.

When he got to the office, James pushed open the door against an accumulation of letters and advertisements that had been dropped through the door slot. Matt had gotten a couple of desks and chairs, two kerosene lamps and a stove. And upstairs there were some sparsely furnished living quarters.

With a pile of paper on one desk, it looked almost like a real office. On top of the pile was an unopened letter from Matt.

November 20

Dear Bro,

> *Congratulate me, big brother, Sophia has agreed to marry me. It'll be in the spring. It'll be a busy year. I'm going to bid on the Marshall Pass railroad project— Leonard tells me it's a shoo-in. Also, he mentioned that Denver is pleased with what you did at Royal Gorge despite being a little cautious at times. Speaking of Denver, I'm there now. I came up from Trinidad in July. We seem to be passing each other in the dark.*

Matt

P.S. I've been asked to serve as a Trinidad City Alderman. Maybe Leonard talked to someone.

◇◇◇◇◇◇◇◇◇◇◇◇

James and Phillip Anschultz left Trinidad at first light, each with double bed roll and provisions, James with compass and the Las Animas County plat, Phillip with shovel, pick-axe, and auger. He's really getting down to basics, James thought. He had included Phillip, the Engle coal mine superintendent, in the group of lease applicants for two reasons, first because he was a good friend, but mostly to have the benefit of some real coal-mining expertise. Phillip, about ten years senior to James, had worked down-pit in a primitive Pennsylvania coal mine—one still using children to muck out the low-headroom coal faces. Disgusted with the working conditions and the ignorance of the mine overseers and under-lookers, he made his way over to the fledgling Missouri School of Mines. Three years at Rolla prepared him for Palmer's Colorado and Iron Company, where he soon found himself developing and then operating the Engleville facility.

It should take the better part of two days, James thought, to make a very general assessment of the canyon. While riding along, he filled Phillip in on the status of DelAgua Canyon Partners and particularly on the potential participation by Llewellyn's coal company.

"I have to tell you, Jim, I really appreciate being included in this project, but I'm disturbed that Llewellyn might be in on it, also. You know how I feel about him."

"Believe me, Phillip, I share your concern that Llewellyn may slip in—I don't trust him, either. Somehow it got out of hand between Matt and the lawyer—I was away too long. I've talked to the lawyer, but I won't know if it has done any good until I've talked to Matt, as well. All I can do is try to be sure that the partnership agreement protects everyone. Moreover, the fact that Llewellyn apparently wants to be involved could suggest that he knows something we don't. And we *do* need development money."

"Actually, I have no right to say anything," said Phillip. "I'm only in this through your generosity. I have everything to gain and nothing to lose, but you seemed to be asking for an opinion."

"As a leaseholder, Phillip, you have every right to speak up. On top of that, you're the only one of the six of us who knows anything about coal. We're all equal partners and I'll do my damnedest to keep it that way."

They turned into the canyon, following the arroyo westward. The snow from a storm the week before had melted, except for some caps on the little hills on both sides of DelAgua and Berwind Canyons and a few patches in sheltered parts of the watersheds.

"Here we are, Phillip, and buried right about here is our survey marker. We're talking six parcels, plus one plot for common facilities, one-thousand-foot frontage each, east of a line right up the middle of this little valley—about at the center line of the arroyo.

There will be four parcels east of the stake, the common area at the stake, and two to the west. Each parcel will extend well beyond the toe of the eastern slope—all the way over to the D&RG property. Mine is the first up from the marker, yours the third. The question is—does it make any sense? As you can see from this county plat, we're on nearly a straight line between Engle and Walsen and only a little offset from Cañon."

"I can say this—right off the top," Phillip declared. "This terrain looks good, just like Walsen and a little like Engle, but that doesn't ever tell the whole story. I think the first thing we should do is look all around for any sign that the ground has been disturbed by someone taking samples or cores. It's pretty difficult to keep secrets in this business."

They spent the rest of the day crisscrossing the area, one mile north and one south of the marker and about a mile into the hillsides. Other than a few rocky outcrops worthy of closer examination, there was nothing of interest. No sign was good sign, they reasoned—no disturbed ground, no wagon tracks, no stakes, no hoof- or footprints. And then—not more than a hundred yards north of the marker—a faint but unmistakable wagon-wheel mark.

"And look here, Jim, I think this was a core sample. See, it's perfectly round—about six inches diameter—and carefully disguised with a piece of sod from someplace. *Somebody* knows more than we do."

After a cold dinner and a very cold night—a seven-thousand-foot winter night—they were more than eager to start poking around the next morning. But no more wagon tracks, anywhere. The outcrops yielded no useful information, so they turned their attention to the arroyo walls, deeply eroded, hopefully in places where rock strata might be visible. Both Berwind and DelAgua Creeks were running, handicapping their investigation.

"We shouldn't allow ourselves to be too optimistic about finding any more real evidence, Jim. Coal occurs in beds, and while some beds are near the surface, others can be hundreds of feet down. And some beds are thick enough for more than one working level. In areas like this, the rolling hills we see were probably formed when the earth's crust was pushed into folds. So you're as likely to find a particular seam on top of a hill as in a depression. Down at Engle, the beds or veins are all quite level and not very deep, and the same thing at Walsen, I believe. Hopefully, under this layer of plain dark dirt—and we don't how thick this layer may be—might be a two- or three-foot layer of a light gray to white shale and under that a foot or so of gray clay or soapstone. And under that some coal—maybe. If not coal, then perhaps coal's usual companions, shale or clay. I don't think, though, that this arroyo is anywhere near deep enough to expose meaningful strata, unless the beds are close to the surface."

They spent until mid-afternoon scratching and digging with pick and shovel, and occasionally with the small auger. They did find some gray shale-like material—and lots of it—in the bottom of the arroyo under a few inches of sand and silt. But no clay.

"Well that's it, I'm afraid, James. Inconclusive, except for the indication that someone else has been here. Funny—that hole's on your brother's parcel."

"Very disturbing. Anyway, Phillip, thanks for your effort."

"No. Thank *you*, Jim, for giving me a shot at it—and you know, there's more to look at. The leases haven't cost anything yet—except for the lawyer. If the leaseholders would all chip in we could have a few test holes drilled. I could find out how much that would cost—without tipping our hand. But if you can't manage to keep Colorado Coal Company and Llewellyn out until they're invited in by vote of the partners, then I for one am out."

"I feel the same way. But we can't just quit. No matter how many leaseholders would be left, whether one or more, Llewellyn would simply find someone else to grab up the discarded holdings. Remember, too, Llewellyn probably has some friends in high places."

"Then what do you think we should do?"

"I think we should hold on and try to make the agreement right. But, if we don't get our way, we probably should ultimately join and even court CCC—if that's the only way to develop the properties. I'll sound out the other leaseholders.

"One thing you might think about, Phillip. We both know that Palmer is a railroad man—not coal or steel. And Llewellyn is not a railroad person. For one thing, he went to school up at Golden and D&RG's new steel mill near Pueblo is his baby. Now, it's common knowledge that General Palmer is splitting his coal and steel interests away from D&RG and forming a new firm, Colorado Coal and Iron. Suppose this new CC&I should merge with Llewellyn's CCC? It's a natural—Llewellyn's always been Palmer's fair-haired boy. I can attest to that. You, as a mine superintendent for the new CC&I must keep this in mind as you agree or disagree with Llewellyn. As you said to me a while back, 'protect your ass.'"

◇◇◇◇◇◇◇◇◇◇◇◇

Later that week, James dropped in on a very busy Jack Meadows, who seemed to be doing the design work for most of the new homes up on Aristocracy Hill.

"Hello, James. Shipped your llamas in yet?"

"Not yet. I'm trying to find some that understand English. Which brings me to the point of my visit. We, the DelAgua Partners-to-be, will soon be presented with partnership papers written in *legal* English—which even the most domesticated llamas cannot possibly understand." James went on to describe the work the lawyer Josephson was doing for the project. Meadows didn't seem to share Phillip's concern over Llewellyn, and James didn't feel it proper to press his own feelings in the matter.

Jack offered to locate the near corners for the leaseholders and to assist Anschultz with locating the exploratory holes at the appropriate time.

From Jack, James learned that a new coal mine with company town was being developed less than five miles south of Trinidad and exactly on line of his Walsen-to-Engle line. "They hired me to help lay out the little town and facilities," said Meadows. "When I go back over there, I'll very casually ask the guy in charge exactly how they went about finding out where to go in with the shaft. I'll find out if they did some core drillings and, if they did, who did it, how much, and all of that. Since you'll be in Denver, I'll pass on the information to Anschultz."

◇◇◇◇◇◇◇◇◇◇◇◇

It was fortunate that James had taken care of the Trinidad loose ends; a telegram transcription was delivered to the office.

> WESTERN UNION
> JAMES MOLYNEAUX TRINIDAD MAR 15
> SOMETHING HAS COME UP NEED YOU IN DENVER
> FIRST WEEK APRIL THEN TO TEXAS CREEK STOP
> EVEN EARLIER IF POSSIBLE STOP REPLY SOONEST
> STOP PALMER

Well, here I am, connected to those goddamn wires again, James lamented. And this was supposed to be a free country. No one saw me pick this up, so 'soonest' is the day after next week—or so. On the other hand, Palmer pays well—so maybe...

James's last order of business had been to open a Columbian Partners drawing account with the agreed-to startup funds from his and Matt's joint family account. This should keep Lillian going, James thought. However, there wasn't much of a balance left in the family account and James' attitude towards Denver suddenly shifted a little.

James went over to the Columbian for his good-byes, taking the rest of the week in the process.

◇◇◇◇◇◇◇◇◇◇◇◇

Arriving in Denver, James had hardly removed his hat before he was ushered into Palmer's office.

"Here's what you are to do, James."

"And 'good morning' to you, sir," James ventured.

Ignoring this breach of discipline (it wouldn't have been like this in Tennessee, Palmer was thinking), he said, "I want you to stop Santa Fe again—only this time don't be afraid of a little bloodshed. You will first stop them at the point of their construction—which is almost to the West Portal, I think. Then you will have other elements of your party in place ready to enter the gorge at any convenient and strategic downstream location. We'll have our forces ready to quickly step into place and secure our rights to positions reluctantly vacated by Santa Fe."

Seeing an obviously perplexed James, the General continued, "We have information leading us to believe that the U.S. Supreme Court will soon—in a month or so—hand down a decision in our favor granting us prior rights in the gorge. Experts tell us that this is a clear and unmistakable point of law and the court really has no choice. However, it is thought that the opinion will be very narrow and not address the lease problem at all. We will win and lose at the same time. But we also think that the San Luis District Court is almost ready to enjoin Santa Fe from operating anywhere in Colorado on a capitalization technicality. Privately, I do not believe that this ruling will stand up, but it will give us the opportunity to move in with preemptive action.

"So, in addition to your force at Texas Creek, we will have others at Trinidad, Pueblo, Cañon City, Alamosa, and Denver to take back our lines, stations, and rolling stock the minute the San Luis message is flashed. At every location we will have writs and sheriffs to legitimize our actions. All clear?"

"Sounds all right. How many men will I have?"

"That's up to you. What do you think you'll need?"

James ran that question around in his mind, then said, "As you know better than I, General, the 'Arkansas River Canyon' above the West Portal is vastly different from the Royal Gorge. Instead of one- or two-thousand-foot canyon walls, we're looking at fifty feet or less, and the canyon passes through a rugged area, rolling hills and lots of rocky outcrops. There are many points of access from either rim, and the canyon itself is rather easily traversed. It would take an army to stop Santa Fe once it emerges from the Royal Gorge but it *should* be possible to effectively stop construction—for a time—wherever the work is between the canyon rims."

"I can see what you mean," said Palmer, "and the tracks *must* run close to the river most of the time, otherwise the grading job would be impossible."

James continued, "I think that a single impregnable barrier at river's edge, protected by highly mobile rifle squads along both canyon rims, starting as far eastward as possible, would keep Santa Fe's tracks out of Texas City as long as you would need—but not forever. Not only would the riflemen protect the barricade from attack from the high ground, they might be able to provide some construction harassment as well."

"You paint a pretty good picture, James," the General said. "Now the question, again. How many men?

"I think we should have about seventy men at Texas Creek—half mounted sharpshooters, the rest 'roughnecks' with pick-axe handles and back-up rifles. At the gorge, two or three squads of ten expert riflemen each, all mounted. Side arms, if any, will be kept in bedrolls—not worn. We will establish a number of high-ground sniper's nests which, together with mounted riflemen, will protect our rear. Our canyon teams will be used to annoy and intimidate Santa Fe people down below—strictly hit-and-run tactics. Since that operation will be ten or fifteen miles from base camp, we will need a cook wagon—perhaps one on each side of the river. I think that's it, but we need communications. I wonder if there's a telegraph anywhere—say in Cotopaxi?"

"I think so...you've got it, James. I'll send a senior clerk with you over to the D&RG roundhouse to arrange for supplies and transport. My aide here will help you select people. We have lists of those whom we've recruited before."

James turned to leave but not before a final word from the General. "I'd like you in position as soon as possible, but no Santa Fe contact until you hear from me. We must wait for the Supreme Court decision. Incidentally, you just missed your brother. He left here two weeks ago with a couple of our lawyers for San Luis. They're going to try to talk to the circuit court judge about Santa Fe's breach of some of the lease provisions."

"I was hoping to see Matt here—we've some personal business to take care of. But first things first, I guess."

"I don't think this will take very long, James. I've something else cooking that I can't talk about just yet, but I think everything will be cleared up by early fall. Matt will be back in Denver in a couple of weeks. If there's a lull at Texas Creek, maybe you could get over here for a short visit. And if you happen to be in Pueblo, you might drop in on Leonard. He won't be doing anything in the gorge this time—he's tied up with the new steel mill in Bessemer."

To himself James complained, there's just too damned much going on in this big business world—it will be good to get out in the field again—but he had a nagging feeling that things would be considerably different this time around. We stopped Santa Fe cold at the Narrows—with a minimum of direct confrontation and no serious casualties—by outsmarting and out-bluffing them and by establishing some near-impregnable defensive positions. Did Palmer really understand just how strong we were, or was he overwhelmed by negative reports from Llewellyn? It seemed, at the time, that D&RG was much too responsive to the court order that caused us to shut down and pull out. And the way Santa Fe's hundreds and hundreds of construction workers and armed guards literally swarmed into the gorge on our heels made me wonder just who in Denver was talking to whom. Santa Fe moved so quickly to get track to Parkdale.

◇◇◇◇◇◇◇◇◇◇◇◇

James split his force into three groups to take different routes into the Wet Mountains Valley, Hardscrabble, Grape Creek, and the Huerfano River. In addition, he spread them out over a two-week period. This was all designed to attract as little attention as possible. He led the first group up Hardscrabble over to Silvercliffe and then north to a point about three miles downstream of Texas Creek. It was an ideal place for a base camp—an impregnable barrier to Santa Fe construction, access to the towns of Cotopaxi and Texas Creek, and a good base for downstream strike teams. The last contingent to arrive brought the news from Denver that other D&RG forces were in place—in Trinidad to move north, Denver to move south, Alamosa to move east, and Pueblo to move in any direction. The Texas Creek group's mission was to stop Santa Fe construction up the Arkansas and to harass work crews in the canyon.

As the men straggled in, James started to organize his people—barricade riflemen, strike crews, fortifications, and support. Pete Warren and Sam Alexander, squad leaders at the gorge, were with him again and he appointed them lieutenants for this new operation. "Like before," James told them, "we're not out here to kill or be killed. We have a few dozen brake clubs and a bunch of billy clubs with our gear and that's what we'll use first. We're going to win this thing and do it without anyone getting killed.

"Now you know this area better even than I. I'll give you the general objective and you two will work it out. Santa Fe has construction forces in the gorge; when we pulled out, they came right behind us."

"Too bad—we had it locked up. We could have stood them off for months."

"So we'll have to do it again. We'll send out scouts to see exactly how far Santa Fe has advanced. Denver would like us to stop Santa Fe inside the West Portal—that's the best defensive spot—but construction may be much too far along. Here in the field we must be realistic, even though Denver may not be so inclined. Let me give you my slant on a strategy for this operation. First, I certainly could be wrong, but I think this will be a very short affair—a matter of days, I believe, once it gets started. We want to impede the construction, shoot their horses and mules, put some bullet holes in their water kegs, kick up some dust, and make a lot of noise. But then we had better get the hell out and retire to a *protected barricade* in a location of our choosing. I think I've found such a place. I'd like you both to see it and give me your opinions.

"As I look at it, our main camp, kitchen, supplies cache, and reserves should be about two miles north and east of Texas Creek. Our main fort—with fifty riflemen—will be down in the canyon just a short distance east of the main camp. The place I have in mind for that is a large ledge that sticks out on the north side of the river's edge about one-half mile below the site for our main camp. We might build tiered breastworks to accommodate up to fifty riflemen totally in command of the river. In addition, we could have five or six sniper's nests on both sides of the river, giving absolute downstream cover for about one-half mile below the fort. These nests would have in-depth protection from behind and a protected corridor for supplies and fall-back, if necessary. I don't expect a shot to be fired from these nests." This raised some eyebrows.

"Yes, that's right. The sniper's nests are for protecting our own people in the canyon, our barricade fighters with cudgels—pick handles and brake clubs—who will make their stand at river's edge just below the bulwark we build. We will pair up; every man with a cudgel will have a buddy with a rifle at his back—strategically placed. At the first sign of a firearm being raised on the other side, all unarmed men will take cover and retreat to the barricade where their own rifles are stashed. Their covering riflemen will move up and take over. In addition, there will be squads of mounted riflemen on both sides of the Arkansas to protect our backs as well as to impede the construction people."

"Could I make a suggestion?" This was from Pete. "How about some mounted strike teams of riflemen to harass them farther downstream, maybe from one or more of the side canyons we found before—hit-and-run tactics?"

"Sounds good. Take a look at it," said James. "But remember, Santa Fe has control of the gorge pretty well up to the West Portal. Its men are probably swarming all over the north rim plateau all the way up to Parkdale and are not likely to be caught sleeping again."

Sam added a comment. "I recall a creek, I think they called it Copper Gulch, coming in to the south side of the river just across from our old Camp C site, about a mile below Parkdale. Maybe we could make a strike from there. The river would protect us from direct attack; anyone trying to ford it would be a sitting duck. We could retreat up the Copper Creek bed and then back to Texas Creek."

"We have to be careful not to get trapped down there. It'll have to be a quick hit and run," said Pete, "but it would be very disturbing to Santa Fe if we could pull it off."

"I'm all for it," said James, "but I think we should confine our freelance activities to one or two days, at most, and then fall back to provide support at our barricade. We'll have to see how this plays out; conditions might dictate our taking a different approach.

"Pete, you have the north side of the Arkansas, and Sam, you the south. I'll command the fort. You'll each need a commissary wagon about halfway to the portal. When the action starts, send runners back very frequently so I can make adjustments in manpower as necessary. And as I said before, hold your fire until Santa Fe has exposed its intent—with two exceptions. First, I've been told by Denver that Santa Fe has scoured the Kansas and Missouri saloons for mercenary gunslingers. So, if you see anyone with a holstered revolver or a revolver in hand, you shall shoot him dead center on sight. Then, when you have time, roll the body into the river. If body counts are wanted, let Cañon City or Pueblo authorities worry about it."

"And the other exception?" asked Pete.

"Animals—horses and mules. As horse lovers, we may hate to do this, but we have to reduce Santa Fe's mobility."

Sam and his ten riflemen rode out of Texas Creek the next morning. To Sam it was apparent that James was kind of impatient, anxious to get this over with—I imagine he's as sick of this phony "war" as I am, he thought. And so is Pete. We talked about it. If it weren't for the fact that we *know* James will do his damnedest to keep us alive, we'd quit right now...maybe start up that gun shop in Cañon City that we've talked about. Guns are about the only thing we know. But that takes money and this job pays well.

Enough of this daydreaming, he admonished himself; let's get to work. He sent one-half of his men along the canyon rim as close as they could reasonably get, to locate a convenient mid-canyon campsite, to probe for evidence of Santa Fe down at the river or up on the rim, to identify likely attack points, and to map out safe escape routes. Two of them were to remain near the farthest penetration point to serve as forward scouts and the others to return to the campsite selected earlier.

Sam led the other five riders overland on the shortest and most reasonably comfortable route to where he thought Copper Gulch might be. Their objective—even though it might require an overnight—was to determine the feasibility of a quick in-and-out strike on Santa Fe where Copper Creek came into the Arkansas. Two forward scouts were left behind; Sam and three riflemen returned to the campsite. At first light one rider was sent back to the main camp to order a commissary wagon. Sam took stock. The chances of a successful Copper Creek strike were very good, and a half dozen harassment sites were identified all the way up to the main fort. It bothered Sam that no sign of Santa Fe could be found. Were they being suckered?

Pete's expedition was similar to Sam's, with about the same disposition of scouts, sentries, and forward camp, but with one notable exception: Santa Fe had occupied Parkdale and everything for about a mile to the west. Worse than that, construction crews could be seen at the river at least a half mile outside of the West Portal. Pete estimated that Texas Creek could be reached in less than a month; Palmer had better hurry up. And we had better be prepared to do some heavy-duty sniping.

◇◇◇◇◇◇◇◇◇◇◇◇

It was well into May, with the main camp and fort, the two forward camps, and sniper's nests completed, but no word from the courts. Of course some delay in receiving a message might be expected. Nevertheless, patience was wearing thin. Pete reported seeing a Santa Fe train at track's end near Parkdale decorated with ribbons and streamers and carrying dignitaries, judging from their dress. They're rubbing it in, thought James.

◇◇◇◇◇◇◇◇◇◇◇◇

Matt's return to Denver had been a little depressing. "The trouble with these state-court rulings is that nobody pays any attention—even we," said Palmer. "But don't worry about it. You can be sure that the Supreme Court has heard about the San Luis action and will take it into consideration. There should be a ruling soon."

That hadn't been enough for Matt. While everyone else in the office fretted—waiting for the court decision—Matt had moped around. In fact, fearing the very worst, he wouldn't be receptive to good news when it did arrive. The eventual news was good, but not good enough. The court handed down a very narrow decision. D&RG was awarded prior right in the gorge, the two stop-work injunctions were canceled, and D&RG was ordered to pay Santa Fe for all the work that had been done. *But the lease was not canceled.*

The news from the district court had no sooner been received than a favorable ruling came out of San Luis. The circuit court enjoined Santa Fe's subsidiary from operating a railroad in Colorado. As expected, Santa Fe ignored this order. But with these legal rulings in hand, albeit as weak as they were and as short-lived as they probably would turn out to be, General Palmer had what he needed. He signaled his strike forces to go into action. The Las Animas group occupied all stations and roundhouses in Trinidad and El Moro and seized all rolling stock. One train, filled with armed combatants, rolled north to Cucharas Junction where a serious encounter occurred. Similar mobile forces moved south from Denver and north from Pueblo, securing all facilities along the Front Range. Within days they had seized all of the leased properties, rail lines, stations, and rolling stock. A few fatalities had been experienced—but not reported—and more than a few broken heads and bones.

◇◇◇◇◇◇◇◇◇◇◇◇

James had kept abreast of Denver's actions by means of telegraph messages through Cotopaxi, and immediately went into action upon receipt of Palmer's engagement order. Messengers were dispatched to Sam and Pete. The second battle of the Royal Gorge was joined.

Pete came in with his first report. "Since Santa Fe is all over Parkdale, our guys couldn't get close, but as we backed up the north side of the canyon, we disabled several grading crews. We have now reached our forward camp, which, as you know, is located on a sharp bend in the river about halfway to Parkdale. The bend gives us an intimidating field of fire. We'll pause there until the enemy catches up, fire some threatening shots, and then resume our backpedaling up to our fort. We should all be back here in two or three days. We'll take up positions on the north rim above the sentry pits."

Sam reported, "We made a wide sweep around the West Portal, tethered our horses, and went down Copper Gulch to a point near to but above the Arkansas, finding a natural breastwork caused by stream erosion. It was a good position. Below us it appeared as though an attack force was planning to cross the river to the south side, and sure enough, included were about a dozen rough-looking individuals with holstered revolvers.

When they forded the river, we plunked six of them dead center, rolled the bodies into the water, and slipped away. Since we didn't fire at any Santa Fe people, the mercenaries probably got the idea.

We'll coordinate our backpedaling along the south side with Pete—
the two forward camps are just opposite each other and connected
with a messenger rope. From there we'll continuously probe in all directions for Santa Fe outriders until we're pressured to backpedal to
the main fort. As we move upstream we'll try to 'herd' Santa Fe along
the canyon bottom right into your hands."

James had devised a half-mile defensive corridor below the fort
with hand-to-hand fighters and their backup riflemen down at river-
side, and with a thirty-man tiered main barricade at the deadline. By
an unspoken mutual agreement, cudgels were the weapons of choice
of each side as Santa Fe made several probes to test D&RG's defenses
and then retired to think it over.

"Look out now," James called out. "They'll regroup and come after
us with everything they've got." And this was plenty. A solid phalanx
of club-wielding roustabouts sharing the canyon bottom with the
river engaged a like number of D&RG fighters. Bodies were bruised, a
few arms broken, and more than few heads cracked, but no advantage
was evident. Not surprisingly, after an hour or so, the first handgun
made an appearance. An undisciplined mercenary hired gun could
not restrain himself.

As planned, Rio Grande hand-to-hand fighters immediately dis-
engaged and were replaced within seconds with their armed backup
men together with riflemen at the barricade who had already picked
out their mercenary gunslinger targets of opportunity. Riflemen and
snipers from the canyon rims joined in. A large number of unnamed
and uncounted mercenary gunslingers were soon on their way down
the river—the hard way—back to Kansas. A quiet stalemate prevailed.
There were no deaths reported to the authorities and newspapers, but
Texas Creek medical facilities were crammed—casualties from both
D&RG and Santa Fe lying side by side in hospital beds and cots.

◇◇◇◇◇◇◇◇◇◇◇◇

Within two weeks, Santa Fe managed to have the San Luis injunction quashed and a federal court order issued, requiring D&RG to vacate the seized properties. United States troops were called in to enforce the order. And thus, the ten-day second battle of the Royal Gorge ended.

Since James' force was not occupying any "seized" properties, the court vacate order did not apply and the Royal Gorge standoff continued. James' instructions were still to stop Santa Fe construction near Texas Creek. Santa Fe finished laying track to the barricade, Rio Grande continued clearing and grading upstream from Texas Creek, and Santa Fe finished its survey to Leadville. Some sort of a compromise was clearly indicated. James' forces waited, rifles loaded and leveled.

◇◇◇◇◇◇◇◇◇◇◇◇

Palmer's decisive actions following the San Luis breach-of-contract decision had at first engendered high spirits in the Denver offices. This is the *old* Rio Grande, people were saying—we're not afraid of Santa Fe or anybody else. But in many quarters, optimism was guarded, at best. The legal people, not sure of Palmer's real intent and recognizing the fragility of their case, were skeptical. Matthew, with a certain pride of authorship, wanted to be happy—but couldn't quite make it.

On the surface, the court order appeared to be a disaster for Palmer and his railroad, but his only reaction was an enigmatic, "Well, I guess we showed New York that the Denver and Rio Grande, from top to bottom, will fight for its rights." Matt had no sooner said to himself, "Who cares—we lost," than he was invited to join a meeting in progress in the general's office.

"Jay, I'd like you to meet one of my financial aides, Matthew Molyneaux, from your part of the country, Pittsburgh. Matt's new with us, but already he's built one line—over La Veta Pass—won one court case, and become very knowledgeable of the ins and outs, mostly outs, of the Santa Fe lease. Matthew, I'd like you to help Mr. Gould in every way possible. Tell him all. Show him all he wants to see."

Matthew knew something of Jay Gould—anyone who read a newspaper was aware of his checkered past. But that gold-speculation thing was nearly ten years before, and he seemed to have "come West" and "gone straight" since then—if secretly buying the controlling shares of a railroad was without a kink or two. That railroad was the Union Pacific from Omaha to Promontory.

"Well, thank you, William. And I'm happy to meet you, Mr. Molyneaux. That's an interesting name you have—I've not heard it before, even in the East. The French pronunciation just rolls off the tongue. It connotes all kinds of foreign connections: Continental banking, perhaps?"

"Oh, no, Mr. Gould. I'm just a country boy," Matthew protested.

With raised eyebrows, "I'll bet," replied Gould.

Matthew finished his three-day session with Jay Gould, hardly interrupted by meals and sleep. Gould and Palmer then retired into the General's office, leaving Matthew in silent reflection. Why the D&RG, Matthew asked himself. He answered his own question—to beat the Santa Fe, of course! Having surveyed and staked out every decent pass through the Rockies, William Palmer was in a position to assert "prior rights" to all of Colorado. But he didn't have the money.

Matthew reviewed in his mind those days spent with Jay Gould. It was all about money—that was for sure. The very nature of Gould's questions gave Matthew a pretty good idea of what the financier was considering. And it answered why Palmer was ostensibly being so open with his company's innermost secrets. This was salesmanship at its best. Obviously, Jay Gould was going to bolster D&RG with a massive sum. And for this he would demand a lot. He was not looking for profits, alone; Gould wanted shipping control to the West.

On the other hand, Matthew thought, maybe this is about coal—D&RG has potential but undeveloped coal properties all over southern Colorado, enough to fuel all of the railroads now and in the future. But that doesn't figure; Palmer is basically a railroader, as is Jay Gould—the only coal person around is Llewellyn. Matt's mind took another twist. That's it, by God. That's why Leonard is so interested in DelAgua.

The meeting between Jay Gould and the General broke up—both men sort of smiling as they came down to where Matt was waiting. "We shouldn't keep you in suspense, Matthew," General Palmer said. "Jay is announcing, today, that he is planning to run a line from St. Louis to Kansas City, then to Pueblo, paralleling Santa Fe."

Matt was dumbfounded—this didn't fit his train of logic.

Palmer continued, "You look surprised, Matthew, and well you may. And Santa Fe will be, too, but I guarantee it will flinch."

And flinch it did, within days agreeing to a meeting with D&RG—brokered by Gould—wherein Colorado railroad rights were divided. D&RG got the Royal Gorge and about everything else, but agreed not to go south to El Paso or east to St. Louis. Santa Fe kept Raton and the routes south and east. Jay Gould didn't say anything about his announced St. Louis line. He didn't need that now—he had bought into one-half of D&RG. And the Santa Fe lease was cancelled. The Supreme Court legitimized this out-of-court agreement, the Boston Treaty.

And, so, the railroad dispute was settled—this one was, anyway.

◇◇◇◇◇◇◇◇◇◇◇◇

General Palmer dropped in as Matt was picking up to leave for Trinidad. "I'm sorry I'll miss your wedding next week, Matthew. Take the next day for a honeymoon and I'll see you here in Denver the day after that. We've got work to do—Marshall Pass, Tennessee Pass, Gunnison, Durango, Santa Fe...you name it." He whirled and was gone.

◇◇◇◇◇◇◇◇◇◇◇◇

James was wrapping up the Texas Creek operation. The men had pretty well disappeared—almost everyone stopping to pay his respects. "Hey, Big Jim, I have to tell ya—this is the best army I've ever been in. The food's good and none of our guys got killed. This was a pick-handle war if there ever was one."

"Okay, you men, pick up your pay in Pueblo and come down to Trinidad—I'll buy each of you a drink."

James was glad to be leaving. He had a bellyful of playing war. From here it looks like Palmer's just been showing his board he's a tough guy, he thought. "I'm sitting this one out" will be my answer to the General's next telegram. But, I did get a nice bonus—almost as much as my share from selling the store. We'll be able to finish the saloon project in a fine manner. Up to now, Lillian has taken the brunt of this; all of the work of setting up the saloon has fallen upon her. She'll be encouraged by this infusion of cash.

Lillian...Lillian...Lillian. All he could think of, everything he could imagine, the only picture in his mind was that magnificent woman. As James surveyed the glorious West in his mind's eye, the fractional thought of Spanish Peaks jolted him into realistic thought. West Spanish Peak—that's where he would build his hunting shack, but maybe now it would have to be a cabin, or more. A beautiful woman, a saloon, and a mountain cabin. That's all he wanted from the West.

Springing out from that massive peak was Santa Clara Creek, hardly more than a trickle, easily waded by Coalfire. I've given her that big gray I got up at Royal Gorge, James thought. Lillian rides well and I'll bet she can shoot a rifle—providing she's allowed to choose her own target.

James turned in at DelAgua Canyon, proceeding along the near-dry arroyo up to the presumed coal properties. It's interesting, he mused, nearly every creek, every river, and every town still carries a Spanish name. Does that suggest that Colorado has a gigantic guilty conscience? I hope the names remain. It'll remind us who was here first and who should own them now.

He searched diligently for the wagon tracks and patched core hole that he and Phillip had discovered. Finally he realized that the scars had been carefully obliterated. Someone is extremely sensitive to this situation, he thought.

◇◇◇◇◇◇◇◇◇◇◇◇◇

Matthew had beaten James down to Trinidad by a couple of days. Time that was spent mostly with Llewellyn, some with Josephson, and even a little with his bride-to-be. He was met at the train by Leonard and Sophia. The latter's mien was more of a mature smugness than the childlike excitement of a few months before. And Matthew, too, was different. A few months had changed him from an ambitious youngster to a confident player in a new world—railroad finance. Leonard beamed as with paternal approval. All parties had chosen well, it seemed.

Leonard took charge immediately—drawing Matt aside after the minimum of welcoming embraces. "You've got a gold mine in DelAgua Canyon," he exclaimed. "Actually, a coal mine, the next best thing. I took an independent geologist and a coring crew up there. You'd think the core sample was from Engel; it showed a few feet of soil, then some shale, then clay, and finally a well-defined coal bed. Just what we were hoping for."

"The work was very discrete, I suppose?"

"Oh yes. Absolute secrecy is a way of life with these crews. Their jobs and future are on the line."

"So what's the next step?"

"We don't tell anyone—especially your brother. He kicked up a lot of dust with Josephson. I think we should let him have his way, except for the CCC participation. We have to show James that this arrangement is the only way to proceed. Otherwise we'll have a bunch of small-time operations—everyone with coal dust under his fingernails. If he wants to go it alone—okay. It won't bother us—it'll just be a little messier."

"Doesn't your Colorado Coal Company bother General Palmer?"

"Not too much. He needs coal—so I've promised him first call, and at a discounted price. Also, he needs help at the Pueblo steel operation so I've promised him half my time as a steel consultant. He's a realist; he understands my ambition. Likewise, he wants you on his executive management team but wouldn't balk at your owning part of a coal company. And that's exactly what I'm offering my near-future son-in-law.

And so, the happy and nearly extended family proceeded home.

◇◇◇◇◇◇◇◇◇◇◇◇

Back in Trinidad, James stabled his horse, had a shave, haircut, and bath, stopped at Maude's for town clothes, and headed over towards the Columbian. Passing his office, he was hailed by Matthew. "I'm glad you're finally here, Jim. Come on inside, you just missed a meeting of DelAgua Partners. Everything is going fine. The agreement is signed."

James entered and took a seat at what seemed to be his desk. "But I'm a partner, too, and I've not seen, let alone signed, the revised agreement."

"Yes, but Josephson has made most of the changes you wanted."

"Most...*most* of them? What changes weren't made?"

"Well, he softened up the changes you suggested regarding rights of individuals who might want to go on independently, and...er..."

"And what?" James' voice was rising.

"And the part about CCC. We've...I've decided that we absolutely need their participation."

"Without my agreement?"

"Well, yes. We had a split vote. With you abstaining, it was three to two to approve the draft, and when Lillian and Anschultz also abstained on the last ballot, it was a three-to-zero count. Unanimous."

"Matt, you can be damned sure that nothing else will be approved because of my 'abstention.'"

"That's what Leonard...er...I thought...I think that we'll never get anything done with you always opposing anything new and aggressive. So I'm prepared to trade my share of the Columbian Partners for yours and Lillian's shares of DelAgua."

Nearly blind rage seized James. This was *his* idea. *He* had found the strip of Mexican-grant land that had fallen in a crack. *He* had worked with Meadows on the survey.

James had difficulty speaking quietly and calmly. "I'll let you know after I've talked to Lillian." He slumped in his chair, a chill struck him head to toe. This wasn't what Father meant when he told me—no, when he commanded me—to see that Matthew got started in life in the proper manner and that our family values would not be lost. And now Matt's relationship with Llewellyn and family can't possibly be what Father had in mind.

"I think you're making too much out of this, James. Face it. This is the way it's going to be."

This is a pretty clear message, James concluded. Join up or get out. He rose to leave. Matthew, always the chameleon, changed the subject. "Sophia and I are getting married this Saturday, James. Your invitation is in your box at Maude's."

So it would appear that I'm not being asked to stand up for my brother. Another signal. James' naturally competitive nature pulled him towards the fray. But what he had seen so far of typical activities in the back room jerked him back. And he had his saloon—nearly. He had Lillian—sort of. He had all of Colorado's hunting and fishing—for the taking. He didn't need the aggravation of a difficult brother with a scheming father-in-law. This line of thinking calmed him down a bit as he walked down the street to the Columbian.

Suddenly, James stopped mid-step and starred blankly into the distance, as that familiar icy chill once again took over his whole body. What am I doing, James asked himself. I've failed to follow Father's commands and I've lost my brother. But is this the Matthew that Father had in mind, or was that Matthew lost in Atchison, Kansas? I can't forget that I was romanced a bit by Llewellyn, myself. But what I can't see is how Matt managed to distance himself from Llewellyn in the La Veta railroad project and what is driving him now? Why of course, it's Sophia who has control of Matthew now. Sophia is the ultimate whore and Matthew is blind to it. Father hadn't warned me of this possibility. Yet, how could he have known, anyway?

James continued to stand still with a frozen look on his face, while his thoughts continued to flow in his head. How did I lose Matthew? He's all that I have. I don't think I've asked for too much from him—just a level approach to life. And I certainly didn't invent Leonard Llewellyn. But somehow he has erased from Matt's consciousness all decent thoughts. I'm not imagining what Matthew said. This is the way it's going to be.

James resumed walking, all six and a half feet, with his shoulders sagged in frustration, to Lillian's saloon. Entering, James saw Lillian and Mike in their accustomed places at the door, the regulars in their places at the bar—everything as it should be. Except for a solitary person at the far end. Phillip was finding his own way to cool down.

"Hello, Mike, and you, too, Lillian. I've some tho..."

"No, wait a minute, James, I've... Oh, go ahead. Your mouth was open first."

"I want you to marry me, Lillian." This came out much louder than intended. All heads turned his way. Mike was wagging all over.

"For Christ's sake, this time of the day? You been drinking, Jim?" Then looking intently into his perspiring face, she said softly, "You're serious, aren't you?"

"I love you, Lillian, and I need you."

She flung her arms around him—something like grabbing a yearling. "Yes, of course."

There was a little exaggerated applause from the nearby patrons. Lillian continued, "Of course—but not until we've been New Columbian partners for a while. Then we'll know for sure that it's real."

She gently pushed him back. "Jim, I have to talk to you about Del-Agua."

"Yes. Let's go to your office...but first let me have a word with Phillip. I'll be right in."

Anschultz was dangerously drunk and extremely angry, to boot.

"Phillip. Phillip, please listen to me. I know pretty much of what went on today. I've got to talk to Lillian for a few minutes, and then we'll both listen to your version. I'll tell you, I'm as pissed as you—but we'll both do better if we settle down a little. Have some hot coffee and then come on over to Lillian's office." James pointed to the far corner of the saloon.

To Jim's knock, Lillian called out, "Come in, James. First, give me a first-class kiss to seal the bargain then let me say how honored I feel— you're the only decent man I've met in this territory, and I love you very much. Then let me say we're getting a royal screwing from your brother and his royal family-to-be."

"Okay. In reverse order—we'll save the good stuff until we've finished today's dirty work. I talked to Matt about the partners' meeting. Of course I've thought about this since the meeting I had with Josephson in the spring—I told you about that. I was pretty sure we wouldn't get what we wanted. We would be stonewalled, I thought, and sure enough we have been, but Matt exposed a chink in that stone wall. He offered to trade his share of the New Columbian Partners for our shares in DelAgua. I propose to remind him that we are well aware of the potential value of 'proven' mine property of immense acreage compared with a small-town saloon.

"I will also suggest that Josephson should read up on his contract law—or maybe his Guffey's *Reader*. While it might be true that partnership action could be taken with a majority vote, the partnership itself can only be set up with a unanimous one. Remember, I will remind him, the seven parcels are mining grants under U.S. mining law and hence subject to certain transfer restrictions."

"How did you figure this out?"

With a crooked half smile, "I really didn't 'figure' anything out. It's just simple good sense. How could anybody be forced to be a partner if he doesn't want to be?"

Lillian digested this question. "So the partnership doesn't exist yet, and the vote was invalid?"

"That's right. You're smarter than Josephson—and a helluva lot prettier, to boot. The partnership doesn't exist, and won't until all six leaseholders say so."

"What now?"

"I'll go over and see Matt. I imagine he's caught on to Josephson's stupidity by now. If not—I'll fill him in."

"And then?"

James took a deep breath. "Then I'll put on my sweetest negotiating face..."

"That'll be the day."

"And I'll tell him that you and I are receptive to the idea of swapping shares between DelAgua Partners and New Columbian Partners but the DelAgua would be voting shares—not equity ones."

"How do you do that?

"I'm not sure—but Matt will know as soon as he knows what I'm trying to do. If it's to his benefit, also, he'll buy it."

"But do we have a strong point for negotiation?"

"Absolutely. Matt could proceed with forming a partnership of two, three, or four leaseholders, with each one agreeing, but it would be without our leases. And mine, in particular, is right in the middle of everything, and nothing, such as a rail spur, could cross over it without my permission."

"And mine is between Commercial and Ash."

"That's it—in concept, it's simple. There'll be two kinds of shares, voting and nonvoting. They will all have the same risk of failure, and the same share of profits. Ours, yours and mine, will be nonvoting— which will make Matt happy. All others will have full voting rights. So, in essence, you and I would be trading coal-mine voting rights for saloon ownership."

"And that's it?"

"Only if all six say so. Now, possibly one or more of the others might want to trade something else for *their* voting rights or sell them to another partner, as we would be doing in effect, or maybe drop out altogether. But that last would be pretty dumb. Before I talk to Matt, I want to try to get something out of Phillip. He knows all of the ins and outs of mining and I'd like to get his take. If I can sober him up enough."

James returned to the bar. Phillip was still sitting up but with head falling forward. I'll get him over to the office, James thought— maybe he'll straighten out a bit. Half carrying and half pulling, James managed the task.

"What'r you doing? I wanna sleep," slurred Phillip. "Oh, it's you, Jim. I told you, Jim, I told you at the very first."

"I know you did, Phillip, and you were right. Now we have to fix the damage I did. Here we are, Lillian. Please sit down, Phillip, I have a couple of questions. Are you okay now?"

"Yeah, I'm all right—I told you, Jim, that first day I met you—watch your ass, I said."

"I know. Now listen, what is the very worst thing that mine owners do—to the miners, to their customers, to the inspectors, to just anyone? What do the owners most want to hide?

With furrowed brow, squinted eyes, Phillip managed, "The scales."

"What do you mean, 'the scales'? What scales?"

"Down pit—they all cheat—they all weigh light. But the tipple's okay... Let me alone. I'm sleepy"

At James' nod Lillian called over to the bar. "Hey Mario, give us a hand here, if you will. Please find a cot for this man—he's a good guy and Jim's friend. Make sure nothing happens to him while he's sleeping it off."

One of the girls passing by offered, "I can help take care of him."

"I know you can, Millie, but that's not what he needs just now."

◇◇◇◇◇◇◇◇◇◇◇◇

James walked up the street and met again with Matthew.

"Now, Matthew, let me explain to you how it's *really* going to be. I'm sure you're aware that the partnership itself can only be formed with unanimous consent."

"Yes, of course I saw that. But with you and Lillian—and possibly Phillip as well—dissenting, I couldn't see how we ever could get anything done."

Seeing that Matthew was softening, James suggested, "First, let's get a valid partnership formed—between all six leaseholders. We should try to have a leaseholders' meeting no later than tomorrow. Would you please set that up with Josephson? Obviously, we should not have Llewellyn present, but you might see if he would be willing to stand by in case the partnership, once formed, would like to speak with him."

James went on, "Your proposal to trade your shares in DelAgua for Lillian's and my shares of Columbian is acceptable to us in principle, but I don't think possible under the Mining Act, Matt. But you should know better than I. A possible alternative would be to trade DelAgua voting rights, not shareholder ownership. Would that work, Matthew?"

"What you're suggesting is called preference stock, Jim. Usually they have preference over other stocks in profit distribution—but I don't think it has to be that way. Partners can define it any way they want. I'll check with Josephson on that."

James continued, "The revised partnership agreement must reflect this and other stock-trading options that one or more of the partners might choose. The other important thing that I stand fast on is that the parcel-seven lease must remain in the name of the partnership. I reluctantly accept your position that the only practical development possibility is CCC—but with a time limit. If you like, you could invite Llewellyn in to the leaseholders' meeting to submit his proposal, but I can tell you now that the only basis that I will accept would be for a five-year-term lease, during which time *all* coal revenues, net of government royalty, would go to pay for development costs. I think that any investor would agree that a five-year gross payout is very attractive."

"I don't think Leonard will go along with this. It's not even worth talking to him about it. And, James, like I said before, face up to it. The way I said before is the way it's going to be."

"Then, Matthew, there is something else I must ask you. How did the core sample test out?"

"Uh...what...what sample? I don't know what you're talking about."

"I mean the core that was taken several months ago near the southwest corner of your parcel. I saw that, myself, before the divot grew over the filled core hole. If you don't know anything about it, you've *really* got something to worry about."

Matthew took a quick breath, but didn't speak.

"Well, then," James said, "if you have no explanation, I will be forced to report to the leaseholders—before the vote—that *someone*, either one of them or Llewellyn, has secretly taken a core sample and has had it assayed, thus putting himself in a very favorable negotiating position. And, if necessary, I will repeat this assertion to Llewellyn, publicly and to his face."

Matthew was still frozen. He had no idea that his brother could be so tough—worse, even, than Jay Gould.

He finally responded, "What makes you think this, James?"

"Phillip and I saw the evidence of a sample having been taken; Phillip, as a mine manager, has friends inside the assay companies. While it wouldn't be ethical to ask for actual assay results, information that a core sample was either run or not is easily obtained. Actually, the evidence was so clear and backed by two eyewitnesses that we don't really have to investigate further, but we most certainly will—if we have to. I understand that cores, themselves, are typically stored for a long time in the laboratories. If necessary, we'll find the damned core, and retest it. The fact that this matter is still secret strongly suggests that the assay was very favorable."

Matt was visibly shaken.

James added, "We both know very well, Matthew, that the real value of a nonvoting share is considerably less than that of a full-voting share, but if a voting-rights trade like this will end the controversy at both the mine and the saloon, it will be worth it to Lillian and me. And we also know that a different definition of CCC's participation is a must, if the interests of all six partners are to be protected. Matthew, I am adamant on these two issues. Without a partnership agreement along these lines, Lillian and I—and undoubtedly Phillip, probably Alan, and maybe Mrs. Wilcox—will form our own partnership, or possibly each go it alone. If either of these alternatives moves forward, Matthew, you're on your own. However organized, the DelAgua Partnership can invite a development proposal from Llewellyn's CCC, or from anyone else—even Palmer."

"This is extortion, James, pure and simple. I never thought I would see my brother behave like this," said an angry and defensive Matthew through his teeth.

"Nor did I think that I would see *my* brother so guilty of a gross conflict of interest with his future father-in-law Leonard Llewellyn—and even worse, a brother who would deceive the other so blatantly. DelAgua Partners might very well go forward as a mining endeavor but not as a Molyneaux brothers' venture, you can be sure of that. Your only course of action to make DelAgua work is to have Josephson make these corrections in the partnership agreement and then sign off on them."

◇◇◇◇◇◇◇◇◇◇◇◇

With both Matthew and himself backed into a corner, Josephson for misdirection and Matthew for conflict of interest, the lawyer quickly redrafted the partnership agreement to reflect James' position regarding partners' rights. He also drafted two alternate resolutions, one to give Colorado Coal Company the permanent right to develop the properties and share in the proceeds as if it were a partner, the other to invite CCC and others to submit proposals for such development. Selection of one or the other arrangement would be the first order of business for the new partnership.

◇◇◇◇◇◇◇◇◇◇◇◇

Josephson called a hastily arranged meeting of the six leaseholders, to be held in the roped-off corner of the Columbian Saloon. Since every leaseholder could potentially benefit from the partners'-rights change, the partnership agreement was approved following an explanation—with minimal discussion.

With the partnership formed, attention was then directed to selection of one of the resolution drafts.

Matthew concluded his eloquent support of the CCC-favoring approach, "...and finally, let me say that if we don't select CCC into what would amount to a full partnership, it is unlikely that we could find *anyone* able and willing to perform the development we need."

James finished his more persuasive argument, "...a permanent arrangement taking *one-half* of our proceeds? We can do better than that."

◇◇◇◇◇◇◇◇◇◇◇◇

Llewellyn, sitting at the end of the bar, had heard the arguments and the results of the balloting but could not participate, of course, until invited by the DelAgua Partners. James then invited him.

"Thanks for coming over, Leonard. You've heard what we've said and how we voted. We now invite CCC to present a development proposal for our consideration."

"It's good to see you again, James," said Llewellyn. "I was hoping you would have come up to Denver to discuss areas in which you could further assist D&RG. General Palmer and I were both very pleased with your accomplishments in the Royal Gorge."

No hint as to how my actions might have thwarted his personal ambitions, thought James. And he still has the opportunity of carving the Pueblo steel plant out of D&RG.

Llewellyn continued, "We certainly are interested, but you said nothing in your resolution or subsequent invitation about CCC becoming a seventh full partner in this enterprise as well as the developer and operator of the common facilities. I'm afraid CCC cannot offer you a proposal based upon the conditions you outlined. In fact, I fail to see how you could get *anyone* to do so. Neither D&RG nor Santa Fe would be interested."

He stood up, and adopting a "smarter than you" posture and tone said, "James, I have to say, it's the CCC way or no way at all. Perhaps you should poll your partners again, with this in mind." He turned to leave.

"Maybe we'll do just that, Leonard, in closed session, of course. But first, I'd like you to hear another development possibility."

"You're going to suggest a mom-and-pop operation? These just don't work very well on a large scale like this."

"No, that isn't what I have in mind. You may have heard of the Knights of Labor. That's a large labor organization out of West Virginia and Pennsylvania that has been trying, rather unsuccessfully, to make its way into Colorado and Wyoming. I will propose to the DelAgua Partners that we consider a business arrangement with the Knights to help us in our development—in exchange for our giving the union recognition as a bargaining agent in matters of wages and working conditions. I think they would jump at an opportunity to inch their way into Colorado's coal and steel industry and perhaps the railroad brotherhood, as well."

Shaking in anger, Leonard managed to say, "This would create a major labor problem in all major industries in Colorado. You can't be serious about this."

"Oh, yes, I can and will—but I would rather receive a development proposal from CCC along the lines I mentioned."

◇◇◇◇◇◇◇◇◇◇◇◇

James and Lillian had similar mixed reactions to the DelAgua outcome. They had relinquished voting rights—a nagging sense of loss about that—but the other partners were left with a fair partnership agreement and operating resolution and it was up to *them* to resist the rapacious Llewellyn. And now there were two New Columbian partners—the way it should have been all along.

"Lillian, I can't believe that the New Columbian will be in its new quarters so soon. You said the middle of next month?"

"Yes, and it's going to be just beautiful, James. It will be the finest dining and drinking establishment this side of Philadelphia. And we'll have our wedding that afternoon. After all, we will have been New Columbian partners all morning."

"Let's go over and take another look."

The marble colonnade of the new Grand Union Hotel entrance dominated the Commercial Street side of the new three-story brick building, but the more modest but inviting New Columbian Restaurant entrance just to the north held its own with respect to customer appeal. Around the corner on Main Street was the entrance to the New Columbian Saloon.

Lillian and James walked in the front door, right across the street from the opera house.

James had been in many saloons, from Pittsburgh to Texas Creek, but "magnificent" failed to describe this one. "This'll put the opera house to shame. And the back bar is unbelievable," he said.

"That's hand carved—imported from Germany—it was in the *old* Columbian. The first son-of-a-bitch who pulls a gun in here... I'll shoot him myself."

"It looks finished," said James. "What's left to be done?"

"Tables and chairs and a few pictures in here and in the dining room, some stuff in the kitchen, and beds for the girls' rooms upstairs."

"Lillian, did you by any chance get an invitation to Matt's wedding this Saturday?"

She shook her head.

"Just as well. That happens to be the day you and I are going on an all-day picnic—up the Picketwire, I would think."

◇◇◇◇◇◇◇◇◇◇◇◇

James and Matthew met in their joint office. The atmosphere was charged but not hostile. "I guess it just wasn't meant to work out, Matthew," said James, "but I'm sorry it had to be so confrontational."

Without making eye contact, Matt replied, "You're just too damned conservative, Jim. You're simply not open to new ideas in a new world."

"Maybe so. But now a final word of advice from an older brother. Matthew, if you expect to survive in the boardrooms, you'll have to be a lot more careful with whom you associate. You've done some wonderful things—La Veta construction, San Luis court action, Denver financial strategy, DelAgua planning, the New Columbian, and some civic accomplishments here in Trinidad. You're on a first-name basis with generals, governors, and financiers...but Llewellyn and his ilk are not *our* kind of people, and as a consequence they will only diminish your otherwise fine reputation. Father would have called the effects *hammer marks*, brother."

AUTHOR'S NOTE

I WOULD LIKE TO THANK book editors Lydia Bird, Robert Brodsky, Nikki Vergara, and my progenies Larry, Adrienne, and Robin, who were all a little skeptical at first, but now are dedicated to following every single comma.

ABOUT THE AUTHOR

ROBERT MULNIX BROWN is a registered and licensed Chemical Engineer in California and several other states. He is the author of countless reports, evaluations, operating instructions, and other works of prose, but he's only lately learned that none of these efforts amounted to "telling a story." HAMMER MARKS has been a lesson in telling a story.

6613142R0

Made in the USA
Charleston, SC
13 November 2010